T0244712

# Praise for *The F*

"[A] humane and refreshingly astringent novel."
—LAUREN LEBLANC, *The New York Times Book Review*

"An engrossing exploration of national identity, the meaning of family and loss, and what happens when a family hides its central secret . . . Read *The Four Humors* for an insider's travelogue of Istanbul and its volatile modern political history, and for the tastes and feel of contemporary Turkish culture. Read it too, to get to know a wonderful set of characters—women in all their flaws and generosities—and for an astute account of what it means to be an immigrant in America. Finally, read it to follow one young woman's beautifully-rendered journey into her past, so that she can wrest herself from stasis and step into her future." —MARTHA ANNE TOLL, NPR

"If stories expand us, secrets shrink us, as this deep, wise, and intricate debut novel by Mina Seçkin illustrates."
—JEFFREY ANN GOUDIE, *The Boston Globe*

"A book with the potential to create a whole new literary canon of its own. Mina Seçkin's debut book *The Four Humors* flung me into an uncharted territory of literary fiction . . . Both intellectually and viscerally intense." —NIDHI VERMA, *Platform* magazine

"A deliciously bittersweet meditation on the elastic, shifting narratives we weave from the fragile threads of our daily existence, the people around us, and the places we call home . . . What holds these unraveling characters together is Seçkin's precise, direct prose, which balances the grotesque with the beautiful, the funny with the genuinely moving."

—MALENA STEELBERG, *Los Angeles Review of Books*

"Fans of Elif Batuman's *The Idiot* should take note of Mina Seçkin's debut *The Four Humors*, another wry and intelligent novel that engages with the Turkish diaspora in America. As twenty-year-old Sibel seeks relief from an unshakable headache, she ends up delving into her family history and dubious medicinal theories, all of which Seçkin captures with a mordant wisdom that belies her own young age."

—*Chicago Review of Books*

"Mina Seçkin's debut novel chronicles Sibel's attempts to understand herself, her family, and the stories her body tells about both with tenderness and grace."

—EVE SNEIDER, *WIRED*

"An engaging read that addresses both the Turkish diaspora and what it means to change."

—WENDY J. FOX, *BuzzFeed*

"[An] expansive novel . . . [Seçkin's] dynamic writing carries the reader on a multifaceted journey through time and psychological and physical landscapes."

—SARAH NEILSON, *Shondaland*

"Mina Seçkin writes about the human body in a way that is exacting and beautiful, and I am in awe at the way she pins pain onto the page . . . The narrative voice is infused with levity, generosity, and (yes) humor. *The Four Humors* is a gorgeous excavation of the body—its flaws and its desires—and what it means to heal."

—KATIE YEE, *Literary Hub*

"At turns playful and serious . . . One of the pleasures of *The Four Humors* is encountering a multifaceted and complex culture which will be unfamiliar to most Americans, for whom Turkey has been viewed through the limited prism of the Cold War or post-9/11 military adventurism." —CHARLES HOLDEFER, *Full Stop*

"Seçkin's lively prose and empathic portrayal of her characters make for an evocative and entertaining first novel." —*Booklist*

"A captivating treat." —*Kirkus Reviews*

"Mina Seçkin's brilliant and understated first novel describes a young person's quest to situate herself geographically, culturally, historically, and physiologically—to map out a place for her inner self in the world, in her family, and in her own body. Funny, heartrending, illuminating, informative, brimming with cultural specificity and human universality."
—ELIF BATUMAN, author of *The Idiot*

"Soulful and tender, honest, but never cruel. *The Four Humors* is a debut that doesn't feel like a debut. With the wisdom of a writer beyond her years, Mina Seçkin has crafted a novel that delicately and lyrically explores the body and everything it holds—the blood, phlegm, bile, choler, all the bodily fluids and memories and generational trauma, the joy that we keep moving and breathing despite it—everything that makes us the flawed, beautiful humans that we are." —JEAN KYOUNG FRAZIER, author of *Pizza Girl*

"*The Four Humors* reminds us that the most startling love letters—to people, to cities, to fading times and places—are as gentle, wry, and intelligent as they are deeply felt. A beautiful, unpretending book." —MERVE EMRE, author *The Personality Brokers*

"Wise and quirky, searching and warm—a novel full of heart, alive with the humors." —AYŞEGÜL SAVAŞ, author of *Walking on the Ceiling*

"*The Four Humors* is a quiet, startling book that will stay with you long after you turn the final page. Sibel holds grief and guilt in her body, and as she reconnects with her homeland, she will uncover deep secrets and profound truths that will change her forever. Mina Seçkin has written a poignant and penetrating meditation on how we take care—of ourselves, our stories, and our families." —CRYSTAL HANA KIM, author of *If You Leave Me*

"I was completely transported by this novel—as if I'd been taken along with Seçkin's heroine on a darkly beautiful holiday . . . Seçkin is a gifted and natural storyteller, but she's also willing to show us the ways we use stories—of politics and history, in social media, in the bedroom and at parties—to hide and heal. In doing so, *The Four Humors* offers a captivating and profound portrait of a family unmoored by secrets and love." —REBECCA GODFREY, author of *Under the Bridge*

"Set in a stunning evocation of contemporary Turkey, *The Four Humors* is spellbinding. With sensitivity and insight, Mina Seçkin weaves the entanglements of romantic love and the complexities of familial love throughout this exploration of cultural identity. This debut novel is one for our time." —BINNIE KIRSHENBAUM, author of *Rabbits for Food*

# The
# Four
# Humors

*A*
*Novel*

*Catapult*

*New York*

# Mina
# Seçkin

Copyright © 2021 by Mina Seçkin

Hardcover ISBN: 978-1-64622-046-5
Paperback ISBN: 978-1-64622-160-8

*Cover design by Na Kim*
*Book design by Jordan Koluch*

Library of Congress Control Number: 2020952457

Catapult
New York, NY
books.catapult.co

Printed in the United States of America
1 3 5 7 9 10 8 6 4 2

For Huriye and İffet

I call my father, we talk around the news.

It is too much for him,

neither of his two languages can reach it.

NAOMI SHIHAB NYE, "Blood"

# Part I

# I.

THE FOUR HUMORS THAT PUMP THROUGH MY BODY DETER-
mine my character, temperament, mood. Blood, phlegm, black
bile, and choler. The excess or lack of these bodily fluids desig-
nates how a person should be.

I don't know what *choler* means, and when I google it, the internet leads me to a link asking whether *choler* is a Scrabble word.

What *is* choler? asks Cooper when I report my findings. We're
at my grandmother's, where she is resting. She is tired from shopping for bargains on towels all day. The window's open and a
breeze moves through the apartment, carrying cat, gull, and car
sounds from the street into the room. Because my grandmother is
napping, Cooper and I can lounge on her sofa together and even
touch arms. We search bodily fluids online, and Hippocrates,
who first worked this theory out. Hippocrates was born in Kos,
a Greek island off the coast of Turkey, and Cooper and I soon
learn that humorism was practiced primarily in this geographical
region and became very popular in the Islamic golden age. Cooper and I have been in Istanbul for two weeks now. We're here for
the summer. Me, to take care of my grandmother and to see my
father's grave. Him, to see that I do these things.

Before we came to Turkey, my mother set some ground rules. I would stay at my grandmother's apartment in Levent, and Cooper would rent a room two neighborhoods over, at the top of Bebek's hill. No sharing a bed. No kissing in public, because the real Turks won't do that openly. We kiss, instead, when we are alone in the room Cooper is renting near the eye hospital, where he's working. I was supposed to volunteer at a hospital, too, until my headaches began.

Choler, it turns out, is yellow bile, and in excess can compel even the most calm and gentle person into a hot-tempered rage. Phlegm makes you sleepy and sluggish, but you are also known for your dependable nature. Black bile is melancholy, and blood is the best humor. Blood pumps you into a kind and optimistic person.

Wow, says Cooper. He hovers his finger over my computer screen to point out a warning that too much optimism can make you insensitive to those around you, apathetic even. We agree that many people suffer from this blood condition. We agree that although this topic is interesting, it may not explain my headaches. And we agree that my grandmother's Parkinson's cannot be explained away as phlegm.

The humors theory prevailed until the nineteenth century, when another man discovered germs: Louis Pasteur, who laid the framework for medical sterility and sanitation. But I believe in fluids more than germs, even though I am supposed to become a doctor. They say that Saint Margaret Mary Alacoque, who was visited by Christ in a yearlong string of revelations in the 1670s, suffered from an excess of blood. She was his chosen instrument, Saint Margaret said, but she could not convince others to believe her. Christ asked her to initiate the feast of the Sacred Heart. Christ permitted her to lay her head on his radiant, torn-up chest. To cure her delusions, the priests decided to bleed her out once a month. They would cut her white thigh and have her sit in a stone basin. But my understanding of Christianity is limited and mostly googled. I am unsure what they did with her blood.

We've come back to the outdoor market because last week we couldn't decide on the right towel to buy for Cooper's family in California. The first time we pointed at towels and we touched them. We discussed absorbency. We shared our preferences on which pastel colors we believed to be the best pastel colors. We left the market with nothing.

It's crowded today and we're having trouble wedging through everyone. I think Cooper wants to be polite. He hates mowing people down. I take his hand and weave through women weighing fruit in their hands and children begging mothers for plastic toys but I step on the tail of a street cat and it snarls up at me, baring a mouthful of tiny white daggers.

Cooper wants this purchase to be perfect. We wave dozens of towels out and the shopkeeper has me wrap my handsome American husband, she calls him, in a big blue one to test the soft cotton, before Cooper finally settles on purchasing three towels.

Last winter, I invited Cooper to follow me to Istanbul for the summer. Then we coined it our adventure, and by spring, he found a job at the eye hospital near the university. He's a curious person and renowned among our friends for being kind. Like me, he thinks there are vast pools and caves of phenomena that cannot be explained by science, and he frequently admits his regret for having been raised without a religion. I summon and repeat the words *our adventure* in my head, an incantation, until the letters press against each other with so much speed and force they blur and break and I'm left here, in this market, on no adventure at all, only a mixture of mutated letters in my head and a plastic bag of towels in my hand.

We decide to take the bus to a café near the eye hospital because Cooper has two hours before he has to head into work. The bus windows are open and a breeze moves through. We take turns leaning against the pole because Cooper has given our seats to a woman with two children. Here, he'd said, gesturing, his smile as wide as an ocean across his face. They scrambled into the seats, and me, I got up, trying to be as kind as him.

He pulls out his towels from the plastic bag and holds up his purchases. I'll give my mom these two blue towels, he says, and my sister this purple one. What do you think?

I say, I think that's great. They will definitely love them. I am convinced of this because my family loves them, these thin towels. They are much more absorbent than people think.

Should I have bought my sister two towels, too? Do you think it's fair that she gets one but my mom gets two?

The light pours into the bus and we sway on its pole as it swerves through the hills. A city becomes hilled due to an eternity of earthquakes, and scientists predict that Istanbul will experience its next fatal earthquake sometime in the next ten years. The two children have their small hands in their laps and stare up at Cooper as if in a trance, and he beams back. My head has ached since May, more or less the same amount of time I've been in Istanbul. My brain is an earthquake or an ocean. Whichever I am more likely to survive.

THE CAFÉ WE LIKE HAS A FRENCH NAME AND ALWAYS serves strong gunky Turkish coffee. My head pounds and all I want to do after Cooper leaves is go back to my grandmother's and watch soap operas. My grandmother would never tell my mother that I spend most of my days watching television, especially since we are committing this indulgent crime together. She would never tell Cooper, either. She likes cooking up ways to make it seem like I'm doing something productive this summer.

I think I am dehydrated, I announce. I order two teas and bottled water. We're sitting in the café's shady back garden, and Cooper's working on drawing faces.

Where do you start, Sibel? The temples? The forehead?

Maybe the temples, I say, but I can't draw people.

Two women are drinking coffee at the table next to us. The German woman has long tan legs, not a natural brown but orange. Her blond hair is so straight it looks like the ends could cut you. She tells her Turkish friend, in English, that she wanted to come to Istanbul because of the interesting political things going on, especially after Gezi Park last year. That's what she said, things were getting so interesting, and she nodded seriously, holding a ceramic cup of coffee in her hands. We're in a very residential area, with no tourist attractions, so I am surprised this German woman is here. Either her Turkish friend suggested this café, or this woman is the kind of tourist who likes to experience authentic local neighborhoods.

This is terrible, Cooper says. This will just have to be something else, like a building. He cocks his head and laughs. Look, he says, an ear, out of nowhere.

He begins to draw an eye, maybe my eye, into a crescent moon. On the television hammered to the wall the prime minister is giving a dramatic speech. The first anniversary of Gezi Park is coming up and the government has already banned large gatherings in Taksim Square.

It's not politics I am afraid of, I say to Cooper, but people.

Yes, Cooper says. Yes. That's who makes up politics, right? It's definitely my eye he's drawn, a dark oval that meets a moon at its lowermost crescent point. Cooper has sketched Istanbul, the mosques, and the Bosphorus. The moon and the stars are above the city, and tiny framed portraits hang from the crescent like hair.

I tell him about the news segment on ISIS that my grandmother and I watched yesterday. The anchor was a woman and the network made sure she looked beautiful. The first week we were in Istanbul, there was a bomb threat in Sultanahmet. The anchor reminded us of another bomb a few months earlier and the segment ended with a woman in a headscarf crying. She held her palms to the sky like bowls. *The bomb went off and my children were blown away like scraps of paper.*

Cooper asks if I can translate the report back into Turkish so he can learn. I translate, and he's nodding as I diligently report in both Turkish and English what the news anchor said. We must, she had urged, look for a drugged eye, a backpack, someone muttering to Allah under a big broom of a mustache. I add that I may look like this some days, a muttering person, and I do have a light mustache I wax off, but because I dress in some sort of Western fashion and have a generally polite look on my face, no one will suspect me.

But I'm not totally sure if that's what she said, I admit to Cooper. I was googling my headache at the same time, so I wasn't really watching.

Wow, Cooper says, scanning my clothes. Yeah, your tight jeans and sneakers. He reaches to touch my hair. What do they mean, he asks, by a drugged eye? Cooper is so curious about words. I imagine he wants to take a magnifying glass to each person he meets, just to see how they speak. It's not enough to hear them.

Now the prime minister is reminding people of all the looting from last year's protests. He screams and screams about what Allah requires of us.

Want to go? Cooper says, still drawing. To the anniversary protest?

Maybe, I say. But you should talk to my uncle.

Cooper looks up at me and smiles. Sometimes I think Cooper is so optimistic that he believes nothing could be wrong with me. When we began dating in the spring of freshman year, he told me in his dorm room on his twin bed that he was amazed at how in the time he had known me I had not been sad once. Two years later, after Baba died in the kitchen while boiling water for tea, Cooper repeated this statement. And I still laugh and smile easily, but if you took a scalpel and dug into me with a tender wrist you would see that I am no longer like this. And it terrifies me that Cooper will soon realize this, because we have not yet acknowledged that I build walls against others. It is the strongest thing I have built thus far.

It's you I'm worried about, I say. They can see your head of hair from miles away.

Cooper thinks about this. Many Americans have warned him about Turkish prisons. He pencils faces into the portraits he's framed. He wonders whether this bomb segment was racist, as it would be in America. I mention that the American news would never mention the dead Turks, or whether they could have been dead Kurds or dead refugees. They only mention white tourists when covering bombs abroad. Cooper gently suggests that the ISIS-specific actions have thus far focused on kidnapping Western citizens, and I know this, that's why I'm worried about his blond head, but then I ask him if the U.S. news has ever—just once—mentioned the exact number of Middle Easterners the U.S. government kills daily? In the very middle of his sketch of Istanbul, what I thought was the water has become a cemetery. The internet continues to tell me the sharp ache in my head could be dehydration, aneurism, stroke, brain tumor, or a hair tie wound too tight and pulling my scalp back.

I CONVINCE MY GRANDMOTHER TO TAKE A TAXI TO THE Bosphorus with me. The taxi hunkers through traffic on Nispetiye before we merge onto a winding two-lane road and drive down the steep hill in a slow, quiet procession. I tell my grandmother that it is funny that this hill is named "Baby Hill," and she laughs. My grandmother wears a blue cardigan and a matching knit shirt. She holds on to the grab handle in the car to hide her hand tremor. When we get to the shore and climb out of the taxi I tell her she looks like a movie star, and she flashes me a mysterious smile. It's not the smile I remember from her. Her face is less expressive and sometimes stony because of Parkinson's, but it is still trying, very hard.

We walk along the water, an alarming electric blue, for as long as she wants and stop at a café with seats on the shore when she gets tired. In the distance, we can make out the Marmara and the cargo ships multiplying in the horizon.

Look at the Boğaz, my grandmother says. It's the widest river in the world.

I think it's actually the narrowest, I say, or a very narrow strait.

I'll die before I ever leave Turkey again. Even to visit you and your sister. Your mother.

We can always come here, I tell her.

Sure, she says. You can stay with me. She gestures again to the water, as if the Boğaz alone is where she lives.

I already am, I point out.

That's true, she says. Allah'a şükür.

A few days ago, I finally told her about my headaches. I had been hiding it well, but she tracks my every movement, meal, and even temperature on an hourly basis, so my secret came out when I thought she was in the shower and I had lain on the couch with a frozen lamb on my forehead. I felt so relaxed, maybe dead, until I found her in her bathrobe, peering at me from under the lamb's shoulder. She'd demanded some answers. Well, I'd explained, it's a chronic headache located at the very back of my head, not the kind behind my eyes. Not the kind that can make a person nauseous. My grandmother, in great distress, insisted we go to the hospital, and I, wanting to make her happy, agreed. At the hospital, they popped me right into an MRI after asking a few questions about my brain, mood, and mind. But I didn't stay in the machine as planned. The thumping noise in the white tunnel fascinated then terrified me. And I'm unfamiliar with spending even ten minutes entirely alone, without even a screen to look at. I pressed the panic button, and the man reading my brain released me. You can pay when you come again, he'd said kindly, as if holding my brain on a petri dish. Take care. And I am trying to, to take care. I google my symptoms whenever I can connect to Wi-Fi. The first time I searched I was led to the page on humorism. Any imbalance of the four humors means you are diseased. The ancient doctors focused not just on physical ailments, but temperaments, too. An excess of choler or black bile means you are emotionally unstable. Blood and phlegm, very stable. Generally kind. This was before science.

Can we go again, to the hospital, I ask my grandmother.

Of course. She orders us tea. Her hand shakes as she hands the menu to the waiter. My grandmother's Parkinson's always gets better when someone from our family is staying with her, and I'm supposed to be caring for her, but she wants to care for me. We have this argument about care often. She looks up at me and tells me to fix my eyebrows, so I push my eyebrows up and feel with my fingers to make sure the hairs are in the right place.

It's a weird headache, I say. I can still study. Not that I have been studying much, I admit.

That's okay, baby. She gives me a cautious look. Do you want me to come with you to the cemetery?

That's okay, I say.

I bought flowers, she says. Did you see them?

No.

I left them by the entrance. You should take them to the grave.

Okay.

When are you going?

Maybe after my head feels better.

Is he coming with you?

I'm not sure.

The graveyard is a ten-minute walk from my grandmother's apartment. It rests in the middle of the modern city, which makes its presence not an ominous, suburban haunt, but one determined to be at the center of everyday life. From the cemetery, you can see steel high-rise buildings in the distance, straight spines working into sky. I've been to the cemetery only once, last winter, days after Baba died in the kitchen while boiling water for tea. It had snowed the night before, so the cemetery was white.

MOST DAYS I WATCH SOAP OPERAS WITH MY GRANDMOTHER and take calls from my sister until Cooper gets out of work. We like meeting up in his neighborhood, walking around, then returning to my grandmother's for dinner or tea. Today is a hot evening, and Cooper and I take the elevator up to my grandmother's apartment on the third floor. It's the same elevator my mother first took to meet my grandmother, months before my parents married and my father fled to New York, I tell Cooper. She was younger than me and went to Ankara then came to Istanbul, from Ömerler, a village near Bolu, for college. I love telling Cooper this because it reminds me that I can do anything, being this age and without children.

Really, it is the man who is required to pay a visit to the woman's family before he proclaims his wish to marry her. My mother has always liked to do things differently. At my age she was already organizing demonstrations in Istanbul before the 1980 coup.

Really, I don't do anything, but I like knowing that I can do anything.

Each time Cooper comes to my grandmother's apartment, he waits at the entrance. He's learned that my grandmother wants to greet him, even when I'm there with the key, so we ring the doorbell and, moments later, my tiny grandmother opens the door and gestures towards her apartment. Then my grandmother and Cooper grasp each other's hands. They cannot speak the same language, but they make it a point to communicate. This can make me jealous.

My grandmother keeps a very clean house. She must strip a

guest of their coat and brush the lint off the sleeves before she can transform into a proper host. She performs this arduous and anal task now with Cooper, who she helps out of his windbreaker. Her apartment has remained unchanged since the late '60s. There's a lacework tablecloth on every surface: the coffee table, each end table, and the dining table. Framed family photographs stand on this lace like small armies. My grandmother brews tea and brings out a plate of banana cakes from our favorite bakery. Then she sinks into her ancient green armchair, her throne, and on television they show the beige wreck of a city after a bomb.

My grandmother tells me that America has learned how to fight the new world war silently, killing Muslims from the sky with a needle-focused laser. She looks at Cooper to make sure he is eating the cakes. She tells me to tell him what she just said, to translate what she thinks about his president, and about her prime minister, who is expected to be nominated as a presidential candidate in a few weeks. The election is in August, and my grandmother has the news on every day.

Cooper is so beautiful. His lips are pink and wide like a flattened heart. They open and close, this beating heart—his mouth—as he listens to my translation, as he listens to what she thinks of those who run her country.

THE SECOND TIME WE GO TO THE HOSPITAL, A WOMAN ENters the exam room and motions for my grandmother to sit down. I smile graciously at her. Her eyes are a rare blue for a Turk. She is a doctor.

My grandmother resists. Oh, but I am not seeing you today. She is.

I am not sick, I say.

What? asks my grandmother.

Who is sick? asks the doctor. She looks at her clipboard.

I have Parkinson's, says my grandmother, but I am taking my medication.

Okay, I announce, maybe I am sick. I don't know with what.

I also have palpitations, my grandmother confesses.

The doctor is confused. Who is sick? she repeats, suddenly very stern.

Me, I say, we're here for me. I have a chronic headache.

The doctor brings me to a small changing room and hands me a white gown and slippers. My grandmother is behind the door. She asks me if I want her to come in.

That's okay, I say. Thank you.

I am told to remove my necklace before climbing onto the flat bed and entering the white tube. The necklace belonged to my mother, and from its gold chain hangs an Arabic prayer, the one Baba taught me. The necklace was given to my mother by her mother, a woman who has been dead for years. I never met this mother, but I've been told she was fat and fond of discipline. I dip this chain under my shirt's neckline each time I'm at an airport, but in New York bodegas, the men behind the counters read the prayer I carry and nod. When American friends or strangers reach out and touch it, I can always feel their hand on my chest, near my neck, as they ask me what it means.

I have to stay in the MRI this time, because I had to pay up-front and drain my savings, and I don't want to further disappoint my grandmother. She's the one who is sick, after all. Certain neurons in my grandmother's brain are breaking down and dying—the same neurons that are responsible for producing dopamine, which makes you happy. This slow drop in dopamine makes my grandmother's hand shake. Her movements are slow. Her back is beginning to hunch. Despite these symptoms, she has managed to convince me she is okay. She is okay, despite having buried her son. I am not sure how to believe her.

I will myself to feel calm as the white steel tube reads me. I think of ways to distract myself. I make up stories of me dispelling black bile from my body by taking laxatives, but an image of Cooper floats in, and he is worried about my well-being. I get bored. I begin counting the seconds on my hands with my fingers in groups of ten, because this is the only way to get your brain read without having your brain walk out on you.

WHEN I GO TO PICK UP MY GRANDMOTHER'S NEW MEDI-cine at the pharmacy the next day, I also buy lavender-scented hand lotion and, on the street, more cigarettes. The man running the newsstand comments on my preference for menthols as well as my strange accent. I tell him I grew up in America, but not to worry, I am still Turkish. He nods in approval. On the walk from the newsstand to my grandmother's, I always pass a mother and her three children. Sometimes she's sitting peacefully on their big quilt on the street in front of a washing machine store while her children go up to people to ask for money or food. Other times her children are asleep in her lap as she holds a cup out and people storm past her looking guilty or disgusted. This woman and I always make eye contact, and then I give her pieces of bread or pastries that my grandmother baked earlier that day, or sometimes sloppy eggplant or meat dishes in glass bowls that I've smuggled from her kitchen, and this woman thanks me and then thanks

Allah. Based on her accent I think she's a Syrian refugee, but I am not certain, and I'm not the kind of person who would ever ask. Today I'm walking slowly and smoking my cigarette with my smoker's glove, which I wear so the smell won't linger on my fingers and betray me to my grandmother. The mother is holding out her cup, but her children aren't around. I hand her a tinfoil package of börek, and she thanks me and then thanks Allah, as usual. I smile and walk away quickly, as usual.

Now I have to make sure my grandmother takes her medicine. She must take these pills four times a day, every day, despite the nausea that they cause. Occasionally, when her daily pills don't prove powerful enough or she reveals to me that she hasn't taken them in a few days, I administer a shot of clear liquid dopamine into her bloodstream. My great-aunt, who is afraid of blood, often comes over to make sure I inject my grandmother's thigh correctly. Earlier today, my grandmother went on another cleaning purge. She wore yellow latex gloves to scrub the wooden floors with soap. I thought of her as Saint Margaret, single-minded in her vision, her Allah-given mission for cleanliness. What? she asked when she noticed me staring. I have to make sure the floors are clean before guests come over. Why? I asked, it's just your sister. She laughed. It has to be clean, she repeated, and when I asked if I could help her, she said no. My great-aunt wants me to put the needle in now that I'm here, and I imagine myself as the only well-meaning, pious man in the mob of villains who bled out Saint Margaret. I'm not entirely sure why my grandmother's doctor prescribed this syringe, which is given only as needed and in extreme cases of Parkinson's when a person feels particularly stiff. My grandmother and I agree that she is still reasonably agile and can clean the floors just fine. But her doctor likely knows she loves to skip pills, and my grandmother cannot be Saint Marga-ret. Those who suffer from excess blood are sensuous and prone to sexual abandon, and my grandmother is too old for passion. She suffers from old age, an excess of phlegm, which makes her cold and dry, but also dependable and kind.

We drink tea in the living room as my grandmother prepares a plate of food. She's wearing another sweater set, this time forest green, and is avoiding me and the syringe in my hand. The news is on, and one of the deputy prime ministers sits with his colleagues. The deputy prime minister's wife sits at a table in the same restau-rant but across the room. She eats alone, her face to her food. She stabs an eggplant with her fork, then glides the eggplant around her plate to soak up the red tomato oil. She eats slowly. The cam-era zooms in on her face as the news anchor tells us about her, and about the fact that she does not eat at the same table as her husband and the people with whom he runs the country.

My great-aunt frowns at the screen. We didn't grow up like this, she says, especially not in Istanbul. We grew up wearing miniskirts. We didn't even wear long socks.

And now, I say, it's not like you wear your miniskirts anymore.

Nobody needs to see my legs now, she says, it's true. It's the men who need to cover their heads—maybe that will open their brains.

My great-aunt Pinar is my grandmother's younger sister. You only have to cross the street, pass the taxi stand on the corner, and walk down a steep hill with crumbly stone steps to get from my grandmother's to my great-aunt's apartment, which looks identical on the outside: a six-story building painted pale green with a small balcony for each unit. Aunt Pinar moved to Levent in the 1960s, after my grandmother lost her husband at the same age my mother met hers: seventeen. The little I know is that her husband died in an earthquake. I have no proof, but I have come to believe that they had an arranged marriage. I think she never loved him.

Aunt Pinar calls Cooper my fiancé. She inspires our entire family to do the same. It's unclear whether they know he is not my fiancé, that dating does not always work that way in this country or the one I am really from.

What kind of dress will you wear at the wedding? Aunt Pinar asks. She pours me more tea, and I hold the glass by its thin waist. What shape will the neckline be?

I don't know, I say. But I do like the kind that illuminates the collarbone.

Yes, she says. Did you know mine was like that? My collarbone, we put eyeshadow on it so it sparkled.

I've seen the pictures framed in my family's living room in Brooklyn, on the shrine of people my parents left behind in Turkey. There are photographs of each relative, because we have to make sure they feel represented if they visit us. Aunt Pinar came to America once, when my younger sister Alara was born, but she hated our photograph of her graduating from middle school, and so the next time we came to Turkey for the summer, she gave my mother her wedding photo as a replacement.

She suddenly looks worried. Is he attached, very strongly, to any family names?

Maybe, I say. His middle name is Bartholomew, after his great-grandfather.

What kind of name is that? You have to make sure your own names are given priority.

I say nothing. I do want those names, and to brand my children with a name like my own, one my family can pronounce. But I do not want to give my child an alien name, an easily mispronounced name, a dead name, a name that other people—strangers, teachers, lovers—bury alive upon speaking. Americans think my own name, Sibel, refers to a Greek prophet of doom, but the Turks think the name comes from Arabic, meaning a single raindrop between earth and sky. It may also be the Turkic name for an Anatolian goddess of mothers.

At least the child could have blue eyes, Aunt Pinar mentions after a while.

I think of my sister, who wears purple eyeliner to summon the green shards in her brown iris. She shaved off the first syllable of her name and now goes by Lara with Americans. She's a year younger than me, and we have matching wide shoulders and cheekbones like slabs of yellow marble. Only Alara's frame has shrunk. She's not eating.

It won't work, I say.

You're right. The Turkish gene is too strong.

My grandmother walks in with a tray stacked with tiny dessert plates and baklava and fresh cherries. Piles of fruit and fat.

I wouldn't trade all of my grandchildren for one blue-eyed child, she announces. My grandmother has only two grandchildren, me and my sister, but I don't want to remind her.

Aunt Pinar is appalled. I never said that's what she should do. I'm only saying maybe something good will come out of it.

She doesn't have much to choose there, you know. My grandmother turns to me and says, We knew long ago that the boys over there would be foreigners. She uses a flat cake knife to lift a baklava from its box and pushes it onto a plate with her thumb.

My friends have so many grandsons, Aunt Pinar complains, but Sibel doesn't like them.

I do, I say. I do like them. They are very attractive to me.

My grandmother draws the cake knife through the air. Don't say it if you don't mean it. Your baba, if he hears, his heart will rise from the ground and you will break it.

Baba is dead, I say.

My grandmother raises her eyebrows.

How can we know what he'd think? I say.

It isn't that easy to understand, being a father. Aunt Pinar exhales.

He's dead, I repeat. He's not *being a father*.

And what about your mother in New York, who works so much, only to come home and cook? Only to make sure you have a place to settle after college?

She stays because she would never leave, I say. Because she and Baba said a million times that moving back would be an act of cowardice.

They decide to ignore me. Instead, they start discussing one of my closest friends from home, Deniz, and whether he could be a good fit for me or Alara. Our dads were friends. They were both thrown into prison with my uncle Yılmaz in 1977 after the Taksim Square massacre on May Day. He's Kurdish, and as soon as he was released, five years after my uncle and father, he left Turkey with his wife and managed to join my dad in America. Deniz was raised in Brooklyn and has thick hair he sometimes puts up in a bun. I've been lending him hair ties for years.

My grandmother is more open-minded than Aunt Pinar, who returns to her list of eligible young Turkish men. My head aches, and I tell them I'm going to lie down. I can feel the banging thing in my head between my ears. In bed I think of Aunt Pinar, who will now be forced to put the needle in her sister's thigh.

COOPER AND I RETURN TO THE MARKET THE FOLLOWING Monday. We want to purchase another towel, this time for my grandmother. This was Cooper's idea; he wants to return her hospitality.

The market is less crowded today. I follow Cooper's yellow head of hair, as yellow as an ear of dried corn, through the stalls. We spend one hour touching the towels at three different stands before picking out two white towels with yellow trim. I tell Cooper that gifts are useful, given that my grandmother doesn't speak English. He nods and points out that it is remarkable that they still seem to understand each other. It is easier to leave the market than to enter it, and by the time we're outside and waiting at the bus stop, Cooper tells me his plan. It is very hot out today, and his blond hair is stuck to the back of his neck. He wants to take a weekend trip to visit the school his grandmother taught at for two years near the Syrian border, the same boarding school my father attended for high school. We unearthed this mysterious coincidence the first time we met. It was week one of freshman year, and I had not yet found any friends, so I was wandering around the university dining hall with a big tray of tater tots—a few paper bowls of tater tots, really—and the bowls kept sliding around my tray and I really did not want to lose a single tot, so when I knocked into this boy-man who had diligently filled his tray with paper bowls of baby carrots and celery, we couldn't help but crack up at each other and our vastly different food choices.

We began to talk, innocently, and not yet combatively, about fats versus greens, hedonism versus asceticism, a topic that truly had been the sole wedge in our relationship until my father died. He lost a few baby carrots because of me, and I helped him pick them up. His arm hair was thick and golden and I liked the ripple of muscle on his forearm each time he picked a vegetable off the ground. It's really lucky that we didn't lose any tots, I remember telling him. He agreed with me. The tot is a very rare find here, he replied, with equal notes of ironic and earnest, and right there, I knew that this person would either be my best friend or my boyfriend. It's funny how I used to be much more certain about things. We got to the topic of his grandmother when I joined his table of new friends, because one of his new friends—no longer a friend, and now a person we make fun of—asked me where I was from. Brooklyn, I had said. Oh, this friend had said, though of course I knew what was coming. But where are you *from* from, like your parents?

We're boarding the bus a few blocks from the market. Why do you want to go to the school? I ask Cooper. It's pretty far, and that area could be dangerous for tourists.

I think it will be good for us, Cooper says. For you.

I've already been there, I begin, but Cooper squeezes my hand.

We say goodbye on the bus, because Cooper is to go to work, and I'm to watch the latest two-hour episode of our favorite soap opera with my grandmother. It's about the love story between a Crimean Turkish soldier and a Russian noblewoman. I will never spend the night in Cooper's rented room, because we think it would break my grandmother's heart. Really, we have very little sex here because of these spatial difficulties, and in this way, I come to realize he is not just the man I have sex with, but something else, something more terrifying: a man who may know me.

THE NECKLACE I USUALLY WEAR EACH DAY IS NOW MISSING. I took it off for both MRIs, and the taking off and putting back on created a schedule I was not used to. I looked for it between the sofa cushions before our dinner plans but all I found was a crumpled photograph of my father as a baby. Cooper came to my grandmother's and he dug into his green backpack to give her his offerings: the towels with yellow trim. They communicated for an entire hour before we left to take the metro to Istiklal. We padded the narrow street downhill to Pera, where the buildings look Parisian and windowsills host flowerpots. My family likes to show visitors our most beautiful streets, the streets the Europeans stayed on when they came to Istanbul for business or tourism on the Orient Express in the 1800s. Istanbul is not a pedestrian-friendly city, but I walk everywhere. In old Istanbul—or Pera, Kadıköy, and Beyoğlu—the streets are narrow and cobblestoned, the six-story buildings cement or wood. Some buildings have bay windows. Some buildings are crumbling or burned. Sometimes you turn down an unexpectedly dark and empty street, like the street full of electrical shops nearby, and you must walk fast or look like a confident and powerful, untouchable person. There are never any women on those streets.

I don't have friends in Turkey. Only Dilek's friends, who she shares with me for the summer. Dilek is my cousin and she has an opinion on everything.

Cooper and I meet the group at a restaurant. I get quiet anytime I'm in the vicinity of a group of Turks my age. Dilek's friends, though, I'm used to, and they rarely make me feel like I'm not a real

Turk. Because Cooper is here, they speak exclusively in English, and this time it is them, not me, who must switch to their stronger tongue to contribute to a philosophical or political conversation. It's me, Cooper, Dilek, and her friend Esra, who wants to be a novelist. She's very pretty, and she always paints her lips red. Esra often speaks very slowly, which makes what she says seem intelligent. Esra's sister, Eda, is here too. Esra and Eda's father moved to America with his parents after the first military coup in 1960, and Dilek loves to tell the story for them every time I come to Turkey. Their father lived in Virginia during segregation, and after some debate regarding whether Turks are white or not white, he was allowed into the white school, though he never felt comfortable there. His family came back to Turkey after he finished college in America, Dilek says with pride, but when Cooper doesn't know the Virginia school, Dilek's face falls, and Esra and Eda also look disappointed, and I see the way pride can rise slowly, building over the years through the small stories a family will tell, then their children will change the story, and strangers will tell the new story, until the first person's story is no longer recognizable.

The meze arrives and we begin to dunk bread in eggplant and tomato dips. The bread is puffy enough to look like pillows. Dilek's friends are in agreement that the nervous energy on Istiklal makes them want to stay home. They mention that Istanbul is not what it used to be. I mention that Istanbul has always been a place for migrants. By the late 1800s half of Istanbul's population were migrants. Dilek rolls her eyes. She tells everyone that I need to start reading Turkish history in Turkish, not English. But the right Turkish history, Esra adds, not nationalistic propaganda. I know this, but I say nothing. They continue to ask me why I came here this summer, when most of my life is in New York, a place that is not dangerous. Dilek is quiet now, and looks down at her plate. I know she wants to come to the grave with me, so I look down at my plate, too. They carefully steer over our silence and talk about the New York dream, and how exciting a city it must be, and I nod and nod but I don't have the same dreams my parents did, the dreams of America other Turks have. The same happens when Americans describe moving to New York, and how there is so much to do in the city, how there are so many possibilities, so many thrills, and with the thrill, an overwhelming sense of smallness. It is not that I cannot recognize the sentiment because I was born there, but that I am not afraid of feeling small.

Eda sits closest to me and complains to the table about her boyfriend. How he got her sick. She coughs on our dips and pillow bread.

I think everyone is sick these days, I say. I still can't get rid of my headache.

It's true, Dilek says. You know Americans don't believe in AC sickness?

Not this again, says Cooper. He smiles.

I explain that each time I get a sore throat from leaving the air conditioner on, or by sleeping with my hair wet, or even with the window open, Cooper doesn't think it possible. Every time he says, you were probably already getting sick.

Dilek's friends shake their heads.

But it's not possible, Cooper says. He looks around the table at our blank faces. Mine is blank in solidarity, because I know it's stupid to think you get sick from leaving an AC on, but also, I really do contract a cold from sleeping with my hair wet. Dilek launches into a passionate argument with Cooper about how American it is of him to think this about air conditioners. You think industry can solve everything, she yells, and Cooper protests. Dilek's father is my mother's brother, Uncle Yılmaz, who met Baba in college at a demonstration when the country was maybe even more split than it is today; the Turkey where about ten people—students, women, children, right-wing nationalists, Kemalists, socialists, communists, Kurds—were killed by one another, or, as some later suspected, by the deep state, each day. Istanbul was plagued with violence, spies, American influence, Russian influence, and the Turks, who didn't know what they were and how they should properly be themselves.

Meanwhile, Dilek loves to introduce me to her friends as her favorite cousin, who's Turkish but grew up in America. She'll tell me my Turkish is cute. She picks at my mispronounced vowels like at the white flesh on a fish bone. She used to tell me that I should know more Turkish curse words as well as proper, consistently implemented grammar. That's how people respect you, she'd say. She would then tell Alara to do the same, but Alara never listens to anyone, especially if they tell her how to be a person.

This summer Dilek has been gentle.

The Gezi Park anniversary is happening in two days, and Esra says she's definitely going. Dilek is not sure, despite having gone last year.

Are you going? Esra asks Cooper, and he looks at me, quickly, and says, No, but be safe.

I'm lucky that Dilek's friends begin lighting cigarettes at the table. I ask Esra for one, pretending I don't have my own in my purse, hidden in a pouch. Cooper's face is compassionate, understanding, but I know he wants to tell me that I will die if I continue this. He wants me to stop smoking. But he cannot want everything. He does not know what this cigarette feels like releasing it-self in my throat and opening my chest as if with two strong arms.

THERE IS SOMETHING HAPPENING IN THE MAIN SQUARE, SO our taxi driver, who is upset, tells us he has to take an alternate route. He curses. I tell him it's okay, we have no place to be. Coo-per agrees and tells him thank you in Turkish. I repeat it too, a tranquil thank-you, and look out the rolled-down window. The call to prayer fills the taxi. After 9/11, my parents stopped pray-ing. They decided to not raise us as Muslim, as they had planned. But I still know the prayers. I still know how to summon them, especially when nothing else can hold me and every taxi I take back to my grandmother's passes the cemetery, and we drive by the glowing white stone gates now, and behind their glow the high buildings are lit up for miles. The gates are engraved with a verse from the Koran that tells me every living thing will taste death. Last winter, Baba died in the kitchen while boiling water for tea, then we spent the next ten hours on a flight to Turkey and I held my mother's damp hand during the airplane ride. We learned that you can transport bodies on the same passenger plane you are traveling on, or you can have it fly separately on a cargo plane. I must have flown on many airplanes where a corpse was in the luggage below me. My sister was our source for this information, because, as she declared to me and my mother, we had not done anything useful for days. My sister is so useful. She also wants to be a doctor, and there is a great chance she will actually help peo-ple. The funeral was here in this same graveyard, but the grave-yard was different. It was covered in snow and when they lowered his body into his grave some snow fell in, too, with him, which my grandmother said was a good thing, a good sign for him and for her and for us. Not him, his soul. Now it confuses me where I will be buried. Next to my mother and father in Turkey, or in America, with the American children I may have?

AFTER ALMOST A MONTH IN TURKEY, COOPER AND MY grandmother are able to communicate remarkably. Just now, after clearing the dinner dishes, I come back to the living room and there they are, perched on either end of the sofa, speaking with their hands. Their eyes widen and shrink to convey emphasis. Cooper, his hands cupped to form tiny mountain peaks, remarks on how similar Turkey's terrain is to California's, and my grandmother looks wistful, absorbed, as if she can see the mountains and trees and blue water north of the Bay Area, a place she's never been. I want to know exactly which Turkish mountains she's conjuring as reference, what images her brain builds to fill his statement with shape. Cooper picks up an apricot and holds it high in the space between them. He uses a mixture of English and Turkish words to say, look, we are both known for growing apricots. They marvel at the apricot as if it has stepped onto a stage, a spotlight illuminating the small and round performer's orange, edible skin.

The television is on behind them and the news tells of violence at the eastern border. A group of men, their faces hidden beneath black fabric, press another man's face to the ground until his legs jerk. Each news broadcaster's voice is indistinguishable from the next. They speak only in panicked tones, rising intonations, a tornado of anxiety. It is impossible for me to tell whether the country is divided due to each broadcaster's apocalyptic tone, or whether this apocalyptic tone is due to the country's division.

But the cable companies make sure each anchor looks beautiful. Today, she is in red lipstick and her hair is dyed a plastic yellow. Her smile is faint, visible only on the edges of her lips.

I turn to watch Cooper and my grandmother again. Seeing the two of them communicating, as if connected by brain or heart or some other powerful organ I can't make use of in myself, forces me to stand up. I want a cigarette but have no excuse to go outside at this hour, when the two people I love most in this country are right here. I want to tell them that their comparison does not stand because Istanbul, unlike California, is the only city on an earthquake fault line that builds skyscrapers without using this very critical material that reinforces concrete to help it withstand seismic activity: rebar. Rebar, rebar, rebar, I chant in my head to myself. Ibn Sina said a pulse should go: relax, rest, contract, rest. A pulse is music in a body. I go to my bedroom, Baba's former bedroom. There's a big bookshelf full of science textbooks and romance novels, a bed that I will share with my sister when she comes to Istanbul in a few weeks, a wooden chest full of hand-embroidered napkins, and evil eyes hammered up on the walls. There is very little here that seems to be his. Nothing from his childhood, nothing from his teenage years when he had a mustache. On the wall is a framed photograph of my parents, marrying. It's a grainy, almost green photograph. They're dancing, and I can see the muscle in my mother's calf flexed from her high heel. Her hands hold Baba's face. It's hard for me to look at it, his face. Somebody is always looking back.

Somebody who spits at my feet and tells me what I did.

THE NEXT DAY I'M AT MY GRANDMOTHER'S WATCHING THE news when the police begin using tear gas and water cannons on demonstrators at Taksim Square. The news does not show this. I find out on Twitter. It is sometime after dinner, and we divide up my grandmother's phone book to call people as we simultaneously take calls, and my mother, she calls, very upset, saying she's heard there were 25,000 police officers but she can't find out whether anyone has been killed and how many are injured and of course my sister calls too, talking about how being an American Middle Eastern kid makes you born to heartbreak from both of your countries, and so often, and my uncle calls asking if I went, if Cooper went, if I know anyone who is there, they're detaining people now, and have I managed to get a hold of Dilek yet, she was at work, she wanted to go, but she's not answering her cell phone, and my great-aunt calls from down the hill, also asking about Dilek and Cooper, and of course I call Cooper first although I know he is still working at the eye hospital near the university and I know he wouldn't go without me and I really believe he is sensitive to participating in the politics of a country he is not from. I imagine he is finally fed up. I imagine he wants to go home already. That his family, who told him to be careful in Turkey, was correct. They will call me soon, I presume. I imagine they will call me selfish. I imagine what people will tell me when I tell them I have not yet visited Baba's grave. When I tell them I have been doing nothing but assessing my blood levels but mostly I am on another planet in television which makes me so much closer to being dead and I imagine what Cooper will say to me later that night, at my grandmother's, eating dinner. I don't know what I'm doing here, he will say. He will put his fork down. He will wait for me to explain to him what, if anything, he is doing here. I wait for one hour with no answer on his whereabouts.

You have four chambers in your heart. And a diseased heart is unusually large, as large as a metronome.

WE SEE EACH OTHER LATER THAT NIGHT. WE STAND IN THE kitchen between the pantry and the wall of hanging pans and my mouth is pressed against his. He lets me start kissing him, here in my grandmother's kitchen, despite the rule that says we cannot kiss in public or in the presence of family, and I begin to think I'm this sort of powerful, I'm not that sort of sad. The call to prayer goes and goes and clears up the furniture stacked high in the small room of my head. I want to know what it is that makes kissing feel good. I want to know, is it the opening? The balancing-out of another bodily fluid: saliva, which easily may contain regenerative qualities when shared with another. The humor theories do not mention this. They only mention your own body as containing fluids that you balance by diet, exercise, bloodletting, and other things that are between you and your body. They do not mention what other people can do for you. I want to turn the news off. I want him to open my head. I want to get him alone, without my family around us—especially the English-speaking ones who translate what he says for the others—and demand an answer. I will ask, What are you most afraid of?

Loneliness, dying, being lonely.

I will put my hand around his white throat to see what makes his blood go.

# II.

Cooper is not, as I believed, like other people or men. It seems that last week's demonstrations have moved him to the point of spiritual transformation.

I want to stay here, he announces. We were about to meet my family at the kebap house.

I don't want to go either, I say. I sit down and slip off my shoes.

No. He pushes my shoes back towards me. I mean here, Turkey.

What?

I want to stay indefinitely. He begins to pace the room. I can take a year off and continue working in Istanbul.

The call to prayer begins and he sits down on his bed to listen. Cooper's sublet is in a neighborhood of Istanbul my dad's family did not recommend, even though they—my grandmother, my great-aunt—moved out of a run-down neighborhood in the '60s. At the beginning of the summer, they made me translate this for Cooper, but he was stubborn. He said he wanted to understand what Istanbul was really like. Uncle Yılmaz, who, like my mother, moved to Istanbul from the village, and, as he likes to say, lived through not only prison but the worst of the city, thinks Cooper will be just fine, and I agree. Cooper's neighborhood, made up of musty-smelling apartment buildings, densely packed and somewhat slanted, borders the expensive villas of Rumeli Hisari with views of the Bosphorus and, farther downhill, Bebek. It's hardly a run-down neighborhood. He has a roommate Dilek helped him find, a Turk our age who, like us, will start his final year of college in September.

Well, I say, announcing what should be obvious, I'm going back home.

But why? What's there for us, Sibel?

A degree? And I need to go to a doctor in New York.

You can graduate anytime, he says, standing to pace again. Later. You can get your degree later. Everything you need to learn about medicine is already here. You can spend good time with your grandmother. You can get a job and make money, instead of taking out loans. America's education system just takes and takes and doesn't give.

He stops pacing and looks out at the minaret again. I think for a second that his blue eyes are filling with water.

Cooper writes weekly lists of ways to improve himself. He writes them in a yellow notepad he found at the eye hospital. Then he combs through each list to examine how he can be a better person. He emerges from his lists kinder, more spiritually refined. His white face looks cleaner, scrubbed, his freckles radiating heat. There is always a big idea at the back end of these revelations. I've looked before, and some items concern me: how he should act with me, how he can do better, how he can make my headaches—which he agrees are very real—go away. I know he wants me to return to my father's grave. Last night at my grandmother's he sat me down and gently proposed that my headache could be a guilt headache, an accumulation of grief and blame. If you don't unknot your guilt from your grief, he said, you're never going to feel better. I listened. I'm listening still.

But visiting Baba's grave is the first thing on his list, the last on mine.


AT THE KEBAP HOUSE, EVERYONE WANTS TO SIT NEXT TO Cooper, so I sit at the other side of the table. The maternal and paternal sides of the family come together anytime we're visiting. Uncle Yılmaz joins our gatherings with Aunt Sevgi, their son, Emre, thirteen years old with a voice that just dropped an octave, and, of course, Dilek. My uncle is the tallest in the family on both sides, the most opinionated, and the central patriarchal figure. He's a socialist and always tells us about his six months in prison, after the Taksim May Day protest in 1977 when the guards twisted his balls with enough force to draw blood, whipped the soles of his feet, and spread hot egg yolk in his armpits. He attended every Gezi Park protest, and always jokes that he's sitting in shallow water, waiting for the resistance.

We're only in the meze moment of the night, and Cooper, in his baby Turkish, reveals his plan to help the Syrian refugees, the words mispronounced but spoken with enough enthusiasm to move a crowd. I comment that this is news to me, but no one listens. Aunt Sevgi, who works with refugees, begins to fill Cooper in on the program in Fatih where he can begin volunteering as soon as he wants. Next to me, Dilek is tapping her hot pink nails on the table, waiting to tell him what she thinks. Aunt Sevgi became my mother's friend in college here in Istanbul. Then my mother and Uncle Yılmaz married each other's best friend, a fact that made my father especially proud. The two couples were student members of the first socialist party granted a seat in parliament before they splintered into a new group. Despite the party's strong anti-imperialist stance, my parents fled, hilariously, to America. It's more complicated than this, I know, but my uncle always called my father a coward.

Your father liked him, no? Aunt Pinar asks me.

Nope, I say. He never liked any boys we dated. She's asked me this before, and I'm not sure why she still wants my father to have loved him. She's trying, in a way that is different from mine, to switch the train tracks of the past by pulling just one small lever.

The kebap arrives over a bed of raw onions and parsley. The waiter places one plate for every few people on the white tablecloth. I fill up my plate first, with three different types of meat. Aunt Pinar watches me spoon up a mountain of buttery rice. When she first saw me this summer, she weighed me with her eyes, but said nothing. Usually it is the first thing female family members tell me when they see me for the first time that year, how much weight I've gained or lost: fifteen pounds since my father died. Aunt Sevgi has been scanning my body too. They don't say anything about the new fat on my hips, my arms, even my nose, which can bulb up with flesh, because this year the cause for weight is obvious. They're afraid of me, and the shape my grief has taken. Blood, you're lean and shaped as if made from stone. Phlegm, you're fat. Because humors had to do with passions, temperament, and behavior, of course people had a lot of moralistic ideas about willpower and control. Moral health, which does not interest me.

I'm sure he did, Aunt Pinar repeats. He knows what's good for you, she tells me with authority.

How could he know what's good for me?

She raises her eyebrows.

He's dead, I say.

Aunt Pinar snaps her fingers at her daughter to pass her cigarettes. Aunt Pinar thinks she's the only one who smokes in my family. To smoke a cigarette, linguistically, one must use the Turkish verb "to drink." Turks drink their cigarettes like water down throats.

You know, Dilek finally interrupts, I've been thinking of joining my mom's work as well. She beams at the table and squeezes Cooper's upper arm with her hand. Dilek used to be fat and now she body-brags every day. On social media she only posts pictures of herself in tight shirts, her navel taut and firm, wearing sunglasses. Sometimes she makes the captions famous lines of Turkish poetry on loneliness. My own body is still okay but I have love handles that make my belly look like a bowl and my areolas are too big, much bigger than any other woman's that I've seen. I was on a school field trip at the Met in junior high when I first became aware of my giant purple areolas, as big as sliced salamis, because every European painter gave their women hard white apple-shaped breasts with a tiny pink areola around each dainty nipple. I was confused and angry. I spent the next few years cataloguing the size and color of areolas on friends or strangers in locker rooms and HBO shows. That first year of me being a breasted young woman took me back to Turkey for the summer, like every summer, but this time when I went to the hammam with my mother and sister I had my first shot at seeing if all Turkish women were cursed with giant areolas. My data was inconclusive. Big areolas are, however, genetic.

Now I don't care anymore. I don't even care about makeup and skin cream. I used to be obsessed with skin cream. I used to be obsessed with enhancing myself. I wanted to ensure that I was smart, hardworking, kind, happy. And I'm all for women who are allowed to do what they want now, but what if I want to do nothing?

Dilek turns to me. Her areolas are like mine, only oval, like fried eggs.

It's remarkable, Sibel, Dilek says. Most tourists would flee a country when it's in this much shit, but your boyfriend decided to stay.

Yes, I say, preparing some big statement, but Dilek's not listening. She's never really listening even when she's making eye contact. Cooper, though, uses his whole face to listen. His eyes glaze over only during conversations about food. You, Cooper once said, live to eat. You're always looking forward to your next meal. But I, I only eat to live, to keep surviving. Wow, I had said, also enthralled by this now very obvious difference. Yes.

Dilek's still talking about the volunteer work she can't wait to do. She's planning to meet with an American woman who hopes to establish a small shelter in Çesme, where refugees have been embarking towards Greece. Her parents are proud of her, but they still want her to have a profession—even Uncle Yılmaz, who loathes the effects of capital, wants that. At my age, my uncle was a poet. He wasn't brave enough to continue in the end, he says, as in, his party was banned, a regime of military censorship began, and he couldn't make money with his poems. Now he's the middleman for a raki distribution company, which had been doing well until the prime minister increased the taxes on alcohol.

He is sixty now, and for the first time he is older than Baba.

My grandmother now tells the table how Cooper helps her cook dinner each night. He cuts and skins vegetables, breaks the necks of string beans, then clears the table and washes each dish. My grandmother admits that she doesn't want him to do this, that it feels strange to her, but she must be grateful.

It's my kitchen, after all, she says, and he's my guest!

Cooper listens, smiling, and looks at me.

Sibel, of course, helps too, my grandmother says with pride, but when everyone turns to me, hunched over my plate eating with my fingers, their faces don't read of disbelief but pity.

She's a little sick, Cooper says in Turkish.

I'm not sure what it is, I say after swallowing. Maybe it is muscle pain.

They begin to diagnose me. My headaches, Uncle Yılmaz declares, are psychosomatic. The Turkish is the same, *psikosomatik*, because there is an unsurprising number of words that Europe and America officially invented and made attractive or otherwise untranslatable to other countries.

Well, Aunt Pinar begins, what did the hospital say?

You had an MRI? Dilek asks.

Aunt Pinar pins my arm down on the table—I think she's trying to hold my hand—and faces me. What did they say, baby?

They don't know yet, I say. But they're supposed to call me soon.

Other words taken from Western languages like *psikosomatik* are *flört*, which means flirt, and *psikopat*, which is psychopath.

Aunt Pinar's son, Demir, who just got a job in health insurance, wants to know how my job is at the hospital. Aunt Pinar elbows him, and Demir looks startled and says, oh, never mind, and I sit there with my oily hands not knowing where to look. Someone asks how Alara is doing and my grandmother answers for me. Alara, like my grandmother says, will be coming to Turkey in a few weeks, and my family begins to discuss what kebap houses they should take her to and also whether she has a boyfriend these days. Then my grandmother tells them Alara is on the same flight as Deniz, and Dilek snorts. Dilek tried to make out with Deniz last summer and he gently pushed her away. We don't talk about this. But they stall again, and they turn towards me, so Cooper mentions that he's very excited to see other cities in Turkey, now that he'll be here for a year. Dilek and my uncle nod in agreement, and the table deliberates over the best places for Cooper to visit. We're going to Konya and Tarsus soon, and my uncle tells Cooper to be sure to see the basketball courts at Tarsus. Uncle Yılmaz could never have afforded to go there, and he is openly envious of the young boys who did. He says my father used to go to the locker room to smoke cigarettes and carve his name into the wall with an off-brand Swiss army knife. Everyone laughs. It's fun to pull kebap apart with my fingers and sort out the fat, but Aunt Pinar slaps my hand. She hisses at me to use a fork. Then she asks me if we booked different hotel rooms for our trip to Konya.

No, I say, emboldened. We'll sleep in the same room.

She raises her eyebrows and takes another drag.

Then there is the Turkish word *hüzün*, which cannot be translated into English. Instead of meaning a simple sadness or suffering it denotes a collective, Istanbul-wide phenomenon that some call spiritual, some call nostalgic, but the one thing we know for sure is that the word exists because it is pridefully shared with others. The ideal is not to escape this suffering, but to carry this suffering. It is possessing the weight of the city as you wade through its past and present and, by doing so, you dissolve among many. I am pretty certain—as Ibn Sina was certain, too—that those with an excess of black bile like me are prone to feel this weight.

Istanbul is a humor. The lubricant, oily and thick, black humor that begins to leak from my spleen. Istanbul is black bile, melancholy, only disguised as a city.

I catch my cousin Emre watching me. When I raise my eyebrows at him he flinches and drops his fork. I'm waiting. I'm waiting for a lull in the conversation about the presidential election, about Gezi, about the refugees in Turkey. How the demonstrators last week only wanted to read a statement and lay flowers in the park. How sad it is today, how sad today, and every day in this city. I need a lull. Finally, when Cooper has his mouth full, when Dilek's checking her phone under the table, when my uncle's draining his tea since the restaurant won't serve him raki during Ramazan, when Emre dares another glance at me, I announce that I visited Baba's grave earlier today.

Everyone is still. Dilek begins to cry. My grandmother reaches for Aunt Pinar's hand, which makes me miss my sister.

But I lied. I didn't spend my morning at the grave, but by the water. I ate the rice-stuffed mussels everyone tells me to avoid; then I walked two neighborhoods over to Ortaköy to eat a baked potato filled with butter, beets, and olives. The MRI report came back with no conclusive information concerning the state of my brain. The doctor wants me to come in again, but I am not hopeful that they will give me the certainty I seek. Maybe you are stressed, they will say. Maybe you are sad.

THE NEXT DAY WHEN COOPER GETS OUT OF WORK WE VISIT an anatomy exhibit near the Istanbul Modern. Dilek's friends told us at a bar a few nights ago that it was very strange. Dilek squinted at me after saying this and decided that I would in fact like such a show. They have a museum like this in America, yes? But it's such a morbid concept, she said, shaking her head. Cooper had carefully translated the exhibit's name to *dead real bodies*.

Great, he'd said, laughing. Sibel, let's go.

In the exhibit, the text on the walls introducing the gallery apologized for itself. WE KNOW THIS MAY BE STRANGE, the curators wrote on a white wall, BUT YOU CAN LEARN A LOT FROM THE MYSTERIES OF THE BODY. For some reason they used a glittering pink color for the text. I translate the more obscure Turkish for Cooper. In the first room, more than fifty skulls are tacked to the wall. It is not clear who these skulls belonged to, but most died from smoking, or, the four humors would say, black bile. I explain to Cooper that black bile makes a person brood, gloom, and withdraw. But black bile also has the power to thicken blood, allowing it to clot. Those with an excess of black bile can repair their bodies with impressive speed and minimal scar tissue. Mozart was diagnosed with rheumatic fever, which was thought to be caused by excess black bile in his brain. Academics passionately debate whether this scandalous rumor is true: that Mozart really died from an infection caused by the bloodletting procedure meant to cure him. George Washington, too, woke up one morning with a sore throat and, after his doctor drained numerous pints of his blood in one day, died.

Then we see the bodies themselves, preserved in a process called plastination, where scientists replace bodily fluids and fat with liquid plastic, later hardened, molded, and posed into lifelike forms. Some of the bodies are so well preserved in orange tendons and skin I find myself looking suddenly at a sculpture.

Don't you think, I say to Cooper, that these seem so real that they're like sculptures?

He looks into a pair of glass eyes. But sculptures are the unreal, he says. This, this is the real thing.

Cooper begins to debate what is real and not real, pointing at body parts, limbs, lips, vulvas. The necks have so many dried vessels and tendons, a web of orange and white strands, like fresh prosciutto. Cooper said this, the fresh prosciutto thing. He has not eaten pig all summer, so he's confusing what is dried and what is fresh. I also miss eating pigs. Mortadella is my favorite pork product after hot dogs.

Prosciutto is dry-cured after all, Cooper points out. Rubbed with salt then preserved.

This is about what we can learn, I say, this is not about prosciutto.

I'm just saying. These guys are preserved with plastic, not salt. Doesn't plastic seem unnatural?

This is about medicine, I say, it's about how doctors learned what to do to make us live longer lives. Look, I say, here is a man who died of excessive alcohol consumption. Here is a man whose knee replacement got infected. Here is a smoker.

I shut up. The late smoker looks back at me with a stern, dried-up face.

Sure, Cooper says. Yeah. I just don't think I'm going to eat meat when I leave Turkey.

I stop walking. I thought you were staying, I say.

Yes, he says, one more year of eating meat, then I can be a vegetarian again.

What?

He continues to hum, walking through the dead real bodies. So you're really staying?

He takes my hand and pulls me to the next body.

The museum plaques tell us that each body's pose serves an educational purpose. For example, when observing the man tossing a ball, we're meant to note the muscles a man uses while tossing a ball. There is a man riding a horse, also in prosciutto, a man running, his bent arms in front of his body like arrows, and a woman who sits naked in a chair, a baby in her arms. They seem to have forgotten about her areolas. The baby is a doll. It is wearing a bonnet, which is not even a Turkish thing, and seems like an oversight on the museum's part. A woman standing next to us shakes her head. She seems to be floating in heavy perfume. When we smile at her, she leans in and tells us that she's heard that most of these bodies are stolen.

How else do you get these disgusting, shameful corpses? she asks. She walks away with a sharp turn to share her message with a man across the room. Cooper begins to follow her. He wants to understand what she meant by shameful.

What, can I not ask her? He loosens himself from the pincer grip I've got on his arm.

Your Turkish isn't good enough, I say. And maybe she's disturbed by all this.

He considers this. You're right, he says. Then he tells me he is so proud of me for having gone to Baba's grave. Was it crowded? He asks.

No, I say, defensively. It's a cemetery.

Well, was anyone else there?

No? I start, with no idea if the cemetery is crowded. Why?

Nothing, nothing. He smiles again and folds his arms over his chest. I'm confused. What does Cooper know? He starts humming again and walks away from me, standing in front of a young girl with glass eyes. Mohammed said that fennel flower cured every ailment but death. I'm going to be a doctor, I have to be, I'm on track at school and everything. I have to do this, because I would rather die than disappoint anyone more than I already have.

Alara and I don't actually want to be doctors. Our parents brainwashed us at an early and susceptible age, telling us that if we didn't become doctors, lawyers, or engineers we would make no money and America would never consider us real Americans. I understand the flaw in this logic now, that it is not law. My mother doesn't talk directly about college loans but implies every so often that becoming a doctor is the only secure way to avoid debt, despite the years of debt that medical school incurs. They fought for an anti-capitalist Turkey in the '70s. America made them change. Cooper's parents, in contrast, are artists. His father is a painter, and his mother is an interior decorator. They were shocked and concerned when he said he wanted to be an eye doctor, and he tells me that they still hope he will become an artist like them. His father believes that you need to be an artist if you want to be free. I'm so amazed by this ideology. Cooper is the oldest child of three, but sometimes I find him so bizarre and surprising that I'm shocked he's not an only child.

We walk back to the entrance of the museum. A wide window opens to the Marmara, so blue it looks painted, and we see giant cargo ships from Russia that cross the Black Sea and funnel down the Bosphorus. The seagulls rise, soar, and fall into the water.

Look, I point, how happy they are.

He laughs. We don't know that the gulls are happy, Sibel.

And it's true, he's right. I take his betterment for granted. Cooper wears socks to bed, his mother is a voracious reader, and he is afraid of spiders. Nothing else. He's not afraid of anything else. He is resilient. His body is full of blood, and my humor, black bile, causes menstrual cramps, dizziness, headaches, alienation. In other people, it can cause uncontrolled passion or a deeply rooted connection to God. Allah, I think, feeling guilty. My mother was once in a weird place, that's all she said, "a weird place," and she started watching a channel on television about Buddhism. She really connected. She watched every night after she put me and Alara to bed. Only she began to have these dreams of Mohammed, and she was afraid, but she also felt blessed. She had never seen him before, and after 9/11, she did not know if she ever would again. Well, she never watched these Buddhism programs again. And now she feels "weird" about Buddhism. Black bile begins as an accumulation in your spleen, bleeds into your liver, creeps into your joints, and rides your spine up to your head, where it ultimately causes great fluctuations in your emotional life. Most of the men in my family have died from heart attacks. The women, ovarian cancer. Blood enters your heart through the right atrium. Your right atrium then pumps this blood into the right ventricle, which shuttles the blood to your lungs, which hand the now oxygen-rich blood back to the left side of your heart. The heart is the only organ in a human body that can move by itself. Anytime I'm lying flat on my bed I make myself as motionless as a lifeless object. A boulder. A tall steel building. Then I make my heart the only moving thing.

It is the closest I have come to forgiveness. What I mean is, forgiving myself.

# III.

WE DECIDED AT THE BEGINNING OF THE SUMMER WE'D TAKE
one trip outside of Istanbul. I wanted to visit Berlin, where many
Turks immigrate, and Cooper chose Konya, a city remarkable
only for housing Rumi's tomb in a Sufi mosque. In 1980, it was also
where an Islamic party led a rally that my parents say was one of
the many reasons General Kenan Evren went ahead with the coup
that sent my parents to New York. I'd already been there years
ago with my family on what Baba called an emotional pilgrimage. Cooper and I were going to decide fairly, with a coin toss, but
when Dilek told Cooper that the boarding school that his grandmother taught at was only a four-hour bus ride from Konya, the
bribery began. Cooper spoke of Rumi's poetry constantly, reciting
his poems like a human-size songbird on my shoulder, in my face,
anywhere we went, sometimes in memorized Turkish. He spoke
of my grandmother, how she is so generous to him, and how he
wished I could have known his grandmother. As he narrated how
his grandmother took only one handheld suitcase with her on a
three-week voyage that carried her across the Atlantic and through
the Mediterranean to Istanbul then Adana, I imagined his grandmother disembarking from this ship in Istanbul and carrying her

leather suitcase, and I saw, for only one moment, what she saw: ferries, seagulls, mosques, minarets, trams, and street cats. That's not what I see when I see Istanbul, but I wanted to know what it felt like to see a city like this one for the first time. To feel awe. So I said yes, okay, why don't we go to Konya and Tarsus.

Today is the hottest day of the summer yet and we put the fan at an angle where it hits my damp neck, his chest. Like my grandmother's, Cooper's apartment has no air conditioner, something he finds meaningful. Cooper wants to call the school to make sure it's open when we visit. He wants to poke around campus. Tarsus American College, now coed, is just outside the historic city of the same name, where Saint Paul was born. They say Cleopatra first met Marc Antony in Tarsus. During an official meeting under olive-tree shade they made eyes at each other. I'm not sure what happened next.

Cooper is googling the school's phone number and tells me that his grandmother never talked about that time in her life. It was before she met the man who would become his grandfather. At that time, he was serving in the Philippines.

My parents say she almost married a Turkish man, Cooper continues with excitement. I don't know how it ended, though. She came back to California two years later, with a suitcase full of silk scarves, towels, and black charcoal sketches she drew of women in headscarves.

Remember, he says, recalling the one time I visited his family's home, we framed those sketches. They're hung up in my kitchen.

They're beautiful, I say. I remember feeling moved and transported before them. I remember having told my father that Cooper's grandmother worked in Turkey, at his same high school. I'd told Baba about the sketches and he got upset. Women don't wear all black there, and especially not on their heads, he'd said, and began pacing our kitchen. He said Americans will never understand Turkey or Muslims, and that we don't have the tools, temperament, or language to correct their misinterpretations. I was upset, and pointed out that yes, Cooper's parents must think you are a bit barbarian for not letting him sleep over. Baba did not respond well to this, citing the doctrine that when I'm back in his house it's his rules, and then my mother sat him down by pressing on his shoulders, motioning towards her own heart. Don't tire yourself out, she'd said, and he'd held her gaze and nodded.

We sit on Cooper's bed as he digs in his pocket for his phone. He's more excited than he's been all month, and each time he sees I've stopped paying attention, he touches my jaw to lead my head from its view of the window to face him. Nothing bad has ever happened to Cooper, which I point out to him sometimes. But it will, he often replies, and then he's silent, sometimes for hours, and even if I crack jokes or play his favorite songs, but especially if I try to seduce him, he will only give me a small, sad smile, and apologize, admitting that he has lost some optimism, but he's sure it will return soon.

Finally he manages to get in contact with the administration at Tarsus.

I have a strange request, Cooper says on the phone, my grandmother worked at this school in the 1940s. He takes his hand off my mouth and his eyes look vacantly into mine. I hear a muffled voice on the other end. Cooper laughs.

Yes, her spirit has sent me back here. I have no free will! He laughs again before becoming serious. This might be a stretch, but do you happen to have anything of hers, any papers, formal documents?

Outside, a group of boys throw around a rubber ball and yell insults at one another. They call one another pussies and vaginas and sons of whores. In the distance is the water, and farther back, the tall minarets far enough away to look like needles. A younger sister, or maybe love interest, stands at the edge of their circle. She has her thin arms planted on her hips and wears a green plastic clip in the shape of a bird in her hair. It looks like she wants to join, but one of the boys shoves her and she lands on her hands and knees. Then this girl's mother flings open the front door and ushers her inside, and I can't help smiling, comforted by familial care, until I catch sight of this mother's throat. She has a tracheostomy. In New York, most of these holes are covered with plastic to make it easier to eat and breathe and consume liquids, but I haven't really seen the tubes in Turkey. Maybe this woman is taking a break from her tube. Maybe she just cleaned the nooks and passageways of her tube and now it is on a drying rack in her kitchen. I wish I didn't see the hole in her throat from this far away. I wish I had some way of not remembering my father.

We're in the domestic terminal a few days later.

But tourists don't go there, I tell Cooper again as we board the plane to Konya. Alara called me this morning, as usual. She expressed concern about rising tensions near the southeastern border, but she thinks this adventure will be good for me. Only my grandmother doesn't tell me what will be good for me. I'm grateful that she feeds me and brews me liquid potions and that's all. She sent us off with a packet of oily börek, which I carefully placed at the top of my backpack.

We move slowly in line. The moment I step off the boarding

bridge and onto the plane, I have to incant a small prayer to Allah and murmur amen three times while simultaneously touching my hands to my forehead so that we land safely.

It's only Muslim tourists who go there, I repeat after saying my prayer. And the Americans who read Coleman Barks like the Bible. And Coleman Barks doesn't even speak or read Persian, did you know that? He just reinterprets English translations.

Cooper helps a woman with her baggage. Then he turns to me on the turquoise-carpeted aisle and mentions lightly that maybe it will be good for me to go someplace where I have an isolated memory of my father. I listen. I imagine Baba as a phantom floating beside us in Konya. I imagine he would tell me that I actually am a Muslim tourist. I wonder if he'd fizzle if someone walked through his image. Or maybe he'd be translucent throughout the hot day.

KONYA IS A LARGE, FLAT CITY OF STANDARD TURKISH buildings—gray and beige apartment complexes, all with dusty red roofs. In the distance there is a squat mountain range. We walk through the city and point out things that we find beautiful, interesting, sad. We learn that Konya was the capital of the Seljuk Empire one thousand years ago. We weave through crowds of people, women shopping, men sitting outside cafés playing backgammon and rolling tiny white dice in their fists. In a pastry shop, I tell Cooper to use his Turkish to get two börek, one meat, one feta and spinach. He smiles at the men behind the counter and orders with exceeding politeness. He apologizes for his accent. The Turks behind the counter look at me, this girl-woman with her blond boyfriend, and mutter what Cooper can't understand, something mean, a limb of the Turkish lexicon he has not yet faced.

What did they say? Cooper asks me. He hands me a börek wrapped in wax paper. I stare at them and they stare back. The börek were made just ten minutes ago, I say. I press his hand to the wax paper. See, how warm they are.

I kiss his ear and wrap my arm over his shoulders in front of them and the men behind the counter persist, lips snarling. This time they address me by saying my great-grandfather would rise from his grave in Gallipoli should he see this.

Cooper thanks me, for the ear kiss or the börek, I'm not sure. Neither of my great-grandfathers are buried in Gallipoli. My mother's grandfather didn't die in World War I, nor did he die in the Turkish War of Independence. He was thrown for dead into a pit in Palestine, where he croaked for help until a British soldier heaved him out and loaded him onto a ship to India for prisoners of war. He returned to Turkey eighteen years later, a bullet hole scarred over on his forehead, the left side of his body partially paralyzed, and is now buried in his village outside Bolu next to his daughter, my dead grandmother who is renowned in our family for falling in love with a Kurdish man whom she was not per-mitted to marry. The others are buried in Tokat, or Georgia, or somewhere else in Anatolia.

There is a long line to get into Rumi's tomb and the sun is strong. I wrap my head up in a silk headscarf as Cooper reapplies sunscreen to his face and neck. As we wait I bend down to feed a cat some börek. There are no tall buildings around the mosque save for the turquoise minaret, bright green against the blue sky. The summer before Baba died, I was living at home. Cooper was staying in the dorms on campus with his friends, but one night, I decided I would sneak him into the house and make him sleep in my bed. I was testing my boundaries, because what girl doesn't want to see what her body can get away with? But my father, he came upstairs to fix the radiators, which were not working properly because the pipes were full of trapped air, and when he opened my door and saw Cooper's blond head poking out of my covers, he dragged me out of bed by yelling, dragged us out of the bedroom by yelling, as if his voice were a rope around our necks, and he dragged us down the stairs and into the kitchen, where he asked Cooper, Do you let your sisters act like this too? Do you let your sisters act like sluts?

Maybe my father would be happy to know that I am far from a slut. I have no excess of blood in me to cause sexual abandon. I think of the dried-up vulvas in the body exhibit. There was one woman who was embracing a man, and they made his penis look erect. You can't tell what the woman is feeling, which seems meaningful.

Inside the mausoleum, Cooper's blond hair is again the stalk of tall corn, high above the moving sea of coarse black hair and silk scarves. The other visitors turn their faces to him, even those at the feet of Rumi's sarcophagus covered in gold-embroidered cloth, as if they all came to Konya to see this young man, Cooper. I'm embarrassed. There is a group of men weeping in the corner. Another man cries as he plays a reed flute. An American takes a flash photograph, something strictly forbidden. One man, praying on his knees with his hands open in front of him, stares at Cooper. The man keeps staring at Cooper the whole way through the tomb, his small pink mouth mumbling under his black, broom-like mustache, but Cooper keeps looking at me. He's charting my facial movements. He wants to know how I feel.

He wants to know if I'm feeling moved by Rumi's dead, holy body and these acts of pilgrimage. He wants to know whether I'm reminded of my father's grave, my lie, but he can't find out that I never went. He already knows what happened at the funeral. He can't find out anything else about me. I smile for him, it's a weak smile, I think, but I'm not very sure what I seem like to him or to anyone anymore. I used to have a lot to say. I used to be choler: energetic and ambitious. People used to tell me to be quiet, and I would react violently. Now I am listless and tired. I'm phlegm, passive but sensitive, and sentimental. Maybe I am growing up.

And my father, he was otherwise silly and friendly, and he loved to dance to music with his hands up, his fingers snapping to the beat.

Later, on the hard bed in our hotel room, Cooper asks me how my head feels. Our hotel is near Alaaddin Hill, and cat and people noises float in through the open window that faces the park. Tomorrow we will be taking a four-hour bus to Tarsus. Cooper is very excited for our grand visit to the school, and his excitement, I'm hoping, makes up for my fear. Cooper is on his own family mission. His grandfather, a man he never met, died in a fire only a few years after marrying his grandmother. At the beginning of the summer, Cooper told me his grandfather reminds him of my grandfather the eye doctor, and how both our grandmothers spent a lifetime with dead husbands. What he said annoyed me. But my grandfather died in an earthquake, I'd replied, and much earlier in their marriage. Hmm, Cooper had said. He looked funny, as if he was lying. For such an open person, it's always been hard to tell when he's lying. He would be a great actor. A brief panic biles up in my throat when I think about how in all the time I've protected my lie about visiting the grave, I've never known if Cooper has a lie, too, one he is keeping hostage. And I should have known that when he shared his grandfather theory with me the week we first arrived in Turkey, the week I called the clinic and apologized, the week my grandmother began taking care of me instead of the other way around, the week my sister called me, saying, You were never like this, Sibel. Like what? I'd said. Well, unsure of yourself, she said. Depressed. Again, I don't know, but I should have known that week that we would end up on a hard bed in the middle of Turkey at a hotel named Dream of Rumi on a mission to walk hand-in-hand through our world of the dead, a path Cooper has mapped out for me, and for him, a path that only leads me back to my father.

I steer Cooper's hand to the muscles between my shoulder and neck until he begins to knead.

Do you know that *tarsus*, I say, in anatomy is also the word for fibrous connective tissue on the edge of your eyelids. The sheet of tissue that helps support your eyelid.

Oh, he says. I didn't know that.

It also has something to do with bones, but I can't remember that one.

He smiles. Finally, he takes my mouth.


THE SCHOOL IS NEAR THE EDGE OF TOWN, AND AFTER WE unfold our legs and walk off the bus, we hail a taxi and make our way to my father's school. I recite my prayer and touch my forehead three times before we pass through the gates. I have to ask Allah that we spend this day with no accidents or trouble. Sometimes I dare to ask for more, like, Allah, may I please have good thoughts today, or, Allah, may I please not see my grandmother's hand tremble today, or, Allah, may I please transform the feeling of guilt into good gut movements? When we pass through the gates we see the great stone building—the main school. Cypress trees line the perimeter of the campus. Cooper wipes his hands on his pants after showing me how sweaty he is with anticipation. Because it is summer break, there aren't many people around, but there are many cats. The women who work in administration are very friendly. One asks me in Turkish if I'm an alum, and I politely tell her no. The same woman gives Cooper a package of his grandmother's papers.

We made photocopies, she explains in English. So, it's for you to keep. She smiles at Cooper and asks if she can help with anything else.

We say no thank you, and when she turns away, we remark on how kind she was, and helpful. We remark on the way the air here feels clean and windy, as if someone were trying to tell us something. I feel this often in Turkey. We stand next to a Turkish flag outside the school's entrance and slide the soft pieces of paper out of the package. His grandmother, Joyce, looks very similar to a Turk in her photograph. Cooper points out that her nose ends in a small hook like mine. We do not know why this is significant.

The package also contains Joyce's application essay and her résumé. Her essay is written in a neat, tiny script. Joyce explains that she wants to teach in Turkey because the world is in a very fragile state right now. We have to come together and understand one another's differences in a time like this, she explains. The date on her essay confirms that she applied one week after the end of World War II. On her identification card for the school, someone wrote out her name and under her name and photograph, her religion. PROTESTANT is stamped in Turkish.

That's funny, Cooper says, she wasn't religious at all.

They had to write something, I say, my identification card says "Islam."

We continue to sift through her papers, heavy in a packet, light when holding up just one sheet. I want more packages, receipts for clothing and kebap, evidence of how she spent her time. I want to know how she liked it here. She must have been choler, which made her courageous and adventurous. I want to see the man she almost married, the Turk. I want to know who broke whose heart in half and who kept which pieces.

This feels like we're traveling through time, I say.

Traveling through time is harder than I thought, Cooper says.

But we're doing it now.

I mean, emotionally hard.

It begins to rain, and we don't want the papers to get wet. Cooper slips the papers under his shirt and we run along the side of the main building until we find a set of stone steps sheltered by trees. In the distance, two cats are playing. Maybe they are fighting. It is difficult to tell. Cooper has a peculiar look on his face.

What? I ask.

Don't you want to find your dad's records too?

I wave my hand through the air. Oh, I already know those. When he and his best friend refused to cut their hair—they had grown it past their shoulders—their physics teacher, a draft dodger from Kentucky, got so mad. Then they came to class with their heads shaved, and the draft dodger punished them by forcing them to copy out each page of the Oxford dictionary.

Wow, Cooper says. This was during the Vietnam War?

I guess so. Near the end of it, I think. He became a leftist here, too. All his friends had anti-NATO banners on their dorm room walls. One of his friends got kicked out for going to a demonstration.

What demonstration was it?

I don't think he told me.

They probably have a whole file, though. And with more information. Maybe you can find out.

Maybe, I say. Maybe I'll go ask.

He stands up. Well?

I make to get up. Why don't we wait until it stops raining?

You don't want to do it, do you?

I do, I really do.

He looks at me. He moves towards me, sitting on the step against the stone wall. He corners me like this. Look at me, he says, please.

This place reminds me of the place where we went camping in California, I offer.

Last year we camped in the redwoods and smoked weed and had sex against a tree. We went off the trail and hiked a hill. We could hear the voices of people on the path below us while Cooper had his whole hand in me. He reached up into my ribs and held my wet organs in a hard fist. We'd looked at each other, me and Cooper, as he continued to use his hand to get something from me. I remember feeling calm.

I know less and less about you, sometimes, Cooper says. He's towering above me and his eyes water. Did you really go to the grave, Sibel?

Yes, I say. Yes. Cooper keeps his eyes trained on me, on my face. I want to ask him how he can love somebody so lonely. I want to nail his thin body down like a board for an answer. We've been together for two years, and Cooper and I have never once had an argument. Maybe it is because we were close friends first, but we slid into each other easily. We didn't have to compromise ourselves for the other. We didn't have to take turns with feelings. At the time, I thought that was what love looked like, but now I think love is something else. We are going to have to unearth the people we will become, slowly, carefully, but with a dedicated and calm labor, as if digging into dirt with special tools, tools that will not maim the tender thing inside the other that we find.

He sits next to me on the stone step. We're sheltered from the rain. I point out the cats.

Do you think they're fighting? he asks me.

Are we? I venture, afraid to say it.

No, he says quickly. No.


THERE IS TURBULENCE ON THE PLANE RIDE BACK FROM Adana to Istanbul. I make my hands into open bowls on my lap in prayer. Cooper is happily chatting in English with the Turkish man next to him. What kind of person is happy in the middle seat of an airplane row? What kind of person is happy talking to a stranger about developments in eye surgery?

I'm trying to complete my prayer, but my language is all wrong, and I have to resort to my own ritual, because if you don't have a ritual to confront death, a ritual aligned with a religious practice, you have to fashion your own. The Turkish rituals are not my own. Medical bloodletting was born in Egypt, and Galen, a Greek who lived in Turkey sometime during the second century, often prescribed bloodletting and cupping in order to effectively release a bad humor. His theory that blood—as well as the humors and pneuma, which is essentially air, but in the human body became the spirit or soul—moves through the body via pulsing arteries was widely practiced until William Harvey, who served not only as chief physician to two British kings but also examined women accused of witchcraft, proved in 1628 that the heart is really a pump. Galen mistakenly believed that the heart produced blood for arteries, while the liver produced blood for veins.

All these ancient doctors, the more they mapped out the human body's circulation, the more they argued about the location of the human soul. Baba believed you don't have a soul, you are a soul. Baba, who said the Koran is the socialist Bible.

As a child on plane rides to Istanbul, I'd cup my hands in prayer during turbulence. Baba taught my sister and me the Arabic prayers, like water on his tongue, gravel on mine. I'm afraid, I told him on one plane ride to Istanbul. We were over the Atlantic, and I was certain that even if the yellow inflatable slide popped us out of the plane we'd still die in water. If we were to crash, I asked, would death be immediate?

He leaned in. His elbow slipped off the armrest. Yes, he said. Right away you become an angel. After so much life, he said, such little death.

EVERYONE CLAPS WHEN THE PLANE LANDS. I LOOK AT Cooper, who is smiling, and we clap too. We take a taxi back from the airport. Cooper gathers our luggage and I tell him to go inside, that I need to call my mother. Really I plan to smoke a cigarette.

If he's suspicious, he doesn't show it. He sees my grandmother on the balcony, looking for us, so he hurries to buzz the door.

I move behind a tree across the street from my grandmother's apartment building, and I smoke my secret cigarette. My black smoker's glove was stinking, so I washed it with my clothes before our trip and laid it to dry under my bed where my grandmother most likely won't clean. But I carry toothpaste and hand lotion in my bag, also gum. I always smoke my secret cigarette behind this tree. It's a good tree. I can still see my grandmother's apartment but I am securely hidden. The crested wave shape of Cooper's voluminous hair is visible through the window when my grandmother reaches forward to hug him.

Baba smoked in secret, too, and I picture his lungs as black, oily stones in his chest. The night Baba died in the kitchen while boiling water for tea, I heard him yell. It was a short yell, as if snapped off halfway. I continue to hear him yell and yell, a broken machine walking into a wall.

When I finish my cigarette, I suck toothpaste into my mouth from the tube. I rub lavender lotion on my hands, focusing particularly on my two fingers that once held the cigarette. Bloodletting myself will not cure me if I'm full of black bile. And when I first came to Istanbul this summer, my grandmother sat me down and said, I am getting closer to death, but in heaven there will be a spot next to me. I will save it for you. You will meet me there.

I'm riding the ancient elevator, thinking of my disguises. What story am I telling myself that is so different than that of my grandmother, and even my mother, the women who won't tell me the full story of who they are and when they became people?

# IV.

MY DAYS FEEL DIFFERENT, NOW THAT I'M LYING TO MY
grandmother and Cooper. My grandmother has her reading
glasses on and is flipping through her telephone book until she
sighs and heads for the kitchen. The television is on, as usual, and
the anchor is discussing the upcoming elections. There's a plan to
meet for dinner with Dilek and her friends.

I've got this headache still, I tell Dilek on the phone, I should
stay home.

Are you sure you don't want to come to this restaurant? Dilek
asks. It's a new seafood place I found. They serve sushi.

No, I say, but I'm sure you picked a very cool place.

Cooper is coming, she says. But sure.

Cooper is spearheading a new project at work to provide eye
care for Syrian refugees. I didn't think he had time for dinner.
I'm collapsed on the couch, stalking Dilek on social media. She's
posted another photo of herself in a bikini. My grandmother
comes back in with a tray of hot Turkish coffee. Her hand shakes
as she places the tray on the lace tablecloth. She heard me tell
Dilek that Cooper has been very busy lately, and now informs me

that despite his various commitments, he graciously wants to tutor Emre in English.

I close my computer lid. But I was supposed to do that, I say.

You can't do that from over there, she replies.

There's video chat, I suggest. I can do something over video chat.

Can you assign homework? Can you print worksheets with vocabulary?

I'm not going back for another month. It's basically in two months that I'm going back.

She's doubtful. I can see it in the way she's about to open her mouth.

He doesn't speak Turkish, I remind her.

We've been talking, she says, defensive. He's gotten very good. She hands me a cup of hot coffee on a saucer.

You can't even speak the same language, I say again.

She ignores me. We watch the news while drinking coffee. She tuts her tongue at the television screen showing recent footage of what Israel is doing to Palestine and changes the channel to a soap opera.

I love this one, she says. She points to the handsome man. He's in our Russia one, too.

The handsome man is from a religious family. He wants to marry a young woman from a wealthy, secular family. The handsome man gets yelled at by his mother, who covers her head in a silk scarf with blue flowers. We listen to her command her son to stop seeing the whore he's dating. She curses the snobby family the whore comes from. She curses the fact that this woman does not pray. She curses god for her ill fate in sons.

What happened to her other son? I ask my grandmother.

He got married to a whore, too.

Oh.

The handsome man leaves despite his mother's threats and takes a shared taxi through the streets of Üsküdar, the ferry across the Bosphorus, and boards another bus that shuttles him down the highways in modern Istanbul to the rich neighborhood in the green hills that the young woman lives in, with her family, who similarly looks down on the handsome man because he is religious and poor.

I forget, my grandmother says, does Alara have a boyfriend right now?

No, they broke up a few months ago.

My grandmother nods in approval. The women in my family love television. The Turkish shows are about family, culture, and inheritance. My mother, who likes American sci-fi and fantasy story lines, says that we, Turks, are simply not creative enough to produce television that strays from common, overused story lines populated with the same characters: a doting and controlling mother obsessed with her handsome son who falls in love with the wrong woman, all under the purview of an angry father. The father has a thick mustache only if he is supposed to be religious and poor. The rich fathers are clean shaven and wear silk suits in their Bosphorus mansions. Sometimes it is the boy who comes from the rich, secular family, and the girl he loves, then, is required to be from a poor neighborhood where all the neighbors are friends and come over for tea to gossip and the mothers are always obsessed with cleaning. There are obviously never any queer characters on these shows. The bad girls—the ones who make this star-crossed, class-based love story between the boy and girl even more difficult—are always tall and blond. The only exception to this formula of rich and poor, religious and secular, is the television show about the sultans where the socioeconomic situation is evermore complicated, as the feud is between the sultan's mother and one of the sultan's wives, who was formerly a Christian slave.

You know what my mother always says? I ask my grandmother. She looks up, her shaking hand in a bowl of cherries.

What? Her eyes are back on the screen.

This is not creative. This is too much like real life to be creative.

The mother wears a different silk headscarf now, this time embroidered with tiny red flowers. She's gossiping to her friends at tea about how her only son cannot marry that girl.

It's too much like real life, I insist. The censorship, too.

My grandmother shrugs and hands me the cherry bowl. What isn't?

Then there are the talk shows about diets and makeup and hair dye and other vital lessons on well-being. We particularly enjoy the dramatic interpersonal programs. Yesterday we watched one where they brought in families who were no longer speaking to one another. A girl with heavy makeup sat on the green stage couch, attempting to make peace with her mother, but her mother refused to be on television, so the program showed her Facebook profile picture on the split screen as her daughter cried about abandonment.

When my coffee cup is ready, my grandmother mutes the soap opera and begins to read the grounds.

Well, she says, her nose in the tiny cup, wow.

What? I say. What does it say?

This shape, she says, is a field of dirt. There is soil everywhere. But here is your body.

I look into the cup. We fight for nose space to see into the thing. Sure enough, I see my body: a thin white line in negative against the brown sludge.

Those are the leaves, the trees, and finely packed dirt, says my grandmother. It looks like life is continuing above you, and you've covered yourself in earth. She holds the cup out of reach and regards me very carefully.

It looks like you are ready to die, she announces.

What? I say. I reach for the cup but she moves it, like we're playing a game. That's insane.

That's what it says, baby. She shakes her head. This happened once to my cousin who was having stomach pain, not headaches. She said you have to take in the earth in order to gain your advantage over it. She bought fresh potatoes from the market and boiled them. But you have to leave the skin on the potatoes, she says you can't even wash off the dirt that gets stuck in those craters. First, we have to make your stomach better.

My head, I say, my head hurts, not my stomach.

I think it will have the same effect, she says. Doesn't your period hurt, too?

Your cousin is what, eighty? Ninety? One hundred and fifty?

My cousin is dead, she says, laughing. She died many years ago.


UPSET ABOUT MY FUTURE, I DECIDE TO MEET UP WITH Cooper and Dilek after all. I take the bus to the water, and when I walk into the fish restaurant I'm shocked at how black the Boğaz glints before me. Maybe it is not Istanbul itself that is black bile, but the Bosphorus. Most of Dilek's friends have left, but Esra is still there. They're sitting at a long table with a white tablecloth, a plate of fish bones before each of them, an ashtray for every few seats. Dilek is wearing a low-cut shirt and has taken her place next to Cooper. Her eyebrows are particularly neat and thick tonight. They're talking about how Eda, Esra's sister, didn't come tonight. She's been going straight home after work every day because she's worried about what could happen on the metro, in crowded squares, in malls. She thinks even the ferries are dangerous. Their parents didn't allow Esra to go to the Gezi anniversary because when she was at a demonstration last year in Nişantaşı, her boyfriend was arrested and she came home bruised from water cannons. I drop a chunk of bread for the street cat that rubs up at my ankles. Soon, more cats gather at my feet. That Cooper, an American, wants to stay in a country like Turkey renews Dilek and Esra's waning hope, and they begin to talk about the upcoming election.

I ask the waiter for another bowl of bread. It's funny that they didn't end up ordering the sushi.

Cooper thinks it makes sense, Turkey's state right now, because the poor always rise against the rich. The political divide reminds him of America. Dilek agrees, and calls Cooper so intelligent. I can't tell if I saw him look at her body, or if he was charmed by the funny way she uses a knife. The cats have tripled and they sit at my feet patiently. I drop more bread on the ground. I know Cooper would never do something with her. He, like me, is a deeply monogamous person. We inherited this from our parents.

I clear my throat and say that according to the Istanbul municipality, 75 percent of the city's 330 cemeteries are already full and space concerns push grave prices higher. Rich people can buy the graves that go for the same price as renting an apartment with a view of the Bosphorus.

Dilek shoots Cooper a concerned look, but I ignore it. The poor people, I continue, who receive minimum wage—the U.S. equivalent of $3 an hour—have fewer options. They have to wait five years to even bury a new body inside another family member's grave.

Esra's staring at me. She says, of course, that's a concern. However, she thinks the biggest problem in Turkey right now is that the educated youth won't pursue careers in politics or academia, a trend that started after the 1980 coup, when the Turkish upper and middle classes gave up on participating actively in politics because of decades of violence and instability. Or arts, she says knowingly. Everyone in Esra's family, including her sister, warns her against writing. Her friends, however, are supportive. She finds it generous that her boyfriend wants to read the novels she loves, particularly because the novels are generally about sad young women who either lash out by acting rude or by being despondent and uncommunicative.

Does he like the novels? I ask her.

Esra shrugs. Sure, he finds them interesting.

Have I met him? I ask. Everyone looks away uncomfortably, and Dilek says he's at school in America. Remember, I told you. He's working at a—what do you call it?—think tank this summer.

Oh, I say. Sorry.

This conversation seems to end the dinner. As we're kissing everyone goodbye on each cheek, Dilek pulls me aside to tell me she spoke to my mother on the phone the other day, and that she's worried about me. What is she worried about? What I did to my father? I'm scanning her face, looking for a clue.

Do you want me to come to the grave with you? Dilek asks.

Remember, I say, I already went. I make to join Cooper, who

is pretending he's not eavesdropping, but Dilek grabs me by the fat on my upper arm.

But the end of Ramazan is coming up. We should go together, once Alara's here.

Okay.

We can bring your grandmother, too. My dad wants to go as well.

Okay.

Dilek wants to push me but I'm not ready. And I know there's only so much passivity a person can take. I smile at her and she smiles back. We stand there smiling. It's nice, smiling. Then she hugs me, and her perfume is so strong, like I'm swallowing chunks of rotten flowers.

Cooper and I take the bus back to my grandmother's, and as we pass the cemetery I think of the people who can't afford graves. Their dead are buried on the outskirts of the city, in new cemeteries, making the dead not abstract, finally classless souls, but distinctly poor souls. Even when dead, the relationship between the poor and the rich continues to shape the parameters of this city. Then there are the Jewish cemeteries, and across Turkey, unmarked Armenian graves. Cooper, who'd been talking about how excited he is to develop a fundraising plan for his new project, has fallen silent. I ask him what's wrong. Nothing, he says, but when he makes eye contact he says that he just can't believe that we've already been here for one month. I say, Same, me too, and I make my face convincingly somber, although really time has been passing very slowly for me. I was nervous about Cooper coming here, a place no American friend of mine has ever seen. Silly, I thought, that I could take his heart into my chest cavity and let his beat in place of mine. Ancient Egyptians preferred the heart as well. Like me, it was the brain they didn't understand. During the mummification process, they'd wield a bronze scalpel to dig into the corpse's nose. I'm not sure whether they pulled the whole thing out that way, or how they were certain they'd latched on to the right organ. I'm not sure how long it took to dig out the brain.

When the bus pulls away and disappears down a hill, Cooper kisses me goodbye on the mouth. I don't think time is passing in the same way for us. Nobody is around when we kiss.

THE NEXT DAY I TELL MY GRANDMOTHER I'M GOING TO A café to study for the med school exam, and I make a big show of putting my textbook in my backpack. My grandmother makes sure that I take a sweater, in case there's a breeze. She is obsessed with breezes and thinks they give people head colds. My plan is to walk by the water. Ibn Sina, the Muslim father of medicine who expanded greatly on Hippocrates's and Galen's works, emphasized the importance of internal and external causes for illness, including environment. Clean, unpolluted bodies of water balance a person out. Water is an antidote. By the time I'm nearing the foot of the hill, my mother calls me. I'm on a tiny sidewalk, less than one foot wide, and I silence her call. Then she calls again. I pick up and explain that I'm doing well, don't worry, and my grandmother is doing okay, too, but when she asks about Cooper, I can't say anything. She informs me that I seem to have begun some new practice with Cooper. I seem to have split myself in half for him but only to show my exterior, the part that is lips and heavy-lidded eyes, and she tells me in Turkish, You've become a well and what he throws in you he'll die trying to get back. I can hear my sister agree in the background. Alara most likely helped cook this theory up. Her school in California finished a month later than mine, and she's at home for two weeks before she joins me here. My mom has only one week off in the summers, and she likes to save it in case there's an emergency.

I think my mother just learned the word *accommodating*. I mention this, and she says, No, of course I know the word. I only just started to use it.

My mother can tell stories only in Turkish. Alara and I, in turn, don't know the more intellectual Turkish words; phrases that delineate adult sentiments about emerging scathed or unscathed from a bureaucratic system. We always have to meet in the middle of language.

My mother asks me if I've visited his grave and I'm scared to lie, because if anyone will find me out, it's her.

Yes, I say. I went. I wiped dirt off the grave with a wet towelette and I placed some flowers on the gray stone. Tulips. I don't know if those are graveyard flowers.

That's fine, she says, those are fine flowers. What else?

I spoke some prayers, I say, the ones you taught me.

She's silent. I can hear her breathing on the other end of the phone.

You were always much better at the prayers than him, I continue. Nothing from her, still. I am terrified of my mother's grief. I am terrified at how similar it seems to my own.

My mother remains silent until she asks me if I'm by the water.

I walked to the Boğaz to read. I'm having trouble studying, I add.

You're not studying for the test? Are you feeling okay?

I'm okay.

Then go to his grave, baby.

Oh, I say. I can't remember if I've lied to her and told her I went to the cemetery. Didn't I just tell her I went? Does she mean me to go again? Again and again?

Go to the grave, baby. He's there. I promise.

We're quiet. I'm sucking on my hair, wondering if she'd hear me drag smoke into my lungs if I lit a cigarette. Finally, she says there's nothing like the way the Boğaz glints under the setting sun. She says she met my father there, by the water, after her brother was released from prison. She remembers weaving between cars to cross the street, while her brother stood, ashing his cigarette, and opened his arms. She remembers acting coy, debating what the Sixth Fleet was still doing in Turkey and what would happen with the labor strikes across the city—the automobile manufacturing workers, the miners, the goldsmiths in Taksim—before finally allowing her brother to introduce her to his best friend, my father, who she at first thought was much too serious. She loves to joke that my father didn't crack a laugh until three months into their relationship. My father rarely spoke about Turkey. I don't even know what it was like for him growing up, because my grandmother never speaks about him as a child either. And Alara and I don't know what our parents did in the late '70s besides attending demonstrations and organizing. Baba did admit to us, only once and just last summer when Gezi began, that he distributed funds for purchasing weapons. That's why he fled to the States in 1979 for a PhD he had applied to the year before on a desperate whim, and just in case.

Actually, my mother suddenly says, we met before then, and as she tells me these scant yet animate details of meeting him at a demonstration on a university campus in Ankara where three students were killed, I begin to resurrect my father. I'm doing it, I'm seeing him. He's swimming.

I blink and the strokes that were his arms cutting through water is bobbing plastic trash.

I COME HOME AND AM SURPRISED TO FIND COOPER'S THERE. He's cooking dinner with my grandmother. I elbow my way into the kitchen and he tells me he hasn't eaten all day. He's decided to fast for Ramazan's last week. My grandmother understands our English, because Cooper was just clutching his stomach, and as usual she's very impressed. My grandmother can no longer fast. If her blood sugar shoots up any further she'll die on her sofa watching the news. She's been having chest pain this year and she can't take her Parkinson's medication without food. We lick date pits dry, then we eat at sundown, the time in the summer holiday when families gather to drink Coke and dip bread in meat oil, while my least favorite broadcaster, the one with plastic blond hair, screams out the news, and each time I lower the volume my grandmother hunts down the remote to raise it back up. I would fast, too, but I can't stop eating. Not this summer. My grandmother, who goes to the cemetery only on holidays and is planning on going soon for the end of Ramazan, asks me whether they fixed the stone of her husband, who died in an earthquake. I'm upset at myself. I made much too big a deal at the kebap house of visiting Baba's grave. My grandmother doesn't have a grave ritual. She would understand that I don't have a grave ritual. I have only my humors. I fill my mouth with eggplant. I say, Well, I didn't see, I couldn't tell if it was whole, and I squint my eyes to look like I'm thinking but confused. She nods firmly and fills my glass up with Coke. She is so proud of me. Cooper looks down at his plate and cuts his eggplant into tiny pieces. He must know I'm lying. The last time I fasted was four years ago, and it was the only time, and I only lasted one day. My grandmother says, Maşallah, then tells me to explain what *maşallah* means. Cooper tells her in Turkish he understood, and they smile. We sit there, smiling.

COOPER CANNOT DECIDE WHAT WOULD BE MORE USEFUL today, taking me to another doctor for my headache, or buying flowers and going to my father's grave himself. He's disappointed in me. I'm lying on his slim twin bed with my feet sticking off the end, an ice pack on my forehead, a hot water bottle on my uterus. I need something better, though. Something holy.

You know, Sibel, Cooper says. I have some news for you.

I roll my eyes over to him. Something in him, or me, has aged.

Nermin, she told me something your father wanted you to know. Something that happened.

Now you're calling her Nermin?

This is serious, Sibel. There's something I need to tell you.

I know about her life, I say.

I don't know, Cooper says carefully, if you really do.

I can't look at him.

Sibel, you need to let this go. It wasn't your fault.

Cooper digs into his backpack and emerges with a fat, ancient book. He splits the book open by the spine and lays it across our thighs.

Sibel, look. I found this at the library, so you don't have to google anymore. Hippocrates penned the first book on healthy diets. And al-Razi, he was a physician and alchemist, said: *as long as you can heal with food, do not heal with medication.*

This is what you wanted to tell me?

No, he says, not this. I just want you to see this first. He repeats al-Razi's line.

Stop it, I say.

But it says what you've been talking about, that the humor theory of medicine is not outdated at all, but rather points to psychology. And endocrinology. It's all hormones. It's a more understanding, maybe parallel, medicine. Well, not just medicine, but the spiritual, too. The soul. They were looking for the location of the soul.

I never went to the grave, I say.

Cooper closes the book, using his thumb to bookmark the page.

I didn't go.

Cooper thinks about this for a moment before he opens the book again and turns towards me on the bed to continue reading, like I'm a child being put to sleep. He begins to move his hand in slow, wide circles on my back. Don't touch me, I say. I hear my voice climb like it belongs to somebody else. He continues to draw circles on my back and me, I'm yelling, stop reading it, stop, open the window, open the window, and me, opening the window and forcing the book out the window, and him, putting his cold palms to my forehead, my cheeks, to make my face, hot from crying, puff down and cool, and me, slapping his hand away, hitting him, hitting him again, and wanting him to hit me back, and his sweat, soaking his sheets, and him, finally bringing his mouth to mine and getting my arms behind me and securing me in his lap on his twin bed with the window open and the call to prayer going and going and me, freeing my arms, my hand around his white neck. And me, opening. I want a titanic part of myself to stay open.

I was the only one home last winter when my father died in the kitchen while boiling water for tea. He fell to the floor. He had a heart attack. I knew what a heart attack looked like from school. I knew that a clot had blocked my father's blood flow, starving his heart's oxygen supply. In medical textbooks, sections on the cardiovascular system state that the first identifiable sign of heart disease is either a heart attack or sudden death. Watching him, I knew there was only a certain amount of time before his heart muscle would die from lack of oxygen. I froze. He looked at me, on the ground, his fist at his chest.

I don't know how many seconds passed before Alara came home, humming, kicking her boots off, texting on her phone, and saw us in the kitchen. She called 911 herself. Baba died two hours later.

THE NEXT DAY, MY GRANDMOTHER SETS OUT FOR THE cemetery with fresh flowers for her dead husband and her dead son. The heavy wooden door swings shut behind her and burns a new hole in my head, and that hole leads to another door, my own door, an iron door that creaks open when I allow the lock to loosen enough, into the room in my head that holds the funeral on the winter day when the cemetery was covered in snow and Alara and I never guessed it would snow, nor did my mother, nor did my grandmother, nor did my aunt or my cousins or my uncle, because it snows in Istanbul only two, maybe three times a winter, and the snow was heavy and thick and already a few inches deep when we got to the funeral and the sun hit the snow in orange and pink waves and the long and thin gravestones poked out like broken gray teeth and there were more cypress trees than I could ever count and I stood there in my grandmother's tiny Mary Janes, which were too tiny for the long feet I had inherited from my mother, because we forgot to pack black shoes, which is silly—how could we forget black shoes for a funeral—and Alara was wearing these cotton sneakers because she didn't want to borrow grandmother's shoes, especially because the only pair left were ancient high heels, and Alara didn't understand why everyone was telling her she had to wear nice footwear like leather to a funeral, why not just black, and our feet were soaked through and I remember wondering if my feet could think, would they think they were swimming or just freezing, and I tried to turn my feet towards Mecca, the same direction Baba's head was turned, but I forgot the direction of Mecca and we stood there and listened to Arabic prayers and Turkish condolences, and as it was ending, as people were heading towards the cemetery gates, as we were saying thank you, thank you for coming, to family and friends, one old woman, a woman I don't even know, a friend of my grandmother, I think, that's what my mother said to me after, when she was trying with all her might to make sure I wasn't cutting myself up about it, about this woman, about what this woman said to me, because this old woman plowed through the snow with a wild, horse-like energy, and she came up close to me, so close I could see a hole in her trachea from smoking and I couldn't stop staring into the hole, and she also didn't use a plastic tube, and this woman spat in the snow and I watched her chunk of yellow spit sink down several inches and the woman was dressed in black, a long black skirt and a heavy coat, and she was in the arm of a young woman who looked a little bored, and the old woman with the hole in her throat said, Are you not ashamed? Are you not ashamed that you let your beautiful father die?

# Part II

# I.

MY GRANDMOTHER IS HAVING FRIENDS OVER. I FORCE HER to sit down as I brew liters of black tea for her guests. Her kitchen is small, wood-walled, with no windows or ventilation, making her apartment smell thick with meat and butter every day around noon, when she slips into this tiny room to cook us lunch and dinner. I'm enjoying this. For once, I'm the one who feeds and caffeinates the women. My grandmother forces her sister to take the green armchair, while she sits in a rickety wooden chair near the double-paneled door that opens to the hallway. She has to keep an eye on me in her kitchen. Her other friends are sitting on the sofa, and they cross their legs at their ankles. One of Aunt Pinar's sons is getting a divorce, and the women discuss the former bride and what she did to make their marriage fall apart. Then they discuss another woman who just married into another family. Then they discuss another bride, and whether she will be good enough for their sons. Finally they admit that their sons can be pretty useless too, and that only a remarkable woman would be able to put up with them. On television, the police stand in a line outside one of Istanbul's oldest high schools. A protest is rumored to take place after the deputy prime minister announced that women should not be laughing loudly in public. He even blamed soap operas.

My grandmother's friends compliment me on helping my grandmother. After asking me if I have a boyfriend, if he's Turkish, if he's going to propose to me, if my sister has a boyfriend, if she'll get one soon, they ask me what I'm studying in school.

She's going to be a doctor, my grandmother says proudly as I hand her a tea glass on a saucer.

One of my grandmother's friends, Hatice, is focused on how dark I've gotten. She asks my grandmother if I am usually this esmer, a term used to distinguish women who are darker-skinned. My mother is darker than my father, but my grandmother does not give in to such gossip about colorism and politely ignores her friend's question by complimenting Aunt Sevgi on her new hair dye. Hatice looks disappointed, and instead asks me if I've been going to the beach, and I reply no, just walking around a lot. They are confused about the walking, but they agree that exercise is very healthy and they wish they could walk by the Boğaz sometime. The women are scanning my body for fats as usual, but I've worn my favorite tentlike dress, which makes it impossible to see my love handles and belly. Even my areolas are bigger now. I pull up a chair next to my grandmother and sit down, but not before Hatice asks me what book I have there, on my lap. It's unfortunately another humor book, one with an amazing passage about Mother Mary and how when she became pregnant with Jesus she transferred her humoral balance to him. This is uncommon. I tell Hatice it's about the history of medicine and she nods gravely. Another friend, Nilüfer, looks nervous. She keeps moving her hands around in her lap and adjusting her hairdo, a slicked-back bun of thin hair. At certain angles I can see her white scalp. She proceeds to tell me to be careful, that being an intellectual in Turkey can be a crime.

I'm hardly an intellectual, I say, and my grandmother agrees. She's not a writer, Nilüfer. Sibel's going to be a doctor.

The phone rings and I thank Nilüfer for her sage advice. It's Cooper, who wants to know if he should come with me to the hospital later. Last night after sex, Cooper said he wasn't upset that I had lied—he just really needs me to go to the grave. I can do it, I will, I'd said, but not with much conviction, and a bit confused as to why Cooper remained so set on this singular mission. I take the phone to the hallway and look at the photographs on the wall as I tell him my grandmother's already coming with me to the hospital, despite me having told her I'd like to go alone, and we laugh, a bit forcefully, at her doting behavior before saying goodbye. I spend a lot of time in my grandmother's apartment looking at old photographs and photo albums. Mostly the photographs are of me and my sister. There is only one photograph of my father as a baby. Then he is suddenly eighteen, or nineteen. Sometimes I make jokes that he never lived here, but my grandmother doesn't find these jokes funny and usually ignores me by simply turning her face away or accidentally dropping a plate.

Now my grandmother is describing Cooper to her friends. Yes, he's a foreigner, she says. But he's learning Turkish. Maybe they will get married, but they do things differently these days.

An alarm on my phone rings to tell me it's time for my grandmother to take her dopamine pills. I go to the bathroom, looking for her medicine bag. Lately my grandmother has been dodging her medication with increased craftiness. When she resists, I have to threaten her with the syringe and remind her of every Parkinson's symptom she's permitting control over her body, including delusions. I'm terrified of delusions. Ibn Sina once treated a prince who believed he had transformed into a cow by binding him in ropes for one month and threatening him with a knife, all while feeding him food that he told the prince was for cows. The cognitive behavioral therapy worked. The prince loved being told that he was getting fattened up for slaughter.

But my grandmother is not afraid of delusions. She thinks that's what prayer is for. It's likely that this bovine prince had schizophrenia, not melancholia, and Ibn Sina diverged from his Greek predecessors in his belief that mental illnesses were not, as previously believed, due to divine intervention but instead a humoral imbalance. I wonder. I splash my face with water in the sink. I haven't performed abdest since Baba died. Before that, only once, when he wanted to teach us how to pray on a mat. Islam is about respecting the spiritual beliefs of most people, and my mother lights a candle in every church she visits, but my father found this stupid, and he'd warn her against the moral code she was impressing on us. He wanted her to teach us about Islam, not Christianity. I turn on the faucet for the bath. I stick one foot under scalding water followed by the other. I wonder how I could get closer to Allah. My forearms followed by my shins. I also wonder when my father turned into the easily angered person he died as.

I dry my feet and find the bottle of pills. It's hidden between the hard yellow towels that my grandmother doesn't like to use.


TWO HOURS LATER, MY GRANDMOTHER'S FRIENDS ARE still having tea. Her friends no longer bring hot food and pastries, as they did following my father's death, but they are still very tender with my grandmother. They try, they really do try, not to talk about their own sons. Now they're discussing this new development called social media, and how they want to learn to use the damn thing to see what their grandchildren are doing every day. Aunt Pinar is a big advocate of this education project. If strangers can see what they do, she demands, why can't we? Her audience, riled up, nods. I offer to create each woman an Instagram account, but they begin to complain about not knowing what buttons to press, and anyway, only my grandmother owns a smartphone. We made her an Instagram account last summer, and sometimes she successfully likes our photos. Usually, she posts glowing red photos of her blurry thumb by accident.

I'm attempting to study at the dining table when Alara calls. She calls me every day, usually right when I am in the most dramatic scene of a soap, and proceeds to ask me whether my headache has moved to the front of my head, whether its ocular or catamenial, if I'm sure I've had no migraines, how she can't believe I'm not even taking Advil, and why I have no desire at all to actually take care of myself and seek the help I need. She does all this militant work to distract us from her own mental and physical illness, her eating disorder, which is a convenient tactic that perhaps I should adopt. She's really smart, my sister. Today Alara wants to know what I've been doing, so I tell her I've been going to the grave often. I'm brazen in my telling, aggressive, although I assume my mother and sister know I've been lying. But if Alara knows, she's not saying, which is unusual. She always has so much to say about everything. My grandmother hovers over me just as Alara asks about her health, ignoring her friends, who have begun discussing Turkish boyfriends for someone like me.

Oh, I say, looking at my grandmother, who smiles in a flirty way, as if her life is some big joke. She is doing pretty well.

The other morning my grandmother was having trouble getting dressed. I was walking down the corridor from the bathroom, where I had discovered that I was ten pounds heavier since the end of junior year, when I passed her open bedroom door and saw her trying to stick her arm into the sleeve of her grass-green cardigan—our favorite cardigan—but her aim kept slipping. I went in to help her, and I led her slack wrist into the sleeve, as she made me promise not to tell my mother. I promise, I replied, and she kissed me on my cheek.

Now Alara repeats her thing about Advil, saying it is honestly even a little hard to believe that this headache is chronic if I'm not taking Advil, and I explain that grandma has been making me liquid potions that actually work better than medications. Alara has some strongly worded opinions on this, but Aunt Pinar just changed the television channel to a talk show discussing diets, and the host now informs our living room that if you rub your stomach a certain way, it helps your body with constipation and makes you lose weight in your sleep, so my grandmother's friends stretch their legs out and start rubbing their fats.

Is it working? Hatice asks.

It's definitely working, I say, my palm over the telephone receiver. Hatice smiles.


THE AMERICAN HOSPITAL IS IN NİŞANTAŞI, A NEIGHBORhood of grand apartment buildings painted in pastel greens, yellows, ochers, and reds alongside the more standard beige and gray. The iron window railings all hold flowerpots, and the hilly, tree-filled streets are lined with coffee shops, pharmacies, shoe stores, wedding dress stores, and hardware stores selling long elec-

THE FOUR HUMORS + 87

trical cables and outlets and bulbs. Certain streets have grand stone apartments with ornate bay windows or exclusive, pricey designer stores where the air conditioner cuts into the hot air on the street when women in stilettos push open a door and strut out. The hospital is very modern, and my grandmother points out all the things they've renovated as we float up the escalator in the lobby.

Have you been here before? I ask my grandmother.

She looks offended. My husband was an eye doctor, Sibel.

Oh, I say. But didn't he work at the eye hospital?

She nods. The ceiling is so high it serves as the ceiling for seven, maybe even eight floors. The chandelier is perfect, modern, and hangs through the building the way I imagine my lungs to hang in my skeleton.

Do you think this lobby's ceiling is higher than the mosque's ceiling? I ask her.

Wow, my grandmother says. She looks up and I see the veins in her neck, strong green rivers running under layers of wrinkled skin.

That's very interesting, she says. I think so. I guess it's good our health is prioritized. She clucks her tongue, her head full of politics.

I have just enough money saved for this, I say.

Your mom isn't paying? My grandmother is appalled. She lives off her retirement checks, but every few months my mother sends her some money.

I didn't ask her for more, I say. I'm going to get a job next semester.

That's good, she says. But make sure to study as hard as possible.

I will, I say. That I'm not working this summer is something my mother and I have not discussed. And my mother, she doesn't know about my humors. She doesn't know I'm studying for the MCAT by reading the sections on anatomy exclusively, and this private hospital is still not as expensive as it would be in New York, but what if it's money I'm spending on nothing? My humors, I've used them to diagnose myself, but they may fail me, like they have failed so many patients before and after Christ.

My grandmother is quiet. We have a minute, maybe more, on this escalator. Suddenly she looks back at me, a hard glint in her eyes.

Which one?

Which what?

Which mosque?

I don't know, one of the big ones.

She laughs. She tells me she hasn't been to any of the mosques in decades. I don't see why I would go, she says. I can pray at home.

Why don't you?

She thinks about this. I'm okay not knowing, she says.


MY DOCTOR TELLS ME HE HAS A FUNNY FEELING ABOUT the source of my headache and instructs me to lie down. My grandmother sits in a gray plastic chair, watching him. Although the MRI showed nothing in my head, there was something in my neck.

Nerve compression? I suggest, lying flat on my back. A squeezed nerve? Disc hernia?

He shakes his head no each time.

Discs are cushions between the vertebrae, I tell my grand-mother. She nods seriously.

Grilled tomatoes between kebap, she adds, poetically.

Melted cheese between phyllo, I say. Kunefe!

My grandmother shakes her head.

No. That one does not work, Sibel.

The doctor's suspicion: the muscle connecting my neck and shoulder is inflamed because I tense up and carry my day's weight by activating my neck, not my abdomen. The doctor wants to test his theory. He tells me to raise my legs as I'm lying flat on the paper-sheeted bed. I try and my legs quiver and fall.

Try again, he says. He puts his hand in the air above me, and I raise my legs again.

Again, he says. Just one more time.

I raise my legs again.

Is this really necessary, asks my grandmother. She stands up.

Yes. Just one more time. I'm fairly certain she puts weight on her neck and shoulders because she has incredibly weak abdomen muscles.

The room is silent as I lift my legs. I look at the light on the ceiling until I see black spots. I've been tracing the theory of the humors chronologically, and the way medical information was passed around the world map seems to follow the trail of empire and power—the humors were first conceptualized by the Ancient Egyptians and Mesopotamians, systemized in Ancient Greece, further expanded upon in the Islamic world, then seized by Europeans during the crusades in the Middle Ages. This morning I discovered Trota of Salerno, who lived in that coastal town in southern Italy during the twelfth century, when Salerno was the seat of advanced medical scholarship. Trota wrote about infertility, snakebites, makeup, how to remove a freckle, and the four humors.

Suddenly the doctor has a new idea. We also have to take your blood, he announces.

Blood? my grandmother asks. She comes closer to the table. Why is that necessary?

My blood was already drawn last time, I say. I try to raise my head but my neck, like the doctor said, is heavy.

It's procedural, he says. He dabs my arm with an alcohol pad. He asks me a few personal questions, where I grew up in America, what I'm studying, what kind of doctor I want to be. I begin to tell him about myself. I hear myself saying that my father has died, that I have an American boyfriend who wants to be a doctor too. I hear myself admit that I'm no longer certain what he's thinking. The tube in my arm fills up with blood. I smoke, too, I say. I hear my voice slip as I ask if that will affect how the blood is drawn, and my grandmother listens, she comes closer to us on the steel bed and plucks off a strand of my hair stuck to my paper gown. Before he died Baba gave blood often. Girls don't have to, he said, because of your natural shedding of blood: periods.

The humor doctors thought this, too. They thought a lot about what liquids balanced a woman out into a good woman. Because women were compositionally wet, Galen believed, the uterus shed its lining for the sole purpose of balancing a woman out. Freud said period pain was due to psychosomatic lovesickness, the link between nasal passageways and masturbation, and general insanity. I do not trust Freud.

When Baba gave blood, he felt all of his toxins being sucked out by tube. Then he felt his bone marrow get light and clean.

My grandmother is shaking my arm. Sibel, my grandmother says. Sibel.

Sibel hanım, the doctor says, come on now. We're done here.

I blink, their shapes come into focus, and my grandmother looms over me. Behind her, the doctor is frowning. Oops, I say, and we begin to make our way out of the hospital. I hold my grandmother's hand so she stops shaking. The atrium is just as beautiful as before. I'm looking in people's faces, to see if they're seeing beauty, too, or if they're used to this beauty. One woman looks at her phone as she rides the escalator. An old man counts the bills in his wallet.

As we wait for the bus on the street corner my grandmother turns to me. I wonder if we're going to discuss how I told the doctor I smoke, which, despite my methods for disguising the smell, she may have sniffed out anyway. She has a powerful nose. But she tells me I have to make a choice. I have to either trust Cooper or let him go his own way.

His own way? I say, confused.

My grandmother looks sad and tired. She tells me with family, it's okay. Your family will never leave you. But it's important to be careful with other people. You will never know when they have had enough.

She looks around at the colorful buildings. I met your grandfather here, she says.

When I ask her where, she says she had migraines, and she convinced her parents to allow her to go see an eye doctor for treatment.

Oh, I say. Did you think you had headaches from blurry vision?

What do I know? my grandmother says. I wanted to see what a doctor's office was like.

IN THE THREE HOURS SINCE THE HOSPITAL, MY GRAND-mother seems to have decided I go out too much. She announces that she does not want me and Cooper traveling to crowded, unsafe neighborhoods. Our favorite soap opera, about illicit love during the Russian Revolution, just ended, and she follows me around her apartment in her fluffy green bathrobe. There are mixed-up people there, she complains. At the beginning of the summer, she was proud of what she calls our bravery. Now she thinks it's foolish.

Why would you need to go out, she muses, when you already have a boyfriend?

I laugh in her face, and before closing the bathroom door, I tell her she's getting conservative. Plus, Cooper is busy lately. He's being weird, I add. She shuts up. Calling her conservative was a mean thing to say. She'd die before becoming, as she's said herself, one of those Turks.

I haven't been wearing makeup lately because I've been having trouble recognizing my face in the mirror. I once found body lotion very relaxing. I loved to marinate my face in hyaluronic acid. Now I am a scaly monster. But in the past few days I've taken to wandering into my grandmother's bathroom and slathering my face with her ancient foundation she's kept unused for decades. I do this after my abdest. I especially like to get my neck and throat. A princess named Sichelgaita ripped up her cheeks with her nails and tore out her hair while delivering a eulogy for her dead husband in 1085. No problem, Salernitan doctors said. They understood this kind of self-mutilation, as women in Salerno were melancholic and passionate, and black bile not only caused sadness, but also lovesickness, irrational behavior, and uncontrolled physical impulses. Trota from Salerno is already my favorite humorous doctor. She brewed many balms made from bird grease to heal the sad women's faces.

My grandmother is in the corridor, preparing to ambush me. She's brought me the tea I forgot to drink, but her hand is shaking, and the liquid slops over the lip of the cup. I take the glass from her.

I smell like talc, I confess.

That foundation doesn't match your skin, she says. You're too dark. She gets at my face with a napkin she just dipped in tea. We're in the cramped corridor between her bedroom door and the bathroom door, the very butt end of her apartment. There isn't enough room for the two of us to stand, let alone fight.

Stop it, I say.

It's making your face look like chalk.

Please stop, Grandma.

You haven't gone to the grave, have you?

No, I say, holding her arm back, I have gone.

Cooper told me a few nights ago. You haven't been, baby.

He's lying, I say, my face hot. I'm battling back tears. Trota says that if you cry often, your womb is suffering from excessive humidity. She thought God made man hot and dry—the ideal temperature—and woman cold and wet so, in the act of sex, the man can balance the woman out, and I'm trying to balance myself out, I think I can do it by myself, without a hot and dry man, just me and my humors, and I'm excited about doing this myself as my grandmother is telling me that I don't have to go to the grave. She only thought it would help me. It's okay if I don't go, she says. She herself barely goes, for example. I thank her, and I tell her I love her, but I have to ask her, What if he's still there? She's confused. What do you mean, Sibel? I explain that if I go to the grave, then he's dead, and I'll know it. And that will mean he won't be here anymore, will he? And she says, That's okay, Sibel, it's okay for you to know it, it's okay, he's here and he's not here, it's both. I have to ask her a few more times if this is true, if it is really both, if he's here and not here, and she considers both possibilities while also emphasizing that she doesn't know for certain, because how can a person know anything for certain, and she makes me want to take her by the hand and go to the grave together right this moment, this morning, in our bathrobes, her in green, me in pink, but instead I figure I can begin by letting her wipe my face in the hallway. She's a foot shorter than me, so I lean down enough for her to rub at my cheek. I remember that I threw the book on humorism out Cooper's window a few days ago and I'm hoping he retrieved it. He's the type of person who would have retrieved the book without telling me. He wouldn't have retrieved it just to tell me he retrieved it, because that would make him the type of person who performs good acts only to appear as someone who performs good acts. Tomorrow I will tell him I appreciate him. That I am grateful for his acts of service. I tell my grandmother I'm sorry I used her makeup, and she says it's okay. I tell her I used to love face lotion but I didn't bring any, does she have some? No, she says, she doesn't. What's the point? she asks, meaning her wrinkles.

At least you don't have a throat hole, I say, trying to make things light again, but she's walked away from me. She never wants to talk about the woman at the funeral, her friend.

I find my grandmother stirring lentil soup in the kitchen.

You felt a bit hot, she announces, come here. I bend down again so she can put her palm on my forehead. She nods with purpose and begins to brew me a potion of turmeric, lemon, ginger, peppercorns, and cinnamon sticks. She kicks me out when I tell her I can do it myself and that she should rest. Maybe I can learn from her. Maybe it is good for the mind to stay busy and help others.

WHEN COOPER OPENS THE DOOR TO HIS APARTMENT THE next day, he looks unsure, at first, of who I am, before his mouth finally breaks open in a smile. His energy is high but strange, and I feel I don't quite recognize him. I thought I knew him. I thought he had a tender masculinity. I thought I was angry with him for telling my grandmother about the grave. I thought he was full of blood, but people with excess blood in their bodies are resolute, never wavering. He's wavering. I realize, suddenly, and with sickening force—I need stable, not wavering. Two people can't both be wavering in a partnership. I sit on his bed and tell him about my latest discovery, Trota. I try to show him a strange painting of Trota on my phone, where she sits in a red gown at a desk, a scroll and ink bowl in front of her. There is also a knife. Her fingers end in sharp points like scalpels, but her pinky is bent backwards. Cooper pushes my phone away. His mouth is closed, and his eyes look for me on my face. He seems confrontational today.

I'm saved by his cell phone ringing. He texted his family this morning about his grand life decision to stay in Turkey, and I can hear his mom's anxiety from where I sit. They don't even know their son fasted for Ramazan. Cooper looks at me and smiles as he speaks on the phone in a calm voice. I smile back. Cooper enjoys suffering. Maybe it is a Christian thing, although his family hasn't practiced Christianity for years.

Because Cooper and I are both the elder sibling, we have to take care of people. My specialty with Alara was teaching her how to talk back to my father. But there is still something fundamentally different between us. For example, my mother was a lab technician when she was pregnant with me. After I was born, my grandmother stayed with us in New York, to help my parents, and she'd often ride the train from Bay Ridge to the Bronx, me wrapped up in a blanket, so my mother could breastfeed me in a toilet stall. They had heard that babies taken off breast milk early get sick often. Alara and I think our umbilical cords are buried in a small lawn on Columbia's campus, where I now attend school, because such a burial apparently ensures your child will get into said university, but when I confronted my mother about this myth she was angry. I'd asked her, Did you bury my umbilical cord at Columbia, like the other Turks? We are not those kinds of Turks, she'd said, appalled. Then she'd paused.

She said, I keep your umbilical cords upstairs. In my jewelry box. Because that way, they say, your children will stay close. Your children will never leave you.

I know my grandmother also kept Baba's umbilical cord, but I've never seen it.

I look up at Cooper, who'd said his goodbyes and I-love-yous to his family, somehow resolving the argument with them in just a few minutes of positive conversation about how much he will better himself here in Turkey, and they must have believed this, because a lot of America is about bettering yourself. In his family, American independence is more valuable than family duty. He's now sitting cross-legged on the floor, watching me.

So, Cooper says, you seem like you're doing better. Why don't we go to the cemetery?

Nope, I say. No thanks.

I lock myself in the bathroom. My head feels hot, and I wonder if it's a new form of my headache, which has recently been moving behind my eyes, or something else. I have to be a hard worker, that's how I was raised. I was raised to know that hard work cures all ailments. The body induces a fever because heat is the best way to kill microbes. Al-Razi told doctors to please put a hand on the fevered patient's forehead and pay careful attention to whether the skin emits hot spikes. Trota diagnosed fevers differently. She believed the womb is tied to the brain by nerves. A woman who was not properly menstruating could easily feel the same cramping pain in her neck, her upper back, or her head.

I am menstruating fine, if a bit heavy, but my sister hasn't had her period in months. Her hungry body has stalled in secreting certain hormones. Trota thought menstruating helped regulate a fatal imbalance in a woman's four humors, and she was renowned for expelling excess wind from wombs in order to induce menstruation. For one such windy patient, Trota cooked up a bath of marshmallow and lichwort, and helped her patient into a stone basin. Trota then made the patient a plaster of barley flour and wild radish and pushed this plaster into the patient's vagina. The woman's windy womb was thus cured, and her menstruation resumed. When Alara gets to Istanbul, I want to threaten her with a plaster full of food up her vagina, and I'm wondering how she'll take it. Laughter? Shock? Genuine fear?

I'm her sister.

COOPER BRIBES ME OUT OF THE BATHROOM BY GIVING ME the al-Razi book I threw out the window. He's read it, too, because he seems to have converted to my private school of religion. I am so pleased to have you as my first student, I tell him seriously, but he shakes his head no. Okay. It was the kind of joke that would have once granted me at least a weak smile.

One hour later, we're walking to the bus stop for the university because Cooper wants to check out yet another book from the school library on optometry and Islam, his words, and when we get to the bus stop I sit down on the bench, then I stand so a woman with three children can sit instead, and she thanks me then thanks Allah, but I don't get enough time to further my earnest dialogue because Cooper is dragging me onto the wrong bus, the bus to the cemetery gates, and he is in a frantic mode, his face so determined, it is alien, so I rip my arm out of his grasp and say, Wow, you really think you can trick me like that? He admits that he was attempting to go to the grave, with or without me. So kidnapping, I say, joking and wiping the sweat from my forehead, but he is serious today. He won't laugh. The woman with children stares at me, and when I smile back she pulls her arm around her children so they can't see me, and Cooper says, Well, I would hope you wouldn't have to be tricked, Sibel, and hangs his head like a sad dog as we wait for the bus and then on the whole ride over.

Now we're at the university gates and we are not speaking. Cooper wears a lanyard holding his hospital ID in a soft plastic case around his neck. He wears it everywhere he goes, which I find hilarious. We wait at the security station, where we show the guards our identification then wait for a few silent minutes before they decide to let us in. The security station is planted at the top of one of Istanbul's many hills, on the road near residential complexes, while the main school buildings are down the hill among tall trees. Cooper repeats himself as we're walking down the hill. He says, I just wanted you to want to go, Sibel. It's not about the grave or respecting your father. It's about you, he says. He keeps repeating that it's about me, not about my father. Only when we get to the campus lawn does he shut up, and we find seats at the school's café, where the cats are tripled in number and force. The cats are particularly abundant at this university, the same one my mother went to, and I love imagining her lounging on the lawn with friends and petting cats and attending class in the stone buildings covered with ivy. The café faces a basketball court, and, on the other side, there is a short stone wall with a view of the water. Students sit and eat on this wall, and cats walk alongside them, sometimes right over the students' laps. There are so many cats in Istanbul that someone made a documentary that follows their daily routines. The documentary is very therapeutic and interviews the people who take care of the street cats, making the film more about how people routinely impose their lonely thoughts on animals than it is about the cats. I saw the documentary in a fancy indie theater on the Lower East Side with Deniz, and when I mention the film to Cooper now, he sets his tea glass on the wooden coffee table and looks at the glittering water, at the students drinking coffee and playing pop songs on their phones, at the street cat on his lap, then back at me.

Oh, Cooper says. Is he still rapping?

Yeah, I say. He's working with his dad now, this summer. But he's making a mixtape.

Cooper bends over to pet the cat. Deniz often suspects he is appropriating black culture by rapping, though he also wonders to what degree it's okay because he's Kurdish, and fighting oppression, he says, is a global struggle. He tries to indoctrinate me about my own skin color, the same as his. You're *brown*, Sibel, he will tell me. But I can pass as white, I will say, I'm basically white, and he'll say, You're Middle Eastern, which makes you brown, which does make sense to me, sometimes, especially because the idea of white was created and continues to be enforced by racist U.S. laws that determined who was allowed to live in America, and who was allowed to live in what neighborhood, a mandate that is ever-shifting, but I'm not always convinced. I think I'm more whatever I'm seen as. Some people in New York call us brown, some people in New York call us white. We don't know which one is most accurate. When we straighten our hair they say Jewish. When we wear hoops, Latina. And when Alara moved to California for college everyone thought she was Iranian or Pakistani.

Didn't you say that he was also coming to Turkey this summer? Cooper asks.

He's coming, yeah. On the same flight as Alara, to see his grandma. She has lung cancer.

Cooper runs his hand through his hair. Cooper gets jealous anytime I call someone attractive, but he will never admit this to me. Jealousy appears often on his improvement lists. Oh, he says. I forgot about that. Is he okay?

He's okay, I say. He's doing as good as me.

Cooper laughs at this. As if that's helpful, Sibel.

What? I ask. What's funny?

You won't even let me know just how good you're doing.

I'm doing as good as Deniz.

Jesus, Sibel.

Could you feel my head?

Oh, wow. I think you have a fever.

AFTER BABA COLLAPSED IN THE KITCHEN WHILE BOILING water for tea my sister took his pulse and she called the ambulance. Then she laid her body over his. Ibn Sina says there are wavy pulses and wormy pulses. Then there is the ant pulse, which gathers energy before it begins to throb.

I didn't open the door for Cooper after he took the subway from school to my parents' house. Instead we had other people over. Deniz was at our house for one week. Deniz's mother stayed, too, and every evening she would sit with my mom on the fire escape, smoking late into the night. That week Deniz's mother cooked for us, and when the mood was right, Deniz quizzed Alara on materials for biology, and he sat at the kitchen table and held up tiny postcards of organs. I watched him take the heart postcards out of the stack and stuff them in his pocket.

One night, maybe the second or third night, I got into the sofa bed we made up for Deniz, and the moon from outside cut into the room and lit up his body. His body felt right, bigger than Cooper's, like I was something small to hold in a palm. That's what I did. I made myself as small as a body in a palm.

COOPER IS NOT HAPPY WITH ME. I WANT TO GO HOME, alone, to avoid him. I have to sweat out my fever in my grandmother's hot apartment. I have to leave the university before the fight can continue, but the moment I understand that what I need is to be away from Cooper, even for just an hour, Cooper gets a phone call from Aunt Pinar inviting us to the kebap house now that Ramazan is over. She asks him if he's with me, and he says yes, and when she says, Well, why the hell isn't she answering her phone, Cooper narrows his eyes at me, and I can see him debating whether he should continue protecting my generally reckless, insensitive behavior. I'm choler again. I'm ill-tempered and destructive. Instead he says, Oh, I think her phone is on silent. As she tells him the time and place, Cooper stares at me. His face, usually easy for me to read, is masked.

We pass by the cemetery on the bus and Cooper points it out to me. There's the cemetery, he says in a serious voice.

SOMETIMES I WATCH THEIR FACES TO SEE WHO IS STILL thinking about my father. My uncle is on his fifth glass of raki telling the story of his friend, the smartest guy he knew, who was organizing while a student at Robert College until he disappeared and turned up years later working undercover in the East Berlin radio station. Dilek, who like my sister eats very little now, has not stopped texting since we sat down. And my cousins with children are too busy to be sad. I'm still looking for something in their mouths and eyes. It's difficult to tell when a person is eating, though, because eating food is the best kind of balm for sadness. Cake is the best texture of food for grief, as well as bread, because these foods will soak and hold your liquid feelings. I look at my grandmother, who is pushing around raw onions on her plate. She may be more alone than me, and in all this time of her taking care of me I keep forgetting it is her only son in the grave, and I have never had a son, I have never had a child. I was supposed to be taking care of her this summer. I want to tell her sorry and I make to stand but Emre is asking Cooper which curse words he knows in Turkish. He just taught Cooper the words for asshole, motherfucker, bastard, son of a bitch. *Kaknem* is another insult, meaning two things: bitchy or dried up.

I push myself away from the table but this time Dilek, leaning on my chair, wants to speak to me in private. She's wearing a silky black jumpsuit she probably bought from Zara, with sapphire blue heels.

Sure, I say, go ahead.

I'm worried about your sister, Sibel. I was just talking to your grandmother, and she says Alara has lost almost ten kilos. What's happening?

What the fuck do you think is happening, Dilek?

Jesus, Sibel. You don't have to be a bitch. I'm concerned about my cousin.

Cooper looks at me with his eyebrows raised. Emre, who was just avidly cursing, shuts up and stares at us. Aunt Pinar, who had been diligently listening, stands up to smoke, though we all know she is really going to pay for the bill in secret, and Dilek glares at me before stomping back to her seat. I reach for Cooper's leg under the table, but he bats my hand off.

Why are you being so nasty, Cooper mouths.

Cooper turns back to my cousin Emre, shouldering me out, to teach him the popular curse words in English.

WHEN DINNER IS OVER, SOMEBODY—I COULDN'T CATCH whether it was my uncle or great-aunt—has a brilliant idea for the young people to go to a bar. I'll drop you guys off, my uncle says, and the old folk nod and nod, likely thinking of how much fun it must be to go to a bar where you pay money to drink poison in a hot room with strangers. My grandmother is on my side, but nobody listens to her insist that I have a fever and should come back home with her to rest. They're drowning her out by arguing over who gets to pay the bill, and while my uncle and cousins are passionately debating who is being more rude by offering to pay, Aunt Pinar tells the table with glee that she already did. She turns to me and wipes my sweating forehead with a napkin. Go have fun, she says. I'll make sure your grandmother gets home and takes her medication.

She'll be worried about me, though, if I stay out late.

Then don't stay out late.

We're stuck. Cooper only wants to be polite to my family, and Dilek—well, I don't know, maybe she is trying to help me in her own way, because the look she shares with her father tells me there is so much I don't know about my family, and what they seem to know about me.

We end up at a bar on the water in Arnavütköy, where the streets are narrow and the wood-paneled houses, each painted a different shade of pastel, all have big bay windows. This bar is full of young people and the cocktails are as expensive as the cocktails in New York. Dilek leads us up the narrow stairs to the rooftop, where we find two corner seats and Cooper stands.

Dilek is a rare Turk with blue eyes. She always says it's because her mother's family was from Macedonia until the Greek-Turkish population exchange. She thinks this makes her different than regular Turks.

I mention this now, that she and Cooper both have blue eyes.

Dilek is not taking my bait. Neither is Cooper, who knows that when I'm angry like this, I'm waiting for someone to open the door for me to lash out. I'm here having told myself I'll confront Cooper. I'll tell him he's betrayed my confidence. I'll tell him he doesn't understand me, that he won't tell me what I look like and feel like to him, which is his duty, me being his girlfriend, but he, maybe because of a strong sense of tact, will not tell me just how much I have failed to communicate with both myself and with him.

I'm on my fourth drink. I hope Dilek or Cooper will take it upon themselves to heroically pay the bill. I repeat myself about the eyes.

You don't have my mother's European gene, Dilek says. She tosses her hair over her shoulder, and the waves fall down her fat-less back. Now she's mean, like I wanted.

But his eyes are darker, I say in Turkish. I'm testing to see what Cooper understands.

It's you two who look alike, Cooper says in a confident voice. He's switched to Turkish.

Her nose is straighter, I say, smiling at Dilek and wondering when someone, it has to be Cooper, catches on to the fact that I'm fucking joking. I'm prodding Dilek to have this reductive, pheno-typic discussion.

Dilek grabs a candle and holds it to my cheek. Cooper, she an-nounces in a stern voice, Sibel's nose is very different from mine. She is not from Macedonia, like me. She passes him the candle and Cooper's eyes cross as he focuses on my nose. I swallow my drink and look for the waiter to order another. And I'm jealous of them. I'm jealous that Cooper and Dilek get to play with attrac-tion, infatuation, desire, as I'm here, drunk and fevered and with a belly full of black bile, the least sexual humor.

We leave the bar soon after because I stopped speaking and began hunting down strangers for spare cigarettes. Cooper apologizes to Dilek, who looks smug but tries to also look sad and sympathetic, but as we're saying bye I'm grateful. I can't wait to rest so my fever goes away. Cooper, though, proceeds to make me walk up the hill to his rented room, a long, steep walk that takes thirty minutes, thirty minutes of not speaking. Isn't it funny, I say as we're climbing the stairs to his apartment, that you used to be the quiet one in this relationship? But Cooper doesn't think this is funny, and after pausing, says so. And when I scowl, he sighs.

Cooper's roommate is home, entertaining guests in the kitchen. Even with Cooper's door closed I can hear Turkish rap and women laughing. I take off my shirt and walk around his bedroom in my bra, my best one, an emerald green. I walk to the window, to the door, pretending to look for something. I bend over, my back to him, because I know his favorite body part of a woman is the back and the soft canyon cliffs the muscles make on either side of the spine. He ignores me. I wonder if I'm being desperate, using sex to try to connect with the person I already know I've lost. I walk to where he's sitting at his desk and kiss his ear. I put my hands around his neck. He turns on his chair and holds my face in his hands, a half foot from his own. He won't let me get closer. I need to know if he's playing a game.

Cooper pushes me off.

What's your problem, I say.

Nothing.

What the fuck, Cooper.

He meets my gaze and holds it carefully. I need a retreat of some sort, he says.

Is this not a retreat?

What?

Is this not a retreat? From home? From the U.S.?

No, I mean a retreat from this. We spend every minute together. I've forgotten what it's like to be in my own head.

What's happening in your head?

He looks out at the lit-up mosque a few blocks away.

I've been in my own head this whole time, I say.

I know.

No, I'm saying I've been in my head, why can't you manage the same?

He stands and unzips his backpack. He unpacks his film camera and some snacks from my grandmother as well as the thin blue towels we bought during our first month in Istanbul. He rolls them up so they look like tubes. He turns back to look at me.

You are so stagnant, he says, it's like even this can't change you.

This? I ask, pointing to his musty room full of other people's things, the student he's renting this space from.

Here, being here, and with me. I knew you weren't happy, but I didn't think you would suck all the attention out of every room. Do you know you're doing this? I'm not sure. You think you're the only one grieving. Your whole family is here—also grieving!—and you're still not grateful. You've got your shoulders hitched up to your head, you lose energy when we're walking after ten minutes. Just ten minutes. It's always ten minutes, and when those ten minutes are up you start slapping your feet against the ground the rest of the day!

I see myself as an old woman in a black cloak slouching around the city. Everyone must wonder what she's doing with a valiant blond young man.

But I love walking, I say.

Cooper points at me, naked save for my green bra. You, he

says, are still smoking. You think you're hiding it, but I can taste it. Your mouth smells.

Why didn't you say anything? I say, touching my mouth. Why didn't you say you knew?

It's sad, actually, seeing how you say hi to me, all cheery after your cigarettes, thinking you're getting away with it. And you said you wanted to come here to take care of your grandmother, who put her own son, a son she barely got to spend time with, in his grave. Instead you're nasty to her, to everyone. You're playing a game with this grave. You think your family really cares if you've gone? *You're* the one making it a big deal, Sibel. Nobody *gives a fuck*, Sibel, about the GRAVE. They give a fuck about *you*.

The music, I suddenly realize, has been turned off, and the apartment is silent. I was making to leave, I had just put on my shirt and was looking for my sandals, but I'm stuck.

What, he says in mock surprise, you don't want to have to talk to them?

Are you stupid?

Me? he widens his eyes. The Sibel I used to know would love to talk to them, would love to talk to me. Remember, Sibel? How I used to be the quiet one in this relationship?

The music starts again. I strap my sandals up. We are silent, looking at each other.

Does this even upset you? he asks.

No, I say.

He's still holding his green backpack with both hands and the zipper slowly begins to open on its own. A few books fall out. He looks like he's about to change his mind about me.

Are you sure? Cooper asks. I'm not really sure, I mean, I'm sorry. I can do better, Sibel.

No, Cooper.

I know you think you don't deserve this, my help, but I want to. He pauses. Sibel? What are you thinking?

I could sit down and have him heal me, like he wants to, but I have do this for myself. I tell him this, that I have to find mental equilibrium on my own, and then I leave.



COOPER FIRST TOLD ME HE LOVED ME ON THE BASEMENT floor of a sports equipment store downtown. I had just helped him pick out his backpack: green, instead of red. He grew up with many red accessories, he had explained. Backpack, lunchbox, shoes. But his mother had purchased those items for him, and he never had the chance to choose his own color. It was only after we debated the meaning of colors thoroughly, of what red versus green said about him, that he went with green. When he finally made his decision about the backpack, he looked at me, where I was sitting on the ground happily talking about colors, and he said, Wow, I love you. There were still two years until my father would die.



MY GRANDMOTHER IS RESILIENT DESPITE THE CHEST PAIN and Parkinson's, and what is left of her energy she uses to wait up for me at night. I stand behind my tree, smoking a cigarette, and watch her as she looks out from the balcony. She scans the street for me but can't see me. The streetlamps are bright and the color they leave on her makes her face look flushed and young. She leans farther out. Her white nightgown blows like a giant white sail catching the wind.

I smoke another cigarette.

I watch her dress fill and empty.

This building, the one my father grew up in, is called the Sunshine Apartments. But my body has become a darkroom that will tinker for months, maybe years, to reproduce his memory.

I'm close enough to the apartment for my phone to link with the internet. A message from my sister lights up the space around me. She will be here in two days.

# II.

I worry that without a boy to show around Istanbul I won't leave my grandmother's apartment. I am, after all, a lazy person. I shut off the television and guard the remote under my sweating thigh so my grandmother understands we will no longer watch the news about the upcoming presidential elections. Then I begin the book Cooper found on ancient Islamic medicine. It's hard not to think of him, and I'm concerned that my mind is loosening, that it's not able to shut particular feelings off like it once could. Did Cooper read up to the part about doctors who used leeches to make women seem like virgins? These brides, who had had improper, unmarried sex, would come begging for a leech, and the doctors would carefully latch one to the patient's labia while instructing the woman to rip the creature off discreetly, moments before penetration. If the woman was not so daring, she could remove the leech the morning before marriage, as the animal would have already worked for twelve hours to induce a flow of clotted blood and constrict the vagina.

My grandmother wanders into the living room. She's scanning the room for the remote. She's been acting strange since I told her Cooper and I broke up. I'm wondering how to ask her about her life, the way Cooper did, because she rarely talks about the past. I'm worried, too, that she is worried about me, and that her worry for me could spike up her sickness. We're heading to the hospital today, this time for her. Heart disease is both nurtured and inherited, after all, and because my grandmother has been having chest pain all year, we want to make sure that everything is flowing properly in her bloodstream. She can't eat for twenty-four hours before her angiogram, and she tried to prepare a breakfast spread of olives, feta, tomatoes, and cucumbers just for me until I forcefully stopped her by blocking the kitchen door and standing guard for fifteen minutes. I need to concoct a foolproof plan to make her stop caring for me. And she's dressed in brown, a fashion choice my mother tried to dissuade her against ten years ago.

Maybe you should wear something else, I say, following her to the hallway. Remember what my mom says, brown makes people unhappy.

I don't care about brown, she says, waving me off. She uses a long metal rod to pop her heel into her shoe. She looks at me, her eyes moving from my bare feet to my pajamas, my neck, my unwashed face. Are you ready to go?

Please, I say. You can wear green. You just washed that nice green shirt!

Why did you break up, Sibel?

Fine, I say. He doesn't understand what I feel. He is annoying me. He is making me feel sick. He is making me go to the grave. So, Grandma, we are no longer going to be romantically together.

She looks suspicious. I am worried, Sibel, about you. And about your openness.

Okay, I say, well, let's talk openness. Are you still friends with that old woman? From the funeral?

She drops her keys. How many old women am I friends with, Sibel?

I try not to laugh, because this is serious. The one, I say, slowly, because we have never discussed this old woman. The one who spat at me.

I touch my throat.

The one with the hole, I add. From smoking.

My grandmother's hand is shaking more violently than usual. She looks so tired today. I reach for her hand, but she bats me off.

Get dressed, she snaps.

I say yes, of course.

I'm dressing, and I pull on my loose pants and clasp my bra as quietly as possible to eavesdrop through the door. I want to know if she's okay, if she's standing or cleaning or making sure her keys are in her purse. In the year 175, Galen was one of the first physicians to describe the symptoms of Parkinson's; that "shaking palsy," characterized as a resting tremor, was different from a nonresting tremor. But the ancients, including Ayurvedic physicians who believed in three humors, not four, didn't know what caused the tremor. My grandmother likes to say that you cannot die from Parkinson's, but with Parkinson's. I think this is true. Some of the symptoms in the advanced stages of her disease, such as loss of balance, immobility, and hallucinations, can cause death, but I want to believe her.

When I come out of my room, ready to go, she's not there.

I run down the stairs and step on a street cat trying to slip through the door. My grandmother is outside, waiting for me on the curb, but she won't meet my eye. I decide not to speak either. We hail a cab and I roll down the window, then my grandmother insists that the strong breeze will make my fever worse, but I insist that that is looney science, plus the breeze is hot, plus I'm the one with the wrist and arm power to control the window, and anyway, who is studying to be the doctor here, I ask, quite aggressively while simultaneously swatting her arm off me. She raises her eyebrows and I raise my eyebrows back, and we sit there, the wind a cyclone in the back seat, our arms intertwined, before I admit that yes, she has a decent point, I truly might not become a doctor, and she misinterprets my pessimism and says yes, Sibel, we can't jinx anything, you know, nazar, and okay, fine, nazar, so I roll the window back up and we drive through the city with the window shut and the smell of stale cigarettes strong.

I FILL TWO PLASTIC CUPS WITH WATER AND HAND ONE TO my grandmother. They are going to do an angiogram by filling my grandmother's veins with blue contrast dye in order to determine via X-ray whether her veins are blocked. If blocked, the angiogram procedure includes inserting a stent. She looks healthy and radiant to me. I tell her this as I sit next to her in the waiting room and thereby break the wall of silence that one of us, I'm not sure who, built up.

Thank you, she says, her voice still clipped.

I fold my hands on my lap, mimicking her hands on her lap. I can only see her profile, and under the fluorescent lighting the green shards in her eyes pop, shards I've inherited. I figure eyes are historically romantic for a reason. We want to know what another person sees, and if they see like we see. I'm looking, but I receive no immediate results.

This is a tough business, I announce.

The cardiologist?

Sorry, I say. No. I'm not sure why I said that.

You don't have anyone to think with, she says, looking at me seriously.

What does that mean?

Cooper, she says. You have no one to speak with about topics that interest you.

That's very untrue. I have you, I say.

She laughs, a snort escaping through her nose. It's true that this is the first day I haven't spoken to Cooper in two full years and I'm not sure where to dispel my mind. My grandmother must know, though I have no idea what she did with herself when her husband died in an earthquake. I peek a look at her. She's doing today's crossword and I'm trying to catch her eye. Old people, or people with heart disease, can develop a purple ring around their irises. My grandmother's irises are faintly lilac-colored.

A doctor calls my grandmother's name. As we make for the procedural rooms, he sticks his arm out before me.

Only the patient, miss, he says, looking at his piece of paper. My grandmother's worried face meets mine. We'll call you in after the angiogram.

I walk back to the waiting room and sit down. I cross and uncross my legs. There is a woman with her head covered who stares at my face, and I smile at her, but it seems as if she's not looking for anything. She's only blanked out. I flip through the newspapers on the coffee table in front of me. Every Turkish newspaper has the same front-page layout, with the right border dominated by a thin but booby woman, usually in a bikini, or a silky dress that splits open to reveal her legs and chest. She looks cut out and pasted onto the page. Most are Turkish celebrities or models. Only one newspaper in this stack shows a woman in work clothing. She is a businesswoman.

I've been keeping a running tally at my grandmother's, too. For every twelve papers or so, there is only one that deviates from the naked woman norm.

When Baba got an angiogram, followed by a stent, I took the train from college to the hospital in Park Slope. He was having chest pain. Baba lay in a hospital bed, his wrist bandaged up. He wore a thin hospital gown, and when we hugged, the slit on his side opened and I saw his dark nipple and tiny areola. He lay on his side, and when I told him he looked like a merman, and the thing about his areola, he smiled. So many men don't know what an areola is, but not my father. I'm not sure if that's something to be proud of.

The newspapers here are all centrist, which is not surprising. Clearly outrage at the naked woman norm is useless given the number of journalists in prison. I put the newspapers down and say a prayer, the same prayer my mother said when Baba was receiving his stent.

Finally a nurse calls me into the recovery room. I follow her, and find my grandmother propped up in a bed. I've never seen my grandmother's areolas. She's very private about her body. I've only seen her giant beige bras drying out on the laundry rack, strategically placed on the lower tier and curtained by pant legs. I sit in a chair and reach for her hand.

How is she? I ask the nurse.

The results are back, she says, looking at her clipboard. She won't need a stent.

I wouldn't get a stent anyway, my grandmother announces.

The nurse laughs. We wouldn't exactly give you a choice, she says. You have your rights, of course, but we would strongly suggest listening.

Nope, I agree. You'd do what they tell you.

My son had a stent, my grandmother says. And he died just one year later.

The nurse says she's very sorry. There's nothing worse than burying your child.

My grandmother agrees. At the hospital in New York the patients with new stents lay in beds in a big room, eating hospital food. I stayed there when they inserted his stent. I was reading about a disease where you're born with your organs on the wrong side of your body.

The nurse tells me to make sure my grandmother doesn't participate in any stress-inducing activities in the next few days, perhaps even weeks, and I can't help myself, I laugh in her face. The nurse is confused.

Sorry, I say, it's just, that's no problem. We have a pretty stagnant life.

My grandmother nods. We pretty much do nothing.

But she does clean a lot, I say, and we're both laughing uncontrollably.

I mean emotionally stressful, the nurse warns, but my grandmother snorts and turns to me. She thanks me for being here.

Of course, I say.

Does your head hurt?

No, I lie. I'm okay.

Can you take her temperature, my grandmother asks the nurse, who seems to be inspecting us.

Oh, okay. The nurse looks at me. Are you sick?

No, I say. But I've had a headache for a few weeks now.

She has a fever, my grandmother says.

The nurse says she'll be right back with a thermometer.

I thank my grandmother, and she says, of course. Then I tell her about my big theory concerning the women in Turkish newspapers. She agrees that there is hypocrisy in what the government will and will not allow. We have to stay here for a few hours while the punctured hole in her wrist heals, or at least heals enough to remove the pressurized plastic block without her blood spurting everywhere. I'm watching her heart on the black monitor. The green lines form tiny mountains that rise and fall. Anytime a noise comes out of the machine, I feel something in me jump. I'm not sure if it's an organ or my blood pressure or my nervous system that tells me to be afraid. Then, there is the prophecy of my own heart. My trachea.

BACK HOME, MY GRANDMOTHER PEELS OFF HER SWEATER and begins to yank open a window.

You're not supposed to use your arm for seventy-two hours, I say. She scoffs and we lift another window together. She's full of blood again. I thought she was doomed to phlegm, because of her old age and because she can be prone to sensitivity, but is thoughtful and even-tempered when discussing difficult topics. Cooper, however, will always be blood. And male blood will never be bled out in a stone basin. Unlike Saint Margaret Mary, he will thrive.

And Cooper is, apparently, thriving. He calls the landline and my grandmother picks up.

She begins giving him the recipe for her meat-and-eggplant dish in a terse voice, and he seems to ask her whether she thinks he should use two or three cups of water to cook the eggplant, because she replies, in a serious voice, three cups will do. Maybe he's inviting his coworkers over to his tiny apartment. They'll

probably eat standing up. I'm counting off his coworkers, especially the girls, and I don't remember any of them being hot but
anyone can look hot if you feel possessive or jealous enough so
I crawl over to the other side of the couch to lift the lid to my
laptop and stalk the girls on Facebook. Finally my grandmother
hangs up.

Well, I say from behind my screen, my voice thicker than I
want it to be.

I don't know, she says. Her arm is beginning to bruise. She is
conflicted now. Maybe she is on my side. When I tell her this she
gets upset.

Of course I'm on your side. Plus, you're the one who pushed
him away.

Thanks, I say. Thanks for reminding me.

You're welcome, she says.

Who's he cooking dinner for, I ask. Dilek?

My grandmother is visibly upset. She has Dilek and her parents over for tea often and considers them her own blood family.

No. He said work friends. She pauses, as if combing through
his words for a possible lie.

Don't worry, I tell her, Cooper would never do that to me.

You mean your cousin would never do that to you. My grandmother looks around her living room, then begins to close the
window closest to me, where I was enjoying a decent breeze. I
block her at the next window.

We are going to sweat your fever out, Sibel.

It's already so hot in here, are you crazy?

No, baby. You're the crazy one.

She leaves to use the bathroom. I'm stewing on the couch, listening to the toilet water run while my grandmother begins cook-

ing dinner, something I told her to let me do, but she never listens. Can we get better knowing we're sick or is it better to pretend to feel good and fine? I want to ask my grandmother, too. She needs this more than me. The landline rings, but I recognize the number as my doctor at the hospital, so I gently lift the telephone then place it back in its cradle.

I TURN THE TELEVISION ON FOR MY GRANDMOTHER. HER favorite soap opera is today, about an attempted honor killing, but the woman flees to Istanbul and ultimately her brother refuses to kill her.

My grandmother sits next to me on the couch. She smells like soap and roses.

I'm sick of this one, she says. Unless you want to watch it.

No, I say. We can watch something else.

My grandmother surfs the channels until she finds an old movie she loves: *Hunchback*, which is about a woman who lives on Cunda, a small Aegean island off the coast of Ayvalik. Her back is bent inward at the top of her spine, making her unmarriable, but nonetheless she falls in love with a handsome, blind violinist. He falls in love with her, too, despite never seeing her face or body. But he is upset because he can't protect her like other men can.

This actress has beautiful blue eyes, my grandmother says. That's why she was so famous in my youth. Really she is not very pretty.

No, I agree, she's not very pretty.

The woman has a dream where she gives her blue eyes to the man. They wear regal outfits and float down crystal steps that begin in the clouds and end in a sunny field of yellow flowers. She is a good person; that's how the movie has framed her character. She is the kind of woman who will do anything for the man she loves. Sure enough, in the next scene she takes the ferry to the eye hospital in Istanbul to give away her blue eyes and now she wears heavy black eye makeup on her closed lids to make it look like her eyes were surgically plucked out. Back on the island, a friend tells the blind violinist that the Istanbul eye hospital has good news for him. The blind violinist cannot believe his fate. He will receive eyes! Free eyes! The blind violinist wants to tell the hunchback woman the news, but cannot find her, and so he travels to Istanbul for his fateful appointment. The doctors swap his blind eyes for her blue eyes. My grandmother whoops, and we agree that he is very handsome with his new blue eyes.

I ask my grandmother whether this surgery is even possible. Not just then, but today.

No way, she says. Aren't you watching?

The formerly blue-eyed, now blind woman takes the ferry back to Cunda. She gets off the boat with her sister, and the crowd, full of pity, follows her through town. One woman carries a goat.

Of course we love drama, my grandmother says, giggling. She pours us more tea and sits deep in the couch.

The blind woman asks that no one tell the violinist that she is the woman he loves. The music is full of violins and the Turkish flute. She visits her father's grave, and the sky is dark blue behind her as she weeps over his grave and asks him to give her strength. Meanwhile, the blue-eyed violinist combs the island for her. He's knocking on doors. He's seeing what people look like for the first time. He's pleading with friends and neighbors to tell him where she is, what she looks like, and why she won't see him.

I've been to Cunda, right? I ask my grandmother.

Yes, she says. There's an amphitheater nearby. Your sister got stung by a bee.

I remember, I say. Have you ever done anything as selfless as this woman?

She pretends not to hear me. That's okay. I'm used to the way my family withholds information. Alara, she can't stand this, and one time my parents were being cagey about my mother's dad, and Alara, in a rage, told them, It's as if your leftist ideology was the family that raised you both. Really you have no family at all. It hit, what she said. My mother cursed at her, and Baba told Alara to wash out her mouth. I look at my grandmother's dyed hair, which looks red in this light, and feel a thrill, the kind you get when conjuring someone old as young again. I am trying to see her more clearly, my grandmother. I'm trying to see what hurt her. Now the blue-eyed violinist holds another man by his collar and screams, There is no way I can live without her!

At the end of the movie, the woman drowns herself after visiting her father's grave. She wades through blue water and she says, Take me, take me, take me, please, to the water or to Allah. I look at my grandmother, to see if she's moved. She's chewing slowly. I can't tell.

WE SPEND THE REST OF THE DAY INSIDE, RELAXING TO-gether. The phone rings and we look at each other, her tiny legs up on the coffee table, me lying motionless on the couch.

What? she says. You think I'm getting up?

It seems our only job is to be called. If this landline weren't here, we'd be entirely useless. Now it's my sister. She's packing for Turkey and asks about Cooper and whether his Turkish is any better, and I tell her that unfortunately he's been learning Turkish at a rapid, murderous speed, and that he can even pronounce certain words better than us, and she curses.

Fuck, Alara says, now we can't talk shit around him.

Don't worry, I say. You won't see him.

What?

Well, we broke up.

What? Does Grandma know?

I was afraid, you know, of her having a heart attack, so I had to tell her gently.

My grandmother looks at me. She's aware I'm talking about her because I've used the Turkish word for grandmother. She also knows the words *heart attack*. She pretends not to know English, but we know she understands a fair amount because she will often contribute a strong opinion to a conversation Alara and I are having in English. Alara says all the required things very angrily, like, I'm so sorry, and He's such an asshole, and What a fucking asshole—all these phrases that feel mandatory and irritating.

He thinks I'm not opening up, I admit.

Well, are you? Not opening up? You do that. I bet you're super shut down.

I'm not shut down. I'm so open. I'm funny, I do things.

Huh. Really. What things?

I talk to people all the time, I insist. I smile all the time. People always tell me I'm smiling.

But you haven't actually been doing anything, right? You're just chilling with Grandma?

We're actually learning a lot about Russia through this soap, I say, defending myself.

I don't mean that badly, she says. Do whatever you want. We

can talk more when I'm in Istanbul. The reason I'm calling is I saw Deniz. He came over with his mom.

Oh wow, I say, that's nice.

I know. I'm trying to get Mom to take time off and join us, but I'm not sure if she's ready.

Ready for what?

I actually don't know what to do with you. You know, what's happening in your head is not what's happening in real life, she says. Anyway, don't forget, I'm landing tomorrow. Five p.m. Deniz, too.

My grandmother asks for the phone. This time it's me with the phone power.

I can hear her asking for me, Alara says. Is she taking her pills? One second, though. Deniz kept asking about you, and he wanted to know what Cooper was up to. He was quite persistent. And wow, he's kind of funny. He's so broody to a hysterical point. Then he suddenly says something so random and effusive. What's going on in your head, dude? Who's home?

Where'd you go? I ask. I remember, too, how sometimes, particularly at night, Deniz sheds his silent armor and becomes someone new, fun and full of threat and thrill.

Some bars. He has such an intense stare, also. He reminds me of you. Well, what you're like now. But I'll turn you around.

My grandmother is prying my fingers off the phone now.

I can't wait to get banana ice cream, she says, but I always gain so much weight there. I feel like a stuffed pig. Bye bye, she sings, and when I pass the phone off to my grandmother they begin speaking shrilly and I don't know how I will get Alara to eat. I don't know how I'm going to stand Alara, who, when on any kind of mission, becomes obsessed. She's going to be obsessed with me, and how to fix me, the whole time denying that she's ten pounds underweight. This is only my mother's guess. My grandmother thinks it's fifteen even though she hasn't seen her since the funeral. She's going to make me hang out with Deniz, thinking he will fix me, and she's going to make me study. My summer charade is over. I have to figure out how to be less of a monster and more of a person. I don't know how I will do this, as I, unlike Cooper, have never made a list of my bad qualities.

Once my grandmother hangs up, she sits next to me on the couch and asks me what's wrong. Why is your face all hung up? she asks. Are you worried about Alara coming? Are you worried she will find out about you watching television all day?

Yes.

You think you can't help her?

Yes.

We're going to have to help her, Sibel. Your mother says she is not herself.

Yes.

She does not look like herself, too. Too skinny.

Yes.

I WAKE UP EARLY THE NEXT MORNING AND CLEAN MY room, change the sheets, and do all the laundry. I have to make sure to do these things before my grandmother does them herself. Once my bed is crisp and tucked in with warm sheets, I start lining my books on humorism and ancient Islamic medicine on the shelf and stacking my test books on the small desk. In ten hours, I will drive my uncle's car to the airport to pick up Alara and Deniz. The car will pass the cemetery, its white stone archway with turquoise ceramics and red tile flowers.

My grandmother knocks on my door. The smell of butter and garlic floods my room from the hallway. She spent the morning cooking rice with currants and dill, rice she will use to stuff grape-leaves. She wants to tell me that Cooper called. Apparently, our friend from school, a friend I have always hated, is here to visit us.

To visit him, I say. He's only his friend, now.

Well, he wanted to know if you wanted to meet with them. Show them around.

Can't he do that himself?

I don't know, Sibel. I'm sorry. I personally do not think you should see him right now, not when you have a fever. Do you want to call him, or me to?

You, I say. I shut my door. She opens it again to say that she's going to her sister's down the hill for some tea before we set out for the airport. I say okay and open up my test book. Maybe I should answer a few of the practice questions?

My grandmother opens the door again. She says her sister can wait. Do I want her to make the boiled potatoes she had promised me? I nod, but my grandmother's frowning, and I'm not sure I understand why she's changed her mind. She walks out into the hall-way and I follow her to the kitchen, where I lean against the door, and when she turns her head to see if I'm there I see her young, as if she's my own sister, and I see what my mother says about my grandmother and me and Alara, how our brow bone is strong and hard above our eyes, how our lips have the same giant dip under the nose, a dip large enough to trap beads of water, and I stand still, in awe of her, but she tuts her tongue again because although she is, by now, used to my starts and stops, she nonetheless disapproves of them, and she shakes her head again as she gets to the kitchen, and I'm in the kitchen too and Grandmother is filling a pot up with water and gently sliding each potato into the pot and she's waiting patiently for the potatoes to boil and she's draining the water out of the pot, then blasting the boiled potatoes from the cold tap so they cool, slicing the white potato flesh for me, then she's brewing tea and all the while I'm frozen again, a different kind of frozen. I'm watching her work in this tiny kitchen, a kind of work she's done for years, even when there was nobody home, even when everybody was dead or missing, and she does this work without smiling. Why would she smile, there is no audience, only me. And she sets the tea glasses on saucers and carries the tray out to the dining room table, and again I follow her. I sit down. She stirs two cubes of sugar into her tea with the tiny spoon and we talk through two calls to prayer. Some part of me wants to count the hours I've gone without a cigarette. I want to count the boiled potatoes I've ingested. I want to count and take stock of things in my head but I resist and I keep pushing the counting away until it becomes clear to me that Grandmother no longer admonishes me, maybe she never did, nor did she ever fault me for freezing in the kitchen while Baba boiled water for tea. Instead, she speaks of her late husband, the eye doctor. She tells me what it takes to care for somebody, especially a sister. She tells me she was once like me, unwilling to accept care, unwilling to face myself, unwilling to live. We talk until it is time to pick Alara up from the airport. I know she is the reason I am here.

GRANDMOTHER MET THE EYE DOCTOR IN THE WINTER OF 1955. It was the same year Cyprus began negotiating its independence from Britain; the same year, too, that the riots started in Istanbul after news circulated that Atatürk's birth home in Salonika, the pink house where he was born in 1881, was bombed. Turkish men ransacked Istanbul's Greek neighborhoods, smashing storefront windows with giant logs, pillaging Greek churches, and setting fire to Greek homes, despite the news turning out to be false. Grandmother, who found nationalism embarrassing, lived in Istanbul with her family: a father who managed the local pharmacy, a mother who was known in their neighborhood for her famous meat-filled grape leaves, and a sister, my great-aunt Pinar, who was, at the time, fourteen to my grandmother's sixteen. Grandmother was two years old when her family—mother, father, uncles and aunts—had moved from Tokat to Istanbul, the Tulip Apartments, a cement residential building on a crowded hilly street in Beşiktaş.

Grandmother was in her final year of high school, and in the evenings, she helped her father at the pharmacy, unpacking boxes of ointment, labeling tubes of medicine and securing them in the glass cabinets that lined the dark wood walls.

The day Grandmother visited the eye doctor's office, she wore a pair of Mary Jane shoes her uncle had bought in Italy, and a green dress she had sewn with pearl buttons in a line down the spine.

I have tried this dress on before, at the beginning of this summer. My grandmother, however, had been much thinner than me. Her breasts, smaller. My grandmother and I had spent a few hot, sweaty minutes trying to heave and smoosh my boobs into the delicate fitted top.

SOMETHING WAS WRONG WITH GRANDMOTHER'S HEALTH. She was experiencing migraines that hit around the same time as her period. She was not ashamed of this fact—or, as her mother, very ashamed, called it, this "coincidence"—rather, Grandmother understood that the knowledge would give her power, as shameful things would for the rest of her life. The sisters had a cousin who was often bedridden, always when she had her period, and they would go over to give her the schoolwork she'd missed. They'd sit on her bed and braid her hair and tell their cousin, whom the family said was cursed by a jinn, the school gossip, which boys the girls liked, and whether the boys liked them back.

Because it was unheard of for sixteen-year-old girls to visit the gynecologist, Grandmother wanted to go to the eye doctor instead. Grandmother, who had never been to a doctor's office before, was insistent that her migraines were due to blurry vision. She said she could rarely distinguish a person's eyes from their eyebrows. She said she could not tell when a person's mouth was moving. She wanted eyeglasses. After arguing with her father for three weeks, he allowed her to visit the ophthalmologist. Accompanied by her unemployed uncle, she took the tram to the office, an expensive one a woman at the pharmacy insisted on, even pressing the money into the palm of her father's hand, and her father took the money only because he had no idea what his daughter was doing at an ophthalmologist's, but the more expensive, he figured, the less likely his daughter would be treated inappropriately. The office was in Nişantaşı, the nicest neighborhood at the time, with clean streets full of clothing stores, a French bookstore, a stationery store, cafés and restaurants, and a department store with European brands.

Grandmother's uncle stood outside the office, smoking, talking about Cyprus to a man who had accompanied his wife to the ophthalmologist. The two men agreed that it was really the Brits who began this conflict, negotiating with both Greeks and Turks behind closed doors for how many decades, and to what end?

The eye doctor was a young man, tall and slim, with high cheekbones and giant, deep-set eyes. He was very handsome, Grandmother said, and she was struck by his resemblance to a hawk.

GRANDMOTHER, WHO WAS CERTAIN HER EYES SAW THE world clearly, but was nonetheless determined to know what a doctor's office was like, lay in the patient chair as the eye doctor prepared his tools for her examination. A framed photograph of Atatürk hung on the wall. Even in the black-and-white print, Atatürk's blue eyes appeared spectral. The eye doctor wore a gray suit and loafers with silver buckles and told her how he'd graduated from Gülhane Askeri Akademisi, a military medical school, in 1950, and started residency at the psychiatric hospital in Bakırköy. He had dreamed of being a psychiatrist. The hospital, on the far edge of Istanbul, past the airport, was a long building of white stone, surrounded by a high iron wall on all sides and hundreds of cypress trees. The economy had fallen so drastically in the past decade that the funds the hospital received were extremely low, forcing some patients to share beds. After a few months of treating these patients, the eye doctor said, I will go crazy here, and the young man worked to become an ophthalmologist instead.

The eye doctor thought Grandmother was likely experiencing headaches due to nearsighted vision that had gone untreated for years. She agreed with him. She said nothing about her period.

The eye doctor told her about his two sisters. How they experienced fuzzy vision and subsequent headaches, but many family members advised against the girls coming into their brother's office. They tried rinsing the girls' eyes in rose water, herbal water, boiled cabbage water. They hung evil eyes over their beds at night. It wasn't until one morning when his eldest sister, Refika, put Urfa pepper in her husband's tea instead of sugar, and he hurled the glass at her face and the hot liquid branded her with a burn on her right cheek in the shape of Turkey, that the sisters were allowed to get their eyes checked.

Grandmother listened. She asked him if he was married, and the eye doctor laughed. He coughed politely to get her to turn to the board and read the letters.

I live with my parents and sisters, he explained.

I live with my family too, she said. We're in the old Tulip Apartments in Beşiktaş.

Where are you from?

We're from Tokat. We came here after my sister was born.

The eye doctor looked at her strangely. We're from Tokat, too. My father works in textiles and moved his business here after I was born.

Grandmother smiled. Neither remembered Tokat, but they spoke of what their parents had told them. Stories of the earthquake, the harvests, the Armenians. The eye doctor's family had migrated from Georgia months before the Russo-Turkish War broke out in the late 1800s.

My family, Grandmother said, was in Tokat for so many years that no one knew where we came from.

He nodded. He asked what letters she could read on the board, if she could read any.

I'm also a pharmacist, Grandmother said.

Really?

Well, my father is a pharmacist. I work at his pharmacy, she said, and before he could answer she read each letter loud and clear, and although she couldn't, at first, read the bottommost line—an A, a Ğ, and an S—she felt a sudden pride, because the eye doctor looked at her, shocked and entirely unsure what she was doing in his office.

BECAUSE THEY HAD NO OTHER PLACE TO MEET, HE LIVING with his parents, and she living with her parents, Grandmother continued to visit the ophthalmologist despite having perfect vision. After that first appointment, the eye doctor wrote in her official chart that she was an unusual patient, with an eye condition he hadn't seen before, and sent her home to her father with the decree that she return for testing next week, no charge. It was a dangerous idea. It usually is, with Turkish fathers. My grandmother's father was at a loss about his daughter going to the ophthalmologist to begin with, so he looked to his wife, who, worried that her daughter's eyes were irritated, was preparing cloths soaked in black tea to lay over her face. He allowed the ophthalmologist visits to continue. It helped that the eye doctor, as his daughter informed him, was also from Tokat.

Next week became every week, and throughout the long winter Grandmother left the pharmacy early on Thursdays and took the yellow tram from Beşiktaş to Nişantaşı, where she'd stare out the windows at the street full of fruit and vegetable vendors among the horse-drawn carriages and new cars from Europe, and she thought that she never wanted something as much as she wanted the eye doctor. She believed that she could make this happen, despite the fact that he was twenty-nine and she, sixteen. Because her father had gone to pharmacology school, his family might allow their son to marry her, and both families were, importantly, dedicated secularists. Grandmother stepped off the tram, cleaned her hands with lemon-scented cologne, spread rose petal cream on her neck and behind her earlobes, and walked into the office to meet the eye doctor, who, despite Grandmother's perfect vision, still set up the board of letters for her to read, still wiped his gadgets clean for Grandmother's well-being, still checked her eyelids for spots, and still dilated her pupils, just to spend time with this young woman from Tokat with pearl buttons up her spine.

ONE AFTERNOON, AFTER TAKING THE TRAM TO THE EYE doctor in Nişantaşı, Grandmother bought expensive rouge from a boutique with the money she'd made at the pharmacy that winter. Her sister, who did not yet know that Grandmother was in love, admired her purchase when Grandmother got home. They rifled through the pages of a French fashion magazine they had purchased from the corner store, where they often bought candy, newspapers, nail files, and acetone. They locked themselves in the bathroom and ran the hot water to clean their faces before they rubbed the rouge into their skin and made American movie star faces in the mirror until their father knocked at the locked door, yelling.

IT WAS THE FIRST WARM DAY OF SPRING WHEN A WOODEN house on the Bosphorus caught fire, and everyone in the neighborhoods nearby gathered to watch the old mansion burn. Those with boats invited friends out to watch the fire from the water.

Grandmother slipped out of the Tulip Apartments and took the tram alone to meet the eye doctor. She was not worried about being caught that night. The eye doctor had a friend who owned an empty apartment, a bachelor pad that he lent to his unmarried friends. They met at the apartment building's front door without saying hello. Grandmother had covered her head with a sapphire-colored scarf, pocketed the key the eye doctor placed in a flowerpot, and walked in before him. She unlocked the apartment's wooden door and set herself up posed on the bed. Her face was painted with rouge to look like an American movie star. They kissed on the bed and the eye doctor undressed Grandmother and she ran her hands over the back of his neck and his thighs before she saw smoke rising outside the window and remembered that even her sister didn't know where she was, and, sliding off the bed, she apologized. She pulled up her nylon stockings, stepped into her dress, put her arms above her head to clasp the pearl buttons down her spine. He diligently dressed and drove her back to the Tulip Apartments. She slid out of the car around the corner and told her family she was watching the fire with school friends.

ONE EVENING GRANDMOTHER WAS PREPARING TO LEAVE the Tulip Apartments to meet with the eye doctor when she heard the front door open. Her sister and mother had returned early from the market, and Grandmother, who had been planning to slip out of the empty home unseen, panicked. Her mother, Emine, a woman tied greatly to principle and the importance of hard work, promptly scolded Grandmother for not being at the pharmacy. Are you sick? she asked. Why aren't you working? Aunt Pinar touched Grandmother's dark curls, which she had just taken out of blue plastic rollers they had bought together at the Saturday market, and asked her where she was going and whether she could braid her hair like Pollyanna, and Grandmother, impatient to leave, lied. She looked her mother in the face and said she was going to their cousin, who was bedridden this week, to sew her a new dress with new buttons down the spine.

What buttons, her sister asked. Can I come?

No, Grandmother said.

When did you buy new buttons? her mother asked.

She replied that their cousin had bought the buttons, and she said to her sister she was sorry, and she promised tomorrow

she'd braid her hair like Pollyanna. My great-aunt, who wanted so
badly to be just like her older sister, said that actually she wanted it
curly, like hers. Grandmother said of course. Grandmother wore
a gray dress, her pharmacy uniform, and in a cloth bag she stuffed
the second dress—the new dress she had already made, not for
her cousin but for herself. When her mother disappeared into the
kitchen, she slipped through the door with this bag under her arm.
It was her idea to meet the eye doctor at the wood-walled bar with
live music in Beyoğlu. She got there early to change in the bar's
bathroom. The eye doctor was there, still dressed in a white coat,
with two friends who were polite but did not know, exactly, how
to talk to this sixteen-year-old girl with a determined face but sad,
hopeful eyes. Grandmother and the eye doctor held hands under
the table and he told her, quietly, so his friends could not hear, that
he loved the dip in her lips, how it made her mouth the shape of
a hand-drawn heart, and how much he'd like to open them, her
lips, and she felt big bells ringing inside her and an urge to take
everything that could be hers, but the next time they saw each
other at the eye doctor's office she had to tell him that her father
had found out. Someone had seen them, and this someone had
told her father that his daughter had run off with a man in a white
coat to Beyoğlu—where, her father had yelled, the whores go—
and if they were not married immediately she would be sent back
to Tokat, where her own grandmother still lived in a village with
chickens and cows, and in the eye doctor's office Grandmother
began picking up gadgets and smashing them to the floor, saying,
If I go back there I will turn into her, she'll make me turn into her,
and we'll spend the day washing dirty clothes in hot water and
she'll tell me about the cypress grove at the edge of town by the
cemetery where she last saw her husband alive before he died in

Gallipoli, killed by an Australian, who had no reason to be fighting in Turkey save for Britain, and it's always because of Britain or France or Germany, I'm so sick of all of them and I'm sick of all of us for looking up to them, for licking their feet and their assholes, and I'm sick of us, all of us, for thinking they will ever let us be one of them, because they keep saying one of us, one of us, that's what they said about Korea, but we will never be one of them, and I refuse to do this, I refuse to be like my grandmother, and, when she caught her breath, the eye doctor lowered her hand holding the scalpel and asked for her hand in marriage.

But the shape my grandmother's story takes is entirely dependent on the eye doctor's mother: Safiye. Safiye had already lined up many suitable brides for her son when the eye doctor first told her about Grandmother. Safiye lost her mind. Is she pregnant?

Grandmother was pregnant, but they would never tell anyone this. Only Aunt Pinar knew, and she knew to protect the secret. Grandmother was shocked to be carrying a child—she was convinced that her womb had been cursed given the pain she experienced during her period. So she prayed five times a day, stitched new dresses to hide her bump, and swore her sister and the eye doctor to secrecy.

Because the eye doctor was Safiye's only son, and most Turkish sons get whatever they want, Safiye agreed to meet the girl.

By the beginning of the summer, the two families had arranged for the eye doctor to visit the Tulip Apartments with his mother and father. Safiye complained during the entire car ride over. First it was about the girl's neighborhood: too close, she said, to a gecekondu—homes that were, as the translation goes, "built overnight" for the many migrants who came to Istanbul from the Black Sea coast or Anatolia. Then she complained about her own husband, a pussy, who made a name for himself with his textile company, which was renowned for providing the carpets to the American embassy in Istanbul, but was now bleeding money. Aren't you? she said to her husband, who had learned long ago not to reply to his wife when she taunted him. Aren't you a pussy? The eye doctor's two sisters were not to attend, but they spent the day concocting different scenarios, imagining what their mother would say to this pharmacist's daughter.

It was rare for two young people to meet and fall in love. Parents arranged marriages.

But Safiye was shocked when she entered the Tulip Apartments and introduced herself to Grandmother's mother, Emine.

They were second cousins. They grew up together in Tokat before Emine moved to her husband's village, then to Istanbul.

THE TWO FAMILIES AGREED THAT THEIR CHILDREN WOULD get married that summer. The evening before the wedding, a henna night was held at the Tulip Apartments, where the women in the groom's family joined the women in the bride's family to celebrate Grandmother. That evening, the eye doctor's family walked into the apartment one by one like a small army, and all night, they complimented my grandmother without ceasing—alarming Grandmother, her sister, and their mother, who continuously knocked on wood.

Grandmother listened to the women gossip about other women. A neighbor lost all of her hair at age thirty after multiple miscarriages. Another neighbor died in a car crash just after getting married. A cousin, a teacher, was raped by the father of one of her students, but the women knew she had had multiple affairs and concluded that her word could not be trusted.

Grandmother was too happy for something terrible not to occur. Throughout her pregnancy, she knocked on wood and prayed.

The eye doctor bought an apartment in Levent, where homes were cheap, and the hills green and untouched. The Sunshine

Apartments. In the summers, people would visit this neighbor-hood to have picnics under mulberry trees. Although Safiye com-plained of the area, saying it was so far out of town that the wolves came in the winter, Grandfather did not listen. Grandfather brought his violin, and his family gave the married couple furni-ture, including a green wood-and-iron trunk that his grandfather had carried from Georgia in 1876. The same green trunk is now in Brooklyn by the windowsill in the kitchen. My grandmother gave it to my parents as a wedding gift.

Grandmother, like many women, wanted a son. She did not want to bring a woman into the world, because it was more dif-ficult being a woman in the world, and she would never want to give a daughter the life she would soon have.

THE NEXT WINTER, GRANDMOTHER GAVE BIRTH IN THE Tulip Apartments. Her water broke while she was drinking tea with her sister and mother, and her sister ran down the street to ring the bell of the midwife's apartment, where the midwife was breastfeeding her own son. The pain started quickly, as soon as the water started to flow, and just like for the other women in her family, the waves of contractions lasted a long ten hours, ten hours when she was certain her uterus would tear through her skin and fly out, before she met her son.

Baba was born with a head full of thick black hair.

The human heart starts out as a tube, and as a baby is growing in the womb, this tube folds itself into the right shape to effectively pump blood and oxygen through the body.

The moment the midwife washed the blood off his new body, Grandfather parted Baba's hair, looking for his scalp. He wanted to kiss his head.

GRANDMOTHER HAD TWO SISTERS-IN-LAW. THE ELDER, Refika, had been married for eight years but was unable to get pregnant. Refika was known for her cat eyes, cheekbones, and a vigorous smoking habit. She was never without a cigarette, and she always pulled one white leather glove up her arm before smoking. She refused to be mocked for this, this one gloved hand, as she said it was a glamorous look. *French*, she'd say, and practical, too. The neighborhood believed she picked it up after she got married, but Refika was never the type of woman to confess much, if any, weakness, my grandmother now says as I'm helping her put her feet up because she's agitated, suddenly, and when I ask her if she'd like the fan, if she's hot, if she wants to stop talking and lie down, she says no.

The eye doctor's youngest sister, Melike, was engaged to a young man who worked with her father at his textile company. This young man was from Bolu, and there were a few weeks of heated arguments between the two families concerning where the wedding would take place. The groom's family won, despite Safiye's vehement opposition. The family packed their suitcases for a one-week stay in Bolu for the wedding. Grandmother, Grandfather, and their baby drove to Bolu in their Chevrolet.

But Grandmother, who had never been to Bolu before, was not allowed to spend that last day with her husband and child. While heaving his sisters' bags out of the car, the eye doctor dropped a jar of blackberry jam, staining the bride's veil, so the women were to sew the best veil as quickly as possible in the groom's family home, a three-story traditional Ottoman-style building built on a stone foundation, with a wooden exterior and boxy bay windows. Grandmother left their baby with her husband, who loved to bounce him in his arm and tell Baba about how his grandfather came from Georgia half a century ago.

At the fabric store in the city's center, the women argued over who would make the best veil. Safiye said she, of course, should make it, but Refika countered that she had become quite skilled with needlework, and what an honor it would be to make the veil for her only sister's wedding. Grandmother wanted to try, too. She was the best seamstress of the three women, she believed, having spent years making dresses. She made her case in the fabric store while the owner smoked a cigarette and gave a few suggestions for which tulle was the best value. Safiye decided to purchase exactly enough tulle for both Refika and Grandmother to each make a veil, and the bride would wear the most beautiful one.

Grandfather got bored in the house that afternoon. He decided to go for a walk with Baba, to point out the cypress and pine trees, the tulips, the sky and the sun, the houses with wooden beams built into their stone and brick walls, a feat, he thought, of remarkable engineering that kept the homes dry.

Grandmother thinks Grandfather had no reason to be outside.

Minutes before the earthquake, Grandmother was sewing her veil on a stiff chair in her sister-in-law's new family home. She wanted to win, especially because she was the only daughter-in-law, and she wanted Safiye to love her.

But Safiye liked her elder daughter's veil best, and when she announced Refika as victor, Refika blushed. Grandmother knew Refika was not the type of person who blushed. Refika was a shrewd woman, a mathematics teacher at a girl's school, who likely orchestrated this competition to begin with, to ensure that Grandmother knew her place in the family. Instilled with this righteousness, Grandmother was trying to fix her veil's scalloped hem, still thinking there could be a chance of winning, when the earthquake hit. Her sewing form slipped, and the needle drew blood from her finger. The women ran under the doorframe and Grandmother held Refika's hand.

GRANDMOTHER RAN INTO THE STREET AFTER THE TWENTY-five-second earthquake toppled the houses in Bolu and killed fifty-six people on May 26, 1957. Refika was close behind, and she was the first to see Grandfather under what was once the tallest apartment building in Bolu at the time.

Grandmother looked at the body buried under beige rubble, the man's gray face, and said, I don't recognize that man.

That's him, Refika said, that's my baby brother.

Then Grandmother heard a cry coming from his arms.

THE WEDDING WAS POSTPONED. THEY DROVE BACK TO Istanbul the next day, and the eye doctor's father dropped Grandmother off at the Tulip Apartments, then brought his son's body to the morgue where he would be washed and prepared for the funeral the next day. Aunt Pinar rocked Baba to sleep while Grandmother sat on the couch staring at the spot on her finger where she had stabbed herself with the needle. Her mother wept, unable to prepare dinner. Her father smoked cigarette after cigarette. At around seven in the evening, the telephone rang. It was Melike calling to invite the family over for tea. My great-aunt helped my grandmother get dressed, and their mother bundled the baby up in blankets, despite the summer heat, and their father drove them to Safiye's apartment.

If the eye doctor had had a brother, Grandmother would have had no choice but to be married off to him. But this was not the case, and this was not the reason the family had invited them over.

A mother should not be raising a child without a man, Safiye said.

Refika has been trying to conceive for eight years now, she said.

Refika will be his mother.

Safiye arranged to take the baby the next day.

GRANDMOTHER KIDNAPPED BABA THE DAY BEFORE HIS second birthday. It was nearly two years after the earthquake, winter again, the same day the airplane carrying sixteen passengers, including Prime Minister Adnan Menderes, crashed a few miles short of London's Gatwick Airport. The passengers were heading to London to sign the Cyprus agreement with the British and Greek prime ministers.

Refika and her husband lived in a pink apartment building in Nişantaşı. As Grandmother made her way to their apartment, she wandered into the florist to buy some flowers to leave for Refika, before changing her mind.

It was a good day for Grandmother's plan. Every Friday, Refika had her friends over for tea on her large balcony. It was impossible to see the apartment's front door or hallway from this balcony, and Grandmother knew that Refika would keep Baba in the bedroom while the women played cards. She knew this because when the young parents had brought the baby over to Refika's, months ago, Refika told her exactly this: that she would never let this baby set foot on the balcony because she was terrified that he would crawl through the railing. When Grandmother used the key her late husband had for his sister's door, she could hear the women on the balcony talking about Menderes, and she saw Refika's white glove through the window, holding a cigarette. She slid off her shoes outside the door, walked to the bedroom, and took her baby.

The city was run with gossip about the plane crash. On the tram ride home, total strangers around her broke into conversation about how Menderes, sitting in the back of the plane, survived the crash with only a few scratches on his face.

When Grandmother arrived home, she put Baba on the couch and set the needle on her husband's record player. She took Baba into her arms and began to dance around the living room to a popular song about seeing the Bosphorus for the first time. She felt peace, holding her son, and, consumed by this calm, she began dancing in circles, repeatedly knocking into the coffee table, and only when she heard the lock turn did she pause. It was her sister in her school uniform, carrying a tray of rice pudding from the Greek bakery.

Aunt Pinar saw Baba in Grandmother's arms and froze. What are you doing?

Grandmother did not stop dancing. I love this song, she said, why don't you dance, Pinar? Why don't you dance with us? Her sister asked if she could hold her nephew, please, she has missed him so much, and only then did Grandmother, still holding Baba to her breast, stop dancing. She began to yell. She cursed Safiye— how could they pretend that she was no longer family now that he was dead, how could they think this baby would take the breast of a barren woman? Can't her sister see how happy he is here? Can't her sister see their great happiness? Aunt Pinar tried to calm Grandmother down. She tried, unsuccessfully, to pry Baba out of her arms. Grandmother slapped her sister across the face and slapped her again, and again, until Grandmother began to lose her grip on Baba, and she stopped only when he was about to slip out of her arms.

I think we are cursed, Grandmother said, because our grandfather killed Armenians.

My sister, Pinar begged, no.

He was a soldier, Grandmother said, what if he did.

He never said anything. Please. He didn't.

You don't know that. Grandmother bounced Baba, and her eyes looked feral and haunted.

He never said anything because he never did.

You don't know.

THAT EVENING, GRANDMOTHER'S PARENTS RETURNED THE baby themselves with the agreement that their side of the family would never see him again.

It worked. My grandmother didn't see her son again until November 1979. Twenty years later and one year before the coup. My father was recently engaged to my mother, and he wanted her to accompany him to my grandmother's apartment. That week, the Grey Wolves' Mehmet Ali Ağca, who had assassinated a journalist on his walk home from work, escaped prison. My grandmother had heard about it from the grocer, who told her she was lucky to not have any sons. All of these sons, the grocer said sadly, they leave the house each day like they will never come home again. Allah korusun, my grandmother said as she knocked on the fruit stand's wooden post. She was buying eggplants to make her best dish for her son, who was coming over with his girlfriend from Bolu. The circularity amazed her. She washed the floors and wiped the windows and changed the bedsheets, in case he needed somewhere to stay. She bought flowers and opened all her windows so the apartment would smell as clean as possible. She wondered if she should wear makeup. When he rang the buzzer, she pressed several wrong buttons before successfully unlocking the door. He was riding the elevator with my mother, and the noise of it climbing three stories marched through my grandmother's head like the Turkish anthem.

They spent the night in conversation. My father told her about his plans to apply to graduate school in America. My grandmother spoke of her years, her seamstress work, her nieces and nephews, who, she said, he would love. She wanted to know how my parents met, and when they replied honestly, that they met at a demonstration, she nodded gravely. When my mother tried to clear the table my grandmother would not allow it. They continued meeting for tea, dinner, or breakfast on Saturdays, up until my father fled Turkey.

MY GRANDMOTHER TELLS ME NOW THAT THIS WAS SIMPLY how Allah willed it. Because back in 1959, after she was forbidden from seeing her son, Grandmother soon became a different woman. She returned to the Sunshine Apartments, the home she had lived in with her husband, and refused to leave. She slept through the day. She let the water boil for hours, once, all night, and when her sister, now fifteen years old, came over before going to school and heard the hot water splashing out of the kettle, when she saw my grandmother asleep on the couch, her body smelling like rotting yogurt, and no food anywhere in the kitchen, Aunt Pinar made the one mistake that, my grandmother tells me, she still regrets. Her sister called their parents. Their mother came over straight away and washed every dirty dish, and as she prepared to scrub down the wooden floors, Aunt Pinar stuck her head out from the balcony and lowered a basket to the grocer for him to fill with eggplants, parsley, and tomatoes. Then the dairy man came by, and she lowered the basket again for a pound of fresh feta cheese. Aunt Pinar boiled water for fresh tea, and she sat Grandmother in the bathtub, where she washed her, scrubbing her armpits, her legs, her feet, and her face. Grandmother thanked her sister for everything. Her sister said nothing. She kept massaging Grandmother's thin arms. She rubbed her scalp and rope of dark wet hair with a bar of soap. Within a few hours, her family, who eventually decided to take Grandmother back into the Tulip Apartments, was at a loss of what to do. Someone—it is unclear whether it was my great-grandfather or my great-grandmother— remembered the psychiatric hospital, the same one the eye doctor once worked at in Bakırköy.

THE NEIGHBORHOOD COULD NOT TRUST AN INSANE GIRL like Grandmother to distribute the proper medications at the pharmacy. They gossiped in the outdoor market near the Tulip Apartments. One woman, clutching bags of white rice, pointed out that Grandmother's job only entailed ringing up the labeled medicine, creams, ointments, and toiletries. A woman buying eggs disagreed, because there weren't many others working at the pharmacy to supervise her, and who could predict what kind of spite was instilled in a grieving woman? The tomato vendor chimed in, mentioning his own wife, who had miscarried recently, and how she could no longer be expected to complete daily tasks like preparing breakfast, cooking dinner, doing the laundry, let alone help him with his tomatoes, and these women thanked him for his counsel and said they were sorry for his loss, that Allah would help him and his wife find peace. This same conversation was surely discussed at length and in loops at the market, at the butcher's, in the Greek bakery, until finally, one of these women cornered my great-grandmother Emine and Aunt Pinar in the market and expressed her concern. When the woman walked away, Aunt Pinar turned to her mother and declared that if they listened to this gossip, if they forbade Grandmother, who never finished high school in order to work at the pharmacy, from working, if they were seriously considering Bakırköy, she would jump into the Bosphorus and she would do everything in her power to die. My great-grandmother, who was already working so hard to make sure her elder daughter did not shame herself any further, urged her younger to please be quiet in front of everyone at the market.

But Aunt Pinar dutifully shared this gossip with her sister—she thought, or she hoped, that it might help.

THAT EVENING, GRANDMOTHER WAS WASHING DISHES IN
the sink when she heard her parents arguing. She rinsed off her
soapy hands and padded into the hallway. Her mother, who had
just reported what she'd heard at the market to her husband, suggested once more, and with quiet panic, Bakırköy. Her father
refused to consider such a place. Those people are truly crazy,
Emine, he said. Our daughter is not crazy. We can't take her out
of the pharmacy.

The same night, long after her family had gone to sleep,
Grandmother slipped out of the bed she shared with her sister
and took the bus down to Karaköy, where the Bosphorus met the
Golden Horn. She sat on a bench by the ferry station and petted a
street cat as strips of moonlight moved on the black water. It was
always colder by the water, which she chose because it would be
busy with cargo ships and fishermen, who would render her invis-
ible amid the early morning activity. The fog was so thick, it was
impossible to see three feet ahead, and the people moving towards
her looked more like ghouls than people at all. Every few years,
a giant ship would crash into one of the wooden mansions on the
shore of the Bosphorus. Sometimes the ship was transporting steel

and wood from the Black Sea to the Mediterranean. Sometimes the ship carried military supplies from Russia to Cuba. Sometimes it was a clear and weightless night, with no fog, but each time my grandmother heard news of a ship wedged deep into someone's home, she would remember this night.

Grandmother sat on the bench for a few minutes longer before she jumped.

A FEW YARDS AWAY, A FISHERMAN WAS REVVING UP THE small motor of his tiny blue boat. When he saw black fabric ballooning in the water nearby, he steered his fishing boat through the fog and towards the mass, sank his arms into the water, and tugged the girl into his boat. He took her to a fish restaurant on the shore, where the owner was beginning preparations for the day by lifting fresh octopus from buckets of ice water. The owner sat her in a chair, wrapped her in blankets, and asked her for her family's telephone number. At first the girl didn't speak, she only knitted her swollen purple lips shut and stared out at the water, so the owner telephoned his wife, waking her, and asking her to please speak to this girl, we have no idea who she is, she's some crazy girl who tried to kill herself in the Golden Horn, please come, and she did. She took the girl into their apartment, where she dressed her in freshly laundered clothes and pulled thick socks on her frozen feet and put her into the bed she shared with her husband. While Grandmother slept, the wife, who had managed to get the girl's name, found her family's telephone number, and when she called it was the girl's sister who picked up, who insisted she would come alone to bring the girl back. Alone? the wife demanded, what about your parents? But the girl's sister came, and when she woke her, Grandmother rose and walked in her sister's arms out of the apartment and onto the tram back home as if in a trance.

THEY ONLY WANTED A WAY TO HEAL THEIR DAUGHTER. Years later, Emine begged her daughter to forgive her, that they would have never actually sent her to Bakırköy. They didn't know. They didn't know anything.

A few weeks after her little jump, as they called it, the family made their decision. My grandmother had resumed sewing, praying, and, on rare but meaningful occasions, laughing. She was ready to hear their news; that my great-grandfather could not risk his business losing any more money, as they were already constrained by recent zoning laws, and many wealthy people had started packing up their homes and moving out to new neighborhoods. So my great-grandfather, while he was drinking tea and Grandmother was clearing the dirty dishes, told his daughter she must stop working at the pharmacy.

Grandmother stood still with the tray full of dirty plates.

But what will I do? she asked.

Her father didn't have an answer. The windows were open and in the distance two cats were shrieking, a noise that filled Grandmother's head for years.

*Part III*

# I.

MY YOUNGER SISTER ALSO LOVES BLOND MEN BUT IS OTH-
erwise unlike me.

I drive to the airport with my grandmother next to me. She is
calm, and each time I take my eyes off the road to glance at her,
she's looking back. She has her hands in her lap and doesn't say a
word about Istanbul's crazy drivers, usually her favorite topic. And
she hasn't expressed any worry about this being only my third time
driving in Istanbul. She looks out at the tall steel buildings, the cemetery, the crumbling façades plastered with ads. As we were riding
the elevator, she told me she was very relieved to have shared her
story with me. I kissed her cheek and held her hand as we walked to
the car. I had only known that her husband was an eye doctor who
died in an earthquake. Alara and I thought she never loved him.
We thought the old woman who spat at me was her friend, not this
great-aunt. I can't see my grandmother the way I used to, and this
recognition fills me with hope. If she can be a different person, who
was the same person this whole time, I can, too.

We pass the cemetery and she smiles. I tell her that some
grave owners post online ads selling their family plots, many of
which are already filled with bones.

People need money, she says sadly.

The new Istanbul skyline could be repurposed to accommodate the dead, I say.

Don't be insane, my grandmother says.

I roll down our windows and my grandmother hangs out her arm.

IT'S ALWAYS MEN WAITING IN THE ARRIVALS HALL OF Atatürk Airport. Taxi drivers, private drivers, but usually dads or uncles or brothers. It smells like sweat. We're the only women here and we're hungry, so we buy börek to eat out of oily napkins. My grandmother hands me a wet towelette from her purse. Her hand is still shaking, and I realize that I had been hoping she would be less sick now, now that she had released something held inside for so long. She wipes her hands clean, then motions for my forehead to feel if I still have a fever.

Gone? I ask.

Gone, she says, patting my arm and proud. Now you feel like ice.

They're coming towards us. Alara is wearing a long colorful dress, her hair piled on top of her head in a bun, her wide mouth open in a laugh. Her thin arms swing at her sides like oars. Deniz is scowling, but otherwise looks happy. His long hair grazes his shoulders in dark waves. He's in a graphic T-shirt, a habit he often says he won't kick. This one's his favorite, a photograph of Nas, and Nas in turn wears a Supreme shirt. Deniz's carrying her things.

Alara and Deniz close in on us, hugs happen around me, and my grandmother won't shut up about how tired they must be, because it is her job to be the best grandmother to us, to take care of us before she takes care of herself, and I'm stuck thinking, again, of how I can be of any use to my elders when they throw themselves over to take care of us, and how I can transform the Turkish obsession with caring for the youth, who would be just fine, wouldn't we, without all their care, when Alara and Deniz turn to me, smiling, their eyes wide and hopeful, and I surprise them, I take them both into a big hug.

THERE IS THE USUAL TRAFFIC ON THE DRIVE HOME. ALARA and Deniz point out the buildings they don't recognize, ones newly built since last summer, and my grandmother shares what she remembers was once in each skyscraper's place. She's sitting tiny in the back seat, her seat belt cutting her long breasts in two, talking while her body remains entirely still. She's back to her usual form of storytelling: geographical data, anthropological details, facts. My grandmother informs us that there used to be only a chocolate factory on the outskirts of the airport. Now there are miles of run-down, paint-chipped buildings, and I see a short man dressing a mannequin in the third-floor window of a clothing store. Alara and Deniz are angry at the new skyscrapers and malls sharing the hills with beige and gray apartment buildings, mosques and minarets. People use the Turkish verb for "planted" to describe the phenomenon of newly built skyscrapers, which have been rising for years now at a rapid, fatal pace. Fatal because the economy will not support them, and many of them—retail, business, residence—are too expensive to be used. And the steel buildings, thanks to this term, masquerade as some organic form of life.

I decide I will do whatever my grandmother tells me I should do.

If she told me to visit his grave, I would go.

One third of Parkinson's patients suffer from depression. I cannot be responsible for making her illness worse.

We drop Deniz off in the neighborhood next to ours, where he's staying with his grandmother. Anytime a family member lands in Istanbul, an arrival ceremony commences at my grandmother's apartment, where we feast on tea and pastries and ice cream, and each time, after we're already full of pastries, my grandmother reveals the second feast, dinner, which she has spent all day preparing. Deniz's will be conducted in a similar fashion, and his aunties will ask him if he has a girlfriend, if the girlfriend is Kurdish, if he is going to propose. Deniz has only ever dated blond white girls, but never seriously enough for his family in Istanbul to know.

Alara and I try to help my grandmother, but she bats us out of the kitchen. Alara's moving through each room of the small apartment, eating a dribbly peach, and talking of the distinct smell of this place, a smell she can recognize only on the first day she returns. She runs her hand over a photograph of my grandmother marrying my grandfather. She asks me if I think Grandma was the thinnest in the family back then and I shrug. She leafs through my test books before throwing her bag down on our bed. In the living room, she opens and closes the dark wooden cabinet with my grandmother's lifelong collection of porcelain plates. When we were little, my grandmother filled us up with carbs, cheese, meat, and sugar, adding enough weight to change our body types. I used to think I came to Istanbul each summer only to eat. Now I'm thinking food is medicine. Trota, Galen, al-Razi, Ibn Sina, they administered bloodletting, of course, but the majority of treatments concerned adapting your diet in accordance to your

liquid makeup, as well as the season. Sugar made a person instantly happy, and it instilled that person with enough energy to
do physical work. I begin to tell Alara this and how they used to
think sugar was very healthy, but she pretends not to hear me. I
will keep trying, because it's time. We have never spoken about
this, her eating disorder, because within weeks of Baba dying in
the kitchen while boiling water for tea, she'd already spun a strong
defensive narrative. She justified her new lack of sugar, as well as
a long, unspoken list of other carbohydrates, as healthy. Ibn Sina
would agree with her. He was the first to measure sugar in urine
in order to diagnose diabetes.

My grandmother's hand shakes as she lines up stuffed grape
leaves in a pot to boil. When we attempt to help again she tells us
we're embarrassing her. We protest, but she starts smacking us
with a wooden spoon. There's hardly enough room for three of us
in there anyway. We sit on the floor of the balcony instead, where
wet sweater sets and blouses and my grandmother's big beige bras
hang around us, and we talk about Cooper.

You know, Alara says, sucking a peach pit clean in her mouth,
I could never tell—seriously, never—if Cooper was genuinely
nice, or if it was all an act. You know, to appear nice because it's
more socially comfortable than being rude. I thought it was an act
at first, when you first introduced him to us. Baba thought so, too.
But then I thought differently. Especially after winter break. He
always knew what to say. He never pushed us. You.

And now? I ask.

She licks her peach pit. I'll admit, I do still think it's genuine.
Do you miss him?

Alara's still in her stylish airplane outfit but her face looks
yellow and oily. I want to tell her that it scares me that the other

night was the first time Cooper and I had ever fought, and does that mean he really wants to give up so easily? Do I?

Jesus, Sibel. Hello? You don't know, do you? So fucking typical of you to not know.

No, I insist. I do know. It wasn't working.

She spits out the pit and begins to eat another peach. The smell of lamb and buttered rice from the kitchen fills the balcony. Alara is right, I don't know if this is better. I know I miss him. And I know I'm an idiot.

Aren't those full of sugar? I point at her peach.

I didn't eat on the plane, she replies. You know, when you first called me weeks ago, saying you weren't going to volunteer at the hospital after all, I wasn't surprised, exactly, I just felt sad.

I'm still interested in medicine, I say, and I recite my favorite fact, that your periods don't necessarily add up to an expiration date for childbearing, but that many of my friends still think they're losing future baby chances with each period.

Alara rolls her eyes but I continue.

When there is no baby, I say, which is most of the time, your uterus sheds the newly formed lining. Some eggs may be nestled in that lining, but it's not a drastic loss of eggs. Really, the eggs die on their own.

Alara's confused now but absorbed. She finished three peaches and has their pits laid on her lap like hard, tiny brains. I thought your period meant you flushed out your unused eggs?

No, I say. Alara is not listening to me. I tell her how a baby girl is born with every egg she'll ever possess. This means that when our grandmother gave birth to our mother at home, the eggs that made us were already in existence.

Alara nods, then asks again about Cooper. She tells me I'm

being very elusive, very annoying. She throws a peach pit at my face.

Fine, I say. I haven't seen him since our fight. All I know is he's going to Georgia. That's what Grandma told me. They're still talking, and I think she's sacrificing her protectiveness to, you know, be my informant. But sometimes she won't answer his calls.

Alara asks me how the hell I manage to compartmentalize my feelings, and I say I don't, not really, I can't, and I can't tell if I need him or want him. I can't tell what I would ever do without him.

Oh, she says. Yeah, that's bad.

We're quiet. My grandmother washes her beige bras with so much more regularity than I do. There is always at least one giant bra out here drying next to the plants.

Wait, hold on, Alara says. Georgia, the state?

No, no. Georgia. I nod my head to the left, as if we're sitting on a paper map of the world. He's going to Tbilisi.

What will he understand about Georgia? she asks. She gets excited again and asks me if I knew that Baba's grandfather was from Georgia.

Did I already tell you that? I ask. Which grandfather?

What are you talking about? Wait, but why is Cooper going to Georgia?

The balcony is too small for both of us, and the plants are touching our legs and arms and the smell of butter floats in from the kitchen and I feel hungry and sick and I have no idea how everyone else can carry tightly sealed packages full of stories around, never to open them, and how that doesn't make everyone else feel so fat and bloated, full of phlegm and feverish, and I am tired, I am so tired of trying to do the same. I want to start a new way of being a family, so I begin to tell her what Grandmother told me. I can't tell it as well, with all the details, but my sister's face is beautiful in that it is remarkably easy to read. She's listening, her mouth popped open, her eyes filmy and bulging like rain clouds, as her tears—she always cried more than me, she cried to get what she wanted, sometimes she cried for me to get what I wanted—slide down over the bones in her face.

ALARA CONFESSES THAT SHE DOESN'T KNOW HOW SHE'LL sit through this dinner without asking every family member what they knew and why they never told us. She waves the white tablecloth over the dining table and I secure the edges. I feel differently. It's not their story to tell, I say, a bit unsure of myself, and she gets angry. We begin setting the plates. It's our story, Alara says, and they should have told us. No, it's her story, I reply, and I mention that most of these family members are on our mom's side anyway, but she disagrees, she says most of them are Aunt Pinar and her kids, and she asks me if I know where Refika is now, and I tell her what my grandmother told me, that Refika can't talk well because of her throat hole but she still lives in the same apartment building, the old Cotton Apartments. Alara says, well, we have to see her, and I say, absolutely not, because earlier, when my grandmother spoke of where Refika was now, her hand shook violently, she lost control entirely, and she had to lie down before she could resume her story. I tell Alara this, that each time she proceeded to mention Refika, she looked confused and afraid, as if Refika had entered the room. Alara is listening but remains stubborn. She still wants to talk about this with our grandmother. She still wants to see Refika, which I would never want to do, and we continue arguing like this in English so my grandmother can't follow along, but if my grandmother is capable of hiding the fact that she didn't even fucking raise my father, she is definitely capable of hiding that she knows English.

But why couldn't Baba have told us? Alara hisses at me. My grandmother is in the hallway, opening the door.

We have to find Refika, Alara repeats.

You need to stop talking about this, Alara.

She glares at me.


FIRST, UNCLE YILMAZ COMES OVER WITH AUNT SEVGI, Dilek, and Emre. They bring Aunt Meral, Aunt Sevgi's mother. She is very old, older than my grandmother, and she doesn't know who I am. Alara compliments Dilek on her weight loss and her long shiny hair and Dilek, in turn, shows Alara pictures of herself on the beach in Çesme. Then Aunt Pinar comes over with her two sons. Demir, the recently divorced son, is accompanied by his new girlfriend, who makes the mistake of wearing strong perfume that everyone will complain about each time she leaves the room; the other son is with his children. My grandmother, Alara, and I stand in a line to kiss each family member on each cheek. Everyone has slipped off their shoes and lined them up on a mat in the entrance. The sun set long ago and the call to prayer fills the room. The baby runs from one person to another to present small objects she's found in the room as personalized gifts: an unused ashtray, a notepad, a framed photograph of my father. I was once this baby. Alara was once this baby. Dilek was once this baby, although because she was a baby at the same time I was a baby, and because I came here only for the summers, the summer baby, I realize she was the star baby. The open windows bring the breeze into the hot living room, and my grandmother; I'm not sure what she told her sister, or if my calm energy is radiating, because my family is not surveilling me. As usual, my grandmother takes one million trips to the kitchen to bring out small banana cakes, pound cake, baklava, cherries, plums, and peaches. We're drinking enough tea to make a small river flow with caffeine. Alara explains to everyone what she is doing in her premed classes, and how of course she will help everyone out when she is a doctor. Finally, a doctor in the family! Everyone turns to me.

Me too, I say.

Dilek, who thinks all I do is watch soap operas with my grandmother, gracefully changes the topic to the latest news of how the prime minister cursed Europe out for closing its doors to the Syrian refugees. One of our cousins, who is a nurse in Bursa, tells us that at her hospital, two thirds of the beds are filled by Syrian children, and their mothers have limited Turkish—some know no Turkish at all because why would they, they never had to know Turkish until now—so when she's treating each child, she can't explain to the child's mother what she's doing, and each mother must trust her regardless, without Turkish. Dilek mentions that that is one of her goals, and she looks at her mother as she says this, assimilating refugees with respect to language. She wants to coordinate volunteer translators to ensure that this Syrian mother in Bursa can understand her child's nurse and doctor. Everybody agrees. Some of my aunts and great-aunts knock on the coffee table's wood. Sevgi's ancient mother pulls on my arm to ask me who this girl is.

Your granddaughter, I reply.

My daughter? Aunt Meral asks.

No, your granddaughter. My cousin.

And she doesn't want to be a doctor?

No, I say. She's lazy.

She's no good if she's lazy, Aunt Meral says, shaking her bald head.

Meanwhile Uncle Yılmaz commends Dilek for working on such an important issue, one that Turks—especially, he says, the older generation—are keen to ignore. The older generation protests, and my grandmother urges everyone to stop praising Dilek lest nazar should hit. There are so many things we do against nazar. In this room alone, four evil eyes hang on different walls, pinned up for mandatory duty. One in the shape of a heart. Another eye, its glass blown blue, pressed into a hand of Fatma. Anxiety is nothing new, because we have always been obsessed with fate and chance and the superstitions we've fashioned to combat uncertainty. My mother, a scientist, makes sure Alara and I always leave the house with an evil eye pinned to the inside of a handbag or bra.

By the time we sit to eat dinner—lamb stewed with eggplant and tomato, buttered rice, string beans cooked in olive oil, the grape leaves my grandmother spent all day stuffing, and bread, lots of bread—no one has yet mentioned Cooper. Alara, meanwhile, talks as much as possible in order to navigate the attention of everyone, especially the women, away from the truth that she is eating next to nothing. She is definitely under one hundred pounds. She brings up Deniz, shooting a knowing look at Dilek, who in turn rolls her eyes, and the older women determine they must go to see his grandmother for tea. I'm watching her, and so is my grandmother. Aunt Pinar keeps asking Alara whether she likes the food. Alara replies by saying she had so many peaches just now and also ate on the flight. She spoons a swollen grilled tomato onto her plate and glares at me until I look away.

Demir's new girlfriend stands to use the restroom, and Aunt Pinar leans in on her son and tells him that her perfume smells like a baby's diaper.

Can't you smell it? she asks. Demir shrugs and fills his plate up. He looks miserable.

Who is she? Aunt Meral asks me again, this time about Alara.

When Aunt Sevgi mentions the work Cooper's doing with refugees, the table goes quiet.

This time Alara takes over. She's wielding her fork and knife into the grilled tomato with great precision as she begins to defend my honor. She pivots from discussing Cooper, how he's betrayed not only me but also the family, to politics and the upcoming election. Yesterday, the prime minister was officially nominated to be a presidential candidate, surprising no one. Dilek pokes my arm with her dirty fork and asks, Didn't *you* break up with him? I hiss back, Well, it was pretty mutual. Alara says we have to consider that there's never been a leader of the Muslim world in modern civilization. It makes sense the prime minister wants to be the first. His supporters, not just Turks, but also Muslims across the Middle East, they go to bed muttering his name in prayer, the same way we Americans, Alara nods at me, love our president and what he stands for, but this is all superficial. It's celebrity, Alara says, I actually hate the way Obama has dropped more bombs on the Middle East than any other president, even Bush, but whatever. They, she continues, meaning the conservative Turks, had been economically shunted out of modern Turkey for decades, no? And now his policies have boosted their income, by just a fraction, but a fraction is the difference between being able to pay for new school supplies for their children or fresh meat for the week. Between acquiring the proper medications for a sick grandmother or renovating a moldy ceiling. Do those choices not matter?

Some of our male cousins have answers to her questions. Some of them mention Gezi, and how that energy could be summoned again, and they begin to discuss the future of Turkey. Uncle Yılmaz argues that the government was able to usurp Gezi because the movement had no official leaders. Alara thinks that the fragile truce with the Kurds is sure to break, and soon. Dilek mentions that it is not really fair for Alara to criticize Turkey so much, and pretend to care, when she's not the one who has to live here.

You get to come to Turkey for vacation, Dilek says. You get to leave.

She's right, but I am so sick of this conversation. It is the same every time.

WHEN THE FIRST PERSON KISSES EVERYONE GOODBYE ON the cheek, everyone else comments on how late it is and begins to mobilize. Alara wanted to ask Dilek about my grandmother, but I threatened her in a way that terrified me. I pulled on her hair while we were clearing the dishes until her neck began to bow back slowly, but her hair has been falling out lately and when I unclenched my hand and began apologizing, Alara said that's okay, that's okay, Sibel, and we both stood there in the kitchen staring at the black clump in my fist until Alara said Dilek would probably make some rude comment about Baba not being her side of the family anyway. Now we're back in the living room: Me, Dilek, and Alara. We're sitting in the corner, playing with the baby, who's in my lap and sucking on my finger.

So, Sibel, Dilek says, I need to tell you something. I'm having a birthday party, for Cooper. I figure it will be good to do something, because you know, he has nobody here.

Jesus Christ, Alara says.

Am I invited? I ask. I hand the baby to Alara.

I'm offended, Dilek says. I'm offended that you think I wouldn't invite my own cousin.

Sorry, I say. You've just never done anything for my birthday.

Your birthday is in October. I never see you in October.

That's a good point, Alara offers.

I'm leaving, Dilek says. Ciao.

MY SISTER IS HERE FOR ONLY A FEW WEEKS, SO SHE WANTS to do everything she can't do in New York. She wants to see every family member. She wants to walk around the city. She says she wants to eat Turkish ice cream. I'm relieved because it's important to screen her body and mood in a variety of settings. I've been sizing her up in our shared bed, where she sleeps with her back towards me, creating a wall with her spine jutting out of her skin. And it's not that she's breathing heavily and sweating, it's this spine. I'm afraid of her spine. At night the streetlights illuminate the room and fasten on to each notch of spine through her shirt, and there isn't enough space between us. I feel her body like a part of mine, but I'm unsure if she feels the same way. She would not want my yeasty, melancholic body. She would not want my fats, my headaches, and, she told me today when she caught me staring at her arms, she would not want to waste time reading about ancient, useless medicine.

Alara and I decide to go to Cihangir for the day. We call

Deniz to see if he wants to join us, but he's hanging out with his cousins. When Cooper calls the house again, Alara picks up, and she speaks in sharp, loud words, the whole time looking at me and miming smacking someone with the hot iron she's using on a pair of expensive pants she found at the outdoor market for cheap. What did he say? I ask her. Oh, nothing, she says, dodging my eyes. Alara, I say more forcefully, tell me what he said.

Cooper is leaving for Georgia for a week and, it turns out, wants to see me before he goes. He wants to make things better, Alara admits, but I personally don't think you should. At least not yet. You should be alone right now. Independent. Huh, I say, but isn't my big problem that I'm too alone? In my head? Withdrawn? Alara emphasizes finding myself and mentions that I've had a boyfriend for my entire postpubescent life, basically, and do I really know how to support myself emotionally without a significant other? No, I say, but I have other support. I'm emotionally resourceful. She ignores me. Those weren't real boyfriends, I add, in high school. She ignores me again. I circle around her as she's ironing, asking her if she herself knows how to be alone, but she tells me she's really not in the mood to talk about boys. Well, we're not talking about boys, I say, we're talking about being alone. She rolls her eyes. Once she manages to get the fancy crease down the front of each green pant leg, we leave for the metro that stops near the museum recommended to me by Esra. Apparently the museum engages with a blurring of fiction and reality. We pass the mother and her children on the quilt, and the youngest girl takes my hand and runs alongside us but I pretend not to know her. Alara gives the girl a few coins, and when she sees me turn my head and mouth sorry to the mother across the street, she furrows her brows but says nothing. We descend into the metro and head towards the museum. The novelist Orhan Pamuk created this museum to be a physical representation of his novel of the same name. Each chapter corresponds to a panel set up behind a glass box populated with objects, and there are three floors through which the narrator visually tells the story of how he, although engaged to a woman named Sibel, has fallen in love with a younger, more beautiful woman who is a shopkeeper. The author has collected many objects—objects representative of the narrator's love for the younger, more beautiful woman— from an Istanbul of years past. There are newspaper clippings, silk scarves, lipstick tubes, glasses of tea, and smoked, crumpled cigarettes. Alara is fascinated by what is real in the writer's life and what he fictionalizes—like this panel, she says, pointing to a placard that reads, "My Father's Death." Whose Turkish Airlines tickets were those? What about the bottle of kolonya? And the ulcer medication?

I don't know if it matters, I say, but Alara is not listening. She's walked away to the next panel and is looking at herself in the mirror above a dirty sink.

Do you know, Esra is writing a novel, I say, and it's about a girl and her boyfriend.

Wow, Alara says. Of course she is.

The boyfriend is her boyfriend, Alp. Do you think that's fucked up?

Sure, yeah. But I guess she has nothing else to write about.

Alara doesn't like Esra. She thinks she is pretentious.

Cooper is fascinated by objects and puts great meaning in his own: his two blue towels from the outdoor market, his green backpack, his grandfather's white safari-style shirt. If he were here, he'd mention the weight of objects, how we can misplace feelings in them without knowing that we've given up something of value inside us. I'd point to a panel where somebody had lined up toiletries, razor, soap, toothpaste, and cologne, on a shelf above the sink. What did these objects take? I'd ask Cooper. He'd think about it but would confess that he doesn't know. That's what I love most about him, that he confesses what he doesn't know. I'm about to text him secretly but Alara points to a panel near the ground with the chapter title "A Few Unpalatable Anthropological Truths." It depicts women's faces cut out from newspapers, and the faces are attached to hanging strings. Each woman has black bands covering her eyes.

What the fuck is this, Alara says. Is this Grandma's time?

We squat down to look at their faces more closely. The novel starts in the 1970s, more than a decade after my grandmother was, as far as we know, sexually active. At the top of the panel, the author has written that these are the faces of shamed women, women whose exploits—sex with a married man, sex before marriage, committing adultery, being a prostitute, being raped—led the newspaper to publish their crimes along with their censored faces. We learn that if a woman under the age of eighteen slept with a man outside of marriage, and that man then refused to marry her, the woman's father would make sure to open a legal case and bind the young man to marriage. My grandmother's father threatened to do the same when he found out about the eye doctor, before they learned he was a distant relative. And he didn't even know she was pregnant.

If a woman was raped, it was still customary for the newspaper to run her photograph with a black banner over her eyes in order to protect the woman from, ironically, being shamed.

Jesus, Alara says. This reminds me of it, of Grandma.

Of Refika, you mean, what she did?

Maybe it was better, then. Maybe what Refika did protected her?

I don't know, I say. I don't know anything about this country, I admit.

Me neither, Alara says sadly.

An elderly man with a big smile walks towards us and clears his throat. He wants to see the shamed women. We shuffle to the next panel of cigarettes, prayer beads, and a half-filled teacup in front of a photograph of the Bosphorus. Alara mentions that it's weird how Refika has never tried to meet us or talk to us. I say yeah, that is weird, although could we call spitting phlegm talking? Alara says hmm, very loudly and slowly, then reminds me of what she did to Refika. How she pushed Refika. She says she hates re-membering this. She says she can't get Refika out of her mind and especially her throat and I turn to her and say, same, but maybe we should try to forget. Alara's angry now. She says, no, Sibel, why do you always do this? We have to confront the things that scare us, not run away. I'm sorry, I say, but she swats my hand off and turns her back to me. I follow her up the final staircase to the top floor of the museum, where there is a small room with an unmade cot in which the supposed protagonist and author of this museum's novel slept as he supposedly wrote this book. I'm confused now as to who is whom. Who made this museum? What's more real, the museum or the book? The smell is funny in here, damp as well as musty, like a person was just here but will never come back.

Tell me that's not supposed to be his bed, Alara says, her voice hushed. She reaches for my hand in alarm, and her fingers are freezing despite it being hot in the museum.

Why are you so cold? I ask.

Alara rips her hand out of mine. I feel fine, she snaps. Let's go to the gift shop.

Okay, I say, following her down the narrow stairs, my hand on the railing. Is there something you want to buy?

She shrugs. Maybe there will be something.

In the gift shop there are copies of every novel Orhan Pamuk has written, as well as old and new maps of Istanbul. A tall blond man who has great posture, like Cooper, is reaching high for an anthology of traveler's tales by famous Europeans who visited Istanbul. There's a giant pomegranate on the cover. Alara runs her hand over every item, flips the books open to random pages, and asks the man behind the desk whether he sells any posters.

We leave the shop with nothing. We're climbing a hilly street where wooden buildings with bay windows flank us. There are cafés, too, with small tables outdoors, and some clothing stores. I'm trying to ask Alara what she thinks about Dilek and Cooper, and why she thinks Dilek is really throwing Cooper a birthday party, but she won't indulge me.

Plus, Alara says, panting, Dilek has a huge crush on Deniz. Remember? How she left the nightclub crying when he said he just wants to be friends? Anyway, at least you're not an unpaid translator anymore. Now that Cooper knows Turkish.

I liked translating for him, I say. But Alara's right. And Dilek has been trying to make plans with us even more now that Deniz's here.

I'm sure, Alara says. I'm sure you love that you can lie when you want to. You can be silent when you want to. You know, Sibel, it's good to keep things from each other because it won't work for you, you know, being totally honest. You're just not an honest person anymore. She squints at me. You used to be. You used to talk about feelings so easily, openly. Honestly, you were really powerful.

Powerful?

She looks guilty, my sister.

Yeah, you said whatever you wanted. You were never embarrassed. You made crying seem good for you. And you were the only one who ever yelled back at Baba. I think he loved you for that.

Alara stops. Two cats graze our feet. We're on a street selling antiques, surrounded by wooden cabinets with intricate carved flowers, metal tables, framed portraits of long-dead women. Men sit at tables spilling out onto the sidewalk, smoking, bringing tea glasses up to their mouths, watching us. We've been here before, with my father. Years ago, Alara and I sat here with him as my mother ransacked the place. I feel as if I've found my body on the side of the road. Alara, she realizes this, too. She touches my elbow. She leads us to the antique furniture piled up outside a shop and we fold our knees under a low wooden table.

Then Alara leans in, close enough for me to hear her heavy breathing.

When should we go to the cemetery? she asks.

We can go on the way back, she says, or do you want to wait for Grandma?

Hello? Sibel? I know you haven't gone. Mom told me.

Alara's shaking her foot fast enough to make the antique table tremble, and each tendon looks strained and hard under her skin. She sees me looking, and says, What?

Let's go now, I say.

Alara looks wary, unsure as to whether she should believe me.

I repeat myself. Let's go, I say, and her body seems to sag or give in a little, her face muscles look loose, she stands with me, and we walk to the bus that stops at the white cemetery gates.

MY FATHER'S HEADSTONE IS WHITE MARBLE, WITH A rounded edge at the top. He's next to his father, the eye doctor. Alara places down flowers we bought on the walk to the bus. Tulips. We still don't know if tulips are the right flowers or whether any flower is fine. We still don't know the right Arabic prayer but Alara asks me if I can please lead one. My tongue feels gummy and the prayer sounds like a song. I'm distracted. I'm often distracted, but distractions help you disappear. Alara doesn't believe in this. In disappearing. Neither does Cooper. But it is impossible to disappear now. There are whirring engines and honks from the highway beyond the cemetery's rear gate, and a group of women are gossiping nearby, over the grave of someone who I think might be their friend. Maybe they are the dead woman's sisters-in-law, because they keep saying she ruined their brother's life and his potential for a successful career. Am I always so distracted?

The cemetery is unrecognizable without snow, and it is bigger than I remembered, with rows and rows of white marble headstones. Ancient Islamic hospitals used to be the only way the Istanbul municipality could collect data on how many people were dying. The dead bodies carted out of the hospitals were the best form of counting, but I don't know where they were buried.

When doctors and philosophers began illustrating the human body during the Enlightenment, they were very confused. Where is the visible soul? they asked one another.

The brain?

The blood?

The liver?

The lymph nodes?

The nerves?

The fingers?

The feet?

The grave?

The eye doctor's grave is next to his parents' grave. Where will my grandmother be buried, I wonder, but I am terrified of asking her a question like that, and I think we all are, me, Alara, my mother. We are so afraid of being honest with one another about her sickness. When we went shopping in one of the modern malls the other day, my grandmother called for my help from the dressing room. She is usually very discreet about getting dressed, so I peeked in politely, coyly. She was sitting there with the beautiful plaid pants we picked out halfway up her thighs. My grandmother looked at me.

Why is this happening to me? she'd asked. We'll go to the doctor again, I told her, and I came in to help her out of the pants. She clucked her tongue no. I said, You do not have a soul; you are a soul, but you have a body for now, and she smiled. That's very spiritual of you, Sibel, and we laughed. It was a light laugh. I helped her back into her clothes and we took a taxi back home instead of walking.

ALARA SAYS SHE'S READY TO GO.

Me too, I say.

Alara's already walking away when I see them. Two women, one old, one young.

It's Refika. She's much taller than I remembered, and she's arm-in-arm with a young woman. Refika is wearing a headscarf, patterned in blue and red flowers, and even from this distance I see that the knot covers her throat hole.

Alara keeps walking. I yell out to her. I say, You go, I'll meet you at home, and Alara turns and looks at me through wet eyes but nods, nods, and keeps walking until she's at the bus stop.

When I turn back, they're already walking away. I'm not frozen this time. I know what I should do. I begin to follow them out of the cemetery.

# II.

ACCORDING TO MY GRANDMOTHER, REFIKA STILL LIVES IN
the pink apartment building in Nişantaşı. The Cotton Apartments. I'm walking a block behind Refika and her companion,
smoking cigarettes the whole way over and wondering if I should
introduce myself, wondering if they would recognize my face from
the funeral, or if Refika was sent photographs of me throughout
the years the way they do in soap operas. It would have been my
father sending these illicit photographs, my father, who—did I
ever know him?—then the young woman on Refika's arm turns
around.

You're coming in, then? she says. She smiles, and one of her
teeth hangs over her bottom lip like a fang. Her accent is thick.
She looks maybe my age, or a few years older.

I nod, afraid to look at Refika's face. The young woman
unlocks the apartment building's door, and I find myself holding
it open as Refika shuffles past me. Her thick white hair looks
like combed cream under her headscarf. The apartment building smells moldy, the same way every building from the forties
and fifties smells, and a white cat stalks by as we wait for the
elevator. My grandmother was here. She stole Baba back from

here, while Refika and her friends discussed the Menderes plane crash over tea.

I FOLLOW REFIKA AND THE YOUNG WOMAN—WHO, I learn, is named Albina and working illegally here from Uzbekistan—into Refika's apartment. Albina holds Refika's frail body as Refika slips off her loafers with a shoehorn. I take Refika's other hand and Albina thanks me. The apartment layout is exactly like my grandmother's, and also has a large wooden cabinet filled with fine china. But this apartment is darker, and the cat smell is strong and unnerving. The walls are bare and brown, and in the living room there are two mottled velvet couches and a skinny, leaning bookshelf that resembles someone with scoliosis. Albina helps Refika onto a velvet couch, then points for me to sit in one of the ancient wooden chairs arranged meticulously around the coffee table, where Albina, or perhaps Refika, has put together a kind of vegetation shrine. Stray cucumbers, dried lavender, and fresh apricots circle a bowl full of tomatoes. Albina doesn't ask whether I like my tea light or dark, but the cup she offers me is dark and perfect, the best way to drink tea, and I will myself into believing that she knew this about me. She knew the particulars of my palate. In medieval times, Islamic physicians would secure their patients by guessing what they ate the day before their first meeting. The doctors would say, oh, wow, I can tell from your mottled complexion that you ate watermelon yesterday, and the trusting patient would cry out in amazement, wondering how he knew about the watermelon. Really, these physicians who made house calls would either see the trash outside the home or note the trees full of ripe fruit around the corner and prophesize accordingly. An orange cat jumps onto my lap and nuzzles at my chin. Another cat stalks a black fly in the hallway. A giant oil portrait of Atatürk hangs over one of the velvet couches, and I try very hard not to make eye contact with him.

Refika catches me looking at her things.

Why don't you go out to the balcony? Refika says. Her voice is extremely quiet and raspy. I almost did not hear her.

Um. That's okay, I say.

She is twelve years older than my grandmother, which makes her about ninety, I think, and she doesn't bother to wear teeth. Not that she's smiling at me. Her lips have shrunk with age, making her mouth mostly gums.

Refika points at the balcony, her fingers gnarled and cloaked in chunky rings. She commands me to stand and look. She says it again, and she's looking at me hungrily, so I pad over in my socks. The balcony is, in fact, beautiful and big.

She spends all her time out there, Albina says, leaning on the doorframe. She loves watching people on the street. Do you want some börek?

Sure, I say. Thank you.

I follow Albina back into the living room. I cross my legs at my ankles and cross and uncross my arms. I pluck a stray hair off my thigh. I smile at Refika, who stares back.

Albina hands me a plate of wet börek. Your shoulders look very tense, she informs me.

Albina is a healer, Refika says. Not very good.

A nurse? I ask. I peel off the first layer of phyllo and eat it with my hands.

Albina cackles. I am, a nurse. But I do other stuff, too. Natural medicine.

You're very dark, Refika says.

It's summer, I reply, defensive.

You must have gotten it from your mother. Wasn't she a Kurd?

No, I say. Where did you get that?

Refika stares at me. I wonder if she has something else to say about how my mother grew up in a village, but she brings her hand to the knot in her headscarf and says nothing. I'm very uncomfortable, and I'm disrespecting my grandmother, being here, but I'm looking for my father.

Albina perches on the arm of my wooden chair to show me an Instagram account about using alternative medicine in order to heal holistically. There are pictures of dried green tea in stone bowls and organs drawn with watercolor and blue statues of Dhanvantari, the Hindu god of Ayurvedic medicine. The account's handle is ayurve-deals. I like that Ayurvedics base their humors on natural elements instead of bodily fluids, but I'm so tired of betterment, and I've been having trouble unbraiding what is medical care and what is commercial obsession with wellness. I say, Cool, and hand the phone back to her.

I learned about it here, on Instagram, Albina says with pride.

Oh, I say. Wow.

Albina nods, scrolling through her phone.

Here, look, I'll show you the first image I saw that inspired me. It's this woman who was having mysterious cramps, and when she used a leech on her inner thigh, the cramps disappeared. I do all sorts of things, really. I can do cupping, she says, leeching, too.

I ask Albina if she has leeches here and she cracks up.

Obviously not, she says.

I ask her if she knows of Ibn Sina, who was born in Bukhara in 980, and she smiles.

Of course, Ibn Sina. The doctor of Islam. Do you know he memorized the Koran when he was ten?

I'm excited. I have found someone from my religious sect. I tell Albina yes, of course I know. I think Ibn Sina is my favorite physician after Trota, does she know her? Does she work on balancing excess black bile in the body? But Albina is confused about Trota, and about black bile, and I remember that contemporary alternative medicine is not, in fact, what I've been practicing with my humors.

Albina looks unsure whether to continue, but Refika nods. Well, Albina says, what I'm really trying to advance into—she points at Refika—is hypnotism. We've been doing it together. I'm going to try and get a professional license. Refika snorts, but she doesn't say anything to contradict Albina, who smells strongly of lavender, as if she soaked her hair in essential oil, or used the oil as a deodorant. Albina tells me she sends the money she makes taking care of Refika to her mother and two sisters back in Tashkent. She also buys them clothes from the weekly market, the latest styles, and then she excuses herself for a moment before returning with a pair of sandals that she is going to send over when she gets the chance. I like them, I say, taking a sandal into my hands and touching the rubber sole. She pauses, and I pause, too, not knowing what else to say. Refika can't speak well, and I'm grateful that Albina is speaking for her. Like a granddaughter. Only Albina is being paid to be a granddaughter. I hand her the sandal and eat another layer of phyllo.

How is your grandmother? Albina asks. Her Parkinson's?

I wipe my oily hands on my legs and cross my arms. She's doing okay, I say.

They stare at me. Albina smiles.

I think it's getting worse, I admit. Sometimes she doesn't take her pills.

How is that making you feel? Albina asks. Is Albina a therapist, too? I'm confused. Refika is watching us intently. She raises her tea glass to her mouth. Is her husband who burned her with tea dead? How do they know about my grandmother, who was diagnosed only three years ago? Where does the liquid go when she swallows?

I nod and ask, Can I have some more time to think about her question?

Of course, Albina says. She looks at Refika, and the two of them look pleased. Albina sits next to Refika, begins massaging her hand, and asks me why my parents named me Sibel, and because I don't actually know why they chose such a haunted name, I find myself telling her about the Greek prophet Sybil, who, cursed by Apollo for rejecting his sexual advances, aged indefinitely, slowly losing muscle mass, bone density, a kidney—I suspect it shriveled up and disappeared in her body—until she grew tiny enough to fit into a jar, where she lived for many centuries, telling the future to needy men.

That's bullshit, Refika interrupts. You were named Sibel because that was my grandmother's name.

Oh, I say. I didn't know that. The eye doctor's grandmother?

Refika nods. Of course you didn't.

I'm sorry, I say. Did my father choose the name?

I chose the name, Refika says. Long before you were born. When it was just me and your father.

I pause. I don't know what to do here. I wonder if I should smile. Maybe I can ask her if that was before or after my father learned about his real mother, my grandmother, but I am unsure of what to reveal. Refika is back to staring somewhat blankly at the tomato shrine. I really don't know what I'm doing here.

Old age is not for everyone, Refika says suddenly. Your grand-mother, she clarifies.

I find this vaguely threatening, and I'm about to fight back but Albina, after giving Refika a stern look, changes the topic. Apparently, my skin is cold and dry enough to make her think something has led to an excessive collection of metal in my body. Albina is wrong about the metal. Cold and dry is common for someone with an excess of black bile, as is heavy menstruation. I clear my throat.

I have bad cramps, too, I say. And the blood is always heavy. Do you think that's a symptom? I point to my swollen abdomen.

Do you drink a lot of wine? Albina asks.

I guess so. A normal amount. But I haven't been, really, here. In New York, I do.

What about pain medications?

What about them?

Have you been taking them?

Oh, no. I don't like those. I get addicted, or obsessed, very quickly.

We're silent. Refika starts coughing, and I genuinely wonder whether she is dying. What is the life span of someone with a tracheostomy? Does she still smoke now and again? Albina runs into the kitchen to get medicine as well as a glass of herbal tea she brewed with turmeric to strengthen Refika's immune system. When Refika takes her medicine and begins to untie her headscarf, she tells Albina that she thinks I am quite ready to be examined.

I'm being examined? I ask. Refika's throat hole is black and as
big as a quarter. The skin around it looks rubbery.

What's being examined? I repeat.

Obviously the examination has not yet started, Albina says,
as if I knew anything about her work other than that she practices
faulty medicine, the kind that requires you to buy, buy, buy. Wellness is a trick, a trick to only advance capital. Many resourceful
businesses in New York have set an expensive trap for the anxious
and unhappy by promising green juices to cleanse you of toxins
and bestow a lean and spiritually connected body. Your mind will
work faster, they say. Your spirit will be clear, they say. They're a
society profiting from our self-doubt. The human body evolved to
heal wounds, so it is ghastly to me that people today pay money for
excess treatment in the form of a jade stone egg to be pushed into
your vagina so that, one website writes, your vagina—and subse-
quently, your life—will be cleansed, cleared, and happy. The egg
costs sixty dollars.

Do you have a lot of patients? I ask Albina.

She looks at me like I'm crazy. Do I look like I have any
patients?

I say sorry, never mind. But don't take my blood, I add.

Excuse me?

I mean, are you going to take my blood?

Refika interrupts again. Are you crazy, girl? You must be
crazy. She's shaking her head and her long white braid like a rope
catches the dim light as Albina explains that she is just going to
talk to me, to get to know me, before we do the hypnotism, and to
not worry, there is no blood here, no needles. She only works with
the body as it appears to her. That, she states, is the body you are
presenting. I'm listening to her, but Refika's throat hole is distract-

ing. She's wiping the hole down with alcohol-soaked gauze Albina handed her. Before the hypnotism, Albina says she will have to prep me by combining the practice of therapeutic body work with a form of Japanese alternative medicine called Reiki, where energy is physiological and can be massaged and altered to cure diseases. First, she is to ascertain the knotted parts of my body, to see if my pain is internal or superficial. Then, in the next session, she will perform a physical therapy where she massages areas of my body to rearrange posture and pain. She tells me it's an American practice, maybe I've heard of it. She says it does wonders for people, especially those who experience psychosomatic pain.

So you think my headaches are psychosomatic? I ask.

After working on the muscles under your skin, she says, I hope to find out.

I don't tell her that the doctor thinks my neck muscles are inflamed. I don't tell her that I don't believe this doctor. I want to see what Albina finds out for herself and whether she could help me find my soul. It has to be in my brain. Now that Refika's throat is clean, Albina ties a bib around her neck so the small white flag covers her hole.

In your third session, Albina says, if your pain continues, I will hypnotize you.

For what? I ask.

She looks at Refika, who nods. For your grief, Albina says sadly.

I was hypnotized once in New York, when I wanted to quit smoking because the addiction compelled me to leave parties and walk blocks and blocks wanting only a cigarette. I was unable to think of anything else, like a vampire in need of blood. The hypnotism worked for three weeks, until my father died. And it's not that I want

THE FOUR HUMORS + 203

to be cured by Albina. I'm getting used to my physical pain. And she is no wellness monster; she only wants to practice her craft, which I respect. What I want is to find my father in Refika. My father was always waiting for our relationship to begin. He would pace around the kitchen island, almost in tears, telling me that if only I was less reactionary towards him, if only I was capable of treating him the way I treat my friends, we could begin our relationship.

As I'm strapping my sandals on in the doorway, Refika shuffles towards me in her plastic slippers. She kisses me on both cheeks and tells me to come back soon. She tells me that she will help me if I help her.

Help with what? I ask.

I want to see your grandmother again, Refika says.


AFTER WASHING MY HANDS AND FEET THIS MORNING, I caught my grandmother whispering to her sister on the telephone.

She's sick, my grandmother said. She's still having terrible headaches, but she's acting like nothing's wrong.

Yes, she repeated. She's still going out every day. With Alara, sometimes. Mostly alone.

My fever has been coming and going in the past few days, but I don't tell my grandmother this. Anyway, it's not like she updates me on her health. We're all heavy with pretending, and Alara has been suspicious of me since the cemetery yesterday. She said she got on the bus thinking I wanted to be alone, but then where was I for hours after?

What happened? she'd demanded when I came home from Refika's. Where were you? I stood there with my mouth open, looking at my sister and seeing the way she had pushed Refika at the funeral, Refika on her back like a beetle, and it took a terrifyingly long time for Refika to get back on her feet in the snow, even with Albina's help. Alara had looked satisfied, proud. I can't trust my sister, not when there's so much at stake. Then Alara called me a gaping fucking fish and stormed off. Maybe she used the word *dead*. I decide to see Cooper instead. I have to tell somebody about Refika. I have to tell somebody I can't have my father's disease.

Cooper said he wanted to go to the archaeology museum, so we're going to meet there. Alara, who had been policing me about not texting him since she arrived, waved me out of the house when I announced what I was about to do.

I sit in a metal chair in the museum's outdoor café, which is lined with giant ancient trees, and order a glass of sour cherry juice. The day is hot and clear, like most days. I can't remember what rain feels like. The chair is making me sit straight, and I think of how Albina told me that Refika gets butt sores from sitting in the same place for so long, so Albina tenderly dabs and disinfects Refika's ass then changes her bandages once a day. I'd forgotten that Cooper's friend is still visiting—he didn't mention bringing him, either—so when I see them, both in white linen safari shirts and walking towards me, I panic. I look at a statue of Demeter, but her stone head is missing.

They drag metal chairs over to my table and Cooper almost knocks into Demeter. When he turns back to look at her stump of a neck, her white fingers holding the toga that falls around her breasts in stone folds, it looks like he wants to apologize to her. His mouth opens as if to say sorry. It is just like him to want to apologize to a stone woman, especially Demeter, the goddess of life and death and mother of Persephone, given he has been calling my grandmother for days now to apologize to her for disrespecting our family. Meanwhile, Cooper's friend, Jonathan, launches into a condensed version of his life to get me, as he puts it, up to speed. How he was just backpacking in Amsterdam and figured he'd come to Istanbul next. How he's considering living in a van for the rest of his life. Jonathan's a few years older than us and quit his job in order to become a world traveler. He was Cooper's freshman-year RA, and took a huge liking to him—as Jonathan called it, he "took the kid under his wing." I was never certain how Cooper felt about him, but I do know he has trouble saying no.

Jonathan orders tea while telling me how he stayed in a hostel in one of Amsterdam's hip neighborhoods. It's really up and coming, Jonathan says, imitating a white woman he met in this hip neighborhood. Apparently she had blond hair pulled back on her scalp in tight braids. Cornrows, Jonathan says with disdain. Jonathan is very politically aware. I think he once worked in investment banking.

Cooper seems distracted. He's staring at Demeter, and every few seconds he'll look back at me, then at Demeter again. Who knows where her head is buried, I want to joke to Cooper, but I also feel invigorated by his silence.

You know, Jonathan says, there were many Turks in the neighborhood I stayed in. Arabs and Africans, too. Germany, where I was before Amsterdam, was also like that.

I ask him if the Dutch are aware that Amsterdam is a white man's paradise built on the exploitation of other people. Jonathan nods passionately. He wonders aloud if this is a true statement or a reactive millennial opinion. Cooper finally has something to contribute, and finally he stops staring at Demeter, and he agrees with me, and with Jonathan, and the boys say that they feel distinctly American everywhere they go. The boys wonder why non-white people are called immigrants, but some white people—particularly Americans—are, they seem to believe, expats.

What do you think you are? Jonathan asks me. Cooper looks over as I pretend to think. Jonathan's family is very wealthy, in the oil business, we think, but he never discusses this.

I say that I'm not sure what this is, being in Istanbul. I'm not sure if I'm traveling or just returning to a place I know.

So you're not an expat here, Jonathan says.

Obviously not, I say. And I have family here. I have citizenship. Plus, I'm only visiting.

Interesting, he says. It's a shame you're not coming with us to Georgia. He looks at Cooper, who pretends not to have heard what he said. What does Jonathan know about us? Cooper is an honest person. Jonathan must know everything.

Oh, I know, I say, and Cooper brands me with his stare again, but it is a soft stare, a guilty stare, and the way he's getting into my head right now feels like the slow insertion of a needle. I learn that in Georgia they will be doing a homestay with Jonathan's "family," a woman who used to babysit and cook him lamb dumplings. Jonathan tells me he's thinking about what it means to be a tourist, which is why he's asking me these questions. Ask away, I say, sarcastically, knowing that Jonathan will not discern my acidic tone. Sure enough, I learn that *tourist* comes from *tour*, which meant "a turn, a shift on duty" in 1330s French. Noblemen were sent on tours in order to collect information on how their kingdom should properly govern a foreign land, how they should assert power, how they should make barbarians bend the knee or die with grace. Jonathan adds that he, and Cooper, must think about this nasty history of tourism as they embark on tours themselves.

Right, Cooper? Cooper drains his tea and nods. I've never

seen him this quiet. He gets quiet only when he is undecided about something. Today that something is me. And I know he doesn't agree with Jonathan.

There's a word for tourist in every language, I say. Right?

Sure, Jonathan says. Of course.

So it's not just Europeans who are tourists, I say. There's a word for foreigner in every language, too.

Sure, sure, says Jonathan, but that's not what I'm saying.

What is the problem then, I say, other people? Who is "other people" when every person is an other, and every person is at the same time a foreigner to somebody else?

Yeah, I know, he says, but that's not really what I was talking about.

But that's what you're implying.

Cooper, sensing discord, comes back to life and steers the conversation towards another subject, our friends in the city, and how they like their summer jobs. We have friends with all sorts of interests, but we talk mostly about why the bankers chose to be banking interns and whether the financial security they seek will be enough for them, and whether we should seek that financial security, too. Now they're on the issue of what is expected of us. Expected by whom, though? Cooper asks. That is easy for him to say. His parents aren't immigrants.

Jonathan is invigorated again. He's talking about how he said no to banking, but understands that he could do so only because he already had financial security. Not everyone can choose to boycott capitalism, he says. Every few minutes he looks at me in a suspicious way. He can't read me, which is fine. I can't read Cooper, I can't read anybody, and isn't it stupid that we think we can speak to people and make friends and continue friendships and have sex and grow emotionally close to other people when all that, what all that time with other people amounts to, is only a brief trip away from being alone?

I sigh without meaning to and Jonathan asks what's wrong.

Nothing, I say, I'm just listening.

Cooper's hand fidgets. I wonder if he was about to reach for mine over the table. Jonathan must know we've broken up, but he is still stupid or rude enough to be here. And Cooper must be stupid, or desperate, too.

Taking care of your grandma is work, too, Cooper says, finally making eye contact with me.

Maybe. But I should be studying, I say, for the MCAT.

Cooper nods. How is that going?

I didn't know you wanted to be a doctor, Sibel, Jonathan says.

Yup, I point at Cooper, like him.

It's harder for women, with the years you'll spend in school, then residency, then fellowship. Jonathan stops, and looks embarrassed for having voiced a very unpopular opinion. If you want children, I mean.

Cooper is watching me again, and I smile very big for Jonathan, wondering how quickly he can forget his own discomfort. It's speedy. Jonathan continues to talk about traveling, and the television screen behind him shows Israeli soldiers holding machine guns on a woman with her head covered. Turkish news never shows the terrible things the Turkish government does but is zealous about broadcasting what other nations do to Muslims. I'm not sure if this is much worse than what U.S. news does. They show what they claim to be international, unbiased news, making Americans believe that U.S. news is the only unbiased—and best—news source for the whole world. For example, not many people knew the United States was already in Iraq when it first invaded Iraq. Not many people know that since 1980 the United States has invaded, occupied, or dropped bombs on fourteen predominantly Muslim countries around the Middle East. We don't realize that being American means thinking we are always right and just.

So, Jonathan says, how's the studying, then?

I'm more interested in practicing mental health, I say, and he nods slowly before looking at Cooper, who stares at me with rapt attention, as if I have succeeded in becoming the emotionally resourceful person he first fell in love with. As if I have healed and can now help him, too. And I have healed. My brain is neither ocean nor earthquake. My brain is a river. There are still some sharp rocks of throb or ache, but I've evolved, like the humors did when they adapted from medical treatment to psychological therapy.

I tell them we should go inside. We pay for the drinks and Jonathan walks between Cooper and me. I take another look at Demeter and I want to ask her if I'm doing the right thing, being here with Cooper. My father loved this museum, I want to tell Demeter. Baba taught us about Osman Hamdi, a Turkish painter who opened this museum in the late 1800s because he wanted the Ottoman Empire to Westernize by exhibiting its artifacts. The Western world had begun its own museum project years before and was already combing through the dirt of other countries, looking for history to showcase in London and Paris.

I want my father back, I tell Demeter. He is missing.

THE MUSEUM VISIT IS NOT GOING AS I HAD PLANNED. I wanted buoyant feelings. Instead, Cooper has been avoiding me,

and Jonathan is lecturing me. First, it was that the Turks were no-
mads then conquerors, carving out a horse-beaten path from Mon-
golia to Anatolia. He pointed to the tiny plaque under each broken
sculpture or mosaic to prove his point. Really, Turks are a combination of those settlers and people from Asia Minor, the Balkans,
the Caucasus, and the Middle East, but this truth is too stitched up
in nationalism and thus too tiring to explain to Jonathan.

I'm in front of a rock from the Taurus Mountains when I hear
Jonathan explain to Cooper that women argued over these turquoise necklaces, and that the ones who got to wear them were the
ones who slept around the most, and with the most powerful men.
I walk over to them.

Take that back, I say to Jonathan.

Excuse me?

That's not even true, I say. Admit that you made that shit up.

No.

Cooper touches my foot with his foot to get me to stop. His
quiet mood is sending me up and down with expectation. Jonathan grimaces, and admits that he can sometimes come on strong.

Some people, he says sadly, have a hard time being wrong.

You mean me? I'm wrong?

Jonathan looks at Cooper, who stares at the ceiling.

In my rage, I surprise myself. I say maybe I am like that,
maybe I'm having some trouble being wrong, maybe that's why I
can no longer let people in, and the whole time my voice rises and
I glare at Cooper, who looks incredibly guilty, either for bringing
Jonathan and not meeting me alone, or for telling me this when
we broke up. But Jonathan, it seems, draws his line when people
expose genuine vulnerability, and he calmly walks away.

Thank God, Cooper says, smiling. Should we go?

I smile, too. Why do you like him, again, I ask, and Cooper laughs. You know, you make those first friends and you can't cut ties?

Some people do, you know, cut ties from those first friends. He laughs again, and I say, But you're not one of those people. In a small voice he says I know him well. Really, Cooper and I were best friends before we ever had sex. Once we started dating, I admitted that what sparked my first move was seeing one of my close friends flirting with him at a sweaty pregame. I got territorial, and that's when I knew if I did not act, everything could change very quickly, and I would never get what I wanted. My friend at the pregame was wearing a pink halter top, and when she laughed, her pointy breasts bounced, and so I quite literally wedged myself between them and began to steer the conversation towards something that did not exactly include her. She excused herself to refill her red plastic cup soon after. She is a very good friend. I must have begun to touch him lightly on the arm and face throughout the night, because within a few hours we were making out in front of all our friends.

We're walking through the museum to the exit, and I feel at the edge of confessing to Cooper that I want to be who I once was, when my phone vibrates. It's the doctor.

Hello, I say. I lean against the wall outside the museum, and Cooper stands next to me, looking amused. How's my blood?

Your blood? the doctor asks.

My blood results.

He tells me I'm fine, that I can relax and take my head off my shoulders. Why haven't you been answering my calls, he then seems to demand, are you okay?

Take my head off my shoulders, I repeat, not understanding the Turkish expression. What is that supposed to mean?

Just relax. Your blood results are fine. You have normal blood. How normal?

Normal, he says. You could use some iron in your diet. But you're not iron-deficient or anything. I'm not saying you have anemia. Are you doing okay, Sibel?

I'm always confused about blood, I say, because it's supposed to be healthy to bleed out, that's what my dad always said. But then there's also menstrual blood, which sheds, but I don't feel any better after this bloodletting.

Excuse me?

I just mean—well, did you know that in medieval Islamic hospitals, bloodletter, cupper, urinator, and circumciser were all legitimate professions? They also prescribed food as medicine.

What? the doctor repeats. Now Cooper is looking at me funny, too.

They were professions. The surgeons were expected to perform bloodletting and cupping, too, but the busy ones didn't do it as much. To treat humoral imbalances in the body.

Yes, yes. I know them. The Ottoman name is ahlat-i erbaa, the doctor says. But that doesn't matter. Like I suspected, your trapezius muscle, it's between your shoulders and neck, is strained.

Wow, I say, an adventurous-sounding muscle. The trapezius is working quite hard, huh. How do you know about the four humors?

Sure, yeah. I don't know. Maybe it was my mother who told me about them? She's very superstitious. Your neck begins in your spine, even your hamstrings. You should do some exercises to strengthen your abdomen.

I say sure. I put my hand on Cooper's abdomen, and he is surprised, but smiles.

The doctor says he's heard a lot of women my age do Pilates these days. An American thing, he adds with another laugh before hanging up.

What did he say? Cooper asks me.

He thinks I should start Pilates. I'll be hot and toned, I joke.

Cooper looks uncomfortable. We used to run together, but he was much faster than me, and would double lap me on the running path in Riverside Park while smiling like a Labrador, and I'd give him a sweaty high five.

What?

This is silly, but I had a dream you were having sex with someone, he says. It was in a cemetery.

Wow.

Yeah.

The cemetery near my grandma's?

No, he says, giving me a shy smile. I don't know what cemetery.


JONATHAN'S SWEATING THROUGH HIS EXPENSIVE LINEN shirt. We've left the museum grounds and climbed a hill to the main pedestrian street in Beyoğlu. For some reason, Jonathan's been debating aloud why the ancient Greeks were obsessed with host-and-guest relationships. I'm walking them to a restaurant that Cooper and I like, where they serve olive oil dishes my grandmother makes at home. Jonathan posits that his host-and-guest theory is more critical to understand when countries share a border. Very dramatically, he says borders are drawn with blood. Sibel, what do you think, with everything going on in Kurdistan?

I ignore him. Americans think they can solve every political horror in the world.

Cooper contributes by mentioning quietly that he loves museums because they allow land to exist with no borders.

I say nothing. Jonathan says nothing. We enjoy a brief moment of silence in which Jonathan has been disarmed.

But the moment is short. Jonathan argues that museums are actually entirely about borders. After all, they cost money. I stare at him, unsmiling. I hold this face until two police trucks pull into the pedestrian boulevard. A few men in uniform start yelling. In the distance is a small crowd of people, maybe ten or fifteen, with cardboard signs and the red, green, and yellow Kurdish flag. Riot police begin to stalk the group down Istiklal. Jonathan shuts up and follows me as I try to wedge my way through the crowd of bystanders—who are beginning to film the demonstration for social media—to lead them to a café in case something happens. I think I see Deniz in the crowd. It's his same face and bun of dark hair. There's someone's hand on mine, it's Cooper's, and by the time we've elbowed our way through the crowd to the door of the café, which is already full, I let go and catch my breath on the sidewalk.

What's happened? Jonathan says. What the fuck's happening?

Sirens are going, cars are honking, and the protestors are chanting but no one has been hurt yet. Riot police have blocked off the entrance to a private school and created a wall with their shields.

I don't know what's happening, I say.

Are you okay? Cooper asks me.

I'm okay, I say. I want to walk back towards the group, to see if the man was really Deniz, but I'm afraid to leave Cooper. He's wiping his nose on his arm. Jonathan stands to the side, shaking his head in disbelief and typing into his phone.

Sibel, Cooper says, please come eat with us?

I can't, I say. Don't forget to take your contacts out if something happens.

I already popped them out, he says in earnest. I'm going to have to squint around the city.

Cooper's smiling. It's a familiar, weak smile, one that makes his face look tired and old and makes me, in turn, sad. But I'm not sure if I'm sad for him or me—because I won't see him old, when I really did think we'd spend all of time together, but forever is stupid, there is no half-life to forever, no middle point, and middles are comforting to me because they're the first concrete moment you can, by doubling the middle, calculate the end.

Where are you going? Cooper asks.

To a friend of my grandmother's, I say. She lives in Nişantaşı.

Oh, where in Nişantaşı?

You know that area—not the fancy stores—the part with tons of old apartment buildings down the hills?

He breaks into a smile.

Cooper, what?

Nothing, nothing. Cooper doesn't know what to do with his hands, and puts them in his pockets. I'm still wondering what's wrong with him and he sees this on my face and says, Really, Sibel, nothing.

We're leaving for Georgia tomorrow, he adds. I guess Jonathan mentioned. But I don't know if your grandma told you.

I laugh. She told me, and Alara thinks you have no business in Georgia.

Probably not, he says. But I'm a conquering tourist, right?

Right, I say.

I'm only gone for a week, he adds. But I'll see you at Dilek's? Can we talk before then?

I've been wanting to ask the same, about whether we can talk before then, but instead I say no, I don't think we should talk before then. Then I tell him that I went to my father's grave, and he looks so proud of me, he looks like he might cry, and we both stand there, almost crying. We stand for a little more and we hear some people around us talking about the demonstration, how, Allah'a şükür, it was small given everything that's going on, and one guy, a guy our age, starts talking to Cooper about how some Kurds don't trust that the government will stay true to its supposed truce, due to everything going on in Syria and Iraq, and this guy's girlfriend agrees, and says that there is no way there won't be bigger demonstrations as things get worse there. Cooper says wow, and adds that the presidential elections, too, will make things even more complicated. They agree, and the girl suspects that voter turnout will be low given that the elections have suspiciously been scheduled during the summer holidays, then they ask him how he knows Turkish so well and he points to me, and it's the same weak smile, the one I love, the one that makes me remember he's renowned for being kind because he really is kind, and he tells them it's because of me that he knows, that I taught him, and they smile knowingly, thinking we are in love, thinking that we are going to do things together, that us being together will send out good ripples into the world. After Baba got his stent my mother said, I was strangely confident that he would heal, that he would stay, that he still had things to do here.

Cooper tells his new friends he's going to get some simit from a stand, would they like any? They thank him, but they just ate. Cooper offers me a simit, and I say no, thank you. I walk away before he can compel me with bread, or before he can say anything to make me stay.


I CALL MY MOM ON MY WALK TO REFIKA'S. IT IS A VERY hilly and disjointed walk, and multiple buses I could have taken hunker past me. My mother wants to know what Alara's doing, and whether my grandmother's health has improved now that we're both there.

She's studying a lot, I say. She goes to play with Burcu's new baby. She's been meeting up with Deniz. We walk around the city. She's eating okay, actually, I lie, but she says she's sick of Turkish food.

Be patient with her, my mother says.

I am.

Good, baby. What about your grandmother?

Grandma is okay. Actually, I think something is bothering her.

What? What's bothering her, Sibel?

I'm talking about Baba's aunt, I explain, the one who raised him. Refika. Grandma told me. No one's ever mentioned her name, ever.

My mom is silent.

Hello?

My mom tells me that yes, she knows what happened, and that yes, Refika, who never let my grandmother see her son, raised Baba. But she stops. She curses in Turkish. She says that this is my grandmother's story, not hers. She is suspicious, too, about why my grandmother told me, and she knows something must have happened to me—I must be in a terrifying state, she says, for my grandmother to tell me. What's happened to you? she asks. What's happened?

Or, she thinks aloud, your grandmother must be losing her mind. Is your head okay?

My head is okay, I reply. The doctor says it's just muscle pain. Are you okay?

He doesn't think it's more serious?

I tell her that no, he doesn't think so, which she doesn't believe. I'm distrustful, too, but I have bigger problems. I have Refika. I light a cigarette and think about how easy it is to lie over the phone. I ask her again about Refika, and she ignores my question. She starts humming, which is insane, she never hums, and I start yelling at her to please tell me what happened.

Have you two been able to go to the grave? she asks suddenly.

Yes, I say. We went a few days ago. Actually, that's where I saw her.

You saw who?

Refika.

My mother curses on the phone.

Why are you talking to that woman? She's insane. I mean it, Sibel. Don't speak to her.

I haven't.

You spoke to her?

I never said that.

She's not a good woman, baby.

I don't believe it, I say.

My mother exhales. Before we hang up, she tells me she loves me. She tells me to never speak to Refika again. She tells me she loves me, again, and that she wishes she could be here with us. Maybe I should listen to her. I need to find out how much Alara weighs, and how I can trick her into eating. I want the power to prophesy. I want, just once, to get something right by the force of hope, responsibility, care.

ALBINA GREETS ME AT THE DOOR. SHE'S WEARING WHITE overalls and a crown made of dried roses. I try not to laugh. I suspect she saw this outfit on Instagram. She leans in to hug me, and I can feel her smelling me. I explain that yes, I just had a cigarette, and I wonder if she already knew I smoked.

Are you a social smoker? she asks instead.

Not exactly, I say, feeling defensive.

So, you're a secret smoker.

A secret smoker, I repeat back to her. Yes.

It's okay, Albina says. She asks me how many I smoke each day and I tell her my number, then retract that number and tell the truth: ten. It is my first time saying it out loud.

This time I admit to her that I've already gone to a hypnotist for smoking. It was a few weeks before Baba died. The woman sent me an intake form with a series of questions to determine what kind of person I was. I ticked off boxes about whether I followed directions best when read, heard, or performed on my own. But as I worked through the list I saw myself tick off boxes that seemed to outline grief and depression. It is difficult to be honest about yourself when taking a personality quiz, especially if you understand how the questionnaire was put together. But I guess it's similar to the way people used the humors to categorize their psychology. Descartes thought the humors made us distinctly human, and good, because what person who works to know themself, then changes based on their findings, is not a good person?

Or is the person who investigates themself thoroughly, diligently, no different from the person who does not? I slipped on my shoes and walked in the snow to a trash can two miles away to throw away the questions. Then I froze on a bench in the park after I pulled on my glove and smoked four angry cigarettes in a row.

But you still went? Albina asks. To the hypnotist?

Yeah, but it didn't work.

Oh, she says. I kick off my shoes and follow her into the living room. Our work will be more beneficial, she assures me. There's a general goal, not a specific one.

Refika is on the couch, and her fat braid hangs between her low, flappy breasts. There's no television, something I didn't notice the first time, which makes me wonder what they do every day. Maybe build tomato shrines. Maybe leech each other.

Albina has me help her move the coffee table to the side, so I can lie down on the rug in the middle of the living room and begin my physical therapy.

This is a little silly, no? I ask from the ground. I'm on my stomach. I have a very good view of Refika's bulby ankles.

This will allow me to access your vulnerability, Albina says. It's not the body that needs help, but the brain.

Wow, I say. Albina is smart. Maybe what Albina does is better than my humors, because she is physically applying care. But I don't think healthcare is why I'm still holding on to these liquids. Maybe it's not about medicine at all, but faith.

Albina kneads my shoulders. First the right, then the left, and I feel my ears pop and open. It feels like I'm carrying a lifetime, maybe multiple lifetimes, in my neck that are being released by Albina's hands.

When did you come to Turkey? I ask her.

After nursing school, I couldn't get a job in Tashkent, she says. So I came here. Your grandmother, she's the one who offered me this job. She pays well. But you know, I send most of the money back home.

I'm thinking of how to remind Albina that Refika is not my grandmother, but she catches herself and apologizes.

Just a slip, she says with a laugh.

That's okay, I say.

Technically Refika is my great-aunt. She's no witch. I turn my neck on the pillow to look at Refika on the couch. I squint my eyes a little, trying to see her differently. Her breasts still look long.

What are you doing? Refika asks me.

Oh, I say. I blink a few times. Nothing.

I turn my head again so my face is buried in the pillow. Albina continues massaging my shoulders. I saw my ex-boyfriend today, I say.

Oh, Cooper? Albina says warmly, as if she knows Cooper. How do you feel about it? she adds.

I wanted him to be mean, I say, to, you know, free me. But he was kind.

Albina asks me what he's like, and I'm wondering when I mentioned Cooper's name to her, but I can't remember so I just tell her that he would like her practice. He is interested in healing, I say, the nontraditional kinds as well as scientific medicine. Sometimes it feels like he was the one born to be a healer, not me, and that there isn't enough room for us both.

Albina thinks I shouldn't worry about space in that way, but it is very healthy for me to not bottle up anger or resentment towards him. She says we have to work on ways to relieve my tension, and proceeds to tell me about how eating certain foods can be transformative and healing. I'm wary of this, of health trends. I'm hitting a wall with the humors, I think, because they are forcing me to choose: Do I believe in constant betterment? Or do I believe that I should accept human nature—and myself—as we are, as flawed, living things that are finitely and irreparably conditioned? I could change myself with potions, with exercise, with positive thinking. With prayer. I need prayer. Proper prayer. But Albina wants to talk about tomatoes. She's had three tomatoes a day ever since she moved here and needed a cure for homesickness.

They're particularly good for the heart, Refika pipes up from her spot on the couch. Especially Turkish tomatoes.

I heard about that, I say, and then I tell them how scientists recently used the cellular matrix of a spinach leaf as scaffolding in order to stimulate a beating human heart. They managed to transform the spinach leaf into a replica vascular system by plucking out its plant cells and leaving behind a cellulose skeleton. Then they soaked the scaffolding in living human cells, and once those cells started to grow, they sent fluid and food down the scaffolding. The veins worked; they moved blood as a vascular system would.

They could really use this, I say, to repair or replace damaged organs. It's a remarkable advancement in tissue engineering. Refika raises her eyebrows.

Are you interested in that? Albina asks.

I don't know, I say. I put my face in the pillow again. I'm thinking about a way to replace damaged tissue in people who have heart attacks—tissue that usually scars over and never regenerates. A way to help people.

I can tell you're excited about it, Sibel.

Maybe, I say.

So if you know what they did, and you seem to know, why do you say *I'm not sure*?

What do you think, I ask Albina, do you think it'll help people? Me?

Yes, don't you want to help people?

Albina laughs. Of course I do.

Me too, I say.

You know, Albina begins, I can help you with your grandmother.

Oh. That's okay, I say. I'm helping her.

I know, Albina says, but her gaze flits away unconvincingly. I can come in, though. A few times a week. She needs it. Her state might be worse than Refika's.

I look back at Refika's bulby ankles.

Sibel?

No, I say. Thank you, but I'm the one helping her.

Albina leaves to get a towel from the kitchen, where it's been soaking in boiling water. It'll be good for your shoulder muscles, she informs me. They are way too tense.

Okay, I say. I hope I didn't offend her, but I'm the one who should take care of my grandmother, and my grandmother can't even hear Refika's name without needing to lie down. Meanwhile Refika begins to stand, a long process, and her hunched back seems to move on its own with each step she takes towards me. I am vulnerable, on the ground with no defenses, so I start to hoist myself up and stand before her. She's still tall, just under my height at five feet seven, and she smells like old cheese, yogurt. No, it's urine, I realize. That's the smell in this apartment. She tells me again that she wants to see my grandmother.

It's been years since we spoke, Refika tells me.

When? Please don't be cryptic.

When your father was fourteen, just before he left for boarding school: 1972.

What about the funeral? I ask, but she looks at me strangely. The call to prayer starts.

I have to pray, Refika says. Maybe you should, too. Goodbye.

Refika pads away to her bedroom at the end of the hall without another word. I strap up my sandals and shut the door quietly behind me. I wanted to say bye to Albina, but I feel numb. I'm looking for something holier than the humors. I want order, reason, meaning. Allah. The stairway lights click on as they sense me walking past each floor. I have taken my grandmother's trust for granted. Her life—the story she offered me—was a gift. And my father, he did not want to give me the same gift. His feelings remain the only mystery.

I'M VERY EXCITED TO TELL ALARA AND MY GRANDMOTHER that I haven't had a headache in hours but when I open the door my grandmother is busy in the kitchen, making me a surprise, she yells out, and my sister is sitting at the dining room table, reading and pretending to eat. She looks up at me with so much hate I'm shocked. I just came from a walk, I begin, but she snorts.

Did you see my text about the demonstration? I ask her.

Oh, so you care about the shit that's going on? Alara snorts and covers her face with the book she's reading, so I walk to the kitchen. Sometimes I wonder how she doesn't feel as hopeless as I do about the Middle East. Apathy, but I'm not blood. Not yet. I must first be so optimistic that I'm blind to pain and injustice.

My grandmother, it turns out, is brewing up a concoction of garlic and lemon in a jar the size of a head. She also made me big yellow boiled potatoes that her dead friend recommended decades ago. She's in a devoted mood and I'm smiling at her like an idiot as she shakes the jar. She tells me that this is an ancient remedy that the eye doctor drank each day to ward off illness. You must peel fifty cloves of garlic, squeeze twenty lemons, and mix the two ingredients in a jar. After storing for one week in a dark place, the concoction is ready to clear all your veins.

You will smell very bad, she warns. Like rotten garlic.

I stick my finger in the garlic water and she slaps my hand.

Is there something that will help directly with the brain? I ask.

My grandmother is stern again when she tells me I must not think about my headache if I want my headache to go away. She also needs me to get my sister to eat something substantial. I figure Alara will eat cucumbers, even though it's hours past breakfast. When I put them in front of her, she raises her eyebrows. There is already bread, cheese, eggplant in tomato sauce, string beans in tomato sauce, and olives on the table. It's hot today, and there is no breeze, but we have all the windows open anyway in case the apartment catches a gust of wind. Alara has a fan angled onto her face and neck. She's wearing my dress, a short white beach dress, and her legs stick out under the hemline. Save for at the university and the modern malls, no woman bares her legs readily here. It's not that we don't want to, it's that the men will always stare.

Did you know, I say, that Cooper was going to bring Jonathan to the museum?

Nope, she says, her fingers hovering over the bowl of olives, looking for the right one. I didn't know that.

Did you ever meet him? You would hate him, Alara. You would probably destroy him.

My grandmother, who keeps coming from the kitchen to

serve us more food, now walks in bearing peppers bathed in garlic yogurt and the boiled potatoes on a tray.

This is too much food, I say. Am I supposed to eat all those potatoes?

Eat as much as you can, baby.

Alara says nothing. She sucks on each olive pit until it is clean and flesh-free.

Remember what Uncle Yılmaz always said, I try again, that until Turkey gives Kurds the democratic justice they seek, socialism is useless here.

Alara covers her eyes with her hands. I have a headache, Sibel. Please.

Wow, I say, you're in luck! We're making some remedies now for headaches. Because, you know, I have one every day?

My grandmother is a vision walking back into the room, lifting heavy jars of garlic and lemon juice onto the table, dressed in all white, smiling like a light beam has slapped her face into a new shape.

What a vision! I say, and I pat my grandmother's hand. Alara recoils.

Jesus, Sibel. Shut up. Stop pretending to give a fuck. And what is Uncle Yılmaz doing now, huh?

Alara stands, swings her bag over her shoulder, and leaves the apartment. I look at her pile of olive pits like tiny skulls. My grandmother hurries to the balcony to watch her granddaughter march down the street into the hot sun wearing only a short white dress, waiting until Alara's white body transforms into a small blurry dot.

My grandmother turns to me as I join her on the balcony. I'm sorry, baby, she says. We were worried about you, after we heard the news. We spoke to your mother. She told us you saw Refika.

I'm suddenly very far away from my goal, my goal to take

care of my family. I got it wrong, again. Maybe I was never black bile. Maybe I just had an excess of it. Maybe it was not my true temperament. Choler not only aids indigestion but also represents childhood, and people who have an excess of choler are excitable, prone to anger but nonetheless fun and generally happy— like children, I guess—and I'm excited, standing on this balcony again as I have so many times with my grandmother, as I did with her and Alara when we were kids and collected snails on the street after it rained and brought them back to live in the plants on her balcony, because snails come out after rainfall, they want to live in liquid, and I'm thinking I can be one again, a child.

My grandmother continues, unaware she's ripping me out of fantasy. She's mad that you got to see Refika, not her. She's mad at me, too, for having told you first, but not so much.

I nod, and I say sorry to her, sorry I saw Refika. She's turned away to check on her plants. Grandmother tuts her tongue and sticks her shaking hand in the dry soil of her tall snake plant, also called the mother-in-law's tongue. The mother-in-law can survive forever, with very little water and sun, and as I'm watching Grandmother water the immortal plant I know that it's not just about the funeral, because Alara defended me at the funeral. It's that Alara's been mad at me for months but can't tell me. She can't say to my face that if I hadn't frozen that night, she would be lifted of a burden—the burden of caring for me.

Before the funeral you have to wash the body. If it's a male body the men wash it. If it's a female body the women wash it. Uncle Yılmaz washed Baba's body with my cousins. Then they put the body in a white cotton bag. No coffins allowed. Your body will become soil faster this way.

My grandmother brings me back to the living room to show

me something in the newspaper. It's a short piece on a couple re-united after forty years of each thinking the other was dead. Look, she says, her hand shaking as she points at the couple's radiant faces, this is them engaged, this is them now. How time changes us.

My grandmother is smiling. She is so optimistic. How often does she think of her husband? Her son?

Forty days after a person's death, you may resume your nor-mal life. A special prayer was read at the funeral to set Baba's soul at peace. The imam asked, How did you know this man? We all said he was a good man. Do you forgive him? Yes. We forgive him in this world. On this side of the earth, we forgive him.

My grandmother has found a pair of scissors and begins clip-ping the article.

Let me help you, I say, and she lets me take the newspaper and the scissors and stands there supervising as I cut along the text.

Make sure to get the photograph, too, she instructs, pointing at the man's young face.

Okay, I say. I ask her if she can tell me more about Refika.

She nods. She says she can tell me, but maybe we should wait for my sister. Alara doesn't like being left out of this, she says.

My grandmother is right.

I ask her if I should not go back to see Refika. I hand her the news-paper clipping and she holds the thin gray paper with both hands.

You can see her, my grandmother replies. I forgive her.

I HAVEN'T SEEN DENIZ SINCE HE GOT HERE, SO I'M GOING to meet him at the mall. One of the newest malls is a twenty-minute walk from my grandmother's, with Turkish and Euro-pean clothing stores, makeup stores, swimsuit stores, baby-gear stores, a few toy stores, a movie theater, and one bookstore with a single shelf of English-language books—most of them classics written by men—and on the top floor there is a food court. I come here to pee sometimes, or to buy iced coffee, a request that makes baristas look at me like I'm a foreigner until they hear my name. Women, who were known to have a more cold and wet temperament, were advised against drinking coffee when it became big in Istanbul in the sixteenth century. Iced coffee is still not big in Istanbul.

I'm smoking on my walk over, and the woman and her three children are on their quilt across the street in front of the washing machine store. I cross the street blindly, without noticing a bus barreling at me, and when I see the shock in the mother's eyes, I laugh. I get close enough to explain to her and her children, who are also looking at me with awe and wonder, that it's okay, no big deal about that bus, and I'm in such a thrill that I forget I don't have any of my grandmother's food for them, that I forgot the package of köfte on the kitchen counter, and so I back away slowly and apologize and keep backing away until I'm basically running.

I run the rest of the way to the mall.

I meet Deniz at a restaurant on the top floor. We order döner rolled up in pita bread and Diet Coke and he tells me about a film he watched last week that he thinks I would like. It's about a Lebanese American girl in Arkansas whose life is okay for a fifteen-year-old until 9/11, when her father is imprisoned on charges of terrorism. She ends up wearing a headscarf and running away to a Zen monastery. She gets there on a motorcycle.

Huh, I say, so you think I should end up at a Zen monastery?

Yeah, Deniz says. I think that would be pretty sick. But you're not very monastic.

What about the motorcycle?

I can see you doing that, too. Deniz pauses and stares at me. But I'm not totally sure you're fit to do something that dangerous.

Really, I say, laughing, I had no idea. Were you on Istiklal a few days ago?

No, why? The protest?

Yeah.

No, I wasn't. I was at home, doing nothing. He starts shaking his leg. Deniz was here during Gezi last year, but found that the demonstrations had too much of a nationalist Turkish presence. If they were aligned on Kurdish rights, he always says, I would have been more down.

I could have sworn I saw you.

I wish I was there. I'm not doing anything useful these days. Deniz runs his thumb over his plate to get the leftover yogurt dip and sucks it before he looks up. Perhaps we are too similar. We are both useless.

I was at the archaeology museum with Cooper, I add, that's when we went to Beyoğlu.

He nods, but his eyes narrow. So did you ever tell Cooper?

Deniz likes Cooper, but after that night he has for my sake intentionally avoided seeing him. He knew I'd freeze up and act like an alien if I saw them together.

Hello, Sibel, he says, where did you go? A piece of his curly hair is caught in his stubble. I reach over and as I move this lock from his face he takes my hand in his. His hand is rough, almost scaly, and I wonder what it would feel like to have him knead my shoulders and neck, my spine. I want to be in Refika's living room again, or wherever it is I can go to escape my body.

You have a body, Baba once lectured me, you do not have a soul. You are a soul.

Just tell me what happened, he says. What happened with Cooper?

I tell him Cooper and I broke up, because I think I was leaning on him too much, and I tell him Cooper's in Georgia now. But Cooper's sad smile from the last time I saw him swims into my head and I stop speaking until Deniz snaps his fingers at me. I tell him about Dilek's party for Cooper next week, a party that infuriates me, and he scowls, which makes me laugh, but immediately says he'll come with us. But you can't be an alien, he adds. We didn't do anything.

I nod, willing myself to believe him. And I'm smoking, I say. Maybe ten cigarettes a day. I'm going to have one now.

He passes me the ashtray.

I went to my dad's grave.

He nods again while sucking up Diet Coke through a straw. Deniz wasn't at the funeral, but I'd told him about the old woman, before I knew she was Refika.

Alara and I are fighting, I think because both of us think the other needs more help. Did you see her? How skinny she is? My mom thinks she's ninety pounds.

Deniz nods. He doesn't comment on her body.

My grandma, I say, is stronger than us but she won't tell me how I can help her.

What do you mean? How's her Parkinson's?

Her hand is always shaking, but she takes her medication consistently. Sometimes she's funky with memories, but so far, no vast delusions or anything. But she hasn't fallen or lost balance, and she can walk on her own. Sometimes she drops things. But she had to give away her baby, my dad, when the eye doctor died in the earthquake in Istanbul. He was raised by another woman, his aunt.

What the hell? The eye doctor?

Sorry, my grandfather. He was an eye doctor.

Deniz is shocked. My grandma never mentioned anything, he says. Your grandma was over the other day, for tea. She seemed okay.

She always seems okay, I say. I think she *seems* okay, you know?

His silence is suddenly infuriating, and I understand how lonely it must be to love somebody like me.

How's your grandma? I ask him, but he shakes his head, and says he doesn't want to talk about it. He looks hurt and angry.

What, Sibel? Why the fuck are you smiling?

No, I explain, it's just that, isn't it funny how they won't let us take care of them? We try to, but they'd literally rather die than let us do something for them.

Jesus, Sibel, Deniz says, but he's smiling. He starts laughing, and I'm laughing. I can't stop it coming out of me.


WHEN I GET HOME MY GRANDMOTHER IS DRINKING TEA and watching a dramatic scene from a soap opera where the young woman is confronting her mother about her uncle's abuse. I ask her if she needs anything and she says no thank you, baby. I go to my bedroom and Alara's there, in one of my bras, staring at herself in the mirror. The bra is too big for her, and the cups look deflated and empty. She moves out of my way to put on a green dress but when she tries to pull up the neckline it falls because the fabric can't find enough breast to make the dress sit right, so she pulls the dress over her head, her armpits deep white caves. It's strange for her to be so quiet. Once I'm naked and looking for a clean shirt, she announces that she brought a box of nicotine patches from New York. She bought them for Aunt Pinar but given that I reek of tobacco, and our aunt is too old to quit a habit, I can have them.

I can't use those, I say, and while I'm trying to smell myself, she throws the box at my face.

No, really, I sweat too much for them to stick.

Alara raises her eyebrows at me in the mirror as she's trying on a tank top that shows her sternum. I'm behind her in the mirror, and we seem doubled, only I'm fatter. There are fourteen bones in the human face, and I'm certain I can see the grooves of each one on her.

Once, I say, I hugged someone, a guy I just met, and my patch stuck to the back of his neck. At first, I said nothing, I just drank my beer and watched him walk around the party, branded. Then I apologized and peeled the thing off. My hand was on his neck and I remember his girlfriend looked at me all crazy-eyed.

Come on, Sibel, she says, that's a ridiculous story.

Really, I say. That's what happened. You can ask Cooper.

What did you do with Deniz?

We just went to the new mall. There's a sushi restaurant now, on the top floor. But we had döner.

Then why didn't you invite me?

You were at the cemetery, I say, and I freeze. I didn't mean to say *cemetery* out loud.

I was, Alara says, wasn't I? But Refika doesn't go there anymore to meet us—no, sorry, you—anymore, does she? she repeats herself as she stares into the mirror. She's very smug now. She says, in a much slower voice this time, No Refika coming for me. No invitations over to Refika's for me.

I try to explain that it is no great privilege going to Refika's, but I shut up. Alara has always been extremely driven by a knack for uncovering secrets and seeking out justice. And I'm scared of what Refika could do to her, psychologically.

How long has it been since you had your period? I ask her.

It's not a big deal. This happens to women all the time, Sibel.

How long? What, five months, six months?

Alara tries to leave the bedroom but I grab her arm. I tell her her body is shutting down. That this is just the first sign of it and soon her bones could break. She's not secreting the right hormones because she's not eating. She squirms out of my grip and slams the door shut behind her. I'm stalking the bathroom door, waiting for her to come out. Anybody with little body fat can get their period back once they gain weight, but she's still damaging her body. Her bone mass is reducing. She's losing hair. And if she keeps it up, there is a high chance her vital organs could fail. To heal one woman who had not had her period for nine months, Galen drew blood from the soft arch of the woman's foot over three days—one pound from one foot on the first day of treatment, another pound from the other foot on the second day, and on the third day, a few pounds more from the first foot. The woman's natural color and heat returned after this practice, as well as her period. But even I would never bleed out my little sister through her foot.

When Alara opens the door, she does so slowly. She pops her head out and scans the hallway for me. I intercept her in the doorframe. I tell her that I'll make the rice—not our grandmother—

and I'll boil it with less butter, no butter, however much butter she wants.

Alara looks at my face carefully.

The hand has so many different tiny bones in it, I say. Did you know that?

She doesn't answer.

I guess you don't really care about that, huh?

Huh? She blinks. Care about what?

About bones, I say, that there are twenty-seven in your hand. That bones are precious, they're brittle. They can break.

A breeze pulls in the smell of fresh bread from outside. I repeat the thing about bones. Alara slaps me on my face, telling me her hand is fine, her hand is strong. I repeat the thing about bones again. I'm pretending she didn't smack me. Alara shoves her fist in my face. She tells me to just see how strong her hand is. I do what she tells me, I look at her hand, and that's when she begins to cry. She tells me she doesn't understand why I think that this grief is just mine, that I think I can take everything from her, without wondering how she feels. You knew I wanted to meet with her, she cries. You knew. We hear my grandmother's footsteps down the hall, and Alara pulls me into the bathroom and locks the door quietly, and as my grandmother starts knocking, Alara makes me swear to never tell her about this, about her eating disorder, as if a body were something to tell in words. As if one could *tell* a body, not see a body, and what was missing.

# III.

WE'RE GETTING READY FOR DILEK'S PARTY. DENIZ JUST arrived, and he's sitting in the living room having tea with my grandmother. In the past few days, Alara's been full of a new kind of fury directed not at me but at Dilek, who she's cursing out the whole time we're looking for something to wear in our bedroom. She is also furious at my father. Every day, she's been asking if she can come with me to see Refika, but I don't think I can go back. It's been one week, and I don't think I can do that to my grandmother. When I told Alara this, she fell quiet.

My grandmother has been worrying us lately. She's been determined to buy her sister a birthday present, but Aunt Pinar's birthday was a few months ago, and my grandmother already gifted her a beautiful purple vacuum cleaner. Today she's insisting that her sister wants a wooden salad bowl. Alara and I were considering skipping Dilek's, but when we came into the kitchen and hinted at staying in, she threw a bag of peaches at us. We all looked at the peaches, leisurely rolling across the kitchen floor, and my grandmother admitted that yes, it is sad that she couldn't get them any farther. I agreed. I really wish the peaches had hit us.

As Alara's changing, I repeat what I've said multiple times today, that Cooper hates birthdays. He hates overt attention. Well, this is good, then, right? Alara says. She's dabbing eye shadow on her lids with her pinkies. Then she rubs lotion onto her thin arms. Watching her, my headache returns, and I lie down on the floor. Alara has her arms behind her back as she secures the clasp of my strapless bra. She pinches the loose beige cups then laughs. I guess I deserve this, she says. Why aren't you getting dressed?

She pulls on a tank top and silk pink pants that show her hip bones. I've been plotting the perfect outfit, a black halter top that makes my shoulder blades look like wings, and tight jeans. I'm on the floor, watching her, until she whips her head around and snaps at me again to get ready already. I run my hand over the hardwood floor to sweep up the wiry black strands of hair Alara's been shedding, counting each one, hair loss being another symptom of anorexia. Deniz calls us from the living room, where we're to take shots from my grandmother's ancient bottle of raki. I'm using my elbows to try to stand up, and Alara has her back to me when I tell her I may text Cooper to say that we're coming to the party, and happy birthday. She loses it, like I expected her to, and tells me how I'd be disrespecting myself by texting him, and then she takes my phone, where I've already composed the text, and it sits typed out, waiting, like a bomb ready to drop.

Don't accidentally send it, I say, panicking. Did you send it?

No, Jesus. Why would I do that?

Your arm, stop flailing it around.

She holds me at arm's length as she inspects the text message. You shouldn't say this, she says. She deletes my message and starts typing. This is much more affirmative and carefree, like, you don't want him to know how upset you are with Dilek.

I'm not upset with Dilek.

Okay. Sure you're not. Should I send it?

Wait, let me read it one more time.

We read the text together and I can hear her breathing heavily. Alara says it looks fine, and that it doesn't matter anyway because I was the one who wanted no communication, so it's okay that I'm now the one breaking communication.

Can I add a smiley face? I ask.

No.

Okay, no. Just send it.

Before we leave, I go to the bathroom. Now is not the time for washing my hands, forearms, shins, and feet. Instead, I slather on my grandmother's foundation. But I look dry and cakey, so I perform my absolutions anyway, praying the whole time. I wash my hands. I gargle my mouth and clean my nose. Then I wet both my arms up to the elbow on each side, brush water around my ears, a little on my hair, and finally I scrub my feet. Trota also wrote a pamphlet on cosmetics, which told women how to beautify their skin, hair, face, lips, teeth, and genitalia. For example, if you want your hair to be long and black, you are to capture a green lizard, cut off its head and tail, and cook the scaly body in oil. Then you rub this lizard oil evenly into your hair. Dilek inviting me stems from either genuine familial duty or a perverse desire to watch me suffer. I understand this. I respect her nerve. I'm trying to go to hell and back alive tonight. I think it is the best cure.

DILEK STAYS IN A UNIVERSITY DORM DURING THE SCHOOL year, but in summer she lives with her parents in their two-story house on the Asian side a few miles uphill from the water. Their home is one in a cluster of identical burnt-orange houses and in the middle is a communal swimming pool. Aunt Sevgi opens the door and we kick off our shoes next to thirty or so other pairs. We head to the living room in the back, where Aunt Sevgi and Uncle Yılmaz are hiding out. Emre is here too, sulking. They say they're going out to dinner and will leave us to have fun, but Aunt Sevgi stumbles on the word *fun* and looks at me. Then she apologizes for Dilek throwing this party. I think she's only trying to be hospitable, Aunt Sevgi says, and Uncle Yılmaz, watching a soccer game, snorts.

Don't worry, I tell her. This is just petty stuff.

This is not petty stuff, Alara counters, glaring at our aunt. These are your feelings, Sibel.

I smile and say bye to them and we walk towards the garden even though I'd rather sulk on the couch with Emre. American pop songs play from a loud speaker in the garden with sugary forcefulness. I wonder where Aunt Sevgi's mother is, and whether this party will bother her.

I need wine, Alara says. Her face looks tired but determined. She's put on the same lipstick as me, our grandmother's lumpy rouge, and our mouths, both made of a fat bottom and a thin upper lip, look identical. But her face is so hollow that her lips puff out. I want wine, too. Deniz follows behind me and Alara tells us this is good, Deniz taking the rear will look good for me. I will look busy. He will look like my dog on a leash, one who can't live without me, who would never let me come to this party alone.

Like a true Turkish man, huh, Deniz says.

Yup, Alara says. That's right.

DILEK'S PARTIES HAVE ALWAYS BEEN THE KIND YOU HAD to drink through to have any fun. An intelligent host should supply drinks, music, places to stand or sit, and definitely snacks, then disappear into the crowd and appear calm and relaxed and only speak when spoken to. Dilek, though, is known for sharing each task she's completed to host such a party for everyone. She's a complainer, but so graceful in her words that nobody, nobody but me, can ever confront her. She always composes a strict playlist of ten songs, songs she says are her absolute favorites, that we listen to in loops. Everyone will be forced to watch her as she plants her soles in the center of a standing circle and dances, all the while sporting a giant smile. Something happens to me as I step into the garden. I realize I don't give a shit, even about Dilek. Even about Cooper and Deniz in the same space. I see Cooper immediately. He's sitting at the circular table in the middle of the garden. The garden is not very big, and there are clusters of people around the peach trees in the back. Esra sits next to Cooper in a silky white dress and she's holding a glass of wine the way people say you have to hold it, with your fingers on the stem and not the bowl. Fuck Esra, I think, as she nods seriously to whatever it is Cooper is saying to the table of Turks around him and running his hand through his hair, something he does when he's nervous. Fuck Esra, I say, this time to Alara and Deniz. Alara narrows her eyes then yells hello very loudly to Esra, Cooper turns, and that's when he sees Deniz and me by the garden door.

You're nervous, Deniz says to me, staring at Cooper.

Nope, I just don't give a shit.

How nice, he says. I'll go get us drinks.

Cooper looks away and nods in mock concentration at a guy who's using his hands as he speaks, while Alara, downing her wine, makes a beeline for him. I know she wants to show him we are here, and we are not intimidated by him, which is an interesting tactic, even if it's true: I'm not intimidated. I am nervous, but I'm angry, too, angry at Cooper and Dilek for this party. I'm choler, again. A strong mix of black bile and choler results in fury. Cooper and Alara say hi, they even hug, and as Alara flips her hair back and begins talking, I can see him looking at the hollows in her collarbone, and her arms as thin as swords.

Dilek glides over to me and we kiss on both cheeks. After asking me why I'm standing here in the corner, she tells me she is so glad I could make it.

Where's Deniz? Getting drinks? she asks.

Thank you so much for having me, Dilek, I say. It's so nice of you to throw this party for my ex-boyfriend.

Dilek balks. I really love shutting her up. Dilek is openly watching Cooper and Alara, and because I don't care about being obvious, and definitely don't care to speak with Dilek, I'm watching them too. Esra has also joined them and they're standing in a circle. I wonder how Alara will choose to make Cooper feel guilty. A man with sand-colored hair introduces himself to both Cooper and Alara. His voice is so loud I can hear him say he's American, too, on vacation here with his parents. He knows Esra's boyfriend from college. Then he compliments Alara on her pink pants.

Dilek's got an e-cigarette that she's brandishing like a wand. I ask for a drag, and when I inhale it crackles and I feel popcorn-lunged but free. No, I'm not a mix of humors tonight. I'm a full dose of choler, full of courage and fury.

Deniz hands me a glass of wine and says hello to Dilek, who forces him into a big hug and presses her hips against him, and he rolls his eyes at me over her shoulder.

How's your grandmother, Dilek asks, is she okay? Deniz nods slowly, thanks her for asking, then pulls me by the arm and gets me in a corner. He wants to talk about my guilt. He says he doesn't care about what we did, but he knows I care, and he knows I bury what hurts in me.

Nope, I say. We're not going to talk about it.

But this time you're different, you're angry. He steps back, assessing whether I am alien or ire, and I'm amazed, because I am angry and it is the first time this summer someone has told me I am anything but sad.

DILEK, WHO WANTS TO TURN THE NIGHT INTO A DANCE party, orders some of the boys to move the circular table and chairs to the side of the garden as she runs into the house to get her portable speakers. She's the first to start dancing to Tarkan, and slowly, the party begins to stand and shimmy. Alara is there next, right beside Dilek, and they link arms and belt out the chorus together. Cooper is sitting at the table again, talking very seriously to Esra. Fuck Esra. I was not diligent enough. I should have been worried about Esra this whole time, not Dilek. Esra is the kind of powerful that Cooper likes.

Cooper hasn't replied to my happy birthday text, and his phone is facedown on the table. I'm surprised he even has his phone out because he prefers to limit his screen time, especially in front of other people. I grab Deniz's hand and we stand to dance. Our bodies press together at the groin for a single moment, and he smells like tobacco and body odor and bread. His lips look like a dark pink flower, and it isn't until he shakes me gently by the arms that I realize he's speaking, he's saying, C'mon, Sibel, since you're feeling so confident, let's go talk to them. I feel a thrill. I'd love to talk to them. I lead the way to the table.

Cooper and Esra are discussing novels when I drag the metal chair across the stone in a screech. Oops, I say, smiling at Esra, sorry. Cooper looks away, and Esra just keeps talking about how she thinks art should be experienced privately. She hates when people post a picture of a page in a book on social media with a cute caption. I've stalked Esra before, and she often posts such pictures, but she never captions them, which she probably finds more meaningful. Cooper, who deactivated his social media accounts years ago, seems enthralled by Esra's comment, and I laugh into my drink, loud enough for them to look at us.

Hi, Sibel, Esra says.

Hey, says Deniz, looking at Cooper, who says hi back and almost looks at me. He's close, close to looking, but tears away. The choler in me rises and I feel more full of liquid than I have all summer.

Well, I say, I can't go on social media without feeling very sorry for myself. But I also feel superior all the time, like, I'm not going to post all the time because I know how to live my life, right? I have things to do, right? I'm not a useless piece of shit, right?

Deniz laughs.

Esra stares at me.

Like, every time I'm on there, people are either telling me all the great things they're accomplishing, or they're telling me to take a nap if I want to, to take time for myself if I want to. I know that, right? Don't I know?

So don't use it, Deniz says, and Cooper looks down and smiles.

I'm just saying our emphasis on self-care may be making everyone more depressed.

Self-care? Esra asks.

Never mind, I say.

So, Cooper starts, how're the beats going?

Deniz nods slowly. I wouldn't be surprised if he just mentioned what we did right there, and actually, I wouldn't be surprised if I did either. What's stopping me? But Deniz's teasing me. He's playing this out, and he thinks he's making me sweat. Does he think this is good for me? They begin discussing hip-hop, and Cooper mentions that he hasn't heard American rap—except for Biggie—played in Istanbul, not once, and Deniz suggests that they hijack Dilek's playlist.

You don't like rap, Esra? I ask, knowing her answer.

I try to understand it, she says diplomatically. Maybe it's because I don't know enough about American culture, and race.

There are a lot of Turkish rappers in Germany, I say.

I know that. My boyfriend listens to them.

Where is he? I ask again.

Esra rolls her eyes then looks at Cooper for help.

What? I ask, but Cooper finally looks at me with his very uncomfortable, pleading look. My phone is faceup on the table, buzzing, and Cooper looks down at the unsaved number. It's Refika. I press DECLINE and Cooper pretends to not have seen but he looks relaxed all of a sudden, and even smiles at me. Okay, Cooper. I smile back.

More people join us at the table, including Esra's sister Eda, who pulls up a chair between me and Deniz, pushing him closer to Cooper. Besides this strained smile, Cooper hasn't said a word to me. That's fine. I'm choler. But people are talking over me, the American boy is asking someone whether they deny the Armenian genocide, Alara is twerking, or trying to, until she resorts to an elaborate belly dance, my phone is buzzing and buzzing, and Deniz is still chatting with Cooper—now they are talking about basketball, and the Knicks, which is obviously Deniz's favorite team, and he makes fun of everyone who likes the Nets now because they moved from New Jersey to the Barclay's Center and he always says that those people are not real New Yorkers. I always wonder who is a real New Yorker. Esra stands with her sister, and they start to dance. Alara bumps into them but I can't tell if she did it on purpose or if she's very drunk, and sure enough, she begins to twerk on Esra, who shimmies away. I get up, and I'm debating texting Cooper something passive-aggressive, but then Deniz gets up too and leads me to the makeshift bar across the garden, not for more drinks but because he wants to stand behind a line of potted plants for I don't know what reason until he lights me a cigarette. Your sinuses are tunnels. I learned this when I was smoking weed one night and someone put dried lavender in the bong and the smoke felt thick and good, sure, but when I smoked a cigarette later that night, the lavender got reactivated in my sinuses and I spent a few high minutes wondering if I was a plant stem breaking through soil. Deniz mentions that Cooper is truly a "good dude."

What the fuck are you saying, Deniz? A good dude?

C'mon, Sibel, he says. You're enjoying this. This is more fun than you've had all week.

I've had other fun, I say. I've been having a lot of fun, lately.

No way, Deniz says. You're having fun, losing control. It's good to see. Deniz looks at Alara, who is still dancing by herself but just by moving her shoulders. She throws a sloppy wink at Deniz, who smiles back. You're waking up, Deniz adds. You haven't had to face your relationship in months. You've lost yourself, a little, don't you think?

Fuck you, Deniz.

He just hands me another cigarette.

Doesn't everyone? I ask. Avoid their relationships?

Deniz shrugs. He asks me, in turn, if it's better to live fully, without a critical eye on yourself, or to diligently observe yourself and others, and through that observation, work to change. Which one leads to more happiness? But he doesn't want my answer, not that I have a fucking answer, and he scans the garden again before marching off. He turns to see if I'm watching. I am, I'm watching, I'm diligent.

A FEW HOURS INTO THE PARTY WE'RE SITTING AROUND the table again. I'm next to Dilek, and Cooper is across the table. Alara was talking to Dilek's most attractive friend until he made fun of the way she pronounced the Turkish r, which is always difficult for us to hit and roll properly, so she sought out Deniz instead and now they are whispering in the corner under an orange tree like spies. People are talking of going to a nightclub soon. One guy, who has been smoking cigarettes all night and has his hair slicked back with just a little gel, wants to go to the fancy one on the Bosphorus with a view of the bridge lit up in neon colors. His friend, though, who has been quiet all night, doesn't want to go to this club, because it attracts more Arab tourists than Turks these days. Cooper suggests we stay here, where we can continue talking comfortably.

Dilek, who will not tolerate the party being moved elsewhere, reveals that actually she just found some of her father's raki stash. We can drink as much of it as we want, she says, forcefully. Wow. She is pleading. I've repossessed Dilek's e-cig and am blowing fat clouds of vapor to surround myself with a shield. Throughout this wildly fascinating deliberation I notice that Alara is no longer outside. Cooper has left the table, too.

I ask Dilek if she knows what Deniz and Alara were talking about so secretively in the corner, and she sighs. I ask her again, adding that I'm sorry, I really am, that Deniz wasn't interested in her last year.

Ask Cooper, she says. He was just talking to them. Honestly, he looked like he was crying, Sibel.

So where the fuck did Cooper go?

Dilek sighs. Now he's with Esra. They were talking in the kitchen. She pouts into her drink. And we have to do the birthday candles soon, she adds.

You're following them?

Shut up, Sibel. No. I'm not. When I got the raki I saw them.

Dilek looks miserable. I decide to be kind, instead, and I give her a hug long enough for me to hear her heart beat through her rib cage.

MY AUNT AND UNCLE ARE GONE AND THE HOUSE IS COLD and air-conditioned and empty. I walk through the empty kitchen, where Dilek had just scavenged on the liquor cabinet, and through the hallway, where I stop in front of a photograph of my dead grandmother posing with her two children. She looks austere and unhappy. The only thing my mother tells us about her father is that he was violent. My father was quick to anger, too. He'd slip into an ancient skin, saying things I thought typical of Turkish men, like, I'm the one who supports you, I make the money here. The things he said when he lost his temper so completely, the things I try to forget, and now I'm wondering whether he was so angry, and so often, because he had the same sickness I have, the one where you develop phantom organs, blood-filled boxes where you can hide whatever you want, and you can live however you want because these new organs evolve to allow your brain to function at what you think is a happier level. But there is no happier level. Now I think there is only living for others, not for yourself. I hear retching from the bathroom in the back, by Dilek's bedroom. I know it's Alara before I get to the door. There is blood in the toilet bowl and on the white oval seat. Alara's hair is matted onto her forehead, her makeup leaking, and she wipes the blood off her mouth with the back of her hand and says that happens sometimes. I'm just drunk, she says, but when she looks in the toilet bowl she's alarmed, more alarmed than I've ever seen her, and she says it has never happened like this, never this much blood, and then she says sorry.

I can't tell her that her esophagus could be ruptured. I can't tell her that when a person throws up consistently, every day, the acid begins to eat away steadily at the esophagus, enough to tear a hole, enough to permanently damage other organs, too, like your lungs. I can't tell her how scared I am.

Let's go home, I say. Come on, Alara.

She tries to stand but falls, and she throws up again, this time on the floor and on the fluffy blue bath mat, and I'm trying again to get my hands under her armpits to lift her but she's refusing, she says there's more coming, and it does come, it's blood again, and after I think she's done although she's not responding, I yell out for my aunt, for my uncle, for Cooper, for Deniz, for either of them, but neither come, so I let myself slide to the ground, my phone buzzing violently in my pocket, and Alara's body falls over mine. I'm covered in her blood and spit and vomit, and I sit and stroke her hair while listening to the party sing happy birthday in Turkish to Cooper until finally Dilek, drunk, wanders into her bathroom and screams.

I'M BACK AT THE HOSPITAL WITH MY GRANDMOTHER. Af- ter arriving at the emergency room last night with Dilek and Deniz, I called my grandmother, and Alara was checked into the intensive care unit. A small blood vessel had burst in her esopha- gus, and the doctors think that if she hadn't come in tonight, the fluid in her esophagus—saliva, food, vomit—could have leaked into her chest cavity, causing bacterial infection or abscess. When we first arrived, the doctors performed a chest X-ray, then they did an esophagoscopy to determine the location of her esopha- geal tear. Because the tear was not severe, the doctors did not need to surgically remove the affected portion of her esophagus.

My grandmother kissed both doctors, attractive young men, and thanked Allah for their help, and the two young doctors looked so comforted and cute, like she was their grandmother. Something I love about Turkey is the way younger men treat older women. The doctors then got more serious, and more kind, and they told my grandmother that some fluid did leak into Alara's lungs, so they would have to suction it out using a chest drain. A chest drain, my grandmother repeated. Her shaking hand floated to her throat as she nodded.

It's almost eight a.m., and Alara's asleep with an IV hooked up to her arm and a feeding tube stuffed into her nose. My grandmother keeps bringing wet paper towels from the bathroom to wipe the vomit and blood off Alara's face and hands. She lugged her small prayer rug here too.

I've spent the past eight hours thinking of my mother, and what I will have to say to her. It's August, and my mother was not supposed to come to Istanbul this summer. As my grandmother wipes Alara's forehead for the fifth time and murmurs prayers, I dig out my phone and go to the hallway, where there are some nurses talking in low voices and a man with a white mustache in a wheelchair looking up at a bulletin board. I ignore the missed calls from Albina.

I call my mother.

I speak to her.

She's coming to Istanbul on the first flight she can find.

# IV.

MY MOTHER IS REMARKABLY SKILLED AT SLIDING INTO the girl who grew up in Turkey, the girl who never left.

I'm waiting outside Alara's room at the hospital when I see her. She's wearing sneakers that are disguised to look like loafers and carrying three bags full of food, as well as the big leather handbag she lugs everywhere. She gives me a brief one-armed hug, smelling strongly of orange disinfectant wipes, before opening the door to get to Alara. Her face looks tired, but the dark bags under her eyes are only genetic. She kisses her mother-in-law on both cheeks before putting her hand on Alara's forehead, then her cheeks, then her chest, rising and falling as she sleeps, until she sinks into the chair by the hospital bed.

My god, my mother says in Turkish. What have we done?

We sit like this for a little, and my grandmother asks my mother how the flight was, whether she was comfortable, and she says yes, she was comfortable, it was okay, there was a fat man sitting next to her, but he was very polite and the food, as usual, was not bad because Turkish Airlines is, after all, the best airline. I mention that Turkish Airlines is the one thing all Turks can agree on. They laugh at this, and my mother in turn asks my grandmother if she's okay, if she needs anything. My grandmother, sitting in the armchair by the window, lifts her chin to say no.

You should go home, my mother says, but my grandmother tuts her tongue.

Shame on you, my grandmother says, and settles deeper in her plastic chair.

Sibel, can you bring your grandmother's medicine from the house?

I'm fine, my grandmother says. Let's eat first. She loots through the bags of food my mother brought: açma, simit, poğaça, mini jam and honey jars she snatched from the cafeteria downstairs. My grandmother is smiling to herself. She knows how to feed people, and she's proud of my mother for bringing all this food. My mother stands to help my grandmother set up a makeshift table near the window.

Sibel, can you get the tablecloth? my mother asks. There are knives and forks, too. My arms are deep in the second bag my mother brought and I want to tell them I'm happy here, with all of them together. It's the happiest I've been. But how can I say this when Alara is practically unconscious? I wave the tablecloth over the plastic hospital table and unpack the bags of food. They're talking about hospitals. How my sister has been carrying a big load. They don't look at me, but it's me they're talking around. There are a few minutes of silence—a beautiful, calm silence— before my mother turns to my grandmother and says, You know she went to Refika's again?

My grandmother, her hands on her lap, nods gravely.

What should we do? my mother asks her.

We? We can't do anything. You can't control girls.

Alara is sleeping in her hospital bed but my mother wants to tell me about Refika. She thinks it's time. She looks at my grandmother, who nods. My grandmother says she has something to add, too. I will take any story, however caustic, however cautionary.

THE SAME DAY I WAS BORN IN 1993, FOUR GERMAN MEN firebombed a Turkish home in Germany, killing two women and three girls. My mother, despite a degree in engineering, could never shed her superstition completely and was convinced that I would suffer due to this connection.

My mother had just come back from the hospital with me, my father, and my grandmother, who had come to stay with us in Bay Ridge to help take care of the new baby. Yesterday's newspaper lay open on the kitchen table, to the thin single column about the fire set in Solingen. Cigarette stubs and empty teacups surrounded the paper, and Baba apologized for not telling her. He knew she would worry.

My mother used nail scissors to clip the article and hid the column in the pages of her Koran, a book she has always kept on the highest shelf in the pantry and never reads.

My mother believed that a person experiences more discrimination if they are part of a larger minority group in a city. She was grateful, in this sense, that there weren't many Turks in New York—thus New Yorkers wouldn't associate her family's foreignness with any group of people they already knew. They might make assumptions, comparisons, veiled threats, but they wouldn't burn her home down.

She was right. But she always says it is not about being right, but about being lucky.

THREE MONTHS LATER, REFIKA ARRIVED IN NEW YORK from Istanbul. My parents were at work. Only my grandmother was home, and she did not hear the door open, could not remember having left it unlocked, could not remember when the tea kettle boiled over; it was after she'd prepared breakfast, after she'd washed the dishes, when she climbed the stairs to feed me my mother's breast milk that she found my crib empty. Maybe she had left me on the sofa she'd been sleeping on, but I was not there. My grandmother looked everywhere, under my empty crib, in the towel closet, in the cabinet full of tea glasses and saucers, before she speed-walked to the phone, where she debated—for the smallest moment—whether she should call my father's office or my mother's office, until all thought escaped her and she reached my father after five tries to the wrong extension, and said, I'm so sorry, I'm so sorry, baby, Sibel is missing.

My father must have known it was her. He must have known she would find out about this baby through the resilient chain of gossip still powerful decades later. He must have known she couldn't have walked very far, because she would want to feed me.

My father found Refika across the street at Nathan's Famous Hot Dogs, where she had me in her lap while she used a plastic fork and knife to cut the hot dogs into baby-bite-sized nubs. She calmly told my father that she'd come to see him.

Now my mother unpeels the sticky top off her orange disinfectant wipes and hands one to my grandmother, who says thank you, and they're both wiping their hands, in sync, but I'm annoyed. Of course they never told me I was kidnapped as a baby. I calmly ask my mother what my father felt, and she's angry.

He thought she was crazy, Sibel. Don't you? She *took* you. You can't just take a baby.

I'm quiet. I accept the orange wipe my grandmother now hands me. My father—I am not sure I will ever know what happened between him and Refika. He's the pulsing black hole I am looking for, still.

Now my grandmother wants to say something. Alara starts to shift in the hospital bed, and the three of us look at her.

Long ago, my grandmother says, I knew that Refika would do this. That she would take you back.

Take me back? I ask her. You mean take me?

Sorry, my grandmother says. I'm so sorry. I'm getting very confused.

Alara rubs her eyes with her fists and stares, unfocused and still asleep, at me.

Sometimes, my grandmother says, Refika comes to visit me at night. We talk. I took my baby back.

She looks very proud. My mother looks like she wants to murder me.

I remember now, Sibel. I went to her apartment, right after Menderes—you know his plane crashed?—and I took my baby back.

# Part IV

# I.

Aunt Pinar comes to the hospital bearing evil eyes and pastries. Uncle Yılmaz comes with Dilek, whose eyes are red and puffy. I want to pull Dilek aside, but there is too much happening, so I text her to tell her she shouldn't take the blame. I'm ready. She reads my text instantly but continues crying, and I'm not sure why she replies with a flying bat emoji. My cousin Demir comes next, complaining of traffic. Deniz comes bearing white roses. My grandmother gets up to rip the curtains open, then she arranges the stems in a vase. We drag plastic chairs in from other rooms and eat around Alara, who wakes up and smiles.

I'm sent to get my grandmother's medicine, as well as a fresh change of clothing. My grandmother, who ignored my gentle points about how there is no way Refika comes to visit her at night when I've never heard it and am a very light sleeper, also wants me to bring some cleaning supplies back to the hospital. The day is hot and dry outside, and I walk uphill, smoking my first cigarette in hours, until I reach the metro. I have some hospital snacks in my pockets to give to the woman and her three children, but when I get to the washing machine store, they're not there. Her quilt is there, pink and gray with dirt, but not her, nor her children. I walk into the washing machine store to ask the man and woman behind the counter, who look like they were just flirting, where she is, and the woman crosses her arms, and the man looks at her, and they smirk. Is it my accent? I ask them. Are you looking at me like I'm crazy because of my accent? They shake their heads no, and the man takes my elbow and leads me back out onto the street. Okay. I bat his hand off. I have places to be anyway.

When I get to my grandmother's, it smells different—musty. Dust is a combination of pollen, dead skin, and disintegrated human and animal hair, and I think I can smell each ingredient, but maybe this is only because we've been away for two days. I haven't watched a soap opera or the news in two days. The only time I left the hospital was to vote in the election. I went with my grandmother, and my mother went when we returned. Sure enough, the prime minister is now president, surprising no one. Maybe it is me who smells different. The apartment is the same. The same since my father first began speaking to his mother, when he found out who she was. I'm worried about her. Phlegm is supposed to be a stable humor, but now she's excitable, choleric. But no. No. This is not about the humors, this is about having Refika in her life again. This is about having a disease that is proven scientifically to intensify when she is stressed. She has been taking each pill I give her four times a day with diligent submissiveness, but who will make sure she takes them when I'm gone? I loot through my grandmother's clothes, looking for her clean nightgown and her lilac sweater set. Her clothes smell like bar soap and lavender. I feel something textured in the stack of nightgowns in my grandmother's drawer: a pink organza jewelry bag, tied at the top with string. I shake the bag out into my palm, and I'm suddenly holding something that looks like beef jerky. It's brown, dried and crooked, gnarled enough to look like a tiny walking stick.

My father's umbilical cord.

I turn the crunchy-looking cord around in my hands for some time. I'm not sure how long it takes for me to place the dried cord on my tongue.


LATER THAT NIGHT, WHILE MY MOTHER AND GRAND-mother are downstairs in the hospital cafeteria getting more tea, Alara wakes up. She needs to read what happened with the election and asks me for the hospital Wi-Fi. She's furious. She can't believe she wasn't able to vote but she bets the president rigged the election anyway. Then she says that she's proud of me.

I'm going to see Cooper tomorrow, I tell her.

Hmm, Alara says. She looks at her phone. Who is "Young Turk #3"? She cross-references pictures of him on Facebook. Oh, I met him at the party.

She puts her phone down and looks at me. I'm still proud, she says. She points at the tube in her arm feeding her liquid proteins and carbs. There are calories in this tube, she says. But they won't tell me how many. Plus the Turkish calories are, what, listed per gram, right? Per hundred grams, not per serving? K-cals. What do you know about those?

I shake my head and Alara pouts. She has to know that I won't indulge her, even if I think discussing her obsessive eating calculations may force her to read the script of her brain, and the patterns it has forced her body to repeat. I want to tell her that every single woman I know has some form of body dysmorphia. I've never met a woman who unconditionally loved her own body, but I don't know if hearing this will help Alara. I have my period again, the third time this summer, and I go to the hospital bathroom to change my tampon. I'm pulling down my jeans and have to make sure my father's cord doesn't slide out of my back pocket. Since my period started yesterday, the pain in my head is sharp and throbbing, and there's a bloat to my belly that could have to do with menstruation, but I'm not sure. My grandmother told me this morning that I should glug whole milk or shovel fresh yogurt down my throat to make period pain go away, but I told her that was silly, and that we can't depend on food as a treatment for every ailment. She clicked her tongue. She was taking her daily dose of dopamine with a glass of water. She now refuses to take the medication that comes in a prefilled syringe. She told me at least three more times to drink whole milk, and Trota would have approved of this remedy, but I have begun to resist anything that reduces the body to private diagnosis and taboo.

Or did I trade my life for my grandmother's? For selfish reasons. By visiting Refika.

WHEN I COME BACK FROM THE BATHROOM, ALARA TELLS me she has to confess something.

I didn't know when to tell you, she begins, but Cooper, he knows about Refika. He told me at Dilek's party. He practically got on his knees all guilty. He knows everything. First, Grandma told him about the earthquake, about Refika taking Baba, you know. She told him the very first week you were here, after the bomb threat at Sultanahmet. You know how she told him? She told Dilek first, had her write it all down in English, and then she handed the piece of paper to him. Then our grandmother gives him Refika's *address*, and she says, go see her, go make sure she forgives Sibel, please. And so, off trots your valiant knight to pass along this message to Refika. Can you believe that? I think it's a little invasive, don't you? Anyway, he's the one who told Refika that you'd be there, at the cemetery, because apparently, Refika didn't believe that you were grieving your father, she thought you were a disrespectful little shit. And since obviously you were not at the cemetery often, Cooper was freaking out, apparently, trying to get you to go, trying to keep his promise to both Refika and your grandmother. He kept updating Refika. He kept telling her this will be the day, this will be the day she comes. So she kept going to the cemetery, or something. I think maybe it made him hate you, don't you? I'd hate you. I'd be driven nuts.

Alara snorts. Nobody cares if I was there, of course. She looks at her phone and pouts.

THE BREEZE HAS PICKED UP AND CARRIES THE SMELL OF salt and fish. I recognize Cooper's blond head looking out at the water. When I come closer to him, standing on the old ferry dock in Bebek, I see that it's not the water he's watching but the mussel-encrusted wooden dock. I'm not feeling like blood anymore. I'm phlegm. I'm old and wise and sentimental. I tap Cooper's shoulder and he turns to face me and we spend a few minutes in a hug before we break. He looks different. His face is tanned and his hair blonder, but the lines on his forehead look deep. He's not wearing his hospital ID today but he is in his favorite outfit: blue jeans and his grandfather's white button-up shirt from the sixties that remarkably has no holes or tears. The Bosphorus is calm tonight, and the violet-and-orange sky makes the water look like molten silver. Men are lined up along the shore fishing. Cooper says he wants to fish, too, and thinks he can borrow a fishing rod from someone at work. He asks if he ever told me that his grandfather used to fish, and always diligently labeled his catch with weight and type before storing the frozen fish bundles in the freezer. I tell him I didn't know this and ask if this was his grandfather who was in Vietnam while his grandmother was in Turkey. The one who reminded him of my grandfather the eye doctor.

Yes, Cooper says. That's him.

We walk to a café we like and find seats near a couple holding hands over the table. Cooper says Georgia has a seemingly more Soviet bent, unlike Turkey, but he's not sure if many Georgians would agree with this opinion. He says he prefers Turkey, but maybe because he was introduced to the country in an emotional manner. Through me, he says simply. He apologizes for not speaking to me at Dilek's; he was only unsure of what kind of person he should be. He admits, yes, he should be himself, but himself interacting with another person—me—confused him. Plus, he could no longer hold in how he met with Refika. And it is difficult for him to admit to jealousy, especially when he spent not just the party, but also the days leading up to the party overanalyzing whether it was really me who wanted to break up, and did that mean I wanted to hook up with someone else? And did he really believe, after all these years, that Deniz and I were just friends? I interrupt to say that hooking up with other people wasn't the reason at all, plus I was confused, too, and I'm not entirely sure it was me who initiated this breakup, and he looks like he's about to argue with me before he laughs, and I laugh too, because I've been talking fast and confused, and we agree that perhaps the ambiguous and nebulous feeling we both have about who instigated our breakup is not the point. Then I'm silent and maybe I look glum, because he clarifies that nothing is going on with Esra—she only wanted his opinion on the recent text messages between her and her boyfriend, who had been acting very distant lately.

Jonathan, he admits, is unbearable, but, he adds, he couldn't say this to his face. He also mentions that Batumi, where my father's family is from, is a casino city now. I say maybe the country needed a trashy beach town. Maybe Batumi was its only city on the Black Sea that could provide such a service, and once you provide such a service your life is chained to its continuation, its production, because otherwise the city would have no money, no food. He agrees with me, but because he knows I don't necessarily feel a pulsing connection to Batumi, he mentions the American feeling of wanting roots, and that because my roots are in Turkey, I don't look for farther roots, like Georgia. It doesn't mean as much for you, he says, but for Dilek, for example, that Macedonian root means everything.

I'm surprised. I think he's right.

And it helped your father, Cooper says, knowing about his mother. He was angry at first, but he came to America with that anger and it helped him, I think.

I'm listening, but I don't think my father channeled his anger very wisely.

And I know you, Cooper continues. He's speaking with a quiet voice, and reaches to take my hand, but I'm not sure what he means by knowing. Does he know that I'm carrying my father's knotted cord around, sometimes in my bag's secret zippered compartment where it hits up against my box of cigarettes to summon a soft, pulsing beat as I march around Istanbul? No. He says he knows I do the same thing as my father did. I keep things in. Your grandmother and Refika, he says, I think they wanted to break the cycle. I pull my hand out of Cooper's and look for my cigarettes. I light one in front of him, and he smiles.

I guess I have no right to tell you not to, he admits.

Yup, I say.

How is Alara? Cooper asks.

She's okay. They're discharging her tomorrow. It's my fault, obviously, that she's this way.

That's silly, he says.

Maybe, I say.

Cooper looks pained to say something. He's ripping up his napkin into tiny pieces, something he rarely does, something he says is wasteful, but he seems to decide it is the right time to tell me that I create solutions in my head to scenarios that are difficult for the emotional cortex in my brain to process. Cooper concludes, gently, that this is similar to the bomb threat.

In our first week here, Cooper and I were in Sultanahmet, seeing Ayasofya. I was happy that day. I had hoped that Cooper, who blended in at the tourist spaces, would not feel too alien in Turkey, and as a result would not hate the place so much. We were leaving the museum when we saw police flood the square.

I wasn't afraid, I explain to Cooper now. I wasn't anxious. I was accepting the possibility that I could die there. I was okay with it.

Well, Cooper says, okay, what I mean is that after that day, no one could reach you. Just the night before, remember? That was just the night you finally told me about what really happened at the funeral. You were healing.

No, I say, I had to tell you because you were here, in Istanbul, and you could find out. I wasn't healing. And there's a big difference, I say, between depression, grief, and hardship. A difference, too, between melancholy and depression. Those with black bile aren't necessarily suffering. Like me, I'm not suffering. Some people even thought that black-bile people were closest to God. They just have a different disposition. It's like the Turkish word I told you about, the untranslatable one, *hüzün*.

But Cooper is not moved by black bile. He looks at me sadly. You remember you asked me, he says, your face was calm, and hopeful, and you said, maybe there will be one.

Well, I say, annoyed, I figured there really could be one. Terrorism is bred, not born out of nowhere. People are fucking angry about the state of things. I wasn't hoping there would be a bomb.

I know what you want to hear, Sibel. You want to be told your father died when you could have prevented it. You could have called the ambulance right away. You could have saved him.

I must look like I've been slapped, because he apologizes immediately. He's right.

I'm not saying you could have prevented it, Sibel. I'm not. You can never know with these things. I'm sorry I got so involved, with Refika. I couldn't say no to your grandmother. And then I got too curious, hell-bent, I guess, on helping.

When I stood still in front of the museum, watching the chaos unfold across the square, I looked at Cooper tugging at my arm to get us moving and instead of breaking down, instead of panicking, running, getting to safety or helping, I felt my first calm in weeks. I realized that if I did blow up, I wouldn't have to be buried like Baba. That night I fell into the four humors. Cooper had just left, and I was in my favorite nook of my grandmother's couch. It was my first Google search that led me to a detailed, informational page sourced from the 1500s on how to cure a headache by dispelling blood from your body. I wanted to, so badly, because I couldn't find anything sacred. I terrified myself. I liked the descriptions of the way patients felt better after getting bled out, and I wanted to try, too. To bloodlet myself. But as I was reading, carefully and hungrily, my grandmother plopped down next to me and turned the volume all the way up on the television, and she told me how excited she was for us to watch her favorite soap operas together this summer. She began to list the ones she wanted to rewatch with me. I was shaking, but she didn't see. I closed the book and smiled. I said, Me too.

I don't tell Cooper this. I never wanted him to bear this responsibility. The sky is now dark blue and purple. Puffs of smoke rise from the cargo ships hailing from Russia. We stand and walk to a bus stop next to the water, and Cooper hugs me. I'm about to kiss him. I'm so close. His skin smells like city and sweat, and it makes me sad to think of all the people who are close to kissing but never will. The mouth is a powerful organ, essential for liquid consumption, purging, essential for opening. I'm opening, still.

Don't cry, Sibel. Please.

Okay, I say. Thank you.


IN THE FEW STORIES MY FATHER DID TELL ME, HE WAS AL-ways disguised. Always cloaked beneath someone else's story, usually my mother's. For example, they once met the general responsible for the coup. It was a fall evening and the air was damp, two weeks before the military would take over the government. She was with her friends at a fish restaurant by the water to celebrate Uncle Yılmaz's birthday. They had saved up for this night. Then they saw the general surrounded by his men, among them colonels and commanders and their wives. She walked up to General Evren and asked for a favor. The general looked up slowly from his plate of sea bass. Gulls soared through the sky and on the water were cargo ships as large as mountains. My mother faced the seated general, and she lied to him. She said there was nothing she admired more than his leadership. The whole time she spoke, her friends back at her table—socialists; according to the military, pigs and terrorists—watched my mother in awe while they tore off pieces of bread to dunk into meze. They were mentally prepared to flee the restaurant, for in Uncle Yılmaz's pockets were banned weapons: a gun heavy against his thigh, and a knife taped to his shin. As my mother spoke to General Evren, the colonel beside him watched her friends, his elbows on the white tablecloth, his eyes tracking their every movement: a glass raised to sip, a knife slicing fish, a cigarette ashed. My mother only wanted to ask the general if he would mind taking a photograph of her and her friends.

General Evren said yes, he would take a photograph. She had a lovely nose, one that seemed very European, French. The black waves that framed her face moved, as if a miniature earthquake below her feet took place just for her, as she laughed at his compliment and handed him the film camera.

The general stood to take the photograph, a photograph I now have, decades later. It's six of them. The only other woman is Dilek's mother, Aunt Sevgi, who cocks her head at the camera, her lips around the butt of a cigarette. My uncle's there, his hand on my mother's forearm as she leans over her seated friends. My father sits at the table, too. He's in a turtleneck. He's the smallest man in the group.

ALARA GETS BETTER AND IS ALLOWED TO COME HOME with us. We bring her favorite outfit—she was precise in her request, even telling us which pair of underwear she wanted, an electric-blue lace thong, which my grandmother instructed me to hand-wash, iron, and fold last night. My mom acts as a railing on which Alara can balance as I kneel at her feet and guide her legs into the lace. We ignore how they are loose on her ass and that her legs are white against the neon because she's been hiding them in large, flowy pants all summer. She thanks us, and her body propels itself forward, determined to go outdoors.

MY GRANDMOTHER, AFTER UNLOCKING THE DOOR WITH her keys, kicks her shoes off and clicks on the television.

It's been too long, Sibel, she says, and sinks into the couch to watch a soap opera. She refuses to watch the news now after the election. This one is about a poor girl in love with a rich boy, and the boy's mother—all dolled up in heels and silk dresses just to drink cappuccinos with friends—always talks shit about her son's romantic interest, but when he comes home she's all kisses and praise, she would never do anything to hurt her son, who also looks fabulous and generally makes the right choices. My mother's laughing, and I'm confused because she always says she left Turkey because of the women telling her all the things she wasn't allowed to do.

On screen, the handsome man's mother is gossiping to her

friends about the poor neighborhood the girl lives in. My mother watches intently and turns to my grandmother.

Do you remember, my mother says, how Refika was so distrustful of me because of my mother, how she got a hysterectomy. A poor girl from Bolu, she had said to him, if she can't cook well she can't do anything.

She said you would lower the IQ of my grandchildren, my grandmother fills in, and they cackle like hyenas. My mother's excited now. Finally she gets to talk shit about this woman. Now she's on about how she invited Refika to her wedding, only because she was curious about the emotional power she might have. Although Refika never replied to the wedding invitation, she did buy my mother a beautiful wooden salad bowl and a matching set of tongs with sad women's faces carved into the handles. A very insulting gift. Only gold would have been appropriate. Refika left the gift at the door of my grandmother's apartment, although no one is sure who let her into the building. No one is sure where this salad bowl even is. Or if Refika was resolute in her decision to leave the gift without knocking, without hesitating, or whether it took her weeks of debate.

But my grandmother, who was just eagerly discussing this salad bowl, and how she even used it once or twice, falls silent. My mother sits next to her, takes my grandmother's pulse, and asks us if we can boil some water for tea. Alara and I look at each other.

Stay, I tell Alara.

I go to the kitchen and begin boiling water for white rice and tea, and chopping up tomatoes and cucumbers for a salad. I'm measuring a tablespoon of olive oil when Alara wanders in to inspect the rice.

You know, Alara says, you don't have to do all this.

I can make it, I say.

What's the latest on your headaches?

I've googled everything, Alara. I don't know what else it can be.

And what, you think it's still just, what, black bile? Come on, Sibel. Something else could be going on. Something serious.

We'll find out, I say.

That's it, isn't it? You don't want to know what it is. If it's something worse.

Please, I say, let me just make this rice for you?

Fine. Did you ask her why she told Cooper? About Refika?

I can't ask her that, I say, and Alara nods.


BEFORE DINNER, MY GRANDMOTHER HANGS UP MORE EVIL eyes in her bedroom. She hammers a nail into the wall, then she hangs the eye by its blue string. When I ask her why she's hanging them up now, she replies that evil cannot live in the presence of evil. When I ask to help her, she hides the hammer under her arm and shoos me out of the room. I stay in the doorframe. I ask her, do you feel dread? Doom? She invites me back into the room to tell me about the first time she came to America to see me, a baby, in Bay Ridge. My mother floats in and crosses her arms. My grandmother is telling a story of how a woman came over once to take me away, but she's calling this woman by her own name, Nermin, and I'm standing there suddenly scooped out. My mother glares at me. My grandmother is confusing herself with Refika. Delusion number two, or is it three, or four? Her hand holding the hammer shakes as she speaks. I take the hammer and hold her hand.

THE FOUR HUMORS + 273

I'm going to lie down, she says. We help her to her bed, shut the curtains, and bring her a glass of water. I put today's crossword on her nightstand in case she wakes up bored. My mother waits until my grandmother's door is closed to grab me by the arm.

She's a jealous, bitter woman, my mother says. That doesn't excuse her behavior.

That's not it, I say, feeling defensive. Not it at all.

You've put your grandmother in her grave, are you happy? You want to make her sick? Don't you see how she's getting worse? Losing her grip on reality?

No. No, I'm trying to help, Mommy.

You're telling me Refika's your priority now? What? Because she wears the face of suffering? Because of her throat? Her loss? My mother is advancing on me, and I am a little nervous. She is powerful, my mother. After Alara pushed Refika and she was on her back like a beetle sunken on the snowy floor, my mother stood over her, held Albina back, and threatened Refika, commanding her to stay on the ground until she vowed to never touch her daughters. It was insane.

She's not my priority, I say. I don't even like her.

You need to tell that woman to fuck off, Sibel.


I plan to go to Refika's one last time. I'm going to confront her like my mother wants. It's early, about seven a.m., and my mother is helping my grandmother set the table for breakfast. My grandmother is herself again. She even told me to fix my eyebrows. When she leaves the room, I help my mother take the honey jar, the toasted bread, and the tiny plates full of different cheeses off the tray. I ask my mother if she'd like to come with me to Refika's.

I may as well drive you there, she says venomously. My mother has managed to commandeer her brother's car for the entirety of her time here—he can take the bus to work, he's still a socialist anyway, she says. She sticks a teaspoon in the honey jar with a surprising amount of force.

Are you going to tell them where we're going? I ask. Alara is still sleeping and my grandmother is in the bathroom putting in her teeth.

Let's say we're going to get some tomatoes. I think your grandmother is running low.

Okay, tomatoes.

We slip out quickly and slide into the car like spies. I tell my mother this and she starts driving, looking weary but pleased. I would have a made a great spy, she says as we pass the cemetery, and I say, Me too. She snorts. We merge onto Barbaros Boulevard, named after Hayrettin Barbarossa, the famous redheaded pirate who was a Turk. Turks love reminding Westerners of the famous people who squeezed into the margins of the Western canon, people who were really Turks. I try to think of others but really, there are not many.

My mother pulls up in front of the pink apartment building. I open the car door, and she says she's going to the pharmacy to pick up my grandmother's medicine, but she'll meet me here in an hour. That's how long it'll take, right? she asks, innocently.

You're not coming in?

Oh no, no. Why don't you just meet me back at your grandmother's. I'll tell them you went on a walk. Come on, she says, suddenly impatient, shut the door.

I do as I'm told. I wave goodbye to her as she pulls away. A truck waiting behind her is labeled the world's largest luxury truck, but it looks like a normal truck to me.

ALBINA OPENS THE DOOR. SHE HAS AN APRON TIED AROUND her waist, and she apologizes for the oil on her hands as she kisses me on both cheeks. She's skinning eggplants. She leads me by the hand into the kitchen to show me how she peels strips off the eggplant's skin to create a zebra effect.

This way, Albina says, there will be both a crunchy texture to the eggplant, and a squishy skinless texture in the same bite.

The eggplant skin is precious to me, I say. It has nicotine in it.

Albina slices open the eggplant bellies and stuffs them with hot rice and currants. I stir the tomato sauce that will be spread over the blistered purple skin. Her face looks so giddy, I don't want to tell her that I can't be in the kitchen right now, that I have matters to attend to, that I am here to tell her employer that our affair must end. And I'm worried Albina will want to hypnotize me, like she promised on that first day. But I don't know what Albina thinks about our family and I don't know why she believes in all this medical garbage or why I believe in medical garbage too. I believed it, that I was choler at the party, that I was phlegm when I found out about Cooper and Refika. I believe it still. But I'm seeing now that I'm full of all four humors, and my excess—any excess is not dangerous or fatal.

Albina slides the tray of eggplant bellies into the oven and hands me a plate of cookies to take out to the balcony. I wash my hands and go outside, where Refika, sitting in one of the wooden chairs on a green cushion, looks out at the street, and the whole time I'm thinking about what to tell her and whether I should. I'm worried I will tell Refika things about myself when it is things about my father I want to hear, things about her, like whether she ate a hot dog at Nathan's, too. Maybe she is the reason I love hot dogs. I'm alone with Refika for what feels like a long time, made even longer because there's nothing for me to do. I eat the full plate of hard cookies Albina had me bring outside, its crumbs constellating on my chest.

Albina finally joins us on the balcony and tells me to get comfortable. Why are you looking so bunched up? she asks, and only then does she reveal that she is, in fact, going to hypnotize me today.

Are you kidding me? I ask.

It's very good for you. We talked about this, Sibel.

I already feel pretty hypnotized.

Don't bullshit her, Sibel, Refika says.

Here? On the balcony? Isn't that dangerous?

Why would it be dangerous? Refika asks.

What if I jump off?

This girl is just as ridiculous as I thought, Refika says, but Albina gives her a stern look. I'm about to get up and run home when Refika grabs my hand. She says she knows how guilt can take a body captive. Is that a threat, I say, but she shushes me. I allow Albina to slide a pillow behind my back. Then it's Albina's voice coming in. I close my eyes like Albina tells me to.

I feel far away, I say.

No, no, you don't, Refika says. We haven't even started yet.

But as Albina counts down from ten the dissolve starts, quicker than I had expected. I fall into what feels like a light hallucination. Each image Albina summons leads to my mind painting a mural.

Albina makes me find my inner child, and my ten-year-old self appears in a tie-dye shirt, my breasts coming in like two sand piles built by ants. My younger self smiles, revealing braces with red and green rubber bands, because I used to pretend to celebrate Christmas. I go to the funeral of my best friend and when I look in the casket it is me, dead. The Sibel who smokes is lying flat in a glass coffin. She's holding blue flowers. She has a hole in her throat. Her lips are painted murky red, a red drawn from my grandmother's blood. It is period blood, which I do not find strange, and I want to touch them. I want to bring my own lips to hers.

I'm in a bare, stark room where I meet the me who dies from lung cancer and I have to confront her. I have to ask her why she did this to me. She has a very dramatic personality. She kicks and screams and rolls her giant brown eyes, and when I compliment her, I tell her she is pretty, but that we will no longer be pretty if she keeps this up. She lights a cigarette and sucks it into her lungs before creeping up close to me and digging the tip deep into my arm. I smell the hairs burning. I think she is Satan exiled from paradise for rebelling, because she's acting like a haughty cartoon character. And then the ten-year-old Sibel with braces and nine birds on her shoulder is dancing alone in a room with big balloons hitting against the ceiling.

Albina's voice, a shepherd, floats in to ask me what I see now, having said goodbye to my past self.

Now I'm on a boat in the Aegean with my friends from home, and I'm getting my hair done, but I think it's during World War I, and we're near Çanakkale. I think we know the war is going on, but we are calm here in the water, and then I feel guilty.

A lot of people died, I add. The water is full of dead bodies.

Do you think about this often? Albina asks.

Yes.

Is it your responsibility? These deaths?

I'm not sure.

Do you want to be sure?

No.

What do you see now?

Now I'm floating in water. The sea is clear and green. There is no one but me for miles.

Why don't you get out of the sea, Sibel?

Okay.

What do you see?

I see a sun, a bed, a mother, a sister, windows, many small windows on a large blue wall, a jar of face cream, the kind that is supposed to make people young again, the smell of food in the kitchen, and when I open the door to the kitchen they are all there, even the ones who I'd thought were missing.

I open my eyes.

Oh no, Albina says, panicking. You have to close your eyes.

But Refika's snapped back into her shrewd stare, and I wonder if I have done what I wanted to at Dilek's party: gone to hell and back. No. I'm still in hell, and Refika is the devil. I haven't paid her price yet. I haven't brought my grandmother here.

I think I'll go, I announce, and I try to stand, but Refika, who's been holding my hand, pulls me back. A leaf is caught in a gust of wind and jerks around. I blink out at the world beyond the balcony. It is a beautiful day, and I am not so upset to be back in it. We're still holding hands but I have to get back to my grandmother, my sister. I have to help them.

Refika looks at Albina, who hesitates before leaving us alone on the balcony.

You didn't keep your end of the bargain, Sibel.

I tell her my grandmother cannot take visitors. It's my duty to help her, I explain. And she is not doing well.

How interesting, she says. I spoke to her on the phone yesterday. Or did you not know?

Oh, I say. I know Refika is lying, but she says nothing else. There's a thick black hair on her chin. Was that always there? Did it grow in the past few weeks? Does Albina usually pluck it out?

I'll ask her, then, I venture, when I get home.

Do you know a New Jersey? Refika asks me suddenly.

Well, I say, New Jersey is next to New York, and is not exactly remarkable.

Refika says she had an old friend there. Then she laughs. My great-aunt keeps laughing until her throat catches.

She moved from here to New Jersey? I ask.

Refika stuffs her swollen feet into plastic slippers and carefully begins to stand. But she's not walking to me, only past me, into the living room, into the hallway, and towards what I assume is her bedroom. I follow her.

Can I ask you, I venture, do you know why my father never forgave you?

She doesn't answer. Albina is nowhere to be found. Her slippers are by the front door, and the plastic is worn, a deep gray indent on each heel. I help Refika open the door to her bedroom, where there's a full mattress with a noticeable depression, the size of her body, and I'm about to help her sit in her wooden vanity chair when I freeze. The walls have so many framed photographs, I can't even tell what color the walls are painted. Photographs of me and Alara. Photographs of my father at five, my father at fifteen, my father graduating from high school, my father smoking a cigarette. In a headshot of Refika as a young woman, she wears a curved, almost wicked smile, and her shaped eyebrows arc at such an angle as to tell you she was not surprised, not scheming, but simply aware of your awaiting suffering. She does not have cancer yet, and her throat is whole and long. I find her beautiful. There is even a photograph of my grandmother marrying the eye doctor, one I haven't seen before, where the eye doctor's sisters loom in the background looking generally happy and supportive. There are no photographs of my mother. Refika settles into her chair at the vanity, where another scalloped-edge black-and-white photograph of the eye doctor and my grandmother is fitted into a frame. That was after your father was born, Refika says, in English, accented, but still English. I feel smacked in the head. Since when do you know English? I ask her. Sit down, Refika says. I was a math teacher, of course I knew some English. I sit down, but I don't see how being a math teacher at a school in Istanbul that wasn't American or British means knowing English. Her telling is not like my grandmother's. She pauses often, but not due to distress, and for long periods of time when I hear my heart racing, my blood filling my stomach, my stomach full of buttery cookies, my head, which is thinking too hard, thinking about what it means to take care of a family or a child or a sister or a friend, my hands, which are shaking—my body, which fills with blood to tell me it's working. It's working really well despite whatever is wrong in there. I know this now. I don't have a body. I am a body.

REFIKA HAD HER FIRST CIGARETTE THE SAME DAY MY FA-
ther went missing. It was 1971, the year the second coup broke
out and the military court began the criminal trial of three boys,
boys who would be hung within one year, and Refika, who knew
her son to be impressionable, had been worried about his future
for months now. Refika was not a superstitious person, but each
day she diligently read her coffee grounds, and that morning she'd
been startled to see an old woman's face in the sludge. Although
the woman had no nose, no hair, and a coiled brown snake in
place of a throat, she looked deeply familiar to Refika. It was as if
she were a woman Refika once knew.

She assumed this woman was set to destroy her son's life.

Refika marched from the girls' school where she taught mathematics to my father's school, two neighborhoods over. She took
the same route every day, picking him up at school despite recognizing that my father, a faint gray mustache already on his upper
lip, was embarrassed by her. He was thirteen years old—early, she
thought, for puberty—and she wanted to preserve him. She did
not know how to raise a son in this new Turkey. A few weeks earlier, the military had delivered the prime minister an ultimatum:

armed engagement, should he not step down. He resigned after a three-hour meeting with parliament. My father asked her many questions about communism, about America's involvement in Turkey, socialism, and the Soviet Union, which Refika always answered in a steady tone. She aimed to steer him towards Atatürk, and away from Russia.

That day, after seeing the woman in her coffee grounds, Refika dodged workers striking at a cement factory, workers striking at a fur company, and workers striking at a taxi stand before reaching Taksim. But he did not spill out the school's doors as usual. Refika was patient. Surely, her son would join her outside at any moment and they'd walk home together as usual. He did occasionally take his time to pack up his bag or talk with friends. But when a crowd of boys in uniform strutted out of the school doors, holding up banners and chanting for the U.S. Sixth Fleet to go home, Refika's heart began to pound, the blood rushed to her face, a heated feeling she was always afraid of, and she elbowed her way through the students and into the school.

She was nearing the gymnasium when a woman in green heels stopped her. The woman was short, with big, low breasts, and she seemed amused by Refika—an amusement the woman later confessed was wildly attractive. Refika's impulsiveness, her conviction, made this woman feel free.

Yes, she was a teacher here, and yes, she knew her son, and yes, he was very intelligent, a curious child, he always wants to get to the root of things, the teacher said, and Refika snorted, she even rolled her eyes, which made the teacher pause and look hard at Refika's face.

Is that a burn? the teacher asked.

Refika blushed. She explained it's only red when she's emotional, and the doctor thought it should heal with time. The teacher, whose name was Meltem, startled her again by asking if she could touch her cheek. Refika stumbled. She asked why. And Meltem, she stumbled, too. She pulled her hand back, crossed her arms. She said, Sorry, I was only wondering about the texture.

Would you like a cigarette, then? Meltem asked her, and Refika paused. She had quit cigarettes.

Come, Meltem said, we'll be here. We'll find him.

So Refika said, okay, I'll have one, and they walked to the empty stairwell and they smoked and Meltem stretched her stockinged legs out on the steps, which made Refika conscious of her own legs, crossed at the ankles, and her bulby calves, and Meltem told Refika about herself, that she was from Trabzon, and had recently taken this job after her mother passed. Her family had not been in Istanbul for long. They migrated from the Black Sea only a few years ago and now lived in one of the new neighborhoods—slums, Refika thought—north of Beyoğlu. It's a miracle I'm here, teaching, Meltem said, I thought it was something I'd never do, but I studied, you know, my parents let me study instead of work like my older sisters. Meltem sucked on the cigarette each time she paused, her fingers like needles, her cigarette like a wand. Refika began to feel comfortable. They spoke of their sons. Meltem's husband worked outside of Berlin at a Mercedes factory, and her son, she explained, had been lost without a male figure. He'll come back soon, Refika said, unsure if Meltem hoped to join her husband in Berlin. Meltem said nothing, and the two women sat in silence.

You know, Meltem began, your son may be snooping out where the new American teacher lives. She's his favorite teacher.

Refika stood, worried.

No, not like that, no. Your son, she said, suddenly confused. Well, don't you know? He says he's going to study in America.

Oh, Refika said, shocked. No, he never said. Is it possible? Could he go to school there?

I think it's possible, she said. İnşallah. My son is the same age. I understand.

He's going to be a doctor, Refika said, like my baby brother. But I'd rather he stay close.

Refika straightened her dress, preparing to say goodbye. Refika loved her brother. She had always reminded herself that maybe, maybe she could learn to love her husband the same way.

What kind of doctor is he? Meltem asked.

He died.

Meltem said she was sorry. She said she could help her find the American teacher's apartment. It might be easier to find together, she said gingerly, and Refika thought about this before saying yes, yes, thank you.

They boarded the tram that would take them to Beşiktaş. Years later, Refika would attempt to describe to herself what she felt then, the feeling of paranoia balanced out by relief; support she'd never had from another person—and Meltem, who was telling her now how terrified she was by these violent demonstrations. I can't even recognize my country, Meltem said in a low whisper, and Refika agreed. This feeling took such force in Refika that she forgot, for just a few minutes, about my father, and as they stepped off the tram and began walking towards this American teacher's apartment, she did not even pause to notice what street they were on.

What is it? Meltem asked, lighting another cigarette. Have you been here before?

That day, the pharmacy was closed. Women from the neighborhood peered into the glass and knocked on the small green door and complained. How were they supposed to pick up the important things they needed?

Refika shook her head. It's nothing, she said. Then she took the teacher's hand.

REFIKA HAD MET HER HUSBAND ONLY TWICE BEFORE THEIR marriage; once, when he came over for tea after having connected her father to a new silk producer who would cut costs for his textile business. The other time for a family dinner, which Refika cooked, and wherein the decision was made. She was promptly married, but in eight years, no baby. But Hasan was a proud man, a businessman, who had persuaded Refika's parents into her hand for marriage by promising to increase her father's business revenue. By 1971, unemployment was high, and Hasan went bankrupt after a decade of poor investments. He began drinking, falling asleep in coffee shops during work hours, and avidly listening to the radio for news of what would happen to his country.

That night, Refika had found my father not at the American teacher's apartment, as Meltem had suggested, but instead at a friend's house, making banners for a leftist organization.

It's your duty to be different from us, Hasan lectured my father at the dinner table that evening. You must be educated, and dedicated to the Turkish state. With education, he continued, drunk, you will run in different circles and speak of different topics. Maybe it will be about industry and technology instead of communism and the price of milk and who married who from the neighborhood. You will do better than us.

My father listened. He was still young, Refika believed, as she stirred rice pudding for dessert. He could not have known what he was doing making anti-American banners.

My father was silent for a few moments until he asked his father whether Deniz Gezmiş knew that he could die for his cause, and was anything worth dying for? Hasan laughed. His laugh, always a rasping noise that sounded like choking, startled the street cat, who, having wandered into their apartment from the balcony, snarled up at him. Hasan kicked the cat out of the house, kicking it repeatedly. Though she thought she heard bones break, Refika kept stirring, she stirred and stirred and stirred, and my father watched her from the living room until his eyes crossed.

What Refika learned later, and, she says, too late, was that my father knew his parents stacked their personal unhappiness on his future: doctor, lawyer, engineer. Even at that young age, he was calculating the exact steps he would take to get away from his parents. Both were devout secularists, but while Refika hung up a new picture of Atatürk each time there was news of a bombing, murder, or kidnapping in Istanbul, Hasan harbored a deep admiration for the ultranationalist movement the Grey Wolves, which, I mention to Refika, is today considered a death squad. She just shrugs. Refika never knew the person my father would become, flitting between graveness and absurdity. The silliness, we think, he released because of my mother, who grew up rash and with a refusal to fit into the shape of the girl and woman the world wanted her to be.

She's the one who made him laugh, I say to Refika, but she just blinks back at me.

By the time my father was fourteen, Refika still took the tram to Beşiktaş once a month. First, she'd walk past the Tulip Apartments, where my grandmother once lived. Then she'd circle around to the pharmacy where my grandmother once worked.

Jesus, I say to Refika, you really kept busy.

I had an obsession, she says simply.

Hawks do that, you know, circle, because they're hungry. Because they eat what they find.

Sure, she replies, I was hungry.

I don't mean you're a hawk, I say, trying to walk this back, although she does have a hooked nose and leaking beady eyes.

Refika says nothing.

I'm only kidding, I repeat, but it does seem like nothing I say can hurt her. Refika wore her most comfortable heels for this hawkish expedition, and she never left home without her lips painted red. She used to bring my father with her, but he was too curious as a child—he wanted to know why this pharmacy instead of the one in their own neighborhood, was it because this pharmacy had cheaper prices? Refika was not even sure if my grandmother still worked at the pharmacy. She'd never once seen her behind the wooden cabinets. For years now, there was another girl helping Nermin's father. She'd watch the girl chew bubblegum, play with her teeth, and steal the pharmacy's fashion magazines.

Once, Refika took the bus a stop farther to the Sunshine Apartments, where my grandmother was living alone. She stood, sweating and thrilled, across the street. The light was on until nightfall, and then nothing.

It had been three weeks since Baba had gone missing. Refika wanted to call Meltem to set up a time for them to have tea, but her days were busy, and despite having friends over often on her balcony, Refika hadn't invited anyone over in weeks. Refika's father recently offered to hire Hasan, and Hasan spent each day at home, deliberating how he should be expected to respond to such an insult, and although Refika was certain her son was no longer spending time with the boys who had made the leftist banners, she was again worried. Refika had just returned home from work when she received a call from her sister, Melike, who had news to share. Nermin was making a living as a seamstress for her neighbor. She hadn't worked at the pharmacy in years.

So she's not there, her sister said to Refika. Did you hear me, sister? You can stop going. You can cut this out.

ON AN UNSEASONABLY WARM DAY IN MARCH, REFIKA MADE plans with Meltem. Her husband would be at the bar until late, and Refika, who had been in a terrific mood since she'd heard the news from her sister, decided to invite Meltem on her monthly walk around my grandmother's former life. The two women met in Maçka Democracy Park near a grove of cypress trees to take the tram. They undid the top buttons of their collared jackets to feel the warm air, damp enough to feel like the inside of a mouth. They stopped for fresh bread. They weighed tomatoes in their hands at vegetable stands before deciding, in unison, that they were too soft. These were tasks the two women often did alone, and both were thrilled that chores could have a charged meaning when performed together. Refika said, Let's walk on this street. It's my favorite.

But when Refika stopped in front of the pharmacy's glass window, she froze. My grandmother was inside with her sister. It was not clear what she was doing. She was not behind the counter, working. She was laughing. Her sister, too, laughing. She was wearing a gray dress with a Peter Pan collar, not the green dress with the buttons down her spine that Refika remembers, a dress

Refika and Melike made fun of, joking that she must have five of the same dress to wear every day. Then my grandmother looked suddenly cross, and her sister rolled her eyes. Was she arguing with her sister? About what?

What is this? Meltem asked. She laughed. Are you in love with someone else?

Refika decided to tell her—and in sharing this secret, she understood that love was trust, trust that a person is most willing to accept and receive love when vulnerable. She wanted that: to be vulnerable. She took Meltem's hand and dragged her behind a cluster of climbing bougainvilleas, where they couldn't be seen, and told her about my father.

By April, Refika had been meeting with Meltem once a week for a cigarette at the park between their two schools. It was never for long, and Refika was frustrated at the guarded intimacy that she could not breach in public. Because women did not frequent coffee shops, and because there was little privacy at either of their schools, Refika invited Meltem over to her home. She wanted to show her the balcony, bigger than other Istanbul balconies, and with the view of a sliver of the Bosphorus. School got out at three, and most nights her husband went to the bar. Recently Hasan came home drunk and possessed, convinced that the Russians were infiltrating the country and using Turks as puppets. Turks are nothing to them but guns and propaganda, don't you see? Don't you see it? Refika did see. She agreed with him, but she adamantly disapproved of the violence on both sides. She said nothing.

If Hasan were to arrive earlier, Refika decided she would calmly, pleasantly introduce Meltem as their son's hardworking history teacher who was in desperate need of advice. Meltem's husband was in Germany, and was looking for a way to have Meltem join him.

When Meltem slipped off her heels on the entrance mat, she was several inches shorter than my lean great-aunt, and Meltem followed Refika inside, where they ignored the teakettle, they ignored the smell of börek burning in the oven, they even ignored what could have been Baba, coming home from school.

Meltem would come over to their apartment only one more time, for a party that summer. Her husband had been pressing her to join him in Germany, where the government had recently begun a family reunification program. Refika doesn't know what my father heard. She doesn't know if it was him who told. She admits she was distracted at the time. And her son had a quiet step. And she wanted, only once, what she wanted.

REFIKA INTERRUPTS HER STORY BY ASKING ME TO HAND her her prayer beads. Sure, I say, and I find them on her vanity. She's silent as she begins to count the stones with her fingers. Then she tells me, with a plainness I admire, that she has decided she is simply too old to keep parts of herself hidden. And I am dying, she adds.

Allah korusun, I say, not knowing what else to say.

Don't be silly, Sibel. You know I have cancer. She leans over to pat my knee and her touch is heavy and damp, but strangely cooling. Well, she says, there was another woman, a girl. We were fifteen in Tokat, before my family moved here. My mother saw us one day, when we were walking home from school. We were best friends, always did everything together, always held hands, but then my mother saw me kiss her. She dragged me home by my ear, but held me close to her body, under her arm, so as not to attract attention in the neighborhood. I was engaged to Hasan the next week.

Oh, I say, did he know?

I'm not sure, she says with a haughty lift to her chin, as if she couldn't care less.

Well, did anyone else know? Your sister?

No, she says. Maybe my mother told Hasan. But I had to trust that they would do the best thing for me, for my protection. Protection is important, Sibel.

In May, my father was accepted to Tarsus, the prestigious American boarding school, and Refika was thrilled. Although his departure was months away, Refika began plotting the party she would throw for him on the eve of his departure. She spent that Friday evening inviting guests. She telephoned her parents, her sister, her aunts and cousins, her coworkers at school. My father, meanwhile, was completing his mathematics homework at the kitchen table. They studied extra mathematics together every evening because Refika had to inspect not only his answers, but also his handwriting. Her son had to have the best handwriting in his class.

Are you going to call her? he asked as she flipped through her phone book.

What are you talking about?

My history teacher, Mama, will you invite her?

Refika came to the table and stood behind him. She asked her son whether he really thought he'd get anywhere in life holding a pencil like a monkey. Refika took the pencil and pressed my father's thumb to his forefinger, enough to make the blood in his skin show.

My handwriting will improve, my father said.

İnşallah, Refika said.

He stared at her. His beard and mustache grew fast now, and he had to shave every day.

She's meant a lot to you, right? Refika asked. Meltem?

My father was silent. Who was he protecting? What was his idea of what a good person should do?

Baba will be here, though, my father said.

Refika nodded.

My father picked up her pack of cigarettes, which she had begun to buy herself.

Let me have one?

Okay, Refika said, although wary, and she watched him pack up his schoolbag and get ready to join his friends. As he was leaving, he said something about an American film at the movie theater, and it took a few minutes for Refika to remember that the movie theater had closed yesterday because of a demonstration last week. The trial was over, and Deniz Gezmiş and the two other boys from the People's Liberation Army of Turkey had been hanged. She tried to call after her son from the balcony, but he had already descended the hill, whistling, and whistling at night could summon the devil. Refika paced her apartment, unsure what to do. Finally she sat down and flipped through a magazine she had bought at the pharmacy in her own neighborhood the other day. She needed a new portrait of Atatürk. It could go anywhere. It did not even need to be framed.

THE PARTY WAS IN THE EVENING OF A WET SUMMER DAY. Refika forbade any talk of protests, bombings, murders, kidnappings, arrests, or mutilations. Melike and her husband brought their three children, and Safiye and her husband came, their business about to shutter. Hasan had been placed on leave a few weeks earlier, and ignoring Refika's wish for an apolitical evening, had gathered a group of men in the corner to listen to the radio. Aunts, cousins, uncles, and neighbors—everyone else was sitting and standing and drinking tea and raki in the living room. Melike complained to her mother that her husband had promised not to engage with politics tonight, and look at him now, but Safiye batted her off. Let him do what he wants, Safiye said, elbowing her way towards Baba. Safiye had a gift for my father: a gold coin engraved with Atatürk's face. Safiye was pinning the coin onto his lapel and answered the question he'd been asking all week: How will we pay the tuition? The money, Safiye answered, is from the eye doctor's savings. My father had heard of his uncle the eye doctor. He'd heard he had a wife, a wife he'd never met, and he asked his grandmother, What about his wife, is the money not hers? The money is yours, baby, Safiye said, and she secured the bust of Atatürk on his lapel.

When a song about seeing the Bosphorus for the first time began on the record player, Safiye had to excuse herself from the crowd to sit on a stool in the kitchen. Refika was agitated. She needed a distraction. She followed her mother.

Why are you crying, Mama?

This was your brother's favorite song, baby.

Refika called for her sister and they calmed their mother down, they said, May Allah look over his soul, he is okay, look at his beautiful son here, look at the happy life he will have, and Refika felt her flush going, she felt something rattling her. Guilt? I ask her now in her bedroom. No, Refika says, defensive—and she lit another cigarette, accidentally ashing it in her mother's hair, apologizing, apologizing again, but her mother just stared at her and didn't say a word. Refika was minutes away, she says, from inviting Nermin and ripping open the careful seams she had sewn around her motherhood, only the doorbell rang.

It was Meltem. She wore a green dress and kissed Refika on both cheeks; Refika, who was trying, still, to compose her face, twist it into her best red-lipped smile. And Refika says she remains unsure what exactly happened in that moment. She was thinking of her sister-in-law. She was thinking of her dead brother. She was thinking of her baby boy who would leave Istanbul by bus the next day, and she did not know if something was apparent on their faces or their bodies, but the whole room stopped buzzing, the music kept playing, and Safiye, who had only just got back on her feet, stared at Hasan—the whole room, actually, stared at Hasan, who was standing in the middle of the living room, inhaling a cigarette with slow fury. He was tapping his foot, smiling at Refika and Meltem like a madman, and my father—he was always watching, wasn't he?—my father stood up and walked towards his father, and at the moment my father reached his side, Hasan told his wife, and his guests, that it was getting so late, and this party, unfortunately, was over.

THE NEXT MORNING, MY FATHER WAS TO LEAVE EARLY TO catch his bus across Turkey. Hasan would drop him off at the station after eating Refika's renowned menemen, my father's favorite. But there was no breakfast prepared.

I want to say goodbye to her, my father said.

Your mother is sick, Hasan said, don't worry about her.

I want to say bye, my father repeated, raising his voice, and he attempted to break through the wall Hasan had made with his body, but it would not have worked, my father would not have been able to get through, small and short as he was, and it did not help when Hasan began to yank my father by the soft cartilage of his ear, out the door and into the stairwell.

REFIKA WENT TO TEACH THE NEXT DAY, DESPITE HAVING two black eyes, a bruise on her throat in the shape of clenched fingers, and a dislocated shoulder. She taught her morning mathematics class for a total of ten minutes before the headmaster opened the door and led her out of the room by the elbow, apologizing to the girls, ten- and eleven-year-olds, some of whom were silently crying at their wooden desks.

She was sent home and told to rest for one week.

She chose to walk the long way home instead of boarding a shared cab, or hailing a taxi, as the headmaster had suggested. He'd even offered to pay for the ride. There was something about the way people looked at her. She did not feel shame, limping down the street with her black eyes, her split lip, her bruise. She did not feel pride or vindication. She felt grotesque. Like an animal. But it was the realization that other people had made her grotesque, other people made her this way, other people did this to her, that gave her a power.

They were not afraid of her. They were afraid of what could happen to a person.

She marched up the hill, through Nişantaşı, passing the pastry shop, the seamstress, the electrical shop, the stationery store, the expensive department store stocked with European brands, the post office, the tailor. She knew someone in each shop, and even those people did not say anything to her. She walked until she reached the newly paved and named Barbaros Boulevard, where she began to lumber down the road along the wide lanes of speeding cars, ignoring the few that slowed, the people who rolled down windows, asked a few questions about her well-being, before shaking their heads then driving away.

In Taksim, Refika did not expect to see, of all the glancing, terrified people, Nermin, her mouth relaxed and open, walking across the square with a vacant look on her face, vacant until she locked eyes with Refika. My grandmother slowed for Refika in a way that other people, especially women, could not slow. Nermin seemed to reach out her hand, but Refika was unsure. She kept walking. And anyway, Refika was never the type of person to admit defeat. You are so afraid of being strong, she says to me now. There are already so many vulnerable people. You can't be one of them.

That's not the point, I say, annoyed.

Refika snorts.

It was hours later when Refika reached Meltem's school and the custodian stopped her before the entrance. I need to see Meltem, she said through a blood bubble on her lip. Her energy was fading. The custodian, an old man known by students to hum loudly and off-pitch, was holding a wet mop with one hand and attempting to keep Refika standing with the other. He yanked the heavy wooden door ajar and yelled out to a student in the hallway to find the headmaster, who came running, who told Refika to please follow him inside, and to please sit down, and to please listen, and to please stop yelling, and to please understand that Meltem wasn't there. She had gone.

Gone?

She came in today, to hand in her resignation. She's joining her husband in Germany. Please, ma'am, let's get you inside. Let's get you some water.

But Refika lost consciousness on the street in front of the high school, where the simit seller, two students, and a man walking with a cane gathered around her and helped the headmaster load her into a taxi to the hospital in Nişantaşı. It would not have mattered. She never knew Meltem's address, and she would never see her again.

REFIKA SPENT THE NEXT FEW MONTHS AT HER MOTHER'S apartment, across the street from her own. Her parents did not understand what had possessed Hasan that night, and Safiye spent weeks discussing the wild look on his face at the party—a face so terrifying, she said, that everyone's blood left their bodies, turning their faces white. Safiye should have starred in a soap opera, huh, I say to Refika, but Refika doesn't understand my joke. At least your mother defended you, I add, and this time Refika answers quickly, in a voice sharp and less raspy than usual. I defended myself, she says.

Hasan pleaded with his father-in-law, he wanted to make things right, but Safiye would not allow him through the front door.

Refika telephoned her son every day, a ritual that took many years to break. He told her that Meltem had sent him a letter.

She's living in Kreuzberg, my father told Refika. She's found a job as a seamstress, and she's happy, Mama. She says there are so many Turks in Berlin, it feels like she never left Istanbul.

Does her husband know?

I don't know, Mama. She says you have to leave Baba.

They were silent. Refika admits that my father, who was no longer on speaking terms with Hasan, never told her she should do the same.

BUT REFIKA WAS NOT THE TYPE OF WOMAN TO MOPE. MY blood, your blood, she says now, somewhat unconvincingly, is too pure, too powerful for that. She aimed to be headmaster of the school by the year's end. There was another woman vying for the same position, who was sweet but stupid, Refika thought.

She shocked her family by moving back in with Hasan, then kicking him out after a year. During that year, he had become a devout man. He had stopped drinking. He even began rising early for the first ezan at the mosque. Still, the neighborhood could not believe that he would leave her so quietly, and everyone had their own theories on what Refika did to bewitch him. Was his reconciliation with himself not enough for her, the neighborhood gossiped, and how greedy a woman was she, after all, to reject a man who had worked so hard to change himself?

But Refika was busier than she'd ever been—and when immersed in work, she lectures now, it is impossible to feel psychological pain. She only wanted my father to be a doctor, despite the potential threats in her way. Most of the teachers at Tarsus were American draft dodgers, people with no sense of country, and with no sense of country, no loyalty. She had heard rumors that American teachers across Turkey were spies. Each night over the phone, she made my father describe each of his friends, their families, their financial situation, in order to determine which political vacuum would swallow her son.

But what my father said continued to frighten Refika. They are organizing *for* Atatürk, Mama, don't you understand? Don't you understand that Turkey is not the country it used to be? That the imperialism the United States is pushing on us will be the end of Turkey's autonomy, modernization, the end of democracy? Refika let her son talk. She took notes. How could he not see that in this Turkey the radical leftists and ultranationalists both were responsible for chaos? She had seen people killed in the street in front of her on her way home from work. She knew her son's theories. That he called it state-sponsored terrorism. He called it U.S. imperialism working with spies all over Istanbul to win the Cold War against Russia. She did not, by any means, support the Grey Wolves like Hasan, but she could not let her son fall to communist influence.

In those years Refika had taken to securing scraps of paper and postcards between the lace tablecloth and glass top of her dining table. Her private mausoleum to the Turkish Republic had expanded. There was a rectangular photograph of Atatürk's face, too, under the glass.

Refika said it helped her see everything at once.

MEANWHILE, MY FATHER HAD NO DESIRE TO BE A DOCTOR. In 1977, after taking the university entrance exams, he enrolled at the Middle East Technical University in Ankara instead.

Refika's vision remained difficult to crush. She was promoted to principal of the girl's school in Nişantaşı that same year and continued to speak of her son only as the future professional. The more leftist activity there was across the country, the more she boasted. She ignored her family's insistence on keeping modest in case of nazar, and she ignored, even, my father's increasingly open hints at political activity: his friend in the hospital, his favorite professor murdered by the far right. What radio on behind me, he'd say, maybe it's coming from your end? Refika called him every day. When he sounded distracted, she made him list the topics he was covering in school, how much he was studying, and whether, of course, he was eating enough. When he sounded excited—she was never told about what, but she heard it in his voice: speed and zeal, an impatience—she worried, and reminded him of his uncle the eye doctor, whose success, she repeated, was due to his belief in modernization, his contribution to a Westernized country.

She did not know that my father was working on a distribution project with a friend from Tarsus who was a medical student. This friend ran an extracurricular group, an exchange committee that sent Turkish medical students to hospitals in Europe for summer residency programs. The European doctors who came to Turkey paid money to stay in hospitals here, and the friend collected this money. The money went to my father, who used it to help buy banned weapons—guns and knives, mostly—that were then distributed to the students in their party.

Years later, my father grew uncertain. Was violence the only path towards the Turkey he wanted? My parents never shared stories about their mothers, but they did speak of this time, and I see now how my father's and Refika's stories of this year press against each other and breed the conflict that was left buried, dormant, a political awakening that died in the chests of so many Turks working for change.

THE WAY MY MOTHER DESCRIBES THIS TIME IS DIFFERENT. This was the same year my parents met at a rally at Ankara University, where Uncle Yılmaz attended school, and where my mother began what she calls her real education: Marxist theory, making posters, pamphlets, and banners, planning demonstrations. It was 1977, three years before the coup, after which General Evren banned all public gatherings and imprisoned thousands of people, effectively stamping out the Turkish left and restoring order to the nation.

My maternal grandmother, Fatma, had shipped her two children off to Ankara when her brother got a job at a furniture factory a few years earlier. Fatma knew high school in Ankara was a better way for her children to get to university. They lived in Altındağ by the time Uncle Yılmaz started college, but Fatma had forbidden Uncle Yılmaz from indoctrinating his sister. No meetings, she'd said, no demonstrations. Do what you like, she'd tell her son, but this is no place for a young woman. Uncle Yılmaz and my mother had laughed, but for the first few years, their mother's word held.

My mother, seventeen years old, had been patient.

Every day, when she got out of school, she was to wait for her brother by the pastry shop across the street from his campus before heading home together. This year, her last year in high school, she began loitering and exploring the campus, taking a few extra steps each day. The campus was composed of beige buildings and one big stone plaza with a bust of Atatürk in bronze. She had already seen how the left and right student groups would linger in segregated groups by the entrance. If you nodded your head to your left side, you were on the left. Right, you sympathized with the right. I've been told many times, by different family members, that the students who wanted no part in the violence were terrified. Some stopped going to school. My father, set to graduate in a few months, understood this fear, and he struggled to justify his own actions, too. He confessed to me once that unfortunately it will be the weak people who inherit the earth. The good die defending what they believe. The bad die defending what they believe. The weak are the ones who wait out violence, profit from self-interest—commonly called success—and keep living.

My mother made her decision one fall day, when the cats were running across the plaza in hordes, and the leaves were a violent orange and yellow. She marched through the entrance of school past the bust with her head high, staring back at a group of young men with their hard, leering faces. My mother at this age was the spitting image of Alara. Like us, she kept her hair long. She wore blue jeans and a Pink Floyd shirt, both bought cheaply from a flea market. Because my mother was tall for her age, with a face of sharp angles and a serious mouth, no one knew she was in high school. She was looking for her brother, who she found at the edge of the plaza with a group of students—three men and one woman, who was smoking a long cigarette—and nodded to her left, a smile splitting her mouth in two. My uncle, who had decided privately months ago that there was no stopping his sister, introduced her to his friends. My father had recently met my uncle through the party, and although they did not agree on how to achieve the vision they demanded, and what degree of force was necessary, they played American songs on guitar together and became close friends. Baba took a drag of the woman's long cigarette as my mother introduced herself. A line of soldiers stood by the entrance of the school, their rifles slung across their chests. They were laughing, their heads tipped back by the necks.

The day they met, the leftist students were holding a protest. There were red and black banners hung up on every school building.

Yankees go home.

Sixth Fleet go home.

It took only a few minutes for someone in the crowd to be killed. Someone said the fascists were there. Someone said it was the police, disguised as activists in the crowd, who fired first to kickstart the bloodshed. When the police began to force a predetermined number of leftist students into trucks to take to jail, my mother asked, Where are they taking them? And her brother looked at her sadly. My father, though, he must have been a little sick, falling in love with this woman amid violence.

But my mother came from a religious family. She came from a village. Her mother covered her head. My father did not know how to tell Refika he had met the woman he would marry. That year, he still tried with Refika. He still pretended. In order to appease her, he put on an extravagant show of complaining about how difficult it was to keep your head down and get any work done with soldiers and radicals swarming the campus.

Refika sympathized. She was proud of her son. She was delighted when he came to visit her in Istanbul with his best friend, Yılmaz. They needed a place to stay because of a school conference, my father had told her, and when she kissed them good-bye the next morning, and when she heard on the radio that a massacre had just taken place in Taksim Square, and when she spent hours looking for him, and when she found out, finally, that he was being held in prison, and when she lifted a floorboard to retrieve a piece of paper she had hidden for years, and when she handed the prison guard this piece of paper, this birth certificate, Refika finally lost her carefully crafted armor, her pride. Because his real father had served in the military as an eye doctor, she knew he would be released.

316 + MINA SEÇKIN

They left the police station. My father, unable to look Refika in the eye, stalked off to board the first bus to Ankara. When he graduated university three months later, he would call Refika. He would forgive her for lying about his birth parents. He would feel grateful for this woman, the woman who was his mother, but not for much longer. Because when Refika had met my father's best friend, Yılmaz, my uncle spoke about his sister, and how she was hoping for university in Istanbul. Refika had noticed, for the briefest of seconds, my father's face. He smiled so slightly—she could see it only in his mustache and the corners of his eyes—and then the moment was gone.

UNCLE YILMAZ HAS HIS OWN VERSION OF WHAT HAPPENED at Taksim Square. He loves telling stories, and I think this is what makes him healthy and whole, because when you don't hold a story in for years and years, it comes out free to grow and change and seep wherever it wants. According to my uncle, there were almost 20,000 American troops in Turkey by 1977. The Sixth Fleet was first dispatched across the Atlantic in 1946 to return the body of the former Turkish ambassador from Washington to his home in Istanbul. But the Sixth Fleet, fearing Soviet influence on Turkey and Iran, stayed, sparked Bloody Sunday in 1969 in Beyazit Square, and by the end of the next decade, many Turks believed that the United States was controlling their government.

As Uncle Yılmaz has explained to me, tirelessly, and throughout the years, the student left was composed of intricate, intersecting, and—by the end of the eighties—entirely boughed and splintered groups of intellectual Marxists, communists, Stalinists, socialists, Maoists, and Kurds, and some groups, depending on how far they were pushed, would commit any act necessary to save their country.

That May Day, which had started out hot and sunny, was rumored by newspapers to end in violence. There are many different roads that lead into Taksim Square, and different factions of the left, as well as the fascists, were gathered at the various entry points. The Maoists, who the Communist Party of Turkey had banned from participating, were rumored to still be on their way to Taksim Square when Uncle Yılmaz and my father heard the shots. The gunfire came from the roof of a hotel, the tallest building in Istanbul at the time, and the crowd of more than 500,000 people stampeded into the square. The police, who had taken over an entire exit, began to plow their armed vehicles through the crowd. Out of the estimated forty people who were killed that day, only four died by a gun. Most were crushed by the stampede.

What my mother remembers: her brother, missing.

What my uncle remembers: a man dressed in black standing atop a car, aiming his rifle at a student, a student he knew well, and nailing him down with bullets. What my uncle remembers is not the crowd stampeding over his friend's body but his friend's face as he knew it, over tea or tavla.

THE ONLY TIME REFIKA MET MY MOTHER WAS AT BABA'S funeral in winter, and Refika refused to speak to her. Do you still refuse to? I ask her now, but she ignores my question.

A few weeks after my parents began dating, my father had tea with Refika. It was one year before the coup. Refika was sitting on her couch, smoking a cigarette and ignoring my father, who had just told him about my mother.

I'm going to marry her, Mother.

She raised her eyebrows. Before my father had arrived, Refika had spent an hour dusting her largest portrait of Atatürk, which hung over the purple sofa. She liked being able to see him as she smoked on the balcony.

You think a woman can join the Revolutionary Left and get what she wants? Refika asked him. They don't treat a woman well there. They'll make her get tea for them is what they'll let her do.

She's not a part of Dev Sol.

Refika sat entirely still, save for her hand bringing a cigarette to her mouth. My father was telling the truth. They were not a part of Dev Sol, but if you traced the group's history down a family tree of splinters and factions you would find my family's former party.

You want to ask me if I'm a part of Dev Sol? my father said. You want to ask me?

It doesn't matter, baby. You can't marry her.

Well, I'm not, my father said calmly. She's not. Neither is her brother. None of us are.

It's not because she's a communist, Refika said, laughing. It's because she's poor.

I interrupt Refika to tell her that what I know about my parents is different. I'm calculating the dates, the month, the year Mehmet Ali Ağca escaped prison, before I say with confidence that the same week she denied them, my parents went to visit my grandmother. Refika shifts her birdlike posture, and behind her, I get a better look at the photograph crammed into the mirror's frame. It is of my grandmother Nermin, in a checkered dress with buttons up her chest. Her hair is bobbed and she sits on a metal chair in a well-lit room. She has a baby in her arms.

Do you know what happened next, Refika says, to your father?

What do you mean?

Where did he go in America?

Oh, I say. Okay. I tell her what I know, that only a few weeks before the coup my father got into a PhD program for molecular biology in Buffalo, where he worked for four cold and snowy years while my mother finished college in Istanbul. At first, he couldn't bear to leave my mother and Uncle Yılmaz in Turkey—but they urged him to take the chance, especially because he had played a trackable role in the distribution of arms.

Your grandmother helped, too, Refika interrupts. Nermin warned him.

Really, I say. How?

Because of your grandfather. Your grandmother was still close with some of his friends' wives, ones whose husbands still worked for the military. This woman called your grandmother. She warned her that the military was planning something.

How do you know this? I ask Refika.

She smiles. Well, the woman called me, too, of course. She was one of my many friends. She's dead now. Something with her stomach. Anyway, Refika waves her hand impatiently. Continue.

Okay, I say, so he spent those years in Buffalo and missed the coup completely. When Americans thought he was Jewish he never corrected them. When they thought he was Indian—at least half-Indian, they would insist in what they considered a polite and conversational tone—he wavered, unsure what to say. Once an Italian classmate came up to him and asked, Where are you from in Turkey? How far did you live from Mehmet Ali Ağca's hometown? Mehmet Ali Ağca, who, after escaping from prison, attempted to kill the pope in 1981 and became the best-known Turk worldwide, at least until Dr. Oz. Baba said, Not very far. He was my neighbor, actually. He walked away.

My parents wrote letters, because phone calls were too expensive. Baba missed Uncle Yılmaz and Aunt Sevgi's wedding. The military's censorship on newspapers, radio, and television back home took effect quickly—even when he asked my mother what was happening, she didn't know, not for certain. In Buffalo, he worked with a professor who was about to move back to Brooklyn. This professor wanted Baba to apply for teaching positions in New York City.

We have an apartment we rent out, the professor told my father after he successfully defended his thesis on molecular genetics and metabolism. It's small, but cheap.

Two years later, my mother joined him and held a series of jobs—secretary, accountant, lab technician—before she got a job with her chemical engineering degree at a plastics manufacturing company outside the city. My parents soon began to host a long line of visitors in Brooklyn. My grandmother, who came to help with the babies. Aunt Pinar, who loved to shop at the Century 21 a few blocks away, where she would buy American clothes for everyone in Turkey. Dilek and her parents came a few times, and every night Uncle Yılmaz and my father drank raki and spoke of what socialism had failed to achieve in Turkey.

Before I was born my mother went to a communist meeting on the Upper West Side. An old woman in a fur coat stood on a plastic chair to yell at another woman, calling her a Trotskyite. Another woman called her a Bolshevik. My mother did not return.

And on Lexington Avenue, Baba made us go to the Turkish American parade, a fact that is embarrassing to me. Nationalism is embarrassing.

We still live there, on the border of Dyker Heights and Bay Ridge, a neighborhood in south Brooklyn that they shared with Greeks, Italians, and Russians. Today, we share it with Arab and Chinese immigrants, too. Just like on the world map, Baba liked to say, his head full of history. The two-story brick house with a pointed roof is next to a gas station and of course Nathan's Famous. My parents' second dream after socialism was to move to a neighborhood somewhere in Manhattan, once their accents had thinned out in the right places, like a voice is a body to be shaped and sculpted. Then Baba got a stent.

But you've been there, I say, haven't you?

Refika nods.

The same year I was born, Refika received a letter from Meltem. Her son had recently secured a job in New Jersey and was moving his family to America. Meltem remembered that my father once wanted to go to America—did it happen? And did Refika want to visit her? Meltem was helping take care of her grandchild, only a few months old, and was hoping to apply for a green card, but was not sure if it would work out. Refika replied that she was very happy to hear from her, and that she did think it possible for her to visit. She proceeded to save for the only airplane ticket she would ever buy. New York City at the end of July. She had a good plan. She would stop by her son's house in Brooklyn, and he would invite her in, make her tea, maybe let her hold the baby. She would tell him she wanted to be a family again. Then he would drive her to New Jersey so he could meet Meltem.

New York City was wet and hot, and by the time Refika exchanged her Turkish lira for American cash and navigated the bus system to Bay Ridge, she had sweated through her dress. The apartment was in a two-story row house next to a gas station. Refika had packed a small suitcase, and she left it by the gate to climb the stairs slowly, praying. She had no knowledge of who would be inside, whether her son would be at work—should she have timed her flight so she arrived around dinner? Would arriving at dinner be too presumptuous? She hesitated on the buzzer before testing out the doorknob. It turned easily for her, and she slipped inside, greeted by the smell of eggs and coffee, a clean living room lined with Turkish rugs, and a damp mold, she thought—was it safe in there? Then she saw me, swaddled in a blanket on the couch, crying, and when she heard someone washing dishes in the kitchen—Nermin? It had to be Nermin, her daughter-in-law would be too shrewd and suspicious to not march over when she heard the door open—her heart stopped.

Her plan still could have worked, but then she heard metal clanging against the sink and Nermin, she deduced, scrubbing a large pot, and she realized she didn't know what to say—how could she apologize? I was crying when she lifted me into her arms, and she assumed I was hungry. So Refika closed the front door behind her, crossed the street, passed the gas station, the bagel store, the 99-cent store, the Claire's where my mother had my earlobes pierced a few days earlier, and walked into Nathan's Famous Hot Dogs. She stood in line at the counter, gave me her thumb to suck, and pointed at the glistening hot dogs on the roller grill. She did not know that American hot dogs had pork in them. I think she still has no idea, because she says now that the hot dogs were very delicious. Very gourmet. She slid into a booth, secured me on her lap, and removed the hot dog from the bun. The hot dog, she presumed, would have to be cut into tiny pieces so I could eat each nub with no trouble. She began this task of diligently slicing through rubbery skin with a plastic knife as I sank into her breast shelf and pawed up at her jaw, which made her laugh, and she was still laughing when she looked up to see my father. She had not seen him in fifteen years.

The girl was starving, Refika said to her son, prying open my lips and pushing a nub into my mouth. What are you feeding her? It wasn't what Refika meant to say. She meant to say, please, let's begin again. Please, let me hold you. But Baba, who understood the precise, lasting hurt caused by silence, said nothing. He yanked me off Refika's lap and walked right out of Nathan's Famous, where Refika sat, for an hour, although she is not sure if it was two or three hours, until he finally returned with his car to send her home.

He drove her back to the airport that day.

THE CALL TO PRAYER STARTS, AND REFIKA TELLS ME IT'S time for her to pray. Plus, she is tired of talking. Okay, I say. Thank you. She looks at me funny. Is she smiling? I can't tell. But I don't think she's crazy. I'm not sure I ever did.

What happened to all your Atatürk portraits?

Refika thinks for a moment, then gestures towards her wall of photographs. Now I have these. It's destructive, politics. Rips people apart.

I nod, but I'm not sure. So many in my family have given up.

You don't pray, do you, Sibel?

No. Not on a mat.

But he taught you the prayers?

A little. I am trying out doing abdest, too. But I'm not sure if I'm doing it right.

Refika nods and leads me out of the room in silence until we reach her front door.

Did you ever get to New Jersey? I ask her.

Refika hands me a crumpled napkin.

You shouldn't cry, Sibel, Refika says. It will make you vulnerable.

# II.

THE NEWS IS ON AS USUAL AS WE EAT BREAKFAST. WE HAVE only one full day left before our flight back to New York, and my mother, carrying hot tea from the kitchen, announces that she has to visit her mother's grave before we leave.

You can come with me, she says, handing us teacups on silver saucers. You don't have to. But I'm going.

My grandmother takes a tiny sip of tea.

I'll come, Alara says.

Are you coming? I ask my grandmother.

Of course, she says. Don't be rude.

My mother looks at my grandmother, who begins stacking the dirty dishes with Alara. My mother is thinking. My grandmother drops a plate and we flock to her feet to help pick up the shards, and she won't listen to us telling her to sit down and rest, instead she's marching to the closet at the end of the hall to get the vacuum cleaner. I run to grab the vacuum from my grandmother, who refuses, so I wander back to the kitchen and am picking up pieces of the porcelain plate when my mother calls her brother on her phone and tells him our plan, to leave immediately, right after breakfast, and yes, we'll be taking his car. Does he want to come? No, he does not. He will bring his kids another time.

Are you just going to stand there, my mother asks me, or are you going to throw that plate out?

We will be driving on the highway from Istanbul to Ankara and will stop just short of Bolu in the village of Ömerler. I can't remember having gone there, but my mother tells me I did, as a toddler, to meet Great-Aunt Şükran—my mother's great-aunt—who is miraculously still alive. I was also there a few years later for someone's funeral.

It makes sense that I've been there for a funeral, I say. Nobody finds me funny.

We're not to stay overnight. We're to drive for four hours—it's only three, my mom insists, but Alara has already Google Mapped it—to Ömerler, then four hours back to Istanbul.

Alara and I force my grandmother to take the front seat. She doesn't go easily, citing my headaches. I have to tell her ten times that I'm fine. As we merge onto the highway that will take us out of Istanbul, I see a pink-and-gray quilt on the side of the road with three children's faces looking out from under the torn fabric. What is it? Alara asks me, but I shake my head. Alara and I begin to play a game where we guess what number on each license plate corresponds to what province in Turkey. My mother says she is impressed with how much we know her country. She's mocking us. My grandmother defends us and calls us spongy girls who learn fast, like her son, she says in a quiet voice that tries to hide her pride, but there is no use hiding pride now. Nazar can no longer harm my father.

My hand is in my purse. I'm holding the dried cord inside my bag and looking out the window at the green hills when I feel someone's hand on mine. It's Alara. Her wrist is deep in the bag, and she's looking at me all confused. She's fighting with her fingers to get to what I'm holding, and she whispers, What is it, what the fuck, Sibel? Oh, well, I reply, also in a whisper, it's his umbilical cord. She freezes. She yanks her hand out as if burned. Baba's umbilical cord, I repeat, and although my mother and grandmother have just put on music, a Turkish artist who sings about being lonely and seeing the Bosphorus for the first time, I bring the cord out into the open and we sit there, in the back seat, petting its dried brown back together.

We're close to the village now. I've had to silence my phone, because Albina won't stop calling me. We enter a tunnel that takes the road through the center of Mount Bolu. It used to be very difficult to get around this mountain, my mother says, especially in the winter, when the road was caked in ice and snow. My mother lived in this village until she was fifteen, when her mother shipped her and Uncle Yılmaz off to Ankara. In winter Lake Abant freezes over and the trees look like a silent legion of snow-covered soldiers waiting to cross a frontier. The winters were dangerous, the stories cautionary: a young girl running across the ice to flee her uncle, who, the village women say, had abused her. The ice cracked, and she was trapped under cold water. Another time a group of boys chased a bear and, thinking the ice was snow, they ran across the lake and drowned. In summer the wheat grew high, she says, and the village would come together to collect the harvest. In summer, the lake was no longer something to fear, the water dark blue, hardly lapping at the pebbly shore, and families from villages nearby came to the water to swim. My mother says that her mother never let her go to the lake when she had her period because the women in the village believed that bears and wolves could smell blood.

I'm thinking about this, about bears smelling blood, when I remember that the earthquake that killed the eye doctor was the same earthquake that originated in Lake Abant. My maternal grandmother would have been, I calculate, a teenage girl. I try to catch my grandmother's eye, but from the back seat all I can see are her crow's feet. The deep crinkles make it look like she is beaming, madly, like a woman who has won.

MY MOTHER SAYS THAT BESIDES HER GREAT-AUNT ŞÜKRAN, we have other relatives in Ömerler, too—her second cousins. The boys had worked in Germany for two years before returning, a shorter stay than most of the men in the village who had left in 1961. Many never returned. There is a renovated mosque in the center of the village, one with a tall green minaret where someone has installed a speaker to ensure that the call to prayer can be heard from every home, all thirty or so, in the village. My mother guesses that the renovations are there thanks to the money earned in Germany.

We open the windows and the smell of flowers and pine move through the car. My mother is pointing to the single-story wooden houses, telling us who used to live where. My grandmother has her hands folded on her lap. She's a city girl and has never been to this village, the closest one to the lake where the earthquake originated.

Your grandmother's cousins still live there, my mother says. She points to a yellow wooden house. There is a porch with a dining table, and orange trees in the front yard. We keep driving slowly down the dirt road. She wants to show us the home of our great-grandparents. It's near the stream, she says, and she pulls the car up beside the house, also wooden, also painted yellow, with a rusty tin roof. We climb out of the car.

A woman in a headscarf comes out of the house. She looks blind. She yells out my mother's name.

We're standing on the dirt road alongside chickens who bob their heads as they walk in circles, and I'm embarrassed about my sneakers and black jeans and black T-shirt and Alara's denim crop top and long silky skirt with a slit down one leg, which is hardly an appropriate outfit, especially considering her lack of fat, which all the Turks will worry themselves sick over, and she's taking photographs of everything with her iPhone.

Within minutes, two more people have left their houses and walked over to us. Hüseyin, who turns out to be my mom's second cousin, and his wife, Latife. I see two more people coming out of their homes and walking towards us. They have iPhones in their hands, and I'm upset at myself for feeling surprised by this. Everyone is kissing cheeks. Everyone is asking me and Alara who is the older sister. I am introducing my grandmother to the crowd, and she blushes.

Hüseyin is ecstatic. He says he was lying out on the wooden couch with cushions he stitched himself when he heard my mother's voice announce that our relatives live there, see, and he thought her words had come to him in a dream until he rose from the cushions and saw a car stop in front of my great-grandparents' yellow house.

I still remember, Hüseyin says, when you and your rascal brother stopped by the cemetery five years ago, in this same car, and you pulled away from the village after seeing them, right? You drove off without saying hello.

Hüseyin is no longer smiling, and the other villagers look at my mother for her answer.

WE DRIVE PAST THE VILLAGE TO A GRASSY FIELD. THE cemetery. My mother parks the car outside the white metal gate, and we step out onto the dusty road. There is a small fountain next to the gate, and my mom washes her hands and face, then my grandmother washes hers, then Alara goes, unsure, looking at me and saying, Wow, this does feel good, and finally I go, wondering if I should wash my feet and forearms, too, to perform a proper abdest. When my mother lifts the latch on the gate, it is the only noise for miles, and then she takes my grandmother's hand and they walk ahead of us through the weeds. There are only a few graves—some slanted gray headstones, others coffin-sized tombs. The oldest graves have Ottoman writing, making it impossible for children and grandchildren to read their family's inscriptions after Atatürk's language reforms. Fatma's grave is between her father, Mustafa, and her husband, Ömer. The writing is in Turkish and tells us Fatma was a mother, a sister, an aunt, a teacher, and a devoted wife. My grandmother is the first to raise her hands in a bowl to pray. Then my mother, then Alara, then me.

What does she have in there? Alara interrupts. Like, does she have any objects? What was she wearing? Did you dress her?

She didn't have anything for objects, my mother says. But she would have liked your question. Don't forget that she tried to dig up her father once, a few days after he died. She wanted to find the bullet in his head. The wound had healed; I remember it as dimple on his forehead.

What the fuck, Alara says. Why would she want to do that?

My grandmother knocks on a tree. Allah korusun, she says. But my mother laughs. It's a mean laugh.

She wanted to find the bullet, my mother says, because she considered the bullet to be the beginning, and end, of her life. The love of her life, Serdar, taught at the same high school as her in Muş. From any point in Muş, you can see beige mountains behind the gray houses built on the hills. The town was thought to have been settled by the ancient king of Urartu, then passed into Armenian hands, Byzantine hands, and then Islamic hands, until the Mongol king Timur took Muş, they say, without any bloodshed. After the Safavids came the Ottomans, and four centuries later, the Armenians who had lived in Muş for centuries were gone. My mother knew none of this when she came to Muş for the first time. What Fatma had was her crippled, protective father, the idea that she would teach Kurdish high school seniors mathematics, and the desire to give her students something she knew she could share: discipline. It was the late fifties, and Turks didn't officially call them Kurds then. Fatma knew this town had few Armenians now. She knew the Russians occupied it for one year in 1916. The rest she learned, slowly, from a friend she met on her first day of teaching, the science teacher named Serdar. She was the only female teacher at the school, and she rarely saw another woman on the streets in town. Their existence was seen only in negative: a line of laundry frozen from the cold, a child running through the streets with a bag of rice, two men walking side by side and complaining about their wives.

My mother and Serdar, she continues after swatting at a wasp in her ear, met every day after class while my grandfather would spend the day limping through town for the coffeehouse where he drank tea and played backgammon. She knew Mustafa wouldn't miss her during these hours, and she would leave school promptly at four thirty to meet her father and return to the hotel. During winter, she left earlier, at three, in order to be home before nightfall, otherwise it would be so cold that the skin on her face would freeze. Serdar would walk her back each time, his long body casting shadows on the snow as they passed the butcher, the mayor's office, the pastry shop, the leather maker. Mustafa had no idea, of course—that kind of courtship would never have been allowed, him being from the east, her from the west. No kind of family connection. But my mother, she believed that her father would listen to her. One night, when she'd returned home from her walk and changed out of her frozen dress, she paced the hotel room, plotting her case as she waited for Mustafa to return from the coffeehouse. They would get married, she decided, on the condition that they live in Bolu. She was confident. Too confident. When she announced these plans, gently, then with more force, to her father, he hit her across the face and locked her in her room. They were on a train home the next morning. Within a week of their return to the village, my grandfather had found a suitable husband for my mother: a man who had just returned from Germany. A man who, I found out years later, could not live with the knowledge that his wife loved another man.

My mother spent the rest of her life as a different woman. Some say her organs became sick with the unhappiness she carried. Ovarian cancer. Some say that's why she dug up his grave after his death. She was convinced that it was the bullet in her father's brain that seeded her misfortune. I remember her saying to me, Allah could never do this to her without an agent. When men in the village took her by the wrists, the arms, and the neck to stop her from digging him up, she channeled her fury elsewhere. She funneled it into getting us out of the village and into an education.

Is this why you're mad at her? I ask, stupidly.

I'm not mad.

You're mad.

It's not madness.

So what's the problem? Alara asks, also stupidly.

The problem, she says slowly, is that nobody told me why she had a new bruise every month. The problem is that she gave me those same bruises. She never touched your uncle.

But I can't bear the thought of my mother hating her mother. It changes me. Alara's mouth is hanging open. My mother has been the same person this whole time. It is us, different.

My grandmother is busy praying, her eyes shut, but I know she is listening.

Anyway, my mother picks up again, Fatma died in the hospital with ovarian cancer. In 1984, before I left for New York. I drove there, to Bolu's hospital. My father did not come.

I thought Ömer died, I say. When did he die?

Alara looks at her greedily. I repeat myself.

He did, she says calmly. He died. But not before he moved back to Germany the same year we left for Ankara. He had a new family there. She looks at me to answer my question. He died a few years ago.

My mother ignores our shock and instead explains how Fatma began her preparations for her death. Apparently, Fatma unclasped her bracelets and pressed them into her daughter's hand. She gave her daughter her wedding ring. By the time she was tucked into the hospital sheets, Fatma had removed her headscarf and pulled my mother over to tell her about Serdar, who delivered her pastries from the bakery when the days were too cold, the kindest soul she would ever know.

My grandmother Nermin had also traveled to this hospital in Bolu. She and my mother had become close by then. She refused to treat my mother, although not yet her son's wife, like so many Turkish mothers treat their daughters-in-law—with a potion of distrust, envy, and speculation. She had already lost too many years with her son.

You should go to sleep, my mother had said when she saw my grandmother in the waiting room, filling out a crossword puzzle with a pencil.

My grandmother had tutted her tongue. Don't be rude. I'm staying.

Fatma was buried in Ömerler a few days later.

But there is a lot I don't understand, my mother confesses.

He's the missing organ, I think. Her father, for her, too. We are both missing our fathers.

But my mother's not done yet. Now she points to a grave next to my grandmother's. The grave looks fresh. There is no stone tomb, not even a headstone, only dry dirt that looks recently tumbled and filled.

I don't know who that is, my mother says. That spot, it was supposed to be mine.

My grandmother opens her eyes from praying.


ON HÜSEYIN'S PORCH, MY MOTHER ASKS HIM WHO IS BUR-ied in the unmarked grave next to her mother.

Oh, that is my mother, Hüseyin says. She died last year.

Oh, I'm so sorry.

God willing, we will all go.

My mother doesn't say anything about it being her grave. Doesn't she want to be buried in Istanbul next to her husband, my father?

But your great-aunt! he says as we kick off our shoes. What a woman, still holding on.

Inside, the light is dim and the floor impeccably clean, and although it smells moldy it also smells like meat and bread because, apparently, when the ancient woman sitting in the corner heard we were here to visit her niece's grave, she said don't you dare let them drive away without tasting my famous lamb. My mother goes to the corner where the woman is sitting. Her bare scalp is covered with a silky green scarf, and her mouth is all gums. I'm looking for her lips. My mother kisses her hand and then brings the hand to her forehead. She motions for me to come over and I take the old woman's hand—it feels like nothing but bones under skin—and I do the same as my mother. I kiss her hand and touch the kissed hand to my forehead, and the ancient woman says that she has been blessed by Allah.

Alara is next, and she is crying in the healthy way, and I wonder maybe if I am freed. Maybe I have not psychologically damaged my sister beyond repair. I'm worried, though, about my grandmother. We are so close to where the earthquake buried her husband. And I have eight missed calls from Albina.

Are you okay? I ask my grandmother.

My grandmother is watching the old woman attempt to mobilize herself. Her tiny hand is shaking by her side when she looks at me.

We turn into a small army in order to get Great-Aunt Şükran from the couch inside to the wooden cushions on the patio. Alara is under her right armpit, my mother under her left, and I wrap my arms around her hips.

When were you last outside, love? Alara asks her.

I'm not a vampire, girl. I go outside.

Hüseyin and his sister, who call this woman their grand-mother, have been taking care of her for almost thirty years, ever since Fatma died. My mother, I learn, visits every few years. Uncle Yılmaz always comes with her. Latife tells me I look just like Fatma, and my mother frowns, but Great-Aunt Şükran is thrilled, and proceeds to call my mother Fatma for the duration of lunch. Great-Aunt Şükran's accent is so thick we can hardly understand her Turkish, and she, in turn, can hardly understand our accents. She keeps interrupting the group conversation to ask my mother why her daughters don't know Turkish. She asks us if we have husbands, and whether they are Turkish, and the women at the table come together over chilled yogurt soup to dis-cuss, in an almost mystical way, men we should marry and men we should avoid. My mother, who hates this enduring conversa-tion, asks about the renovated mosque, and like she'd guessed, it was built with German Turkish money. According to Hüseyin, exactly sixty-seven of the village's one hundred or so men at the time went to Germany and exactly eleven returned. Over the years, these new German Turks drove from Berlin to Bolu, and in the decades to come, it was their sons and daughters driving, and the Turkish they spoke was accented. Broken, the village said. They're foreigners now, the village said. But the children would walk around the village fondly, pointing to the tin-roofed houses their parents and grandparents grew up in, the Turkish lives they never had.

Next to the mosque is a small playground. Apparently, just last week, a black bear climbed down from the forest and lumbered through the village and into the children's playground, a new addition, thanks, they say, to the president. It's normal, Latife says, every few weeks we see a wolf or a bear. There are black boars, too, but they don't leave the forest. Even in their old age, Hüseyin and his friends go hunting wild boars. They don't eat the meat, of course. Once they killed a 300-kilo bear together, thinking it was a boar.

Of course, that's not allowed, Hüseyin explains, but we thought it was a pig. I go to their caves sometimes, just to explore. But if a human enters the cave, the bears will never go there again. And if you enter a cave with cubs in it, you're dead.

Is that new, too? my mother asks, pointing to the internet satellite.

Oh, yes. We installed it two years ago.

Latife comes out with hot food: lamb on a bed of eggplant rice. Latife tells us with pride that she, too, grew up in Germany. Her parents had immigrated in 1961, and she lived in Kreuzberg and went to the foreign high school in Berlin while working afternoons and weekends at her uncle's grocery store. After her father died, she came back to the village with her mother because there wasn't enough money. She wanted desperately to stay in Berlin. She had friends there. The Turkish community in Kreuzberg was so large, you'd think you lived in Istanbul.

Now, she says sadly, many of my friends have been priced out to Neukölln. They may get priced out again. They live in apartment complexes next to the old airport, but I haven't been to visit them yet.

Something in Latife sags. She says something about the tea boiling in the kitchen.

She's a woman of the world, Hüseyin says happily, reaching for his wife's hand, as if trying to cheer her up, and we agree. Latife is encouraged again, and tells us she went to Paris once, too, because her uncle had immigrated there. She says her international upbringing is why she's the only woman in this village who doesn't cover her head. Maybe it's because of the pride with which Latife says this that my sister, right as they're discussing the political state of things, goes, Well, what can we do, with this new president—which is how everyone discusses the leadership of this country, as if they're talking about the weather. Hüseyin, Latife, Hüseyin's sister, Semra—they don't freeze exactly, but they seem to move in slow motion as they politely disagree. Latife says that she's supported the president for years. She's clearing the bowls of garlic soup to make room for the main dish as she tells us how the president's party appealed to her family even when they lived in Berlin because they were not comfortable as Muslims there and there is no greater advocate for a Muslim than him. Semra points out everything in the village that has improved since the president has been in power. Hüseyin lists all the amenities they now have—internet, television, playground, jobs due to tourism, access to work on newly paved roads—amenities they once relied on receiving from family members who immigrated to Germany. We nod politely. My grandmother is silent. She's wiping bread crumbs off the table and into her palm instead of arguing, and my mother looks embarrassed about what Alara said. But my mother could have told us. As usual, she could have told us that we were about to meet family members who support the president. We're used to arguments about Kemalism, capitalism, the military versus the left. She should not have assumed we would know what people think outside our own political bubble. We are Turks who live in New York, of all places, feeling kinship with this country when it is not the country or the nationality that we feel at home with at all, but the people, our family, the things we remember or were told. We don't have to live under this government.

Great-Aunt Şükran has her hand on mine and smiles her gums at me. She's been watching me throughout this conversation about the president.

Can you speak Turkish, girl? she asks.

Yes, Auntie, I say.

She nods her head in approval, but she is still scanning me for something.

In English my sister whispers, How is she still alive?

I don't know, I say. But I think she's over one hundred.

Maybe they don't know her birth year, or something, she says. They probably messed something up.

No, they think that when people are older they live slower lives and cells can heal themselves a little. When people reach a certain age, usually after eighty or eighty-five, the mortality rate plateaus.

Who are "they"? Alara asks. Doctors?

Scientists, I say. If Great-Aunt Şükran can still be alive, there is no reason my grandmother cannot keep living. I feel like I'm close to something, and Alara laughs at me, asking me why I'm smiling, and I keep smiling until someone at the table asks my grandmother if she's ever been to Bolu before. My grandmother says no, she has never been. But the air fills her with vital feeling.

AS SOON AS WE FINISH SPOONING RICE PUDDING FOR DESsert, my mother's trying to leave. She promises Hüseyin and Latife that they can stay with us in New York anytime. We kiss Great-Aunt Şükran on her frail, loose-skinned hand. Then it's my grandmother's turn, and, while petting her brown-spotted skin, she says, May your eyes be clear, your complexion healthy. May you live to see everything you want. Great-Aunt Şükran thanks her and wishes her the same.

We begin making our way to the car but I'm still confused about my mother and the relationship she had with her mother. I'm dragging my feet, thinking, when my mother pulls me to the side of the road. For a second, I wonder if she will leave me here.

When you are raised by an unhappy woman, my mother says, by an unhappy mother, you will do anything in your power to change who you may become.

I can think of lots of examples where that isn't true, I say.

No, she says. I know this, Sibel. I'm not saying there is a way to determine whether or not you are different from your unhappy mother. I'm saying that as the daughter of an unhappy mother, you will always know that your mother is unhappy, and knowing this will make you try to change something, anything, about yourself. I left the country, she says, I had to leave things behind, even things I didn't understand. Does that make sense?

It does, I say.

I know what you're feeling, she says. You think you didn't get to reach a resolution with your father.

Oh. What should I do about it?

I'm not sure. You either think or forget.

Okay.

Sorry. That's not helpful. But I don't want you to be angry.

I am silent. I have questions. I wish I knew why women fought over how to be women. Should I ask her? Will she tell me I am lucky, but not grateful?

She does.

She tells me I am lucky, and also not grateful.

Not grateful enough, she says.

Is my mother smiling? She's turned her head away, but I can't tell what she's thinking and she's already walking to the car, so I follow, trying to see her face.

What are you doing? my mother asks me suddenly, turning towards me.

Seeing if you're smiling.

I'm not smiling.

Okay. Sorry, I say, and she turns to open her car door after waving goodbye one more time. The clarity I see in the world when I am confused, when I don't know something, especially a finite answer, that's where a mind's equilibrium is buried. What I like most is when the dirt is rubbed off enough—but not entirely— to make things clear, seeable, breathing again, like a heart washed under cold water. I want that heart.

# III.

WE ARE BACK IN ISTANBUL AND OUR FLIGHT TO NEW YORK is later this evening. Deniz is flying with us, and he will sit next to Alara. She requested this. She said if she sat next to me we would watch stupid movies about twenty-something-year-olds trying to make it in New York, and she just can't handle that right now. She just wants to sleep on the plane next to Deniz, who is quiet like me, but in a less imposing way. She says he comforts her. I'm happy for them. I want to sit next to my mother. She always gives me the moussey dessert she doesn't like, and always asks the hostesses for extra bread rolls. The flight to and from Istanbul is one of my favorite things. Hearing the Turkish language in transit spaces that are rubbed clean of any cultural signifier fills me with something. A tribalism free from nationhood, government, control. Maybe this is what they call kinship. Each time I leave this country, my grandmother, my great-aunt, and my uncle drive us to the airport, and we always leave with extra time so we can sit in the café before security to drink one more tea together and pull apart one more simit toasted with hot, melty cheese. When it is finally time to go we kiss everyone on both cheeks. We wave goodbye as we wind through the maze of those black retractable-belt lines, and we're always walking through the maze backwards because we have to continue waving. We always choose whichever line is shorter, Turkish Citizen or Foreign Citizen, and my grandmother always waves with her shaking hand standing right next to her sister, and there is always a moment, a moment when I must turn my back to them and stop waving and stand still and serious before the person who checks our passports, the whole time imagining how the person behind the glass wall will look up from the booklet that identifies me as a domestic or foreign citizen to ask me why I am water-eyed or whether I am okay or whether this checkpoint does not feel like the heaviest gateway I must pass, and so often. Each time I turn back, my grandmother and her sister are always still there for one more wave.

As I get older, I'm drawn to families with children, children who swing their legs on the seats by the boarding gate playing Game Boys and Pokémon, or cooking up new games. They always speak in a mixture of Turkish and English, and their mothers are always nearby with their own mothers, who reprimand, compliment, or feed the children. I like to sit near these children and listen. When I was in JFK at the beginning of the summer with Cooper, waiting to board the flight to Turkey, I dragged him to a corner with only one open seat so we could stand near a big family with six children, and Cooper obliged me. There were two fathers in the group, and they were discussing the new apartment buildings and malls being planted in Istanbul, and whether the economy was strong enough to support these developments. Each time one of the fathers spoke, the other father watched their children playing. A girl, maybe twelve, was commanding her little brother to write down a list of her favorite foods, all of which she would eat when they got to their grandmother's house. The brother mouthed out each word as he wrote it in clunky dinosaur handwriting. The brother asked his sister if they should include the desserts their grandmother makes for them behind their mother's back, the unhealthy foods, he whispered dramatically, and the sister thought about this for a while, she even put her hand on her chin, before deciding that yes, they should write down the secret foods, too, because, she said with authority, their goal was to create an honest list. We have to be honest people, she said to her brother, who nodded gravely.

MY GRANDMOTHER LEFT THE HOUSE THIS MORNING IN A panic. She had been worrying for weeks about which food to purchase for us to take home to New York. Her usual self-appointed task is to stop at each market, the ones that she likes best with the cheapest prices, for gallons of green olives in plastic jars, dried figs, apricots, mulberries, raisins, pistachios, hazelnuts, spices from different regions of Turkey, tin jars of feta cheese, and, obviously, towels. We then work together to pack these foods into our suitcases. It is best to disguise the edible under and inside the inedible. For example, arranging spice packets in the pockets of a light summer coat, or the pouch of a sweatshirt. And towels are always best to soak up excess liquids. My grandmother likes to do this task methodically. She likes to tackle one market for one or two goods each day, so as to not tire herself out too easily. This summer, she had confessed to me throughout this week, she has been lagging. She doesn't know why. Maybe it is her Parkinson's, she said before leaving the apartment this morning, using a shoehorn to pop her heels into her Mary Jane shoes. Maybe it is her chest pain.

By the time my grandmother leaves, we're all in her bath-room, fighting for space. My mother is dyeing her gray hair with henna, and my sister and I are waxing our leg hair with sugar, lemon, and water. My grandmother has been gone for one hour when the television, which is on as usual, announces break-ing news that a bomb has gone off near the Levent metro stop, an intersection between a cluster of modern malls and the old Levent Market, a street with many different shops selling dried fruit, nuts, coffee, bread—my grandmother's favorite street. My mother wanders out of the bathroom, her hair wrapped in plastic. My sister and I follow her with long lines of sticky yellow wax on our shins. My mother raises the volume on the television. The bomber may have been working with an extremist Islamic group. The bomber may have been working with the PKK. The bomber may have been working with the Turkish government, or the U.S. government, although that is not stated and infers complicated conspiracy theories concerning the deep state. And of course no-body knows for sure who the bomber had been working with or anything about what exactly motivated him or her or anything at all, really, other than the fact that the bomber is now dead and has killed four civilians: a young woman and her son; an old man who always took the metro to visit his daughter's apartment, where he would have lunch and play with his new grandchild; and a busi-nessman who worked above the mall and was late that morning due to unforeseen traffic. A handful of people were injured, and each time Alara bends down to start ripping off some of the yellow wax from her shin, the broadcaster, who is blond and beautiful as usual, tells us that the number is growing. My mother has al-ready called my grandmother's cell phone, but she never uses her iPhone—she doesn't want to break the glass and she doesn't want to waste money—so it rings violently, like an animal trapped in a cage, from the drawer in the tiny table for the landline. We call every person we know. We call her friends who have not spoken to her in weeks. We call her sister, who says she was going to go shopping with her because my grandmother was looking to buy somebody a gift, but Aunt Pinar's knees felt terrible, so she decided to stay home at the last minute. We call my uncle, who says that she was thinking of getting a surprise banana cake from our favorite bakery before we left for the airport, so maybe she never was at the market to begin with, maybe she is safe, or maybe she is there, helping. I text Albina, asking if there is any chance my grandmother has called. I see the typing bubble pop up and then vanish. Alara looks over my shoulder and remembers now that my grandmother mentioned something about a salad bowl before she left the apartment, and isn't that the wedding gift from Refika she said she'd lost? We rip off the last of our wax and slide on our sneakers, our sandals, and we run down four long blocks to the old market with bakeries, spice shops, butchers, newspaper stands, and that's where the crowd is forming, that's where the police cars and ambulances have pulled up onto the sidewalk, and there is not one street cat to be found. We're asking people if they saw our grandmother. Alara is showing everyone a photograph on her iPhone of my grandmother from just last night, looking off her balcony at the street, right after we returned home from Bolu. We had ripped open the windows and the breeze had moved through the apartment with a million spirits and we could hear the crickets outside as we changed into comfortable clothes and my grandmother took her teeth out and slid them into a glass of water in the bathroom and we sat there on the couches in the living room like so many times, talking while the television played in the background. Alara had said it meant something to her, this room, the night with cricket air in the apartment, so she took iPhone portraits of us in our natural poses in my grandmother's apartment. And as we're combing through people and the splinters of a tree that has fallen into the middle of the road I realize that my grandmother is not here, because if she was here, she would be making herself known. She would be helping. And if she's not helping, my grandmother could have collapsed anywhere, in any of the shops, while filling a plastic bag with pistachios or pine nuts. My grandmother had never been back to Bolu, where the earthquake happened, and what if it was too much for her? What if she left? But my grandmother would never do that. She would never leave us. But I have never known what she wanted. How could I? It is nearly impossible to know what selfless people want.

HOURS LATER, FIVE P.M. WE WERE SUPPOSED TO LEAVE for the airport ten minutes ago, and the alarm on my phone for my grandmother's medicine has rung twice. Uncle Yılmaz, Aunt Sevgi, Aunt Pinar, Dilek, Deniz, they are all here. Dilek brewed us tea, and every time she tries to offer someone a glass, her hand shakes and hot water splashes over the lip of the glass and she apologizes, and then breaks down in tears. Deniz and Alara are sitting on the couch. He's holding her hand. My mother, she's on the phone with all sorts of people—calling hospitals, police stations, my grandmother's friends, who are calling their friends, who are calling their friends, especially the ones who work at hospitals or police stations. I texted Cooper while Alara and I were in the elevator back up to my grandmother's apartment, and he's here now, too, making himself useful by cooking one of my grandmother's dishes, a recipe she wrote down for him. When I look at him, serving the eggplant with lamb in a meticulous but devoted manner, I know that each time we're in the same room we will have so much between us. We will always have this, that's just what people who loved each other will always have between them—the past tense of time. And as I'm thinking about this, Cooper smiles at me, standing arms-crossed by the window, and I feel that smile beat through me again before I have to turn away from feeling, or something braver, maybe. Maybe I can turn into feeling.

I'm on the balcony, scanning the street for her.

A woman walks by and says hello to the men who run the electrical shop below us.

A group of young men and women in business clothing walk by for an early dinner at the pizza restaurant across the street.

Two old women walk slowly down the street, gossiping. I'm nervous. One is tall, the other short. I think it is my grandmother and Refika. Is it them?

Stray cats saunter by, orange, black, cream-coated and covered in soot, until they blur into a parade.

I think I see her. She's tiny. She has one million plastic bags full of bread and olives and dried fruit hung around her wrists, and I'm not sure how she's carrying so much weight. I can hear my family behind me in the apartment speaking in low tones, and I don't want to point out this woman shouldering groceries on the street until I am sure it is her. Until I'm sure that she's here. Only I don't know if it's her. I look and she's gone. I look again, she's there, signaling for me to come down to help her with her bags of food. I look again and it's not her, it's another grandmother, and her grandchild, a boy of maybe five or six, runs down the street towards her and she drops her packages to wrap him up in her frail arms, and the boy resists the hug, he seems to want to help her carry her things instead but she refuses to let him help and slowly she collects all her plastic and paper bags back into her arms as the boy stands, his hand in his mouth, looking at his grandmother as if unsure how he should best handle this situation.

Alara comes out to the balcony. She hands me my phone. It's a text from Albina. My grandmother, she's there. She called them this morning. She said she had something to give Refika. A gift.

Did I do it? I ask Alara.

Alara looks confused.

Did I help them?

A breeze picks up and the trees rustle. The afternoon call to prayer starts. A black cat is stretching on the hood of a car. The grandmother on the street allows her grandchild to carry the green plastic ball she bought for him at the Monday market. Her grandchild takes the ball and holds it high in the air, as if he has never seen a gift so ordinary yet spectacular. A prayer. Somewhere he can store faith.

## ACKNOWLEDGMENTS

My deepest thank-you to Ellen Levine and Alexa Stark, for believing in this book and championing it with such dedication. Thank you to Alicia Kroell, who took a chance on this story about bodily fluids and illness right as a global pandemic set in—your invaluable eye and wisdom were instrumental in making it the book it is now. To everyone at Catapult, thank you for your dedicated work on this book and so many others: Nicole Caputo, Jordan Koluch, Wah-Ming Chang, Rachel Fershleiser, Lena Moses-Schmitt, and Katie Boland. John McGhee, for your superb copyedits—I still can't stop thinking about how Tator Tots are trademarked. And thank you, Na Kim, for your stunning cover design, and Ekin Su Koç, for sharing your extraordinary art with this novel's cover.

Thank you to my exceptional teachers throughout the years: Stacey D'Erasmo, Rebecca Godfrey, Binnie Kirshenbaum, Yelena Akhtiorskaya, Bruce Robbins, Hisham Matar, Adam Wilson, Justin Taylor, Zeynep Çelik, Sam Lipsyte, Darcey Steinke, Elissa Schappell, Karan Mahajan, and especially Hilary Leichter, who urged me to keep writing fiction in my first college workshop. Thank you, too, to Marty Skoble, for first showing me the power in a poem, and for providing a sacred space for young people to write.

This book is indebted to everyone who read it at its various stages of conception and completion, including Jean Kyoung Frazier, Anya Lewis-Meeks, Elif Batuman, Crystal Hana Kim, Antonia Hitchens, Paul Beatty, Karim Dimechkie, Claire Carusillo, Ayşegül Savaş, Merve Emre, Chanel Schroff, CJ Leede, Alexandra Watson, Andrew Kaplan, Gabriela Safa, Mina Hamedi, and Rafaella Fontes. Thank you for your brilliant notes and your unwavering encouragement.

My superhero friends, who supported me as I wrote this book, whether through feasts of food and bevs, chaotic nights, or through the simple joy of company and conversation. Gaby, Gabs, Nina B., Katarah, Julia, Ariella, Bianca, Harun, Dani, Pooja, Jean, Allie, Anya, Rafa, Peter, Sergio, Nifath, Antonia, Adam, Nina W., Henry, Chanel, Claire, CJ, Evan, Deniz, and Larry, you are all homes in my heart.

Thank you, always, to my Apogee family, who continue to teach me how to sustain a volunteer journal through a labor of love and a dedication to recasting the canon. Alex, Muriel, Zef, Joey, Anya, Crystal Y., Brain, Miriam, Chelsea, Sasha, Adrianne, Zavi, Minahil, Legacy, Ingrid, Crystal K., Alejandro, and Victoria—superstars!

In gratitude to the spaces I wrote in and the people who maintain them: the Columbia University libraries, the Hungarian Pastry Shop, Joe Coffee in NoCo, and my parents' home. The Hungarian Pastry Shop has the best croissants in NYC (more doughy than flakey, and with a glazed finish). I am also grateful for the MTA, but only because it's the best place to read.

This book would also not exist without the numerous texts

on Turkish history I consulted and the many people who gener-
ously shared their oral histories with me. Thank you, especially to
Serdar, and to Leyla Erbil's novel, *A Strange Woman.*

Thank you, too, to my medical fact-checkers, Serin Seçkin
and Nina Balac, who replied swiftly and diligently to my every
text about organs, illness, anatomy, and AC sickness.

Thank you to my entire family, but especially my grandmothers, İffet and Huriye.

Thank you to my siblings, Serin and Timur, my best friends.
I could not write without either of you here.

My baba, Tamer, who is a poet at heart—who, in never being
afraid to speak English with zero sense of grammar, taught me the
beauty of using surprising syntax and idiosyncratic words. Thank
you for your boundless love.

And my mom, Elif, thank you the most.

MINA SEÇKIN is a writer from Brooklyn.
She completed her MFA at Columbia University,
where she received the Felipe De Alba Fellowship and also received her bachelor's degree. Her
work has been published in *McSweeney's Quarterly
Concern*, *Refinery29*, *Electric Literature*, *The Rumpus*,
and elsewhere. She serves as managing editor of
*Apogee Journal*. *The Four Humors* is her first novel.